The Players' power

The Moon bowed to the roar of applause. "And so we hope you good folk will find it in your hearts to reward us players richly, paying for our parts."

Taking a deep breath, Mareka turned to Rani Trader, bracing herself for the inevitable rush of adulation that outsiders showed for the players. She was surprised, though, to see the merchant girl staring silently at the dais. Rani Trader did not look at Olric or Jerusha; she did not even spare a glance for the players. Instead, the merchant gazed at the glass panels that the jackhand had hung across the stage, eyeing them as if they held all the Horned Hind's secrets. . . .

Praise for the Glasswrights' saga

"Rani Trader is a real, complex, bewildered person, trying to make sense out of a real, complex, bewildering world. From its rich imagery to its all-too-believable class system, this first novel will absorb and intrigue you, right up to the unexpected ending."—Nancy Kress, author of *Maximum Light*

"This is a splendid tale, one which captured me from start to finish. Bravo—nicely done."—Dennis L. McKiernan, bestselling author of *Silver Wolf, Black Falcon*

"A fine fantasy novel . . . a fast-paced action thriller that has wide appeal."—BookBrowser

"An exhilarating new fantasy . . . full of breathless adventure, near escapes and real emotion."—Writers Write.com

THE
GLASSWRIGHTS'
JOURNEYMAN

Mindy L. Klasky

A ROC BOOK

ROC
Published by New American Library, a division of
Penguin Putnam Inc., 375 Hudson Street,
New York, New York 10014, U.S.A.
Penguin Books Ltd, 80 Strand,
London WC2R 0RL, England
Penguin Books Australia Ltd, Ringwood,
Victoria, Australia
Penguin Books Canada Ltd, 10 Alcorn Avenue,
Toronto, Ontario, Canada M4V 3B2
Penguin Books (N.Z.) Ltd, 182–190 Wairau Road,
Auckland 10, New Zealand

Penguin Books Ltd, Registered Offices:
Harmondsworth, Middlesex, England

First published by Roc, an imprint of New American Library,
a division of Penguin Putnam Inc.

First Printing, June 2002
10 9 8 7 6 5 4 3 2 1

Cover design by Ray Lundgren
Cover art by Jerry Vanderstelt

ROC REGISTERED TRADEMARK—MARCA REGISTRADA

Printed in the United States of America

To Grandpa and Irene,
who have always supported me—
in school, in career(s), and in writing

ACKNOWLEDGMENTS

The Glasswrights' Journeyman would never have been completed without the help of many people: Richard Curtis (my agent) and Laura Anne Gilman (my editor)—who never failed to smooth the rough edges and provided me with excellent advice and support, Bruce Sundrud—who read too many drafts in too short a time without a single word of complaint, Bob Dickey and the rest of Arent Fox (especially the Library)—who could ruin anyone's preconceptions about what a "large law firm" is all about, Jane Johnson—who tolerated my scribbling notes for *Journeyman* (even at the bottom of the Pozzo di San Patrizio), Bob Wentworth—who hypnotized me over dinner at the Nam-Viet Restaurant and provided invaluable advice for the Speaking in this book, James Cummings and Keith Gabel—who provided me with factual information about the economics of players' troops, the Washington Area Writers Group and the Hatrack Tuesday night gang—who have provided support and good humor for lo these many years, and of course, my family (Mom and Dad and Ben and Lisa)—who have always, always listened.

If you would like to learn more about the Glasswright Series, participate in my newsgroup, or send me E-mail, come to my Web page:

www.sff.net/people/mindy-klasky

1

Rani Trader looked through the panes of glass, grateful that the direction of the wind had shifted, that she was temporarily spared the stench of burned wood and melted stone from the city below her tower chamber. She ordered herself not to lean out the window, not to gaze into the palace courtyard and see the refugees who huddled in their makeshift tents. She drew a deep breath, fighting the urge to turn away, to close her eyes, to shut out all thoughts of the fire that had eaten its way through Moren.

No one knew how the blaze had started. There were rumors that it had begun in a tavern brawl, deep in the Soldiers' Quarter. Some said that it had sprung from an unattended fire in the Merchants' Quarter, at a sausage-maker's stall. Others said that it had begun in the Guildsmen's Quarter, or among the homeless, roving Touched.

Rani did not care how the fire had begun. She cared only that the newborn flames had been licked to full life by the springtime winds. The blaze had fed on winter-dry wood, devouring entire streets of the city. Good people had died trying to protect their families, and fine trade goods had disappeared in smoke.

In the end, the fire was stopped only by an experimental engine created by Davin, one of King Halaravilli's retainers. That massive machine, intended for war, had saved some few Morenian lives, bringing down rows and rows of buildings with explosive charges, collapsing wood and mud and wattle so that the fire had nothing to consume, nowhere to go. Even

Davin's creation might not have been sufficient, if not for a furious spring storm that flooded the darkened and charred streets after three days of fire.

Moren was crippled, wounded almost to death. The city faced a new year and old terrors—starvation, freezing cold, madness. The Pilgrims' Bell tolled as refugees huddled in the palace courtyard, on the darkened flagstones of the old marketplace, in ramshackle doorways and unsafe structures. Children were sick, and the leeches who tended the survivors identified a new disease—firelung. The sickness was first brought on by breathing heated air or too much soot, but then it spread to others, to people who were exhausted and hopeless. Firelung killed if its victims did not receive rest and warmth and good, nourishing food. Often it killed even if the patients were cared for.

The only shred of grace from all the Thousand Gods was that the cathedral had been spared. The cathedral and the Nobles' Quarter, and the palace compound. Moren had the tools to rebuild, if it dared.

Rani turned her head away and pulled the shutters closed, turning back to the tome on her whitewashed table. A JOURNEYMAN'S DUTY, she read. The letters were ornate, the parchment page ringed with fine illustrations of journeymen glasswrights going about their business of pouring glass, cutting shapes, crafting fine-drawn windows.

The book was the newest in her collection, given to her by Davin. The old man had carried it all the way to Rani's tower, breathing heavily from his exertion. He had pointed toward the heavy parchment at the beginning of the text, alerting her to the beautifully crafted pages. "Read it, girl. Read it, so that you can get on with your business."

She had bridled at his acerbic tone, but she had long ago mastered swallowing her retorts to the old inventor. Instead, she had brought a lamp closer, and she had made out the words on the page:

A JOURNEYMAN'S DUTY. A Journeyman Glasswright shall exhibit all the Skills learned in his Apprenticeship. He shall show Knowledge in pouring Glass. He shall show Knowledge in cutting Glass. He shall show Knowledge in setting Glass. He shall show Leadership in teaching Apprentices. He shall show Obedience in following Masters. He shall contribute one fourth Share of all his worldly Goods to his King. Only then shall a Glasswright be recognized as Journeyman by his Guild and all the World.

Rani had read the text so many times that she had memorized the words, inuring herself to the longing that swelled in her chest. She had once been part of a complete guild—apprentices, journeymen, masters—all working toward a common goal. Now, she was the only glasswright in all of Morenia. She must prove to herself that she was ready to advance, that she was ready to stake claim to the title of journeyman. She must prove that she was ready to step forward in her bid to rebuild the glasswrights' guild.

After all, no other glasswrights were likely to trust their fates to Morenia. Not after the proud kingdom's own guild had been destroyed. Not after its guildhall was torn down, stone by painful stone. Not after its own masters and journeymen and apprentices had been executed or maimed, the supposedly lucky ones traveling far from Morenia with only scars and butchered hands to show for their devotion. If Rani were to rebuild the glasswrights' guild, she would have to start on her own, vanquishing the nightmares of the past.

And so, even after the fire, Rani began each day by reading the book's exhortation, as if the words alone would make her succeed in the face of Moren's calamity. That morning, she had set herself to work on a new window, a window illustrating the disaster of the fire. She was still trying to determine a strategy for cutting the pieces—long tongues of red and yellow and orange, streamers of color to commemorate the flames that had changed forever the world that she had known. She would immortalize Moren's destruction in glass, exorcise the memories from her own mind, and cement her claim to the title of journeyman. . . .

She still did not have the skill to cut the long, flowing pieces. Instead, she would work on tinting the glass, creating the yellow and orange from clear glass and silver stain. She needed to determine the proper amount of gum arabic for the caustic mixture. She grunted slightly as she reached for a lead-embossed book, the first treasure that Davin had given her. That treatise held almost everything she wanted to know about glasswork, almost everything that she had taught herself in the three years since she had returned from Amanthia.

From Amanthia, where she had been kidnapped and forced into an army of children, children who were sold as slaves to further their dark king's evil goals. Rani had liberated that army, and she had contributed to the defeat of the evil King Sin Hazar. She had learned much on her journey to Amanthia, much about the dark power of loyalty and devotion and love.

Rani set the new book on the table, carefully bringing her lamp near and ignoring the slight tremble in her fingers. She was too aware of the power of fire. Before she could huddle over the pages of tight-written script, the door to the tower chamber crashed open. "Mair!" Rani exclaimed. "Where have you been?"

The Touched girl grimaced. "Tending the children. Six more cases of firelung. All Touched." The disease was spreading, working its greatest damage among the people of Moren who had the least. Rani read Mair's concern in her friend's creased brow. Mair may have come to live in the palace, but her heart was still in the streets, with the children she had raised, with the troop she had led. With a visible effort, Mair set aside her worries, asking Rani, "What have you been up to, that you look so surprised at my coming here?"

"I was reading Davin's newest treatise, about advancement to journeyman."

"Books." Mair snorted as she glanced at the volumes on the high table. Rani knew that her Touched friend was able to read; Mair had mastered her letters at the same time that the girl was learning how to survive in the city streets. Reading and writing were tools that helped a Touched girl thrive, let her read the text of royal proclamations, let her draft markers for loans.

Mair had harnessed her skills well, Rani thought, managing a troop of children with all the aplomb of a general. The Touched leader had consistently directed her followers with a combination of maternal love and mercenary zeal—skills that were sometimes wasted in the constraints of King Halaravilli's court. Mair said, "There are more important things than books."

"Certainly there are, Mair," Rani sighed. "There are funeral pyres for all the victims who were not consumed outright by the fire. There is food to distribute. There are blankets to give out. But I can't be down there all the time. I can't watch over the damage all the time."

"They're your people, Rai."

"They're not mine!" Rani heard her voice ratchet higher, and she reminded herself to breathe, to relax her throat. "I'm a merchant girl, not a noble."

"Merchant girl, guild girl, noble." Mair shook her head. "You're whatever you decide to call yourself. The fact remains that the people need you. Your king needs you."

Rani snorted. "If he *needed* me, he would have included me in his discussions with the ambassador from the Pepper Isles."

"You're still upset about that?"

"If I'd been there, we would have negotiated for more spices. We could have taxed the cinnamon and the pepper—we could have raised the salt tax. We'd have money to rebuild the city by the end of summer."

"Rai, he obviously didn't see it that way."

"Of course he didn't! He doesn't understand how to bargain!"

"He understands how to be a king." Mair shrugged. "He's overlord of the Pepper Isles. If he demands too much of them, they'll rebel. Morenia can hardly fight a battle now, not to keep its outlying territories in line."

Rani did not bother to respond. If *she* had been involved in the negotiations, the matter would never come to open rebellion. She was more skilled than that.

After all, she had been born into a merchant family. In her earliest days, she had learned how to manipulate her older brothers and sisters, how to lure customers into the family shop, how to hone the barest edge of a bargain. Negotiating was in her blood.

"In any case," Mair conceded, "the king says he wants you there tonight."

"Tonight! He's meeting with the Holy Father. He'd banish me before a messenger from the Pepper Isles but permit me to stand before the worldly representative of all the Thousand Gods?"

"Of course the king wants you there. You were the First Pilgrim."

Rani had been selected for that honor almost five years ago, when she had been caught up in the mystery of Prince Tuvashanoran's death. She had been snared by the evil Brotherhood of Justice, a cabal that had conspired to get her taken into the royal household, to have her adopted by the then-king as the First Pilgrim. The Brotherhood had wanted her to execute Halaravilli, to end his life and advance the cause of so-called justice. Rani had freed herself from the Brotherhood a long time ago. A lifetime ago.

"The church hardly needs to be reminded of mistakes it made five years ago."

"The church made no mistakes. They got you in the palace."

"For all the good it's done Moren these past few weeks! Why does Hal want me? The Holy Father's so old that *you* could go in my place and he wouldn't know the difference."

Mair ran her fingers through her always-tangled dark hair as she peered at Rani's blond tresses. "I think he'd notice."

"He might," Rani admitted. "But Hal certainly wouldn't. He's forgotten what I look like."

"Is *that* what this is all about?" Mair clicked her tongue as she crossed the room. When she perched on top of a high stool, she looked like a benevolent bird of prey. "Rai, he's worried for the kingdom, for all of Morenia's future."

"Worried enough that he had to entertain that slattern of a princess from Brianta?"

"Worried enough that he sent her away." Mair's voice was surprisingly gentle. "She's not able to give him the funds he needs; her dowry isn't enough. He was put out with her, Rai, outright rude. He'll be lucky if her father doesn't revoke our right to travel along the Great Eastern Road. She left the palace this morning, and the rumors say the guards at the city gates learned a few new words, listening to her swear."

Rani had not heard that the princess was gone. Even as a victorious smile began to curve her lips, she managed to shake her head in a simulation of disgust. "That's what we need. Warfare on the western front. Any fool could see that this is not the time to provoke our neighbors."

"So now you're calling your king a fool?"

"If he acts like one, that's what I'll call him." Rani tugged at the sleeves of her gown, forcing her attention back to the formula for silver stain.

Mair laughed. "Treason, and within the palace's very walls."

"Is it treason if it's true?"

"It is treason if you speak against your king. It is treason if you leave him alone in his apartments and let him be outfoxed by the Holy Father, who was negotiating contracts before King Halaravilli was born. The church now says that we'll have to pay a delivery fee of one gold ingot for every shipment of food they bring in."

"An ingot! Why, only an idiot—"

"Mind your tongue," Mair interrupted, laughing. "His Majesty commands you to attend him in his apartments."

Mair's words shot through Rani, jamming against her spine and stealing away her breath. "He asked for me?"

"Directly."

"So, now that he needs me, he can keep a civil tongue in his head."

"Let it rest! You pushed him this morning. You know that you did. Your feelings were hurt that he sent you out of the room while he spoke privately with the ambassador from the Pepper Isles."

"He dismissed me like a servant."

"He dismissed you like a friend. Like a trusted comrade who would understand that he needed to honor a guest who is narrow minded, pompous, and rich." Mair hopped down from her stool. "Oh, stop frowning at me. You know perfectly well that the king can't take any chances on tonight's negotiations with the church, especially after he came up short dealing with the Pepper Isles. He needs more money, and faster. There are more than two hundred children who have firelung now, and the number of new cases increases every day. The Touched are going to die if they continue to live in dilapidated tents. The Touched, all of them, and other castes, too. They need shelter, and food, and clothing. And if the merchants don't get trade goods for the summer fairs, it will be even worse come the autumn."

"You don't need to explain the marketplace to me, Mair."

"I'm not explaining it to you. I'm reminding you that your stubbornness can kill. Your stiff neck will hurt children, mothers, fathers—all of Morenia."

"This isn't my fault!"

"The fire isn't your fault. Anything you do to keep Morenia from rebuilding . . . now that's another tale."

"Mair, you're not being fair!"

"Nothing is ever fair, Rai. Your king needs you to attend him."

"It's hardly necessary—"

"It's hardly necessary for you to sulk up here with your glass and your treatises. You need to leave this tower. You need to walk down the stairs, to your own apartments. You need to put on your mourning gown and attend your king and his guest in his apartments."

Rani sighed and shoved away all her other arguments. There had been no reason for Hal to embarrass Rani in public. There had been no reason for him to turn his back on her, no reason for him to treat her like a dismissed servant while he primped and preened for that Pepper Isles lackey, for the Briantan princess.

Nevertheless, in her heart, Rani knew that Mair was right. Hal was frightened. His kingdom needed to rebuild immediately. He needed to protect his subjects. If Hal could not, there were too many restless border lords who would try. Border lords or foreign kings from the lands to the east and the south, restless neighbors who would look at Morenia's troubles as a wide-open door to opportunity.

Rani could show Hal just how wrongly he had treated her if she helped him complete his negotiations with the Holy Father. She held on to that thought as she accompanied Mair down the stairs. She let the Touched girl help her into her stiff gown of black mourning silk. As Mair combed out Rani's gleaming hair, arranging it to fall straight and clean like a maiden's, Rani reminded herself that Morenia deserved her negotiating skill.

She'd show Hal. She'd show him just how narrow minded and foolish he'd been to ignore her, when she had only Morenia's best interest at heart. . . . "Thank you." Rani managed to smile at her friend.

"My pleasure, yer ladyship," Mair drawled, slipping back into the Touched patois of her youth. "If ye think ye're prepared t' take on yer king . . ."

"I'll let you know how the dinner goes."

"Oh, no!" Mair leaped for the door of Rani's chamber. "I'm coming with you."

"Mair, you said yourself that this is a private dinner, in Hal's own apartments. He won't have time to attend to you—"

"Aye, the king isn't likely to waste his time on the likes of me. But who's to say the king's *men* won't spare a lady a few kind words?" Mair curtseyed deeply, lowering her gaze in a gesture that might have been humble, if not for the carnal glint in her eyes.

"You're still after Farsobalinti?"

" 'After him' makes me sound like a bitch in heat."

"Attending to his interests, then? Sparing time for a loyal supporter of the king?" Rani grinned. "Is that better?"

"He's a good man, Rai. He's a good man who cares for his king and his kingdom."

"And he just happens to care for dark-eyed wenches with hair to match."

Mair laughed, running a stiff-fingered hand through her hair. "You say that as if it's a failing."

"No failing, Mair. No failing at all. The green in your gown sets off your eyes." She bit off a laugh as those eyes flashed rebelliously. "Mair, there's nothing wrong with making yourself attractive to a man! Nothing wrong with snagging his attention as he moves between his soup and his meat."

"A man's meat, I know. Now where's his soup?"

Rani smothered a laugh, reminding herself that she was about to enter the king's apartments as an advisor, as a lady.

She had to swallow a few choice comments, as she and Mair wound through the palace hallways. The Touched girl tugged at her green gown repeatedly, jerking the fabric about as if it had offended her in some way. She might have lived in the palace for five years, but she had yet to leave behind all the ways of a street urchin.

Rani found it easier to remember her mission when she stepped into the king's receiving room. A great candelabra blazed against the wall, the finest beeswax candles giving off a gentle fragrance. Farsobalinti inclined his head graciously as Rani entered the chamber. "My lady," he said, taking the hand that she offered and raising it to his lips as he helped her over the threshold. "Lady Mair."

Rani read unspoken volumes in the glance that the knight gave to Mair, in the hand that lingered on the Touched girl's arm as he gestured both of the women into the chamber. Farsobalinti had been elevated from squire to knight the year before, and little remained in his voice or his bearing of the boy who had served his king so well for the first five years of Halaravilli's reign.

Giving Mair a chance to respond to the man's attentions, Rani crossed the room, pausing by the door to the inner chamber and catching her breath, the better to hear the conversation within. She recognized Hal's voice immediately, knowing well its serious, earnest tones. But the response was not made by the ancient Holy Father. It was a younger man, a strident man. Rani knew that she had heard that voice before; she knew that she'd met the speaker. She started to turn to Farsobalinti to inquire about his identity, but the door to the inner chamber crashed open.

"My lord," a page gasped, "the king is demanding to know—Lady Rani!" The boy stopped his breathless question and managed a quick bow. "King Halaravilli is demanding to know where you are."

"I'm here, Orsi, just waiting for you to announce my presence." Rani immediately regretted her flippant tone as the boy looked confused. After all, the page was one of Hal's cousins, the king's heir, in fact. It would not be proper to tease the child. Rani glanced at Mair for reassurance. "Shall we?"

"Go ahead," Mair said, her smile for Farsobalinti alone. "The king asked for you, not for a dark-haired Touched girl." Rani almost snorted; the young knight did not even wait for the inner door to close before he sidled closer to Mair. Rani's belly flipped as she watched Mair raise a hand to straighten the nobleman's band of mourning, but she forced herself to set aside the picture of Mair's fingers on the man's firm arm, of Farso's widening smile. Rani did not have time to speculate on what the couple did in the shadows.

Instead, she focused on the room in front of her. Orsi—Orsomalanu—Rani reminded herself, held the door open. The boy cleared his throat before addressing his liege lord. "Your Majesty." Hal looked up expectantly, and the page bowed to his king and the visiting dignitaries. "Holy Father, Your Grace. The Lady Rani arrives."

Hal crossed the few steps toward Rani, his dark eyes immediately registering the single ruby around her neck. A flush rose in her cheeks as she remembered him giving her the stone, presenting it to her at the end of the summer in celebration of her eighteenth birthday. He had insisted that she wear it, and she had felt his fingers against her flesh, warm and dry. He had fumbled at the closure, and the ruby had started to slip down the front of her dress. She had caught it before it slid away, and they both had laughed easily, comfortably.

Now Hal looked as if he would never laugh again. In the five years since he had ascended to the Morenian throne, Hal had come into his man's height. He was a full head taller than Rani, and over the past winter, he had increased the breadth of his shoulders, spending day after day practicing his fighting forms with his broadsword and shield.

Half a decade of ruling had aged the king in other ways, as well. Rani could see dark smudges beneath his brown eyes, smears of sleeplessness that indicated his suffering over the latest disaster to strike his city. His cheeks were sunken, the bones standing out beneath his unruly chestnut hair. Hal continued to wear the black mourning that he had donned the day after the fire, and Rani wondered if Farso had fought Hal to place the bejeweled crown across his brow. Even in the best of times, Hal was inclined to wear only a thin golden circlet, a brief reminder

of the status that he insisted was proved in words and actions
more than in jewels.

Nevertheless, the crown that Hal wore that night was fitting.
It was woven of interlocking *J*s, the letter that stood for Jair, the
founder of the royal family and the pilgrim who had first cemented the faith of the Thousand Gods in Morenia. It matched
the heavy chain of office that hung about Hal's neck, the sole
jewelry resting on his mourning velvet. Both crown and chain
contained clusters of pearls and rubies in the loops formed by
each *J*. Hal had worn them when he was invested with his religious title, an office that ran parallel to his worldly crown. Hal
was the Defender of the Faith; he had received that charge at
the hands of the Holy Father within weeks of ascending to the
throne of Morenia.

Most important, the crown and chain reminded all present
that Morenia was a long-lived kingdom, a land that had seen its
share of disasters, but had survived all—with the house of Jair
intact. Hal might be reduced to asking the church for money,
but his kingdom would survive. Morenia would prevail.

As if remembering this strength, Hal managed a smile as he
handed Rani into the room. "Holy Father, Father Dartulamino,
you remember Rani Trader, our treasured sister?"

Sister. That was not how Rani would have asked to be presented. Nevertheless, she thought as she collapsed into an automatic curtsey, *sister* was appropriate. Particularly since the
Holy Father had presided over the religious service five years
before in which Rani was welcomed into the House of Jair,
where she became the First Pilgrim for a year. Then she had become a member of the royal family, if only temporarily. She
had been expected to spend a year living in the palace, living as
a member of the royal House of Jair. One year, five. . . . The
Thousand Gods worked in mysterious ways.

As Rani rose from her obeisance, she concentrated on the
fourth person in the room, on Father Dartulamino. His had been
the voice that she heard from the outer chamber. Of course it
had seemed familiar! Rani knew Dartulamino from other hallways, from other meetings.

Dartulamino was a member of the Fellowship of Jair.

Rani cast a hurried glance toward Hal, wanting to confirm

the priest's secret identity. The Fellowship was a shadowy organization, and its members generally kept their daily lives hidden. In fact, in the three years since one of the Fellowship had come close to assassinating Hal, the cabal had drawn its ranks even closer. Glair, the leader of the cell that operated in Moren, had disavowed the crazed nobleman who had drawn steel against Hal; she claimed that the attacker had acted on his own, without approval or permission from the Fellowship.

After much debate with Rani and Mair, Hal had decided to accept Glair's explanation. To do otherwise would have required the king to challenge the Fellowship openly. Hal's reign was still too new for that sort of upset. Instead, Hal had attempted to embrace the Fellowship even *more* closely, to integrate himself into its workings more completely so that he became invaluable to them.

Rani knew that Hal had taken on special missions in the past three years, that he had offered advice and the distinct advantage of royal secrecy to at least one information-gathering sojourn that the Fellowship had conducted in far-off Brianta, homeland of First Pilgrim Jair. Rani did not know the details, but she understood that Hal was maneuvering toward the heart of the Fellowship's cell in Morenia. He had worked hard to make himself indispensable, to make himself the rumored Royal Pilgrim.

The Royal Pilgrim . . . Neither Rani nor Hal nor even Mair—with her long history in the Fellowship—knew precisely what the Royal Pilgrim was. Hal had heard about the Pilgrim from a madman, learning the Fellowship's aspirations from the rogue member intent on assassinating him. The Royal Pilgrim would unite the kingdoms—north and south, east and west. The Fellowship pinned its future on the figure. Hal and Rani might not know the details, but they understood one crucial fact: Hal must ingratiate himself even further with the Fellowship if he was to claim true power in its ranks.

And while Rani had not been privy to all Hal's maneuvers within the Fellowship, she had attended at least two secret meetings of that brotherhood where the sallow Dartulamino had spoken. The man was a priest; he had dedicated his life to the holiness and the sanctity of the Thousand Gods. Now, he was clothed in the simple green robes that all the priests wore in springtime, his unadorned surplice falling from his narrow shoulders like a curtain. His lips were chapped inside his sparse black beard, but they twisted into a passing smile. "Lady Rani, you honor us with your presence." The priest turned toward his superior and raised his voice. "Father, do you remember Lady Rani?"

The Holy Father leaned forward, his skull-like head trembling on a neck that seemed too thin. Rani caught her breath; she remembered looking up at the Holy Father with all the awe of a child, with the certainty that he alone stood between her and the tricksy power of all the Thousand Gods.

King Halaravilli's reign had not been kind to the Holy Father. The old man was bent, his spine collapsing upon itself, and his hands shook with uncontrolled palsy as he leaned heavily on an oaken walking stick. His gaze was cloudy, and his right eye watered, as if he were bothered by dust or new-mown hay. His voice quavered as he raised a trembling hand in blessing, "Lady Rani. First Pilgrim. But that was not your name then, was it?"

Rani blushed at the subterfuge she had played so long ago. "No, Holy Father. You knew me as Marita."

"Blessed be Jair," the Holy Father intoned, and Rani was not certain that he had heard her or that he had understood her words.

In any case, Dartulamino aped the Holy Father's sacred sign across his own chest, and then the younger man turned back to the king. "Aye, blessed be Jair, who watches over all Morenia," the priest said. Rani thought she heard a warning behind those words, a message from the Fellowship. But before she could be certain, Hal gestured his guests over to the marquetry table that stood in the center of the room.

Ordinarily, Rani admired the inlaid wood, letting her fingers play across its impossibly smooth surface. Tonight she found the beautiful work distracting, just as she found that she could not concentrate on the finest golden goblet or the carved ivory fork beside her trencher. She was present as a negotiator, as a merchant. She would have time to dwell on all the finery later.

For now, she needed to devote her attention to the trade being conducted around her.

That work was not long in beginning. As the servants brought in steaming trays of fresh-roasted meats, Dartulamino nodded shrewdly. A footman served him a portion of pheasant prepared with fresh herbs, and the priest observed, "It's surprising to see the Defender's kitchens unaffected by the recent tragedy in Moren's streets."

Defender. The title was perfectly appropriate, but it underscored Hal's submission, labeling the king a servant to the church. Not a good stance for beginning negotiations.

"Unaffected?" Hal sat back in his chair to let the footman place food on his own trencher. "Hardly, my lord. My kitchens, my palace, all of Moren suffers from the fire. I merely hoped to honor you and the Holy Father, and to provide you with a token of my pleasure that you could join us tonight."

"One man's token—," Dartulamino began, but he was interrupted by the Holy Father staggering to his feet. "Father?" the priest asked solicitously, easing a supportive hand beneath the elderly prelate's arm.

"In the name of Jair, let us pray."

Rani obediently bowed her head, watching Hal and Dartulamino follow suit. The footman, caught by surprise as he held a platter of new-dug carrots, tucked his elbows closer to his side, inclining his head. "In the name of all the Thousand Gods, let us offer up gratitude for the food placed before us this night." The Holy Father's voice quaked less as he continued his speech. "In the name of Til, the god of goldsmiths, let us give thanks, for Til has guided us in the creation of things of beauty and things of worth, and Til has seen that the coffers of the church are never empty."

Rani intoned, "In the name of Til," thinking that it was a good sign that the Holy Father had mentioned the church treasury on his own. She swallowed hard and raised her head, prepared to settle down to business.

Before she could reach for her goblet, though, the Holy Father continued: "And let us pray in the name of Kif."

"In the name of Kif," Rani muttered. In the name of Kif, in

the name of Win, in the name of Bur. On and on the Holy Father droned.

"And let us pray, first and last, always and longest, in the name of First God Ait. Ait brought the world out of nothingness, breathing it into being, with the power of his lungs and his thoughts alone. Ait blessed all of creation, the earth and the sky, the darkness and the light, and each of the Thousand Gods. Ait blessed men and women, adults and children. He blessed each of the castes, welcoming the nobles and priests, the soldiers, the guildsmen, the merchants, the Touched. He blessed the seasons, the turning spring, the summer and autumn and winter. Blessed be First God Ait."

"Blessed be First God Ait," Rani echoed, and she thought that she detected a note of exasperation in the voices of Hal and Dartulamino, as well as the servant who continued to hold the carrots.

"Very well, then," the Holy Father said after an expectant pause. "Don't stand on ceremony for an old man." Rani swallowed several sharp retorts before she managed to reach for her goblet.

Dartulamino appeared to take refuge in his wine, as well. After a sip, the young priest raised an appreciative eyebrow toward his host. "Defender, you honor us by serving Liantine red."

"This is the last that survived—our cellars were flooded by the storm that stopped the fire. I'm grateful for the opportunity to share it with you." Hal inclined his head. Rani took a sip of her own wine, but the fine bouquet was lost on her. What was Hal thinking, admitting that the storm had caused such damage? If he intended to negotiate for a loan from the church, he should hardly start by admitting desperate need.

"Of course, we expect to purchase more stock, now that it is spring and the sea passage is safe between here and Liantine," Rani said. Hal glared at her, and she buried a tart reply beneath a bite of carrot. Dartulamino certainly did not miss the exchange; he studied her closely. Rani swallowed hard and forged ahead. "We intend to trade a great deal with Liantine in the coming year."

Hal was clearly furious, but he did not have a chance to

make additional bidding mistakes before the priest said, "That surprises me, lady, after the blow the gods have dealt fair Moren."

"Was it the gods?" Hal finally asked. "It seems to me that we men and women made mistakes. I hear now that the fire may have been started by a smith's flame, left unattended as the breeze picked up."

"And could that not be the work of Ith, Defender? Or of Pron?"

"Why would the god of blacksmiths rise up against all Moren? Or the god of wind?" Hal asked. "What could the entire city have done to have angered those righteous gods?"

"Prayer!" the Holy Father exclaimed, and Rani was not certain if he was responding to Hal's question or if he was replying to words that only he heard. "Prayer is the answer to all the people of Moren, to all Morenia, to all the world!"

"Aye, Holy Father. Prayer is always advantageous," Hal replied courteously, pausing to see if the ancient priest would continue. The old man returned to his roast fowl, forking a huge bite into his mouth and chewing with relish.

When it became apparent that the Holy Father was not going to comment further, Hal said, "We prayed, of course, after we toured the city, after we saw the damage done by the fire. It will take much to rebuild from this loss."

"The church has offered up many prayers of gratitude that it was spared the flame." Dartulamino made a holy sign across his chest, his hand standing out like a skeleton's claw against the green cloth.

Rani waited for Hal to continue. As much as she disliked making an opening bid in any transaction, she realized that she was likely to have no choice. After all, the priests had everything to offer here. Hal had admitted as much. After swallowing a crust of bread, she said, "All of Moren is grateful that the church was spared. Otherwise, we could not turn to you in our need."

Hal set his goblet on the table with a crash. Rani refused to meet his gaze, even when his hands rose from the table. She knew that he would be adjusting his crown, using the movement to remind her that he was her king, her sovereign and her overlord. He was the one who should be conducting the conversation.

Well, if he was so determined to run the negotiations, when was he planning to begin?

Rani saw the priest barely hide a smile as he said, "All of Morenia may turn to the church in need. That's why we exist, to offer succor in the name of all the Thousand Gods."

Again, Hal did not take advantage of the opening, and Rani sighed, setting down her ivory fork. She eyed the priest steadily and said, "We are pleased to hear you say that, Father Dartulamino. Because we asked the Holy Father to supper so that we might negotiate a loan of the funds that we need to rebuild Moren."

"Rani." Hal merely spoke her name, but there was an entire argument behind his words.

She braced herself and met his gaze. "Your Majesty?"

"I am certain that the Holy Father did not intend to barter bars of gold over his pheasant."

"I am certain, Your Majesty, that the Holy Father did not realize the straits of his flocks. He did not realize our need, our desire to help the faithful who would offer up their thanks eternal to Jair and all the Thousand Gods, if only they had a roof to shelter them and food on their tables and wine to drink."

Hal's fury was clear; his jaw turned to stone. Rani knew that she had overstepped her bounds. She would have to argue with him later. She would explain so that Hal understood, so that he knew that she was right to begin the bargaining now. She turned back to Dartulamino, to the man who clearly would decide the church's role in the rebuilding of Morenia. "Surely, Your Grace, you have heard about the firelung in the camps. Two hundred children stricken, and more falling ill every day. Their parents are succumbing, as well, good Morenians all, who need our help, our support. The Touched have been harmed the greatest of all, for it was they who maneuvered Davin's machinery into place, they who made the sacrifice that ultimately saved what is left of Moren. The Touched, of course, have the fewest resources to fall back on in times of trouble, the least food and shelter. We must help them if they are to survive."

"My lady," Dartulamino began, and Rani could see quite clearly that he did not intend to give her what she asked. The church would not help unless Hal paid dearly—paid with money, paid with loyalty, paid with prayer. . . . She drew a breath to cut off the priest before he could make an argument that she could not answer.

"Dartulamino," the Holy Father said, and Rani was shocked to realize that she had forgotten the old man. "Help me, son." The ancient priest fought to push back his chair, to stagger to his feet. "Where—?"

Dartulamino hastened to assist the elderly cleric, settling a familiar hand under the Holy Father's elbow. The younger priest smothered a flash of annoyance as he said to his king, "Excuse us for a moment, Defender. The Holy Father inquires about the location of your nearest garderobe."

If Hal was surprised by the request, he managed not to reveal his emotion. Instead, he rose to his feet, gesturing toward the outer door of the chamber. "You'll have to help the Holy Father down the hall. There is a curtained alcove, around the corner to the right." The old man began to shake his way to the door, leaning on both his oaken walking stick and Dartulamino's arm.

The younger priest looked over his shoulder as they reached the threshold. "We'll finish this discussion when I return. If you cannot agree to the church's terms, Defender, I trust that Jair will provide."

Rani heard the hidden message from the Fellowship, and she caught her breath before she could ask if Dartulamino's words were a promise or a threat. Even Hal was spared the need to find civil words when the Holy Father clutched his aide's arm more tightly. Dartulamino leaned forward to help the elderly prelate through the doorway. Rani was vaguely aware of Farsobalinti jumping to attention in the outer room, and she saw a dark flutter that certainly was Mair, ducking into a shadowed corner of the antechamber. Before Rani could be certain, Hal slammed the door closed.

"What in the name of the Thousand Gods do you think you're doing?"

"What did you think you were gaining by making that poor

old man walk all the way down the hall? You could have let the
Holy Father use the garderobe in the inner room." Rani gestured toward the door that led to Hal's private apartments.

"I wanted them down the hall so that they didn't hear me
order you back to your chamber like the manipulative child
you're acting tonight."

"You're not ordering me anywhere! You don't know what
you're doing here. You *need* me!"

"For what? To exaggerate and lie? To lead them to the conclusion that I don't need their help at all? To let them decide
that all of Moren can die of firelung?"

"My lord, they *know* you're desperate. Anyone who's
walked through the city knows that you've lost more than half
of Moren. Your people are dying. They're starving and they're
sick. Your borders are bracing for an attack like peasants fearing wolves. You need the church's help."

"And you think I'm going to get it by boasting of my supposed wealth?"

"We have to boast of something!" Rani's voice broke as she
shouted out the last word, and she forced herself to lower her
voice. "We have to come to them from a position of strength.
You *know* that. You're just afraid, because of the fire, because
of all that we have lost. My lord, the fire was not a judgment
upon you. It was not some vengeance of all the gods. It was an
accident, and now we have to make things right."

"I'm not sure I believe it *was* an accident. I heard a new
rumor today, Ranita Glasswright, one that I chose not to share
with our religious leaders."

Her blood was chilled by his using her guild name. He never
called her that. "And what was that?"

"I heard that the fire started on the grounds of the old glasswrights' guild. I heard that it was set to teach all future glasswrights a lesson. To teach the crown a lesson for consorting
with the guild that cost Morenia her rightful king."

The accusation stole Rani's breath away, and she could do
nothing but gape for several heartbeats. She had fought that
battle. She had paid dearly to clear her name, to salvage the
reputation of her guild, to identify the true killers of Prince Tuvashanoran. "My lord, you cannot believe—"

"I'm telling you what I hear, Rani. And if I'm hearing it, you can be certain that the church is, too. Just think of how they could use that tale, if they decide that you hold too much power in my court. Even *you* should understand enough statesmanship to understand the danger."

"Even—," she started to repeat, shocked by the scorn in Hal's voice.

"I need hardly tell you that the Holy Father is not my vassal. I cannot control the church. I cannot rein it in. You've heard Dartulamino—he has not called me by my royal title this entire evening. He addresses me as Defender, as a subordinate of the church. If the priests want command over all of Morenia, I'll have no choice but to give it to them."

Still reeling from the angry accusation behind Hal's words, Rani made her voice stiffly formal. "Your Majesty, you will always have choices."

"Like what?" Hal snapped. "Borrowing from the Fellowship? You *know* that I have worked toward a position of power there, but I have not gained their complete confidence yet. Can you possibly be so poor a merchant that you think they should hold my note?"

"Why are you so angry with me? My lord, you summoned me here! I came to help you!"

"You embarrassed me! You made me look like an impotent fool. Morenia has no place for a so-called guildmistress who doesn't even understand how to work with her king."

Guildmistress. Rani began to understand the true threat behind the gossip that Hal had heard. He was linking all of this to the glasswrights' guild—the fire, the disease, his fears for his kingdom. He was going to take out all his frustration, all his hopelessness, on her one dream, on a dream that was so distant that she had yet to complete her first step, achieving the rank of journeyman. Anger stiffened her spine like steel bracing a stained-glass window.

"It was not my intention to embarrass you, Your Majesty."

"Intention or no, that's what you've done. That's what I get for thinking a caste-jumping merchant would help me negotiate."

Hot tears threatened to scald Rani's cheeks. "You've no

right to call me names, Your Majesty. You've no right to question the choices I've made in the past—choices that benefited the crown. I've helped you, and I will again, once the glasswrights' guild is reformed."

"*If* the glasswrights' guild is reformed! How do you think I'm going to pay for that, Rani? How do you think I'm going to finance a guildhall and masters and the finest Zarithian glass? Or were you planning on charming *that* out of the church, as well? Or maybe you were planning on undercutting me with the Fellowship and asking *them* to pay for your guild! Is that what this is all about?"

The accusation shocked Rani, slicing through her rage like the sharpest sliver of glass. "You're mad! Is that truly what you think of me, Halaravilli? Do you honestly believe that I would whore the glasswrights' guild to the first party wealthy enough to build me a hall?"

Hal's eyes blazed at her, fiery above the smudged hollows of his exhaustion. "I really don't know what to think any longer, Ranita Glasswright."

She was across the room before she consciously heard his words; her hands were on the iron latch. She registered the sneer in his last word, the disdain he held for her name, for her. She started to turn back, started to ask one more question, but she was stopped by the king's bitter voice: "Perhaps my father was right, after all. Perhaps he needed to destroy the glasswrights' guild. Perhaps he needed to see it torn stone from stone, to protect Morenia itself."

Rani's fury was a physical thing, shaking through to the pit of her stomach. She pulled on the door latch with all her strength, sending the oak planks crashing against the wall. Then she ran through the antechamber, past the astonished embrace of Farsobalinti and Mair, past the shocked pair of returning priests. She lifted her skirts as if she were a child, and she fled through the palace corridors, taking the steps to her tower room two at a time, until she was safe, secure behind another oaken door.

How dare he?

How dare Hal drag her into that dinner, force her into negotiations, only to betray her? How dare he imply that she would sell herself, sell her *guild* to the Fellowship? How dare he think that she would turn from him, turn toward the church, abandon him?

How dare he?

Only when she had torn the ruby necklace from her neck, only when she had ripped the band of mourning from her sleeve did she force herself to sit at the table that was spread with fiery glasswork. She sat on her stool, and she rested her hands on the book she'd been studying. She tried to concentrate on the words, tried to measure her skill, tried to convince herself that she had learned enough to call herself a journeyman.

As the Pilgrims' Bell tolled its mournful count long into the night, Rani found that she could not think past the tears that slicked her cheeks, could not reason past the sobs that tore her throat. Without a guild, without merchants' wealth, without the trust of her king, she was very, very alone in the center of a dying Morenia.

2

Mareka Octolaris woke before sunrise on her last day as an apprentice in the spiderguild. She lay in her bed and listened to the other apprentices sleeping around her. Early spring rain had fallen during the night. Mareka could still hear the drops falling from the eaves of the apprentices' quarters, through the needles of the spindly cypress trees that ringed the guildhall. Someone moved outside the apprentices' hall, heavy footsteps splashing through a puddle.

Perhaps the canals would remain filled between the riberry trees. Maybe Mareka would not have to drive the donkeys down the spiral steps to the heart of the Great Well. Maybe she could find time to work on her armstraps, on the delicate embroidery that she could wear after she was made a journeyman.

A journeyman . . . Mareka had waited so long, and now the test was before her. One long morning was all that remained, one morning with no requirements, no plans, no obligations. Then, after the sun had peaked at noon, she would be called before the guildmasters, quizzed on all the knowledge that she had gathered in the eight years she had served as apprentice.

Eight years.

She knew that she should spend her morning studying. She should review the ancient texts, make certain that there was not a single detail about the octolaris spider that she could not recite from memory. She did not want to study, though. She wanted to perfect the embroidery stitch that

Master Tanida had shown her only the day before—the riberry seed, the master had called it. The knots needed to be precise, tight, but not so small that they popped through the fine-woven spidersilk.

Mareka closed her eyes and rolled over on her hard cot, taking care to make no noise that might disturb her sister apprentices. She would work the riberry seed into her journeyman armbands, scatter the knots across her stitchery using brilliant, shimmering thread. Her armbands would be the most beautiful that any journeyman had ever worn. They would glimmer in the light of the guildhall, reflected in a thousand mirrors. All the other journeymen would look at them, and they would be jealous of her handiwork, awed by her imagination. They would wish that they had hoarded spidersilk thread, that they had taken the time to learn how to craft the intricate patterns, the smooth stitches and the knots, the . . .

"Mareka Octolaris, if you don't get out of that bed this instant, you'll be sweeping stables for a month!"

"What!" Mareka jerked awake, scrambling from her cot even as she realized that she must have fallen back to sleep. By the Hind's eight horns, how could she? On this, the last day that she was ever to spend as an apprentice?

The sun was already beginning to bake the roof of the apprentices' hall, hot despite the early season. All the other spiderguild sisters had left. All but Jerusha.

"If you'd rather sleep all day, I'm sure there's someone else who will stand in your place at the journeymen's Inquiry this afternoon." Jerusha's hair was pulled tight in two apprentice braids, stretching the skin beside her eyes. She looked pinched and uncomfortable, and she transferred all her nasty temper into her words.

"I was up before dawn, Jerusha."

"I can see that."

"I was—" Mareka swallowed the rest of her explanation. By the eight horns, there was no trying to talk sense to Jerusha. The other apprentice was not going to listen. Jerusha never listened. She was the daughter of two of the strongest masters of the guild, two weavers who had perfected new techniques for creating the strongest spidersilk. Jerusha never hesitated to remind her fellow apprentices that she came from the oldest line of guildmasters. She anticipated being first in the Inquiry, succeeding to all the power of First Journeyman within the entire guild.

Well, Mareka would see about that. Turning her back on Jerusha deliberately, she reached down to twitch her sheet into place on her pallet, automatically smoothing the spidersilk so that it flowed across the straw stuffing and glimmered like milk in the morning light.

Still ignoring her guildsister, Mareka moved to the center of the room and ran through the graceful gestures of the morning prayer, turning to each of the compass's cardinal points and to every halfway marker as she paused in the sacred posture for each portion of the day.

She spoke the words to herself, forming the syllables clearly in her mind: On my first leg, let my morning begin, with hope and promise. On my second leg, let my morning progress, with food and drink. On my third leg, let my morning continue, with work and service. On my fourth leg, let my morning end, with learning and instruction. On my fifth leg, let my afternoon begin with work and service. On my sixth leg, let my afternoon continue with worship and reverence. On my seventh leg, let my afternoon end, with food and drink. On my eighth leg, let my night begin, with rest and solitude, that I may serve the octolaris once again.

She had executed the morning prayer for as long as she could remember, even when she was a little girl, still living with her parents in their dyers' hut beside the wall that enclosed all the spiderguild. Her mother had chanted the prayer aloud each morning, turning the words into a laughing song, and her father had grunted them under his breath. They must have already offered up their prayer that morning. She wondered if they were excited for their daughter, for the child who had been taken into the apprentices' hall so long ago.

Eight years. Eight years of rising with all the other apprentices, washing with them, eating with them, working with them, sleeping with them.

It was time to be done. It was time to become a journeyman.

"That's no way to impress the masters, you know, reciting

the morning prayer." Jerusha should speak! Her own pallet was lumpy, and her spidersilk sheet bunched up as if she had just sat on her bed. "They hardly care about how you pray. It's the octolaris they'll focus on, our skills with the spiders. That's how they'll choose who advances. They're only going to choose one today, you know. One journeyman. Me."

"You don't know that," Mareka snapped. Immediately, she regretted being goaded into speech. She had promised herself that she would not be drawn out, made a sacred vow to the Horned Hind herself. She would not let Jerusha anger her. Not today. Not when so much hung in the balance.

"You've heard the stories, same as I. You know the masters think they've been too lenient in the past."

Mareka held her tongue, all the while that she braided her hair into the apprentices' distinctive double braids, all the time that she shed her rough sleeping gown and donned her simple white tunic.

She did not care for Jerusha watching her, did not like the way the other girl ran an appraising eye over her body. Yes, Mareka wanted to shout. I know that I'm small. I know that I'm scarcely the height of a ten-year-old girl. "A spiderling," her father used to call her, and the endearment was charming on his ruddy lips. He was a short man himself, stretching to reach across his enormous vats of dye, working with his wife, with Mareka's mother, to lift the waterlogged silk from its colored pools.

At least Jerusha chose to keep her counsel as Mareka tugged her tunic over her hips. The older girl did not taunt Mareka about her height, about her narrow shoulders, about her flat chest.

Jerusha did, though, take a moment to dust some crimson powder on her lips. Mareka started to protest. Apprentices must be clean. They must be presentable to the octolaris. They must not distract the spiders with scent, or sight, or sound.

Of course, Jerusha knew the rules. She knew them as well as Mareka did. And she knew that a panel of five masters would quiz the apprentices that afternoon—Mareka, Jerusha, and the four others who were ready to rise to journeyman status.

Jerusha wanted to be noticed—and if that endangered her scores for purity, perhaps the risk was worthwhile. Jerusha rubbed more powder into her cheeks and glared at Mareka defiantly. "I'll see you at the guildhall."

"Aye." At the guildhall, where their testing would begin in a few hours.

Mareka waited for Jerusha to close the door behind her, taking the extra moment to focus her thoughts. One, she was a Liantine. Two, she was a daughter to her parents. Three, she was a sister to her brother, and to her two sisters. Four, she was a cousin to all her far-flung family. Five, she was a worshiper of the Horned Hind. Six, she was a spiderguild apprentice. Seven, she was a student of her masters. Eight, she was a servant to the octolaris.

One, two, three, four. Five, six, seven, eight. The counting calmed her. There was order in the world. There was rightness in the world. She had studied. She knew the rules. She would rise to journeyman and then continue along the trail to power and glory within the octolaris guild.

The sunlight was bright as Mareka stepped out of the apprentices' quarters, and she raised a slim hand to shield her eyes. It was late—too late for her to go to the dining hall, to join the other members of the spiderguild. Besides, she was supposed to be fasting, preparing her body along with her mind, for her encounter with the masters. She was relieved of all apprentice duties for the day so that she might be well rested for the examination.

Nevertheless, her belly growled, reminding her of the second leg of the morning prayer. She always ate in the morning. That was habit. That was custom. It would hardly do for her to faint from hunger halfway through her examination.

Her dilemma was solved when she saw a slave girl huddling at the corner of the apprentices' quarters. The wench was probably waiting to sweep out the room.

"Girl!" The slave jumped at Mareka's bark. She could not have been more than eight years old—young, even for the child-soldiers that the guild had acquired from Amanthia.

She seemed to be a bit slow in the head, too. It took the brat long moments to find her voice, to ask, "Spidermistress?"

The fool had not even learned proper titles in the guild. Mareka was not allowed to be called mistress until she was elevated to journeyman. Until that afternoon, after her testing. Well, if the slave were that foolish, then she should not question Mareka's command. "Girl, go to the kitchens and get me some seedcake. Meet me at the fourth canal, among the riberry trees."

"Spidermistress, I may not!"

"What!" Mareka took a step toward the child, sudden anger spiking her thoughts. How dare a slave defy her?

"Apprentice Jerusha said I was to follow you. She said I was to walk behind you all morning, and report to her all that you do."

Jerusha! Spying on her! As if she hoped to learn some secret from Mareka, gain some edge in the questioning that both apprentices would face that afternoon. How dare she! Just because she was the daughter of two weavers! Just because she was the favored apprentice in the guild! Knowing the answer to her question, Mareka asked the slave, "And is Apprentice Jerusha your owner?"

"No! The spiderguild owns me!" The slave rushed to shout her reply; she had clearly had it beaten into her skull sometime in the past. No individual owned the slaves; King Teheboth would not permit such trade in human flesh. Rather, guilds owned slaves. Guilds, and merchant trading companies, and platoons of soldiers. Slaves were like mercenaries, purchased by organizations to achieve a purpose. The cowering girl was bound to all the spiderguild at once, subject to Mareka's command just as much as to Jerusha's.

The wench huddled against the wall of the apprentices' hall, as if she wanted to limit the target that she presented. Mareka took a step closer, her shadow blocking out the brilliant sunlight across the slave's face. In the depth of the shadow, Mareka could just make out the glint of a tattoo beneath the girl's eye, the silvery spray of a swan's wing across her cheek. Odd, that swan. The boys all had their tattoos carved from their faces, scarred before they were sold to their Liantine masters. Only the girls had kept their marks. Only the girls—and this was the first swan that Mareka had ever seen.

"What's your name, slave?"

"S-Serena, spidermistress."

"Why haven't I seen you here before?"

"I was purchased in Liantine, spidermistress, in King Tehe-both's courtyard. I have served the honorable spiderguild in the city for the two years that I have been in Liantine. I only came to the guildhall last night, with my spidermaster."

Serving in the city . . . The girl must have been bought by one of the guild's experts charged with selling spidersilk in the world beyond the guild enclosure. No wonder she called Mareka spidermistress, then. The fool knew no better. She thought to honor all her owners, never realizing that she would anger some with her impertinence.

Still, even a free child should have understood the simple order Mareka had given. A slave should certainly know to follow straightforward commands. "Slave, do not make me order you again. Seedcake. Riberry groves. You can see them, there." Mareka gestured across the courtyard. "I'll be waiting at the fourth canal."

"Y-yes, spidermistress."

The child did not move.

"Serena! Now!"

"But spidermistress, will you tell Apprentice Jerusha that you sent me? Will you explain to her?"

I'll explain to her, Mareka thought. I'll explain that she had no business setting a Hind-cursed spy on me. "Aye, but only if you get me my cake without anyone seeing. Without anyone knowing that you are fetching it for me." Without another word, the slave girl bolted out of the shadow of the building, her red-slashed tunic fluttering about her knees.

Jerusha might be conniving. She might be manipulative. But she was brilliant, as well. Mareka would never have thought to track her own rival, on this, the day of testing. Who knows what Jerusha might have learned, to further her own mastery? Who knows what secrets Mareka might have shared, all unknowing, that would have resulted in Jerusha's being chosen over her. Jerusha's only mistake had been in ordering about a slow child, a slave too new to do her cursed job properly.

As Mareka strode to the riberry grove, she drilled herself on her lessons, on all the things the masters might ask of her that afternoon. She ran through the eight gifts of the riberries: seed, pith, bark, wood, shade, fruit, green leaves, markin leaves.

The green leaves made a stimulant tea, a bitter preparation that helped many an anxious apprentice study through the night. The markin leaves were the greatest gift of the riberry trees. The yellow leaves that uncurled at the very tips of the branches were the only food fit for the markin grubs, for the fat, white larvae of the markin moths.

And markin grubs were the only food fit for octolaris.

Mareka had seen enough of the white grubs in the past eight years to make her hate the things. Every morning, she worked for the octolaris, collecting the slimy creatures from the yellowing riberry leaves. Every afternoon, she fed them to the spiders, so that every octolaris would grow large, every spider would spin silk, every spider would increase the guild's wealth.

But after today, no more. After today, Mareka would move beyond grubs. After today, she would be a journeyman.

Mareka strode to the fourth canal without hesitation. She was disappointed as she looked into the green-scummed channels—the night's rain had not been sufficient to fill their thirsty depth. She *would* have to ferry water from the Great Well that evening. She sighed, but then she realized the work would not be hers. An *apprentice* would drive the donkeys. An apprentice would descend into the well and fight to transport the awkward panniers of water.

Mareka would be a journeyman by the end of the afternoon.

Reaching down, Mareka adjusted the climbing pads that were strapped around her knees, part of her apprentice uniform. Some masters thought that the cushioned silk was an abomination, a sign of weakness and lack of dedication. But Mareka knew that she could stay in a riberry tree that much longer, that she could harvest that many more markin grubs. After all, her goal was to serve the octolaris. By keeping the spiders healthy and fat, she benefited all of the guild.

And then, because she knew that she would not be climbing

the trees after her examination, because she knew that she would never scramble for markin grubs again, Mareka decided to climb the nearest riberry tree. She would harvest one last meal for the octolaris, provide one final offering, in gratitude for her passing to the spiderguild's next rank.

The riberry bark was smooth beneath her palms. The trees were convenient for climbing; they had been bred for it. They branched often, providing easy hand- and footholds. Mareka's roiling thoughts were soothed by the unblemished bark beneath her fingers—she could not remember a time when she had not climbed, had not sought out the markin grubs.

As she moved out toward the ends of the branches, she thought about the eightfold aspects of markin moths: black grub, black cocoon, grey grub, grey cocoon, white grub, white cocoon, moth, cadaver. The black grubs fed on the bodies of their mothers, hatching from eggs still embedded in her flesh. They spun small cocoons within a fortnight and emerged as thin grey grubs. They feasted on their cracked cocoons, then on anything green and growing. After another fortnight, they climbed to the tops of riberry trees and spun their grey co-coons, attaching the triangular shelters to the undersides of branches. The white grubs hatched within ten days, fat and ravenous. If permitted, the white grubs ate until they tripled their size, becoming awkward, clumsy. They spun a final shelter attached to the trunks of the riberry trees, and then they emerged as moths—dusty grey with streaks of white and two marks like staring black eyes. And the process began again.

Black grubs, black cocoon, grey grubs, grey cocoon, white grubs—

Mareka's clever fingers found a cluster of white grubs, squirming amid the yellow leaves at the end of the riberry branch. She made short work of harvesting the writhing beasts, tucking them into her tight-woven apprentice basket with an expert's disregard for their clinging feet. She found three more knots of grubs on the one branch—someone had not harvested this riberry tree for quite some time. That other apprentice's failure to perform his or her duty worked to

Mareka's benefit. She could complete her harvest all the sooner.

She had just finished stripping grubs from a smaller pocket of yellow leaves when she glanced down at the foot of her tree. The slave girl was staring up, her eyes as wide as octolaris. "Please, spidermistress!" the child called. "Have a care!"

"I'll show you care," Mareka muttered, disgruntled to think that the child doubted her skills. She placed her feet carefully on the branches as she descended the tree, gripping the smooth wood with her palms and her knees, automatically swinging her collection basket to the safety of her back.

When she reached the ground, she held out a demanding hand. "My cake."

The slave girl proffered up a silk-wrapped bundle, her hands trembling. Mareka took the cloth and unwound it, once, twice, three times. She swallowed her irritation at the odd number of wrappings. Any spiderguild slave should have known to turn the silk four times at least. Eight would have been better. Still, the slave had managed not to lose the cake.

And what ho! The girl had taken more than cake. Nestled on top of the golden yellow seedcake was a fistful of strawberries—plump, crimson fruit that glistened in the morning heat. Mareka glanced at the girl, reappraising her skills. "So, what have we here?"

"My mistress in the city liked berries with her morning meal. I thought you'd like the same."

Mareka placed a piece of fruit in her mouth, biting down on the sweet flesh, feeling her mouth flood with juice. She could not remember the last time that such a delicacy had been permitted a mere apprentice—had she truly not enjoyed a strawberry since leaving her parents' home? She placed another berry in her mouth, closing her eyes against the pure, sweet taste.

"What are you doing, stupid girl!"

Mareka jerked back to the riberry grove, even as a flurry of white announced the arrival of another apprentice. She rapidly secreted her seedcake at the top of her collection basket, determined to preserve her forbidden morning meal. It took her only an instant to realize that the interloper was Jerusha, and the other apprentice was furious with the slave girl.

"I told you to *watch* her! Are you too stupid to understand that?"

"I did, spidermistress!" The slave girl yelped.

"Watching means that you see her. Not that she sees you! What are you doing standing here in front of her, you idiot!"

"She saw me by the apprentices' quarters, spidermistress. She ordered me to get her cake."

"Cake!" Jerusha whirled on Mareka. "Cake! You know we are supposed to fast until the masters consider us for advancement."

Of course Mareka knew. And she had no doubt that Jerusha would use the irregularity against her, cite her before all the masters. Feigning contempt, Mareka sneered at the slave girl. "And now you're going to believe a child? An Amanthian slave?"

The slave looked at Mareka indignantly, pulling herself up to her full height. "You *did* ask for cake! And I brought it to you! With strawberries!"

Mareka shrugged and looked at Jerusha. "Strawberries! Are you going to believe that? You made a mistake, choosing this slave for your spy-work. She's too green to know the first thing about the spiderguild."

"She'll learn," Jerusha hissed. "She'll learn how we treat slaves who disobey simple direct orders. Come with me, slave."

"Wh-where?" The foolish girl twisted her hands in her short tunic, clearly reluctant to follow any additional commands from a spiderguild apprentice. Well, she should have thought of that before she let herself be sold into slavery, Mareka thought, squelching a moment of pity. After all, the stupid child had been swayed to Mareka's side easily enough. And she *had* brought the berries, when she could have eaten them herself. Any slave worth her purchase price would have had the presence of mind to steal the berries. A simpleton, that's what this child was.

Besides, what sort of girl would be placed on the auction block? Her own family must have found her too stupid to keep.

Or evil. Maybe she had been incorrigible in her own home, terrorizing an infant sibling. All the more reason for Mareka to help enforce the rules.

She managed to slip the last berry into her mouth without Jerusha noticing.

"Come along, slave," Jerusha was saying menacingly. "We're going to the octolaris."

"The spiders?" Mareka had seen that look of fear before— on older faces than the slave girl's. The child's cheeks paled, making her shimmery tattooed wing stand out like scales.

"Slaves do not ask questions," Jerusha said. "I don't know what your master taught you in Liantine, but here you'll learn the real rules. You'll learn what it truly means to serve the spiderguild."

Mareka was so intent on watching the slave girl that she forgot to rebel against Jerusha's high-handed leadership. She let the other apprentice guide them out of the canals, past the riberry grove and across the expansive guildhall courtyard.

Other guildsmen were about now. Journeymen supervised a trio of young apprentices who were learning how to balance bolts of spidersilk on a dray. Mareka could make out the ornate embroidery on the journeymen's arm straps, the stitchery glinting beneath the slashed sleeves of their robes. Her work would be even better, even finer, fashioned in brighter thread, in greater detail.

Two masters spoke on the steps of the guildhall, their heads close together as they conferred on some obscure point. Of course, they also wore arm straps, but they wore the collars of their profession, as well—brilliant necklaces of woven and embroidered spidersilk, covering their throats from chin to chest. Mareka's fingers twitched as she scratched the hollow of her own throat. One day . . . One day she, too, would have a master's neckpiece.

Mareka followed Jerusha and the slave girl past a clutch of journeymen, who called out good-natured taunts. The journeymen would soon be Mareka's peers, would soon permit her in their own hall, with its private rooms and common hearth, its studious camaraderie. Mareka skipped a few steps to catch up with Jerusha.

The other apprentice led her little procession past rows and rows of spiderboxes. Each of the containers was the same—a wooden enclosure surrounding a flat rock that baked in the morning sun, a dead riberry branch that propped up the rock and created a carefully anchored cave to shelter the octolaris within, a woven floor of delicate reeds, fashioned to support the spiders' heavy silken webs.

Jerusha took them past a team of eight apprentices who were harvesting the webs from the day before, apprentices who were hard at work because they were not going to be tested that afternoon. The octolaris were spinning heavily now—many of the mothers carried egg sacs on their backs, and they instinctively cushioned their boxes with extra silk, providing a lush carpet for new-hatched spiderlings to hide in.

Mareka knew that some wild octolaris spun their webs in unsightly clumps, leaving balls of sticky silk attached to riberry trees, to stones, even to the bare ground. The guild's spiders, though, had been bred for centuries for their spinning habits—they made clean silken sheets, covering the floors of their wooden boxes as if they still needed the webs to capture their markin grub meals.

Without consciously noticing, Mareka passed the brooding females and then the males. She followed Jerusha beyond the unbred females' boxes, and past the yearlings, who would be differentiated by sex when they molted for the final time, in the fall. She passed the spiderboxes that were set aside for the afternoon's testing—all the apprentices who hoped to pass to journeyman would have to transfer three octolaris from box to box. Three spiders—a yearling, a male, and—most dangerous of all—a brooding mother.

Mareka realized that her head was buzzing with suppressed excitement. She was ready for her test. She was ready to prove herself a journeyman. Proximity to the spiders only heightened her confidence.

She forced herself to take a deep breath, to run through the eight rules of handling spiders. One, bind your sleeves, gathering up the extra silk that might frighten the spiders. Two, cover your wrists with spidersilk strips, wrapping the bands to protect against bites from leaping octolaris. Three, block the direct sunlight, approaching the box without glare and with full view of the spider's every movement. Four, sing the hymn, the soothing song that lulled most octolaris into complacence. Five, bow four times, giving the spider a chance to recognize you. Six, rattle the riberry branch, forcing the spider from its rocky cave. Seven, complete the Homing, weaving your fingers in the complicated pattern that signaled dominance, not prey. Eight, for brooding females, consume the nectar.

Mareka had tasted octolaris nectar only twice before, both times under the strict supervision of a master guildsman. Even now, she could remember the powerful draft, feel it tingle against the back of her throat, sweeter than the berries she had eaten. She could remember how the nectar made her aware of every breath she took, of every sound around her. Under the influence of the nectar, she could smell the very octolaris, she knew where the spider was even with her eyes closed. The whisper of silk against her flesh was temptation itself, and she had used all her willpower to focus her attention on the octolaris before her, to sate the brooding female with a wriggling markin grub, to lift the poisonous spider from her box.

Mareka was jolted from her memories when Jerusha came to a halt in front of a cluster of twenty-four spiderboxes. This was the section of the nursery where the masters bred new lines, where the guild experimented with greater wealth and power. Mareka did not know these particular spiders. Looking into the nearest box, she saw a thick carpet of silk spread across the reed platform.

"Jerusha!" she said. "You should harvest the silk every day! You don't want your spiders to stop spinning."

The other apprentice turned to her with a gloating grin. "I *do* collect the silk daily. These are the new spiders that Master Amrida and I have bred. They spin more than twice the silk of other beasts."

Mareka swallowed hard against her jealousy. Master Amrida had always favored Jerusha. He was friendly with Jerusha's parents, had served as an apprentice with them decades before. He always let Jerusha work on special projects. It wasn't fair. Masters were supposed to treat all apprentices equally.

"There's only one problem," Jerusha was saying, and Mareka forced herself to pay attention. "These spiders need markin grubs four times a day."

"Four!" No other spider ate more than twice a day.

"Aye, four. And *I* am going to be too busy to feed them, after I'm made journeyman this afternoon." Jerusha seized the slave girl's arm. "And that's why *you* are going to learn how to feed octolaris."

"Jerusha, you can't!" Mareka protested. "You can't have some stupid slave feed spiders. You know the octolaris require careful attention."

"Master Amrida will never know, unless you tell him. As far as he's concerned, I'll go on doing an apprentice's duties, at least with regard to this line of spiders."

Mareka glared at her fellow apprentice. Mareka might dislike Jerusha. She might compete with her. But apprentices were apprentices, after all. There was a code. Mareka would tell no tales. Jerusha nodded after a moment and said, "Here. Give me your markin basket."

"Collect your own grubs!"

"Four times a day," Jerusha said. "And if they don't eat, they'll die. You would not want to be responsible for an octolaris's death, would you?"

What sort of question was that? By the Hind's eight horns, Mareka could not be responsible for a spider's death! Even the thought made her belly twist. She handed over her basket.

Jerusha reached inside, then pulled out her hand as if she'd been bitten. "What's this!"

Blushing, Mareka remembered the seedcake that she had stashed inside the container. Before she could come up with an excuse, Jerusha whirled on the slave girl. "So you did carry cake to Mareka Octolaris, when I told you to spy on her? You're stupider than I thought!"

"She ordered me to, spidermistress. I had no choice!" The swangirl seemed to shrink beneath the beating sun. Her face twisted as if she was going to cry.

"Who commanded you first, slave?" Jerusha cast the cake to the ground and pulled the girl's hair, yanking hard enough that the slave's neck cracked with the force. "If you're going to serve the spiderguild, you're going to learn obedience."

"Y-yes, spidermistress."

"And you can start showing that obedience by feeding these spiders. Now. One grub in each box. There are twenty-four of them. Take the basket, girl."

The slave lifted the basket with both hands, her sobs shaking her arms enough that the grubs would be bruised.

"Jerusha, at least let her bind her sleeves."

Jerusha sighed and snatched back the basket of grubs, setting it on the ground. She grabbed at the slave girl's sleeves, wrapping them close about her pitiful wrists and securing them with the apprentice silk wraps that she produced from the pouch at her own waist. "There," she snapped at the slave girl. "Step up to the box. Directly in front of me, so that you block the sunlight."

The girl's entire body was trembling now, as if she had already been bitten by the octolaris. "P-please," she said. "I can't! I don't know how to handle the spiders! My master said I must not touch them!"

"Well, I'm your mistress for the moment. Apprentice Mareka and me. You're bound to all the spiderguild, and you'll do as we say. Listen, now, so that you can learn the hymn."

Jerusha sang the sacred words hurriedly, brushing over the long descant. Mareka watched with a sickened fascination, wanting to tell her fellow apprentice to slow down, to take her time, to make sure that the octolaris were comforted by the hymn, by the words. Jerusha, though, completed the traditional song and then bowed toward the spiders—one, two, three, four.

The slave only repeated the action when Jerusha pinched her arm, hard. The child bobbed three times, raising her head at each motion to look at her tormentor. Three times, not four. Jerusha muttered an oath under her breath, and said, "Now, reach out and shake the riberry branch. Let them know you're here, with their prey."

The child glanced in the box and then turned to Mareka with

a pitiful stare. "Please, my lady! You mustn't make me feed the spiders!"

Mareka stepped forward. "Jerusha—"

The other apprentice would hear no arguments. She addressed her scornful words to the slave. "Don't be stupid. There's nothing to fear. I have fed these spiders every day for months. I would not even bother to show you how, if I were not going to be so busy with my new duties. Now. Shake the branch."

The slave's fingers trembled so hard that she barely needed to touch her hand to the riberry wood, to make the branch shake. The girl leaped backwards, as if she were chased by hordes of hungry octolaris.

Jerusha nodded. "Then all you have to do is complete the Homing." She waggled her fingers in illustration. The slave girl gaped, clearly not catching the nuances of the traditional pattern. Jerusha swore and repeated the Homing, impatiently waiting for the slave to mimic the motion. The girl let two huge tears fall down her cheeks, but she managed a vague semblance of the traditional protection.

Jerusha said, "And then you feed them grubs. Reach inside the basket."

Mareka watched in fascination as the slave girl did as she was told. Mareka had let grubs run across her fingers every day for eight years, but she had never been so attuned to the scrabble of their legs, to their tiny clawing feet as they struggled for a purchase. She watched the slave girl grimace at the slimy creature, saw the rigid determination as she caught her lower lip between her teeth.

"There. Now, lean over the box. Farther. Farther." Jerusha leaned, too, reaching for the end of the riberry branch. "A little more. The grub must be close enough that the spider can leap for it."

Another crystal tear trembled at the edge of the slave's eye, brimming over to shimmer down her swan tattoo. Mareka watched the sunlight glint on the tear, shine on the tattooed wing, and then Jerusha said, "Move up!"

Jerusha seized the girl's neck with one hand, shoving her up against the very edge of the box. The movement sent the woven basket flying, arcing into the air, and grubs tumbled onto the ground and into nearby boxes. The slave girl cried out, a wordless wail of terror.

Afterwards, Mareka could remember everything with perfect clarity. She saw the giant octolaris—nearly twice the size of any ordinary guild-spider. She saw each of the beast's eight legs, crooked and glinting with hairs. She saw the swollen body, the cruel head with its pincer jaws and protruding eyes. She saw the spinnerets, small projections beneath the spider's body, curving out from its hairy underside. The organs looked like deformed legs, like fingerless hands, and even in her amazement, Mareka wondered that they could craft the silk that made the guild so rich.

And then, Mareka saw the octolaris's mouth, the two slender fangs that sank into the slave girl's wrist. She saw the spider open and close her jaws, knew that the beast was pumping venom into the wound. She saw the spider scramble for another hold, bite again, pump again, once, twice, three times, four.

The slave girl screamed. High and thin, she wailed at the pain. Swearing, Jerusha leaped forward, snatching the riberry branch from the cage to brush the octolaris from the slave's forearm. The spider landed in her box and tried to scurry beneath her stone, but there was no longer any cave, no longer any escape.

Footsteps crashed along the gravel paths as other people came running, apprentices, and journeymen, and masters, too. Mareka was absurdly aware that the gathering spiderguild avoided the markin grubs that were strewn upon the walkway; they reflexively did not step on the food for their beloved spiders.

Master Amrida pushed to the front of the crowd, his barrel chest accentuated by the heavy neckpiece that he wore. Embroidered knots stood out like drops of blood as he towered over the slave girl. "What happened here?" he demanded of Jerusha.

Jerusha had no answer. She looked down at the twitching slave, shaking her head in disbelief. She still grasped the riberry branch, a forlorn stick now that looked like a child's plaything. Amrida swore a horrible oath in the name of the Horned Hind and pushed Jerusha aside.

The slave's eyes had rolled back into her head. Even as Mareka watched, her lips swelled, dark and purple, as if they were filled with sour wine. Her body began to convulse, her head slamming against the gravel of the walkway, and Master Amrida tore at his spidersilk cloak, wadding up the fine garment to try to cushion the child's skull.

Mareka could hear the girl struggling for breath, hear the chatter of her teeth as her jaws clenched and unclenched repeatedly. She was moaning, keening, forcing an eerie, high-pitched sound past her teeth. The tone of the single word changed, tightened, and Mareka knew that the girl's throat was swelling closed.

The bites on her arm already festered, great bubbles of pus gathering at each puncture wound. Mareka saw the child reach with her good hand, stretch across her agonized body to rip at the bloody fang marks. Her convulsions were too strong, though, and she could not reach her own flesh, could not rip out the spreading poison.

Master Amrida called for a knife, ordering someone—anyone—to get him a blade. Mareka knew that she should move, she should run to the kitchens, she should do what she could to save the child. But she could not tear her gaze away, could not abandon the slave girl, Serena.

Three times, she wanted to cry. She bowed only three times, not four! That had been enough to precipitate the virulent octolaris's attack. That had been enough to bring about this bloody, violent death.

Before Mareka could think of speaking, the child gathered her breath, sucking in air in a frightening, devastating whoop. Mareka reached forward, her hands trembling as if she were moving in her own Homing, her own arcane ritual to ward off the virulent power of the octolaris. As if Serena were responding to Mareka's silent command, the child arched her back, every muscle in her body tightening in one final spasm. The crack of breaking bone was audible to every stunned listener, and Mareka watched in horror as Serena fell back to the gravel.

Her arms lay still, their twitching done. Her legs were spraddled on the stony path. Her back was twisted in an unnatural, impossible position, and her chin was streaked with pink foam, foam that mimicked an octolaris master's neckpiece. But Mareka found that she could not look away from Serena's mouth; she could not tear her gaze away from the swollen, tooth-marked lips, the lips as red as berries, the lips that bloomed beneath the silver wings of a swan tattoo.

3

"Your Majesty, it is good to see you looking so well, and after all that you have suffered in the past several weeks."

Hal waved off the compliment, following through with the gesture to indicate that Duke Puladarati should rise from the cold flagstones in the palace corridor. The former regent may have spent the past three years in the northern kingdom of Amanthia acting as Hal's most trusted governor, but whenever the lion-maned retainer returned to court, he insisted on making a full obeisance. Such symbolic submission embarrassed Hal, even though he was grateful and pleased to know he had no reason to fear the man who once held all the reins of power in Morenia. It was particularly reassuring that Puladarati would take to his knees before his own servants, before the cloaked and hooded secretary that trailed him like a shadow.

"Walk with me, my lord," Hal said. "As you taught me long ago, we mustn't keep the council waiting." Hal matched his stride to the older man's.

"I should hope there were a few more lessons you gleaned from me, Sire."

"There were, Puladarati. Of course there were. You heard about the bargain that I struck with the church?"

"The entire kingdom has heard, Sire." The older man's tone was dry.

"Then you don't approve."

Puladarati stopped abruptly, forcing his secretary to shuffle back a few steps. "The question is not whether I approve,

Sire. The question is whether you negotiated the best deal that you could for Morenia. There are no easy answers, not with all the guilds in Moren destroyed, all the richest merchants burned out, the soldiers' barracks leveled. No easy answers at all."

"No. There aren't." Hal swallowed hard. In the darkest corner of his heart, he knew that he had not managed the best possible arrangements with the Holy Father. The ancient prelate had followed Dartulamino's ironclad lead, raising the stakes so high that Hal was barely able to agree, desperate or no. Hal wondered whether Dartulamino's hard bargaining was driven by his hidden connection to the Fellowship. How much did the priest know of Hal's aspirations? How much did he know about Hal's dream of leading the secret body? And how much was the priest willing to distort Morenian politics as he jostled with Hal for power in the hidden organization?

For Hal *did* intend to lead the Fellowship of Jair. It was only natural, only right, for a nobleman to step to the helm of the shadowy cabal. Certainly the current leader, the Touched woman Glair, was superb at her craft; she had manipulated the Fellowship into a better position than Hal could have imagined when he was first spirited into the secret ranks. But Hal could do more. He could use the power of his throne to move the Fellowship forward even further.

He had watched, these several years. He had studied. Glair could not control the Fellowship forever, and when she sought out her successor, Hal was determined to be the man.

Only so could he protect his fair Morenia. Only so could he protect himself.

And so, he had proffered secret payments to the Fellowship for the past three years—ten bars of gold here, twenty there. He had sent his own messengers deep into Brianta to deliver a clandestine missive for Glair. After all, he was the king. He had thought that he had the wealth and power to spare. He had thought to use his riches to cement his claim—even if he did not know the precise manner in which Glair used his gifts.

He'd know soon enough, when he ascended to true power in the Fellowship's inmost core.

In the current crisis, though, Hal had ultimately received

five thousand gold ingots from the Holy Father's treasury. He must repay five hundred bars in three months—on Midsummer Day—as symbol of his honest intentions. A full five thousand bars would then be due in one year—the loan plus the cost of borrowing from the church. And if he were not able to repay the debt, the church would levy additional charges—550 additional bars by the following winter solstice, 615 by the spring after that. All in addition to the original five thousand.

Usury, clear and simple.

But Hal had no other option. He needed to save his people, his kingdom. All the time that he had bargained, he refused to look at Dartulamino's smug smile. Both men knew that Hal needed the gold, needed it immediately. If he abandoned the church's cruel negotiations, he must turn elsewhere. He must admit his need to the Fellowship of Jair.

Now, Hal forbade himself to dwell on how he might have brokered a better deal if not for Rani. If she had not fled his apartments just when he needed her most . . . All the time that Hal grappled with Dartulamino and the Holy Father, he had yearned to have the merchant at his side. She would have bargained down the price; she would have argued successfully for a longer period of time to pay back the debt, for more time between interest payments.

Nevertheless, Hal had closed the deal, and the church had conveyed its riches immediately. A covered wain brought the first installment of heavy gold to the palace courtyard the morning after negotiations were concluded. Hal had overseen the unloading himself, immediately dispatching crown riders to procure herbs and lumber, to hire skilled workers who could begin the hard labor of remaking Moren.

And now, all he had to do was find a way to repay the Holy Father. He met Puladarati's scowl with his own serious gaze. The man's brows were still dark against his high forehead, the shadows beneath his silvery hair lending him a penetrating gaze. "I made the only bargain I could for Morenia."

"There is never a single bargain, my lord."

Hal flushed. Was Puladarati condemning him for not forcing Rani to rejoin the negotiations? Could the former regent possibly know about the Fellowship, about the terms that they might have offered? Or was Puladarati merely enforcing a lifetime of lessons—look for options, look for escape, look for a dozen open ways and choose the best?

"Aye," Hal agreed. "There is never only one bargain, but some are too costly ever to consider. Besides, the church has lived up to its commitment. The final transport arrived this morning, with the last of the gold that we negotiated. My fastest messengers are riding for Brianta to secure their leading architects."

"From Brianta?" Puladarati seemed surprised. "I had understood that there would be no—er—commerce with Brianta."

"There will be no *nuptials* with Brianta," Hal clarified, and his cheeks blazed. Why should he be flustered at remembering his last exchange with the princess? She had been the one to call *him* names. Even now, he clenched his fists, remembering the tightening snare of chivalry, the almost-overpowering longing to make retorts that would have driven his childhood nurses to wash his mouth with wormwood. "Other negotiations are conducted with the guildsmen of that land, and its merchants. They're willing to take Morenian coin."

He would be a fool to endanger the trade that came from Brianta, even if the princess was no treasure. Her tongue was sharper than any builder's adze, and she knew words that would make Hal's own soldiers blush; he could not subject Morenia to such a queen. Hal continued, brushing away the bitter recollection: "Tomorrow, we will begin to cart away the ruins in the Merchants' Quarter. It will take weeks, but we'll rebuild there first. We might be able to hold a small fair, come spring."

"You have the men to labor, then? To get construction under way?"

"We have some. Enough, if the firelung does not spread." Hal swallowed hard, trying to push away the gnawing rat of fear about the disease.

"And how many are infected?"

"Nearly four hundred now. More each day. Mostly Touched. They were the ones who put Davin's engines into place, who made sure that the fire was stopped."

"You need to get them decent housing, let them heal."

"I *know* that!" Hal caught the tremor in his voice and forced his words to a lower register. "I know that they must heal, that they may not work, that they must have fresh food and clear water. I know all that. I'm doing the best I can, my lord."

"None of us doubts that." Puladarati eyed him steadily. "None of us doubts that at all."

Hal retreated into reciting known facts. "Mair is overseeing the workmen as they build the Touched hospital. They're putting it up fast, backing it against the curtain wall of the old castle so that they don't have to build as much. She says that the Touched will heal better in long dormitories, anyway, rather than individual rooms."

She had said more than that. Mair had sniffed at his suggestion that the sick could be nursed in his palace. She had said that too many had fallen ill—men, women, and children. Besides, the roaming Touched would never be comfortable in fine halls, in well-appointed chambers. They would grow restless, and their minds would not heal with their bodies. The firelung might continue to rage through their ranks; they might become a reservoir of illness that would spill over into the other castes, into all the rest of Moren. Mair had disdained Hal's wealth and royal presumption.

"It's easier to tend to them that way." Puladarati shrugged. "No reason to keep them separate from each other, if they've already fallen ill."

At first, Mair's arguments had made no sense—invalids should have rest, peace, quiet. They should not be awakened by the desperate coughing of other firelung victims, by the screaming nightmares of mothers who had lost their children, of orphans who faced their desperate illness alone.

Then, he had watched the Touched girl, watched the easy way that she traveled down the rows of stark cots. She talked to one woman there, told a ribald tale to a man. Children who were well enough followed behind, ranging among the patients as if they were searching for hidden wealth. Everywhere that Mair passed, everywhere that the children roamed, the patients rested easier. They relaxed against their stained sheets, and they breathed more easily, comforted by familiarity.

Hal had to trust that Mair would make it right. She would

see that the people who had given the most to save Moren were not destroyed in the city's rebuilding.

Hal understood that much about the Touched, but he could not think of a way to tell his former regent what he had learned. The man was a noble; he'd lived all his life in his birth caste. Puladarati wasn't about to start changing his ideas about the Touched now—he wasn't going to forget about roving hordes of children who needed to be turned out of the city streets on a regular basis. Puladarati was a great man, a strong general, and a devoted friend, but the foundations of such men could rarely be shifted.

Hal reached out to clap the man on his velvet-covered shoulder. "Aye, no reason at all. They'll be grateful for the company. As will our fellow councilors, when we begin our meeting on time."

"One moment, my lord," Puladarati said. The old man ran his three-fingered hand through his hair, squinting as he avoided Hal's gaze. "I've brought with me—"

Before Puladarati could continue, a bell began to toll, announcing the new hour and the supposed start to the council meeting. Hal looked up at the page who stood on the threshold of the council chamber. The boy smiled eagerly at him.

"Later, my lord," Hal said. "We'll have time enough to talk after our business here is done." Before Puladarati could protest, Hal nodded to the boy. The page looked from Hal to the regent and back again, and then he thrust open the heavy oak panels.

As Hal stepped over the threshold, his advisors scrambled to their feet, pushing back chairs in a cacophonous shriek of oak against stone. "My lords!" he exclaimed, doing his best to imitate a man who had slept well the night before, a man who was looking forward to the coming hours and the determination of policy, plans, administration.

He took a moment to seek out Farsobalinti, his former squire. Farso had been Hal's most recent appointment to the council; the young nobleman had been elevated just one year before. Hal had come to value Farso's steady good temper, his calm acceptance of council machinations.

Today Farso did not meet his gaze. Hal was annoyed that the

man was distracted, fully engaged in listening to Count Edpulaminbi. There would not be much of interest there, Hal was sure—Edpulaminbi would be discussing the new soldiers' barracks that he hoped to build. The count had had little else to speak about for the past fortnight—barracks, and wells, and other details of civil construction.

Shrugging off Farso's inattentiveness, Hal nodded to the scribe, who rapidly swore in the council meeting in the name of the day's deity, Nome, asking for the blessing of the god of children. When the formalities were completed, Hal granted Puladarati the honor of making the first report.

The former regent glanced over his shoulder at his cloaked and hooded secretary, as if he would require assistance from the man. Nevertheless, he stood and bowed to Hal, addressing his first words to his liege lord before he included the rest of the council with an expansive three-fingered gesture. "Amanthia is healing well, Your Majesty. Whatever flaws Sin Hazar might have had, he organized his country well. His administrative officers have continued to maintain taxing rolls, and the priests still record births and deaths, tracking all the people by the northern castes of sun, lion, owl, and swan."

Hal nodded. He still did not understand the northern system, could not comprehend how a man's entire life could be ordained by the stars that shone in the sky at his birth. Nevertheless, the Amanthians had operated under that system for generations. Hal knew that, at one point, Puladarati had considered tattooing his cheek with a swan—the northerners' hereditary caste of leaders—but he had rejected the notion as unnecessary for a conquering governor.

And Amanthia was well and truly conquered. Sin Hazar may have been a shrewd administrator, but he had not fully contemplated the end result of his plan to sell off the children of his land. He had not imagined what it would be like to rule a country bereft of an entire generation of boys, of men. Even in its absence, the Little Army continued to harrow Amanthia. The absent children constantly reminded the northerners of how much they had lost. Mothers, sisters, ancient grandfathers—all were daunted by their visions of what the proud

Amanthia had been, what it no longer was. Without the children, Amanthia had faced famine and riot, utter political disorganization.

Puladarati concluded his summary: "We have seed corn in the barns for the first time since Your Majesty took control over Amanthia. It should be planted within the next month, and we have every reason to expect that it will mature into bountiful rations for animals and men. In addition, we have high hopes for the wheat crop. The trade fairs, which were stopped entirely after Sin Hazar's execution, are now prepared to begin again, at least the one in Amanth itself. Your northern territory, Your Majesty, is well on the way to recovery."

"We thank you, Puladarati," Hal said. Mention of the trade fairs, of course, called Rani back to mind. Hal's pulse quickened, and he curled his fingers into involuntary fists. Even if he had been wrong in fighting with her about the Holy Father's loan, even if their dispute were his fault, she should have acknowledged his apology. It had not been easy to find anemones this early in the year, especially ones the color of her precious blue Zarithian glass.

Hal realized that his thoughts were wandering, and he forced his attention back to the council. Before he could broach the next topic, though—the construction of Mair's hospitals for the Touched—Puladarati cleared his throat. "Your Majesty, if I may beg your indulgence?"

"My lord?" Hal answered easily, trying to ignore his stomach's sudden, queasy turn. It was unusual for Puladarati to stray from the expected path of a meeting.

"There is another matter that I must raise, one that we've discussed often in the past. I know that the timing is poor now, with Moren's current plight, but I cannot return to the north without having broached the subject."

"Go ahead, my lord." Hal tried to keep a chill from his voice. He did not care for surprises, particularly surprises originating in the northern territories. Amanthia had taught him enough about surprise for a lifetime.

"Your Majesty, as you know, your predecessor in Amanthia sold thousands of children over the sea, bartering their bodies to feed his own desire for power. When you assumed the crown of Amanthia, you assumed responsibility for all her people, including those children, including the Little Army."

Hal understood Puladarati now; he knew where this discussion would lead. He gestured to cut off the nobleman. "Enough, my lord. I have said that I will seek out the Little Army, but I can scarcely do that now. Moren needs me."

"Your people need you, lord! *All* your people!" The shout came from behind Puladarati, loud and defiant, starkly angry in the council chamber.

Hal jerked back in his chair, his hand reflexively twitching to the dagger at his waist. The other council lords reacted as well—Edpulaminbi, sitting closest to Puladarati, stood and drew his sword in one fluid motion, toppling his chair. The sharp blade came to rest against the robed chest of Puladarati's secretary, the point snagging on the heavy wool.

At the man's first word, Farso had drawn his sword, kicking aside Edpulaminbi's chair and adding his blade to the throat of the robed intruder. Even across the room, even with the thud of adrenaline pounding in his veins, Hal could see the taut rage in Farso's arm, the quivering fury that anyone would dare invade the council chamber of Morenia's king, would dare to raise his voice in rebellious anger.

"Hold!" Puladarati cried above the confusion. "Hold, Count Edpulaminbi, Lord Farsobalinti!" The former regent whirled back to Hal. "Your Majesty, forgive me! I told my companion that he could accompany me here, but I instructed him that he must remain silent while your council met. I *thought* that the discipline of the northern army would have made him keep his word."

"Your companion," Hal repeated. He suspected now that he knew who stood beneath the "secretary's" robes. "Have him stand forward."

Edpulaminbi edged his sword back, shifting his hand on the weapon so that he could dispatch the intruder if necessary. Farso backed away also, but he kept his sword conspicuously ready. Puladarati made one curt gesture with his three-fingered hand, enforcing the command with a glare. The robed clerk hesitated only a moment, then stepped up to the table, casting back his hood and glaring defiantly at the assembled noblemen.

A scar shone high on his cheekbone, sickly white against his dusky skin.

"Crestman," Hal said.

"Your Majesty." For a moment, Hal thought that the northerner intended to confront him in the very council chamber, meant to call him out to defend his honor and his actions on behalf of all Morenia. Instead, the former lieutenant in the Little Army bowed his head, stepping back from the council table just enough that he could sink to one knee. He folded his arms across his chest in a stiff military obeisance.

"Rise, my lord," Hal said, keeping his words measured. Seeing the other man brought back a flood of memories—visions of the northern city of Amanth, of the pitiful crowd of Little Army soldiers that Hal had been able to save. In addition, he could remember Rani, torn between her obligation to her homeland and to strange Amanthia, her obligation to Hal and her debt to Crestman. Hal had not asked her to explain what had happened with the northern lieutenant, what words—or more—had passed between them. But he had his suspicions, fostered by letters that Rani sent regularly to Amanthia, long missives sealed with the waxen symbol of the still-dead glasswrights guild.

Hal forced his voice to stay even, and he gestured to Farso to right Edpulaminbi's chair. The former squire complied, but he stood beside his fellow councilor, both men keeping their weapons at the ready. Hal said to Crestman, "You may speak your mind, my lord."

Crestman glared at him, strong emotion darkening the soldier's face, making his scar stand out even more. "You told us you would not abandon us, my lord. You said that you would help Amanthia rebuild. You promised to gather together the Little Army and retrieve your loyal subjects from Liantine."

"And I will keep my word."

"When?" The demand crashed against the walls of the council chamber with enough vehemence that Hal barely stopped himself from flinching. Farso's blade twitched.

Puladarati stepped forward, resting his maimed hand on Crestman's arm. "I'm sorry, Your Majesty. This soldier is ex-

cited. He has recently received news from the east, news about
the Little Army."

Hal forced his voice to stay reasonable. He was determined
not to lose his temper in front of his council lords, yet he was
bound not to back down before Crestman's inappropriate, ac-
cusatory tone. "What news?"

Puladarati nodded to Crestman, and the youth took a deep
breath. He was clearly fighting to keep his own temper, struggling to maintain respect for the king he had sworn to honor
and support. "I have sent out scouts, my lord. One full year ago,
I sent a dozen riders to determine where the Little Army rests,
to find who bought my soldiers and what work has been required of them. The last of my scouts returned on San's feast
day."

San. The god of steel. Four weeks before. "And?" Hal
asked.

"The Little Army is scattered throughout Liantine, my lord.
There is no one camp that houses them, no one town. But many
have been sold to certain places—to some of the guilds, to
some of the courts."

"We knew as much before."

"Aye, my lord. But now we know that the Little Army is
being ill used. The spiderguild is one new owner of your people. They bought many soldiers, many of our youngest re-
cruits, to tend the octolaris spiders that form the base of their
wealth."

The spiderguild. Hal had heard of them, of course. They
were the strongest guild in all of Liantine—they rivaled the foreign king for power and prestige. They held a monopoly on
spidersilk, a rare luxury, and they milked their investment for
every sou they could harvest. He kept his voice noncommittal.
"I've heard of the spiderguild."

"Have you heard how they exploit children? How they require boys and girls to stand for long hours throughout the
night, waiting for markin grubs to finish feeding on riberry
leaves? Have you heard how they command children to pluck
those grubs, to place them, one by one, in front of venomous
spiders, without regard to the danger, without regard to potential death?"

Hal kept his voice even, countering Crestman's quaking rage. "The spiderguild is wealthy, my lord, because it deals with a dangerous commodity. They're wealthy enough to purchase what they need to meet their goals. Children. Mercenary soldiers."

Crestman glared at Hal. "You have said in the past that you oppose slavery. You said that you would free the Little Army."

"I will, my lord. All in good time."

"My soldiers do not have time! It has been *two years*, my lord! Two years since we learned of Sin Hazar's treachery, and years before that since he began to ship children overseas. Your Majesty, just eight weeks ago, my scouts witnessed a horrible death. A soldier in the Little Army—one of the girls who was the last to sail to Liantine—was required to feed the octolaris spiders. She had not been trained, my lord, or she forgot her training. The spiders attacked her. A child, my lord! A little girl!"

Puladarati stepped forward, putting his hand on Crestman's arm, but the angry youth shook off the grip. "Have you heard how spider venom works, my lord? It makes your tongue swell. It makes your tongue swell and your throat close. That child suffocated, my lord. Your soldier suffocated, in the open air, beneath the springtime sun. Her lips turned black and her skin turned blue. A little girl, my lord!"

"And what have you done, Crestman? You were authorized to speak in my name on matters of the Little Army—what have you done to redeem this child's death?"

"I wrote to the spiderguild, my lord. I demanded to know what precautions they were taking to protect children. I demanded to know how they could justify letting little girls die."

"And?"

"And they took their time responding. I waited a fortnight for a messenger bird to arrive. When it came, the message was short, the language terse. They bought the girl, and they could do with her as they wished. They paid good money to King Sin Hazar, and I had no interest—*you* had no interest—in what they did with their purchases."

Whispers rose around the council table, and Hal fought to control his sudden flash of anger. He hardly knew this spider-

guild, and he'd never met its master. Hal had never been to
Liantine, never dreamed of confronting its wealthy power-
mongers. Why this disrespectful tone, then? Why this blatant
incitement to conflict?

It wasn't disrespect. Even as Hal's soul trembled against
the death of a child he had sworn to protect, he realized that
the spiderguild was not being *disrespectful*. It was merely
using its investment. In Liantine, slavery was the law—that
land's king permitted trade in human beings, and it was perfectly legitimate to place a child, even a defenseless girl, in
bondage.

Accidents happened, particularly in the dangerous world of
the spiderguild. No one could argue that a slaveholder *wanted*
to destroy his investment. The guild had likely been chagrined
at its loss—perhaps only for financial reason, but chagrined all
the same.

Hal kept his voice even. "I cannot mount a military campaign against the spiderguild at this time."

Crestman's response was immediate. "I'm not asking you
to, my lord."

"What, then? What would you have me do?"

"Journey to Liantine, my lord. Recall the Little Army—buy
back, if you must, the boys and girls who served Amanthia.
Save your people as you once promised to do." Crestman flung
back his humble secretary's robes and swept his sword from his
sheath—a curved, northern sword. Before there could be any
chance to question his intention, he knelt in full obeisance,
leaning his head against the beautifully crafted hilt.

Farso and Edpulaminbi leaped behind him, the council
lords' weapons forming twin rays of light that seemed to em-
anate from Crestman's shoulders. Ignoring the threat, the soldier raised his chin to look directly at his king. "I pledge my
sword in your service to redeem the Little Army. I pledge my
sword, and all that I can do to save the children of Amanthia.
Go to Liantine, Your Majesty. See your subjects as they labor
in unfair service. See them and redeem the Little Army.
Speak with the king of Liantine, and end this travesty of justice."

Hal saw the tableau the soldier had created, the fealty that was offered anew, even as a transformed feudal promise was demanded. Well, Hal had already pledged to bring the Little Army home. He had vowed to get the children out of Liantine, as many as he could find, as many as could be freed. His days had been filled with other obligations, other demands upon his time and energy and treasury. And now, with Moren burnt and failing, with increased pressure to bid for power within the Fellowship, with the world turned upside down . . .

He looked down the council table, saw the faces of his nine most treasured advisors. Edpulaminbi and Farso. Puladarati. Men appointed by his father to serve Morenia, men that Hal had chosen himself. All gazing at him. All expecting him to act.

And what was he to do? He could not buy back the Little Army—his treasury likely would not have withstood that *before* the fire. Now, with the Holy Father holding him hostage? To gain himself a bit more time, Hal said, "I accept your pledge, Crestman. I accept that you intend your naked sword to offer honor to my crown."

He waited a moment, for the weight of his words to register. The northern soldier inclined his head and returned his sword to his sheath. He was no fool.

Edpulaminbi and Farso retreated a few steps, each man sliding his own weapon home at Hal's flicked glance. Puladarati cleared his throat, shifting slightly from foot to foot. The man was obviously disconcerted by the turn the council meeting had taken, by Crestman's presumption. He glanced from his young northern charge to his king and back again. Before the regent could fashion some diplomatic words, another councilor spoke, Count Jerumalashi.

"Your Majesty. If I may speak?"

"Aye, my lord. All councilors may speak at this table."

"Sire," the nobleman said. "As long as the subject of Liantine is on the table, there is another matter there that concerns you."

Hal pulled his attention from the still-kneeling Crestman. "Aye?"

"We have discussed this matter in many council meetings, Sire, meetings well before the fire and our latest challenges."

Jerumalashi laughed nervously. He was a man of three score years, a sturdy, scholarly farmer who had advised Hal's father for over two decades. Hal had kept Jerumalashi on the council as a gesture toward the House of Jair, as a visible symbol that the son learned from the father. Even so, Jerumalashi and Hal had no great love of each other, no great friendship that had drawn them together. The nobleman was clearly nervous as he completed his thought. "Your Majesty, you come from a long line, a noble line that traces its roots all the way back to the house of Jair the Pilgrim."

Hal tried to make himself relax, tried to breathe out a little of the tension that twisted through his gut. He knew now what Jerumalashi was going to say; the argument had become painfully familiar in the past two years. The older man continued, "Your Majesty, your heir is an unruly child."

"Orsi is my cousin, my lord." Hal tried to keep his voice light. "He's a good cousin. He's even learning to be a good page."

"It is time that you established an heir of your body."

"How many of you lords councilor advised me to wait for that, when a girl first caught my eye?" Hal tried to turn the words into a joke, and a couple of the nobles at the table dutifully smiled, but Jerumalashi stiffened in visible disapproval.

What? Hal wanted to ask. There have been other girls who've interested me since Rani! Do you really think that I would make Rani Trader my queen? Do you truly think that I—even I—would try that? Jerumalashi and other older nobles had trouble remembering to give Rani the title "Lady" when she dined in the palace. Hal would hardly expect his nobles to accept his marriage to the girl. Woman. Glasswright. Merchant. Whatever she was.

Besides, he wasn't even speaking to Rani. She had not acknowledged his gift of anemones.

Puladarati remonstrated with him, where Jerumalashi might not have had the nerve. "This is not a matter for jest, Your Majesty. You know that it is important for you to secure your dynasty. To that end, two years ago, you authorized Count Jerumalashi and me to open discussions with the great houses."

Hal's lungs compressed in his chest. Of course he had authorized his lords to act. He had been seventeen years old, by Jair. He had been eager to "secure his dynasty," or at least to practice.

The Briantan princess's visit had been an unfortunate result from Hal authorizing his lords to search for a suitable bride. The Briantan, and before her, a toothless duchess, and a dimwitted countess from only the gods knew where.

Now, with a wounded city, with Crestman's challenge to redeem the Little Army, with a thousand details of state . . . Hal did not have time to discuss brides and wedding vows. Morenia could ill afford the expense and distraction of royal nuptials when it needed to rebuild. Nevertheless, Puladarati and Jerumalashi were both waiting, and Hal forced himself to say, "Aye, my lord. So I authorized you."

The former regent nodded his silvery head. "And Count Jerumalashi and I have attempted to make reports to you on a regular basis about our progress."

"Aye." Hal knew that he should not feel the urge to justify; he should not try to convince his councilors that he had been too busy to focus on those reports. After all, he *had* listened. He *had* heard about the endless supply of breeding stock that ranged in age from newborn princesses to a dowager duchess who was nearly fifteen years older than Hal.

"You have not listened closely, Your Majesty. No, no, I understand—you have had many matters on your mind; you have been consumed with affairs of state. But it is time for you to turn to affairs of the heart, my lord."

"I hardly think that 'heart' enters into these negotiations, Your Grace."

Puladarati shrugged. "As you will, Sire. Nevertheless, you must negotiate."

Jerumalashi stepped forward again, apparently eager to present his point, now that Puladarati had frayed some of Hal's wrath. "And, Sire, you could scarce do better than to join with Berylina, the only daughter of the king of Liantine."

"Berylina!" Hal exclaimed. There was a whisper at the table, a couple of the lords conferring with each other. There was no outcry, though, no grand surprise. Clearly, the council lords had discussed this matter among themselves. They had obviously been informed of the princess's name before. Both Puladarati and Jerumalashi stayed silent, and Hal took a moment to marshal all his arguments for one fight. He drew a deep breath and gripped the edge of the table, offering up a fleeting prayer to Hin, the god of rhetoric.

"She's only thirteen years old, my lords. Her family has held its throne for only two generations; they're more controlled by the spiderguild than by their own interests. She's got four older brothers who will distribute the wealth of Liantine among their heirs before anything reaches the princess." And she has buck teeth, Hal wanted to say. And her eyes are crossed. He had not completely ignored his lords these past months. He had listened to the rumors about every candidate they considered.

Jerumalashi glanced at Puladarati. When the former regent merely shrugged, the other nobleman said, "Her dowry could bring you much of the money you need—now—to repay the church. Her mother was obviously fertile; the girl has four brothers."

Hal turned his blush into a rebellious attack. "And I'll need to wait five years before I can think of serving stud."

"Not that long," Puladarati said mildly, smothering the breath of surprise from some of the more prudish council lords.

"She's a *child*!"

"The Liantines marry early, Your Majesty." Jerumalashi might have been discussing grafting apple trees, for all the emotion in his reply. "Two years is not so long to wait. Not when one of those years will be consumed with planning a royal wedding. It's been a long time since the house of Jair has taken a wife."

"Two years! That's impossible! She'll only be fifteen!"

Puladarati said mildly, "And what were you doing when you were fifteen, Your Majesty?"

Hal swallowed a hundred acid retorts. He had been trying to save his kingdom. He had been fighting for all Morenia, battling the Brotherhood of Justice, negotiating with the Fellowship of Jair. He had been trying to save himself, and Rani.

Rani. He could not imagine telling her that he was taking a child as his bride.

He grasped at arguments. "Puladarati, you yourself have said that I must yield an heir. Why would you have me wait nearly three years for that?"

"It will take the better part of one, no matter whom you wed. The merger with Liantine will provide Morenia with much needed gold now, and with the potential for more in the future. Who knows what other possibilities for profit might lie overseas, even in the silk trade? Why not marry into the family that has been exploiting that trade for longer than you've even been aware of it? Why not let this union benefit everyone?"

Everyone? Not likely. Not Hal himself. "There have to be other options."

"Oh, there are, Your Majesty." The former regent agreed too quickly. "There are other girls suitable for a royal marriage. Some, though, are even younger than Berylina. A few are old enough that they might not be able to bear the heir that you need. Some come from weak families that only hope to gain power and glory by merging with your family. We've spoken about this, my lord, all your council seated here. We are agreed, Sire. Berylina is the best bride for you."

"You've *spoken* about it—" Hal exploded in rage, pounding the table and looking at his assembled advisors. "You! Farso! You've stood in my palace and debated my bloodlines, as if I were some stallion?"

Hal began to understand why Farso had avoided his eyes at the beginning of this horrid council session. Nevertheless, the newest councilor stood by the side of the table and bowed. "Your Majesty, I've speculated on a bride who will make you strong. A bond that will strengthen all Morenia. We're all concerned for you."

"Concerned for me? What am I, some rutting boar who might go mad if I don't tup the sow you offer?"

Puladarati stood. "Your Majesty!" The words cut through Hal's spluttering rage, and Puladarati continued in a calmer tone. "Your Majesty, you are the leader of our kingdom. You have brought us out of a time of fear and treason. You have expanded the boundaries of your kingdom by conquering the northern land of Amanthia. You have embraced our needs, met our requirements, negotiated with the church to rebuild your city.

"We have always been loyal to you, Sire, because of the crown that you wear. And now, we have come to love you. We have come to love you, and we want your line to continue. We mean you no insult, and we mean you no harm. We want you to be happy, Your Majesty. And we need you to take a bride."

Hal listened to Puladarati's words, heard the calm logic. There was a reason that the man had been appointed regent. There was a reason that Hal had left him to govern Amanthia, and looked to his wisdom at the council table. Puladarati was a natural leader; he was loyal and dedicated. And he spoke the truth.

Hal sank back into his chair. "I'll not pledge myself to her until we've met."

"Of course not, Your Majesty. That's the very reason you should journey to Liantine. To meet."

"And this cannot wait until autumn? Until Moren is well toward rebuilding?"

"Sire, the sea passage is not smooth at any time. Why take the chance that you'll end up in Liantine for all the winter? Go now. Do your business. Know by autumn if Princess Berylina is to be your queen. And if the princess is the woman you will marry, if she is the next queen of all Morenia, then you may find it easier to negotiate for your Little Army. You may be able to save the lives of children, even as you bargain for the mother of your own."

"But *Berylina* . . ."

"We believe that she is best, Your Majesty. Best for all of us."

All of us but me, Hal wanted to say, but he knew better. He was a king, and he could not always say what he thought. Instead, he sighed and drew himself up to his full height. "Very well, my lords. I will travel to Liantine."

Hal glanced at the scribe, who had painstakingly recorded every word that had been spoken. "Let it be noted, then, that on this feast day of Nome in the fifth year of my reign, the god of children smiled upon me, and I agreed to travel to Liantine, to determine the fate of my Little Army and to bring embassy from Morenia to the house of Liantine, to the Princess Berylina."

The words were automatic as they spun from his tongue. But Hal glanced to his right, looking past the pleased Puladarati to Crestman. He saw the youth's tight grin and the smooth scar that glinted on his cheek. Hal looked at Crestman, but he thought of Rani, and he wondered just how much he had forfeited by agreeing to journey to Liantine.

4

Rani squinted into the constant breeze that blew across the courtyard. She wished that she had taken the time to find a cloak before venturing onto the balcony. The early spring sunshine was a relief after the dreariness of winter, but the air remained chilly.

Mair was bullying the workers far below, shouting orders at a team of carpenters that had arrived late that morning. The men were arguing back, apparently disputing whether they had enough lumber to build the walls the way that Mair demanded.

Rani pitied the poor workers. They had no idea how brutal the Touched girl could be, what demands she could make. Unbidden, a smile quirked her lips as one man threw his leather cap onto the courtyard flagstones, emphasizing his point with a loud oath. Mair did not hesitate to grind her heel into the cap, and she matched his oath with three of her own, employing more creativity and a broader vocabulary. Her Touched patois echoed off the palace walls like a file rasping wood.

"Some things never change."

Rani started at the voice, even though she knew she should have expected it. "Crestman," she said, turning slowly.

"Rani."

He was taller than she remembered. Taller, and his shoulders were broader. His face was the same, though—the planes of his cheeks with the white patch of his lion-scar, the hard line of his jaw, the calm depth of his dark eyes.

His voice was lower. Or maybe his words were husky because he had not said her name for three long years.

"I trust that you are comfortable in your quarters, my lord? Poor Moren has little to offer now, but you should at least have found clean sheets upon your bed."

"Aye."

He was not making this easy. She tried to make her voice light. "They're speaking of you in the streets this morning. You should be quite pleased—it takes a lot these days to make folk forget their squabbles over the price of eggs."

"I have not heard the gossip."

"They say that you shamed the king into journeying to Liantine."

"I did not intend to shame him. He is my liege lord, and I only hope to serve him."

"You think that hunting down the Little Army will serve us now? When we face the aftermath of fire and disease?"

"He made a promise. Good men keep their vows."

"King Halaravilli is a good man." Rani answered automatically, setting aside her own doubts, her own anger. Certainly, Hal might be spiteful. He might be immature. He might be a short-tempered, pigheaded, close-minded, name-calling child who thought that he could make all right by sending her a clutch of wilting flowers. But he was *trying* to be a good king. He was trying to save Morenia, even if he saw no path but an ill-considered loan at usurious rates. Besides, the flowers had been the blue of Zarithian glass. "The king acts as he thinks best, holding all of Morenia in his thoughts."

Something in her words heated Crestman's reply. "My lady, if we do not find the Little Army now, it will be too late. It might be too late already. Halaravilli rules two kingdoms now—Morenia and Amanthia. And we in the northern one must know our fate. We cannot live with any more indecision. We must commit our children to the pyre or bring them home."

"And are you prepared for what you might find, Crestman? Are you prepared to learn that all the Little Army is lost?"

"I'm a soldier, Rani Trader. I'm prepared for the reality of war." The words chilled her more than the wind that skirled through the courtyard. She knew that Crestman had trained with the Little Army; he had told her some of what he had suffered in Sin Hazar's horrific camps. Nevertheless, his brutal resignation was frightening. It made her question her own determination, made her doubt her own mettle as she stared down at the aftermath of Moren's brutal fire.

Desperately, she reached for a brighter topic, for some note of hope and success that she could spin out on the springtime breeze. "Davin has helped us tremendously. His engines finally stopped the fire—his calculations and his orders."

"He's a shrewd old man."

Silence. Rani racked her mind for something else to say—something witty and entertaining. She would settle for a pithy observation, a shrewd comment about Moren. About Amanthia. About the Little Army. About the cursed workers who were going about their task, pacing off the floor plan for Mair's hospital.

Rani was spared the need for more stiff conversation when Mair appeared at her side. The Touched girl held a fur-lined cape in her arms, kin to the one that was draped across her own shoulders. "Rai," she said, darting a glance at the northern visitor. "Crestman."

"Mair." Rani heard the old rivalry there, the old bonds that the pair had built around a soldier in the Little Army. Mair and Crestman had both loved the boy, but Monny had perished despite their best intentions.

The Touched girl shuddered and pulled her cloak closer about her shoulders. "You looked cold up here. I went to fetch your cloak."

"The breeze is chilly, but I'm not actually cold."

"I thought that you should put on your cloak," Mair said pointedly. Rani took the garment and shrugged it over her shoulders. "You should leave the balcony, Rai. We should let the men do their work without us hounding them."

"I'm hardly hounding—"

"By Jair, you can be difficult!"

By Jair.

Rani looked at Mair and realized that a flush painted her friend's cheeks. There was a scarce-suppressed excitement in her eyes as she cast a meaningful glance toward Crestman. All in a rush, Rani understood. The Fellowship of Jair had summoned them. A messenger must have arrived while Rani was distracted, while she was trying to speak with Crestman.

She could not imagine what the Fellowship might want. Ever since the fire, the shadowy body had lain quiet, convening no meeting, issuing no instructions. Rani had begun to fear that some of the leaders had been destroyed in the fire. After all, the Fellowship drew its members from all the castes in the city. The leader of the Moren cell was an old Touched woman—who could say that Glair had not succumbed to firelung, even if she had escaped the flames?

But someone had finally decided that it was time for the Fellowship to act. And whatever had provoked that decision must be important. It was risky for the group to congregate at any time, but it was absurdly dangerous to gather in the middle of the day, with the sun up and all the people of the city about. . . .

Rani swallowed a dozen questions and pulled her furred cloak closer about her shoulders. She turned back to Crestman. "I'm sorry, my lord. Mair is right. I must not distract the workmen by watching from here. Besides, I promised I would sort herbs from the new shipment that arrived this morning."

"Duty always calls." His words were bitter.

"I'm sorry," she said again.

He reached out, cupping her cheek with one warm hand. "Tell me that you'll speak with me this evening, Rani Trader. Tell me that we can sit beside the fire and talk about our plans."

We have no plans, she wanted to say. You are going to Liantine with Hal. Traveling to a distant land that holds the remnants of the Little Army. And a princess. I am going nowhere.

Instead, she nodded once, feeling his fingers move with her. "We'll talk."

Mair took her arm, pulling her across the room and toward the stairs, toward the palace gates before she could worry about any other words, any other promises. Rani's thoughts were roiling inside her skull as she approached the guardhouse, but she forced a smile across her lips. "Good morning, Wodurini."

"Good morning, my lady," the man bowed briefly, turning

halfway toward Mair to include her in his greeting. "You're not going out in the city!"

"But we are. Lady Mair and I promised His Majesty that we would see how the excavation crews are progressing in the Merchants' Quarter. We cannot begin rebuilding the market-place until the fire damage is cleared."

Rani's tone was blithe as she invoked Hal's name, but her heart pounded. Hal would attend the Fellowship's meeting. She would see him for the first time since their disastrous fight, communicate with him for the first time since he had sent her the anemones. Annoyed with herself, she pushed aside the thought. Hal was her king, and he was her fellow in the eyes of Jair. All else was separate. All else was immaterial in view of Morenia's plight.

"One of my men should accompany you, my lady. It's dangerous out there."

"The danger is from falling timber, Wodurini. None of your men can protect us from that. We'll watch our step." The guard started to scowl, but Rani shook her head and lied easily. "Besides, the engineers who work on the hospital have said that they will need assistance in raising some frames this afternoon. You'll likely need to send every man you can spare to the court-yard."

"But my lady—"

"We'll be fine." Rani made her voice firm, but she smiled. "We mustn't delay. The king will be asking after us if we don't hurry."

Rani settled her fingers on Mair's arm, pulling her friend beneath the heavy portcullis. She ignored the soldier's grumbled complaints as she threaded her way into the crowds on the city streets. With so many people evicted from their fire-destroyed homes, the paved ways were bustling.

Mair took advantage of the general commotion to hiss, "It was easier to answer the group's summons when I only needed to duck away from my own Touched troop."

"It's easier," Rani said, "when they don't summon us in the middle of the day. How did they get a message to you?"

"I was speaking with the carpenter, and he was explaining why the king's money would be wasted on one long hall. He honestly thought that I have no idea what I was asking for. You should warn the king, Rai—that carpenter is just scheming to take his money and leave with the job half-done. He's a Briantan! He has no pride! He thinks that he can come here to Moren and exploit us when we need him most. Well, he—"

"Mair," Rani interrupted. "The messenger."

The Touched girl swallowed the rest of her vitriolic speech before continuing. "I thought at first that Rabe had sent the child."

Rani nodded. She remembered Mair's lieutenant, a shrewd boy who had taken an immediate dislike to a young merchant girl turned guildsman who had fled her new caste. To be fair, Rani had done her best to provoke him. Still, the boy—now a man, Rani supposed—had done a good job leading his crew in the streets.

Mair continued. "This was no child I had ever seen, though. Whoever is leading her troop isn't doing a grand job, either. Th' puir bairn 'ad only a shift on, not a scrap o' cape i' th' mornin' chill."

Rani realized that Mair had slipped back into the Touched patois that she had spoken all her youth, and she resisted the urge to smile. Fierce emotions always brought out Mair's rough past. "I'm sure you remedied that."

Mair blinked. "Aye. The child proved lucky—the cloak I was wearing was a bit ragged at the seams. She might be able to keep it if the older children in her troop find it too shabby to fight over."

"What did she *say*, Mair?" Whatever the message, it must have been disturbing. Mair was usually far more direct.

"Not much at all. But she handed me this." Mair produced a scrap of parchment from the pouch at her waist, and Rani stopped to read.

Jair summons all his faithful children.

Rani turned the scrap over, but there was nothing else. "She had no other message?"

"Nothing. She took the cloak I gave her, and she ran."

"But how do we know where to meet?"

"We've received no notice of a new place, so we'll go to the old."

"But the old one burned to the ground!"

"We met below the ground, Rai. The guildhall cellar must have survived, or we'd have heard of another gathering spot."

Rani lacked Mair's complacence, or the Touched girl's faith in the Fellowship's communication. Nevertheless, she followed Mair through the city streets. As they left behind the palace compound, there were fewer people about. In short order, the pair skirted the edge of the fire-blackened ruins, arriving at the quarter that had housed merchants before the conflagration. These streets had been home to Rani for the first twelve years of her life, but her heart quailed at entering them now.

"Mair, I haven't been in there since the fire."

The Touched girl shrugged. "We'll be fine."

"It isn't safe! You heard Wodurini."

"It's safe enough. Besides, we have no choice, Rai. We'll stay on the main streets. We're just passing through to the Guildsmen's Quarter."

Rani let herself be convinced, but the first few steps were the hardest. Black grit crunched beneath her hard-soled shoes, yielding up the sharp smell of charcoal. Rani could see where Davin's engines had felled entire rows of buildings—storefronts, with their homes above, collapsed upon themselves in heaps of rubble. Rainwater had drenched the destruction, working its own damage, washing away shattered, blackened timbers. Dirty puddles shimmered in front of scorched, smoke-stained buildings. Rani's heart began to beat faster.

She caught her breath as she ventured farther into the ruins, nauseated by the stench of burned timber and melted stone. The paving stones of the road had shattered under the combined assault of hot flame and cold rain, and the path required all her attention. Twice, Rani and Mair startled rats, and the animals were slow to slink away from the shapeless prey that they gnawed. Rani was grateful that the priests had already passed through this quarter. At least the dead had been carried out, committed to clean and purifying pyres.

The farther the two girls went, the greater the damage from the fire itself. Rani knew that one corner had boasted two silver shops and the finest woven goods in all of Moren, but now nothing remained of the rich shops. There, on that long street, had been the vendors of all things made of tin. And on yet another, there had been leather goods, stretching as far as the eye could see.

Now, all the wooden frames were charred to shadows, and sooty stone crumbled on cracked foundations. The sky was often blocked, and the breeze that whistled through the ruins was even colder than the one that blew in the king's courtyard.

And everywhere, Rani smelled the acid reek of soot. Charred wood, melted stone, ruined curtains and furniture, clothing and trade goods. The stench was thick enough that she thought her lungs would never breathe free. She raised her sleeve and held it across her nose, as if that would be enough to keep the smell of utter destruction from intruding.

Mair led the way as if she had already prowled through these ruins. She chose turnings down the devastated streets, navigating by memory, for there were no more references, not a single cheerful merchant sign. She took them the long way around the open space that had been the marketplace—Hal's men were busy excavating that field, preparing it for rebuilding. It would not do to be seen in the ruins.

At last, they reached the burnt-out warren of streets that had formed the barrier between the merchants and the guilds, and then they walked on the broader streets of the Guildsmen's Quarter. Rani knew these passages less well than those that crisscrossed her childhood home.

Of course, she remembered where the ill-fated Glasswrights' Guild had stood. When she had been bound by her new caste's expectations, she had found few opportunities to explore the surrounding streets. Mair, as the leader of a Touched troop, had lived under no such restrictions. She led the way through the devastation with confidence.

Rani noticed that the ground beneath their feet bore many footprints. Fire or no, people had been prowling through the Guildsmen's Quarter. Rani commented on the traffic to Mair, who shrugged. "The Touched. They'll have scoured these streets from top to bottom. I would have brought in my troop as soon as it was cool enough to walk here."

Rani looked about the desolate ruins. "What could you hope to find?"

"You know the Touched, Rai. The guildsmen, the King's Men—they'd pass over all sorts of treasures. The Touched might be the only folk in all of Moren to have grown richer from the fire." The statement sent a shiver down Rani's spine; she could not help but think of the Touched she had seen in the firelung wards, coughing, gasping, hacking up black soot. Nevertheless, she was grateful for the feet that had passed this way, crossing and recrossing the girls' path. If not for the Touched, Mair's and Rani's footprints would have been conspicuous. They might have led any overcurious strangers to the Fellowship's secret meeting place.

"Here we are," Mair said at last. Rani turned her head at an angle, and she managed to recognize the wall that had surrounded the Tilers' Guild. She could make out the kilns that had fired the guildsmen's pottery, the ruined sheds where apprentices had mixed huge vats of clay with shredded straw. She could see the pitiful remains of the garden that had fed the guild, the spidery trellises that had been erected for vines. A pang shot through Rani's heart as she looked around—so much of this blighted landscape resembled her own destroyed glasswrights' guild after the old king's soldiers had had their way with it, after they had torn it down and torched it for her supposed wrongdoings.

Mair, unencumbered by such haunting memories, picked across the sooty ground, grimacing at the cross-beamed structure that threatened to collapse at any moment. "Back here, Rai. The cellar opened onto the edge of the garden. Remember?"

Rani swallowed hard and forced herself to follow. Of course, Mair was right. The Fellowship's secret meeting house had been hidden from the street, hidden from casual onlookers. The tilers' gatekeeper was a member; that was how the Fellowship had been spirited past the guild's high walls.

The entrance to the cellar was set into massive stonework, as if its builder had anticipated that it would provide a refuge after some great disaster. The deep alcove had protected the oaken door—although the planks were darkened, they stood fast. Rani followed Mair down a handful of steps, gathering her skirts close to keep them from brushing against the blackened stairs. The door was slightly ajar, as if it had been forced inward by the fiery forces that had been at work throughout the quarter.

Mair paused for a moment and reached beneath her furred cloak. She fumbled among her garments, and then she withdrew some scraps of black fabric, as dark as the fire-charred wood around them. Her fingers moving with certainty despite the chill in the air, Mair separated out two pieces of cloth and passed one to Rani.

By time-honored custom, the Fellowship of Jair hid their faces from each other when they came together in a large meeting. Traditionally, that hiding took the form of long, full cloaks, with dark hoods that swept over the wearers' heads. The alternative, though, a fashion newly come to the secret conspirators, was a simple cloth mask, a loose hood that covered only the head, hanging down to the wearer's shoulders. The mask was a reflection of the truth that all the conspirators knew—the disguises were more symbolic than practical. Rani could recognize more than a dozen members of the Fellowship, black hoods or no.

Still, tradition was tradition. Mair must have snatched Rani's hood from its hiding place at the same time that she collected both girls' cloaks. Rani caught her breath as she pulled on the garment. It took a moment for her to find the eye holes, and she fought down a momentary surge of panic when she could not see. Of course she was fine. Of course she could breathe. Mair was beside her, and all would be well.

Apparently unaware of Rani's scrambled panic, Mair glided down to the bottom stair. Her whisper was harsh as she said, "The spring rain nurtures the thistle and the thorn."

Rain. Thistle. Thorn. The Fellowship's passwords were always vaguely ominous.

As if the entrance were controlled by Cor, the god of doors, the heavy oak swung inward, and Mair and Rani moved rapidly over the threshold. Rani blinked in the dark interior, willing her eyes to adjust to the single flickering candle at the end of the short corridor. Once again, Mair led the way as the girls walked toward the guttering flame.

Rani's heart leaped in her chest. She had certainly been to a number of Fellowship meetings in the past five years, and she'd spent her share of time lurking in dark hallways. But this meeting place seemed eerier than the others; it was more dangerous, with the timbers above the cellar creaking in the stiffening spring breeze. In the past, Rani had feared only that the Fellowship might be discovered. Now, she feared that they all might die, caught in the collapse of a ceiling loaded down with ruined wood.

Her morbid speculation was cut short as they stepped into a large room. The two girls were nearly the last to arrive—dozens of people already milled about the chamber, perhaps two score conspirators. There were a few whispers, a few surreptitious greetings among people who recognized each other beneath their symbolic black disguises. Mostly, there was a quiet sense of expectation.

Rani used the time to look about the room, to try to identify members of the Fellowship whom she knew outside of the cellar. Hal was the easiest to find—he stood by himself, at the dais at the front of the room. He must have escaped the palace from one of his secret passages. Over the years, he had become an expert at avoiding his retainers' watchful eyes. He wore his hood like the other members of the Fellowship, but he was known to all in the room. Other fellows kept their distance from him, uncertain of the proper etiquette regarding an anonymous king. Uncertain, Rani thought, of the rumors that had begun to swirl through the anonymous company, rumors that said Hal had high hopes for the Fellowship, or at least for his place within its ranks.

Rani pushed aside such thoughts and extended her search, looking for the broad shoulders of a tall merchant man. Borin. He had led the Merchants' Council when Rani's guild was destroyed, and he had helped a lost, confused girl find her way clear of conspiring forces. Rani had not consciously realized that she was worried about Borin's safety after the fire, but when she saw him across the room, her relief was palpable. She wondered if his bald head glistened beneath its black hood, as it had in the marketplace so long ago.

She did not have time for further speculation. A figure shuffled to the front of the room, moving jerkily as if weighted down by its hunched shoulders. The person's black mask was ragged; the eye holes looked as if they had been ripped with a rusty nail. The disheveled garment matched the newcomer's clothes, rough robes that seemed more patch than fabric. Rags wove between the knobby fingers, filthy scraps of cloth clearly intended to cushion swollen joints.

Glair—the leader of this cell of the Fellowship.

Rani had met the ancient Touched woman many times in the past. She admired the crone for maintaining an iron grip on her fellows, but she feared the old woman, as well. Glair's leadership of the Morenian Fellowship turned order on its head. A Touched woman should not order about nobles, should not issue commands to merchants and soldiers and guildsmen, to the king of all Morenia.

Glair was apparently not at all concerned about what she *should* do. Hunched almost double, she turned sideways like a crab and pulled her wretched body up the single step of a low dais at the front of the room. She rubbed at her right hip as if an ache shot down her side, and then she raised one gnarled hand in a silent command. The door to the chamber was closed, the latch snicking audibly.

The old woman's voice echoed in the suddenly silent chamber, her Touched accent thick: "Blessed be Jair, 'oo watches o'er all our comin's 'n' goin's."

"Blessed be Jair," the assembly replied. Rani added her voice to the group's, and she heard Mair beside her. She resisted the urge to reach out and take her friend's hand.

"Th' ways o' Jair are mysterious," the old woman creaked on. "Blessed be Jair."

"Blessed be Jair," the Fellowship replied.

"Th' ways o' th' Thousand Gods are mysterious," Glair continued. "Blessed be th' Thousand Gods."

"Blessed be the Thousand Gods."

"The ways o' Tarn are mysterious. Blessed be Tarn."

A shiver twisted down Rani's spine as she invoked the god of death. "Blessed be Tarn."

"Let us remember our brothers 'n' sisters i' this Fellowship, 'oo 'ave been called by Tarn, 'n' 'oo 'ave passed through th' 'Eavenly Gates i' 'is service 'n' i' service t' us. Blessed be th' fellows 'oo 'ave died i' service t' th' Fellowship."

"Blessed be the fellows," Rani echoed, but the words caught in her throat. She was responsible for at least one of those deaths, and her once-beloved brother had caused another.

" 'N' so I stand before ye today, fellows. I stand before ye, e'en though we risk all t' gather i' th' daylight. One o' our members 'as brought us news, important news fer all th' Fellowship." Glair pointed at one hooded fellow, who came to stand beside her on the low dais. "Speak, brother. Tell us all yer tidin's."

Rani knew the man, even though he wore a midnight mask. The green of his gown glimmered in the dark cellar, catching the fitful torchlight like a growing thing. Dartulamino, the priest who had come to the palace with the Holy Father, cleared his throat before he addressed the assembly. "Blessed be Tarn," the priest's voice rang out, and Rani suddenly feared what he was going to say. "Blessed be Tarn, brothers and sisters, who has taken from us our beloved colleague—our father, our leader, our guide. Blessed be Tarn, who has taken the Holy Father through the Heavenly Gates."

Rani's throat constricted, and her lungs swelled in her chest—she wanted to breathe, but she could not. She could hear her blood pulsing in her veins; she could feel her fingers tingle, her toes throb. She had to remind herself to push air past the horrible tightening in her throat, the sickening turn of her belly.

The Holy Father was dead.

She knew that she should not be surprised. He had been an old man, after all. He had suffered much in the past five years; he was weak and tired. Only a fortnight before, she had watched him in Hal's chambers, seen how unsteady he was on his feet, how disoriented he became without Dartulamino's careful guidance.

But he was the *Holy Father,* the only one whom Rani had ever known. He had held the office for decades. He was the voice of all the Thousand Gods, the father of all the faithful. He was the leader who had brought Rani into the church, who had sanctified her as First Pilgrim. He was the priest who had conducted her into the royal family, brought her to Hal.

And now he was gone.

Rani managed to pull a breath past her trembling lips. She

must have made a noise, because Mair turned to look at her, her eyes quizzical behind her black mask. Dartulamino continued before Rani could whisper some meaningless explanation.

"The Holy Father passed late in the night. He knew that Tarn was waiting for him. He called me to him before he went to his evening rest, and we prayed together long into the night." Dartulamino made a holy sign across his chest, a blessing that was aped by all the Fellowship. "He was an old man, and a good one."

"Old 'n' good, aye," Glair croaked. "Dead, though. 'N' that maun change some o' our plans, Fellows. That maun change 'ow we work 'ere i' Moren, i' all o' Morenia."

"Begging your pardon," came a woman's voice, and Rani did not recognize the speaker. "Certainly the Holy Father's passing will change our lives as Morenians. But how does it affect the Fellowship?"

For answer, Glair pointed a trembling claw toward Dartulamino. "Priest? 'Ave ye 'n answer fer yer sister?"

Dartulamino inclined his head as if he were humbling himself before Glair; however, he addressed his response to all the crowd. "Aye. Fellows, I have an answer. As you all must know, the Holy Father's successor is selected by the Curia, by the dozen most senior priests in all the land. The Curia discusses this duty often while a Holy Father still lives; it studies its obligations and its options, and it decides with the living Holy Father who might best take charge over the church. The choice is made before the Holy Father joins Tarn beyond the Heavenly Gates."

Hal's voice rang out in the dim chamber, making Rani jump. Tension ratcheted his words to a higher register than normal. "And who has the Curia selected, Fellow?"

"I have been chosen, brother. I am humbled by my obligations as Morenia's newest Holy Father."

The revelation crashed against Rani like a building felled by one of Davin's war engines. Dartulamino. The Holy Father. The church would have more power in the Fellowship—in all of Morenia—than it ever had before.

The other fellows must have been as astonished as Rani herself. A few fell to their knees, worshipful in the presence of their new religious leader. Others surged forward, as if eager to touch the hem of Dartulamino's green robe. Still others pulled away, seemingly afraid of the power in their midst. Rani found herself frozen, paralyzed, unable to take any action.

Glair took back command of the meeting. "Ye can see why we called ye 'ere. All o' ye are members o' our Fellowship, all o' ye know th' power tha' we bear. One bindin' principle I've lived by, as leader o' ye fellows: Mind yer caste. Well, Dartulamino 'as minded 'is. 'E's labored i' th' church since 'e was a boy, 'n' 'e's reapin' th' fine 'arvest 'e sowed. We'll reap wi' 'im i' th' long run, but only if we're ready i' th' fields. Stand ready, Fellows. Stand ready t' move th' Fellowship forward, faster than ye e'er dreamed we could. We may call upon ye i' th' weeks t' come, call upon ye t' make sacrifices. Sacrifices o' yer time 'n' o' yer money. Sacrifices t' move our Fellowship forward."

If Rani had heard Glair's speech under other circumstances, she would have felt proud and strong. She would have felt that she had knowledge and majesty, power and glory to lead Morenia into a new age.

Now, she was sickened by the Touched woman's proclamation. The church already controlled Hal's future; it commanded his destiny by the power of its loan. Now, Dartulamino controlled the church. The crown of Morenia fell directly under the Fellowship's thumb. "Sacrifice" could not bode well for Morenia. Not now. Not with so many other crises in the air.

And even if Morenia's future were not clouded by the fire that had raged, what of *Hal's* future? What would Dartulamino's elevation mean to a king who harbored hopes of high office—of leadership even—amid the Fellowship?

Mind your caste, Glair said. But Hal was minding his, striving for advancement in the organization. What would Dartulamino's new status mean?

Even as Rani fretted, Dartulamino was speaking to the assemblage, his voice smooth and confident. "We have given out word that the Holy Father is gravely ill, but no one knows yet that he is dead. I have left a trusted acolyte with him, tending him, keeping others away. I will try to gain a full day this way.

You have one day, fellows, to figure out how the passing of the Holy Father can benefit you—can benefit us all. Use it well."

Rani scarcely heard the meeting's ritual concluding words. Glair called upon Jair, seeking his blessing once more. The ancient crone slipped out of the room first of all, and Dartulamino close after. People began to leave the underground chamber in knots of two or three, gliding out the cellar door and stripping off their black hoods.

Rani hung back with Mair, easing toward the dais and the front of the room, away from the door, away from the escaping fellows. Her spine jangled with misgivings when she realized that Hal was waiting, as well. How would he lash out at her now? What aspersions would he cast upon her? How would he call her loyalty into question, with this latest challenge to his goals?

When the three conspirators were all who remained, Hal glided up to the door. He peered down the dark hallway with exaggerated caution, taking the time to turn his head, obviously trying to penetrate the shadows. Only when he seemed to have determined that no one lurked in the corridor did he swing the door to, leaning against it until the latch clicked close. He rested his head against the wood for a long minute.

All the while, Rani tried to think of what she should say. She wanted to berate him for falling so deeply into this latest trap. She wanted to point out that he could have avoided being beholden to the new Holy Father, to the Fellowship, at least to the extent he was. She wanted to tell him that he had been stubborn and foolish and wrong.

"I'm sorry, Rani," he said, turning to face her.

"What?"

He tugged away his mask, as if the thin black velvet had muffled his words. "I should have taken your counsel when we spoke with the Holy Father. The old Holy Father."

Rani reeled from the words, deflated by the simple apology. Her throat worked, and she sampled a dozen different responses, finally settling on the neutral, "The Thousand Gods work in mysterious ways."

Mair tugged off her own hood. "I dinna see wha' th' Thousand Gods 'ad t' do wi' this! Men work i' ways more mysterious than th' Thousand Gods every day. Ye should 'ave 'ad th' chance, m'lord, t' send yer own chirurgeon t' tend th' 'Oly Father."

Hal shook his head. "He was old, Mair. He was a sick, old man. It was time for him to meet Tarn. I don't believe that Dartulamino helped him on his way."

"But th' Father should 'ave realized wha' elevatin' Dartulamino would do t' us, would do t' all o' Morenia!"

"He didn't even know about the Fellowship! He couldn't predict what the change might cost us. Might cost my kingdom." Hal's arguments were reasonable, but the strain in his voice was clear.

Rani risked a glance at his face, and she was shocked by the transparent glimmer of the skin stretched over his cheekbones. She tried to agree with Hal, to calm Mair. "We cannot know what the Fellowship intends. We know nothing more now than we did three years ago."

"Th' Royal Pilgrim, tha's wha' they intend." Mair practically spat the words. "What sort o' ignorant claptrap is tha'?"

"It's all we know of the Fellowship's ultimate goal." Hal sighed, but Rani wondered if he was privileged to some other information. Had he managed to worm inside Glair's highwalled core of security?

She could not ask. She could not demand. He would tell her if he wanted her to know. If he trusted her that much.

She said, "It's a good sign that they included us today. Dartulamino could have issued orders that we not learn of the meeting."

Mair answered immediately. "We're full members o' th' Fellowship. They 'ad t' include us."

Hal shook his head. "They could have claimed later that they sent messengers. They could have argued that they were unable to reach us at the palace, that they were fully justified in going ahead without us."

"It wouldn't have worked," Mair insisted. In forcing her argument, she slipped back into the language that Hal was most likely to understand and agree with—courtly words rather than her Touched patois. "We know other fellows. We have allies in the Fellowship—some strong ones. We would have heard from Borin or another friend."

Rani said, "We have no reason to believe that the Fellowship works against us. They denounced Tasuntimanu when he attacked Hal. They have let him rule uninterrupted."

"*Let* me," Hal said bitterly, and once again, Rani wondered if he had some other track to information about the Fellowship, some personal reason to take Dartulamino's churchly elevation as a threat. Hal continued, "I've been waiting to hear how they intend to control my trip to Liantine."

Rani responded before she could dwell on Liantine, before her thoughts could slip toward the paired pangs of the Little Army and Princess Berylina. Her vehemence felt wild, reckless. "What are you saying, then? Are you ready to break with the Fellowship, now that Dartulamino has this new power?"

Hal shook his head slowly. "No. We were agreed before, and nothing has changed at the core. Better to stay within the Fellowship. Better to know what it plans. We're like wrestlers, clutching our opponents fast to know what they intend. It's good to have this notice today, good to know that Dartulamino will become the Holy Father." He paused for a moment, and then he added, "I'm gaining strength. I'll make my bid when it's time."

Rani nodded. Making his bid. It made sense that Hal intended to move toward controlling the Fellowship. He was a nobleman, after all. She recognized the pattern of Hal's strategy. She could respond to it as if she were studying military markers on a map, as if she were reviewing construction plans for rebuilding Moren. Her voice became a model of dispassion. "And? What changes with our knowledge then? Is there any reason to keep away from Liantine?"

Hal's jaw worked, and she wondered at the sentences he tested, the words that he discarded. In the end, he shook his head, shrugging his shoulders in something that resembled defeat. "I have no choice. I am pledged to find the Little Army. And obligated to meet Princess Berylina." He swallowed hard. "Her dowry is more important than ever before. I must break free of my debt to the church. Dartulamino must not own me— as Holy Father or as member of the Fellowship." Hal finally met her eyes. "Rani Trader, I know of only one thing that is likely to further my Liantine mission."

"What?" Rani barely managed a whisper.

"Come with me to Liantine. Negotiate for me with King Teheboth."

The request struck Rani like a blow to her belly, even as she struggled to keep her face impassive. Of course Hal needed to meet his obligations. Of course he needed to find the Little Army. Of course he needed to establish an heir. Of course he needed calm, clear advice on all those fronts.

Mair saved Rani from fumbling for a response. "You need Morenia's greatest negotiator to drive a contract for Berylina? Isn't she the girl with teeth like a rabbit?"

"Rumors about her appearance have been exaggerated," Hal said through a set jaw. As if from a distance, Rani saw Hal turn from Mair and reach for her hand, catch it between his own. "Please, Rani. I need you beside me in Liantine. Say you'll travel with me."

Hal's fingers trembled against hers. His voice caught in his throat, and she wondered if his emotion was merely because he feared what would happen to Morenia in the hands of the Fellowship and Dartulamino's church. But she did not allow herself to worry about that. Her king was asking for her. Her country needed her. Princesses and fellows, they could not do for Morenia all the things that she could. After all, she was the merchant who had broken Amanthia's hold on the Little Army. She was the negotiator who had brought in the builders and masons, the workers who were even now rebuilding Moren. Hal had seen the danger of negotiating without her—he knew that he had been outbargained by Dartulamino and the old Holy Father. Rani had been chagrined to be left out of that work; she could hardly refuse to join forces with Hal now.

Even if now he was going to Liantine. Even if now he was going to bid for a bride.

"Aye," she whispered at last. "I'll come to Liantine."

Hal's lips were warm across the back of her hand, but Rani shivered as she tucked away her black Fellowship hood. Other men had kissed her like that. Crestman had. Crestman would journey with them to Liantine. Crestman and Hal. The Little

Army and Berylina. And over all, the pall of debt to the church. And to the Fellowship.

Rani followed Mair into Moren's burned-out streets. No matter how close she pulled her cloak, she could not still the tremors that crept along her spine.

5

Hal swayed on his feet as he glanced around the Great Hall of Liantine, trying not to appear overly impressed. After ten days at sea, he was still growing accustomed to the feel of solid ground underfoot. Farsobalinti reached out a steadying hand, but Hal shrugged off the attention.

He had lost precious time departing Morenia, unable to leave before receiving formal news of the Holy Father's death, then delayed by official mourning and ceremonies. Provisions needed to be loaded aboard his finest oceangoing ship, and Hal had consulted with advisors regarding appropriate gifts for Princess Berylina. He might have convinced Rani to travel with him and to lend her expertise, but he would not ask her to woo Berylina directly. If this journey came to wooing. If Hal decided that was the best course for Morenia.

He had also needed to consult with Crestman, to learn all that he could about the Little Army's presence in Liantine. Hal had studied endless charts and obscure notations, messages from Crestman's scouts who had indicated where children were being held and how they were being put to use. He had even checked with Davin to determine what he could about the children's usefulness to Liantine daily life. The old man had only offered sour conclusions, maintaining that the Army boys were too wild for life in any civilized society.

In the end, nearly a month passed before Hal was prepared to travel. The delay had permitted him to see the hasty completion of the firelung hospital and the installation of the Touched victims. Even that accomplishment proved hollow, though.

Thousands of Touched had succumbed to the dread disease, and now there were reports of stricken merchants and guildsmen, too. Even a handful of nobles and soldiers had contracted firelung. Everywhere Hal turned, he heard demands for herbs and poultices, for sturdy walls and warm, dry blankets. Every request jangled with the sound of golden coins—coins that he should be hoarding to repay the church. Coins that he had no choice but to spend upon his kingdom.

At least he managed to flee Morenia before Dartulamino's formal investiture as Holy Father. That ceremony would take extensive planning, and it would not be held until the end of summer. The church seemed satisfied to dispatch a single priest to accompany the royal party, one Father Siritalanu. Hal wondered how often the young religious was expected to report back to his superiors.

So, messengers to Liantine had preceded the royal travelers from Morenia, bearing Hal's greetings and his first, tentative letter to Princess Berylina. Arrival dates had been fixed and welcome feasts promised.

But Hal had complicated all of that by arriving sooner than expected, the beneficiary of tremendous spring winds that had filled his ship's sails and hurtled him across the ocean. The flustered Liantine harbormaster had met him at the dock, conveying the royal party to the Great Hall with a combination of exasperation and concern. Hal left behind the majority of his retainers, along with his sea captain, ordering his people to arrange for the transport of his possessions, diplomatic gifts, and other treasures to King Teheboth's Great Hall.

To Crestman, Hal had given specific orders. The Amanthian was to wait on board Hal's ship. He was not to show his face in Liantine. He was not to risk his temper before formal negotiations could commence.

So Hal now stood in the Great Hall, trying not to feel like an interloper. The long room was the most ornate chamber that Hal had ever seen. Great lengths of spidersilk swooped from the ceiling, billowing out to cover the roofbeams. The fabric was dyed an intense emerald green, the color of Liantine, and a delicate silver thread ran through the cloth, subtle reminder of the kingdom's coat of arms. Silk panels on the walls repeated

the theme, but the silver threadwork was more obvious there—
Hal could make out the rampant dragon that was the Liantine
emblem, repeated over and over again by tireless weavers on
endless looms.

Every inch of wall space was covered by the rich silk—even
the doorways were masked by heavy curtains. The effect was
smothering, even while it commanded respect. Hal reminded
himself that King Teheboth intended to intimidate visitors to
his court, intended to cow the Morenians and anyone else who
came to do business in Liantine. That reminder did little good
as Hal calculated the wealth draped about the room. The number of octolaris it would take to create so much silk . . . The
hundreds of people who would need to harvest the silk, and to
clean it, spin it, weave it . . .

Hal shifted from foot to foot, more than a little ill at ease that
no Liantine official had stayed to welcome them. The harbormaster had tugged at his ear and returned to his labor, dispatching a boy to find someone—anyone—who had the
prestige to meet a visiting king.

Hal's reverie was interrupted by the chatter of Mair and
Rani behind him. "And then I told him . . . ," Mair was saying,
clearly recounting some prior conversation. Most likely a conversation with Farsobalinti, Hal mused in irritation. The nobleman was watching the Touched girl with an indulgent smile on
his face.

"Enough!" Hal said, making both girls jump. "You can continue your gossip later!"

Farso stepped forward as Mair started to retort, but Rani laid
a silencing hand on her friend's arm. Hal was grateful for that
modicum of support, but he resented the fact that Mair needed
to be restrained by anyone. Touched or no, she should understand the etiquette of their situation. Before he could make an
acid comment, a length of the green silk in front of him was
swept to one side, revealing a doorway that Hal had not even
suspected.

Apparently unaware of the royal visitors, a girl stepped into
the receiving hall. She glanced over her shoulder as she moved,
her motions furtive, as if she were hiding from someone on the
other side of the curtain. She raised pale hands to her hair, tuck-

ing her loose tresses behind her ears with an automatic rhythm, more the motion of a child than of a young woman. Her hair was as straight as a horse's tail and glossy in the flickering torchlight, gleaming black so deep it seemed blue. The color set off her milky skin.

Hal cleared his throat to announce his group's presence, regretting the girl's startled jump. His regret froze as he was pinned by eyes the color of cornflowers. A high blush stained the girl's pale, pale cheeks, and she raised a hand to her lips, swallowing a startled cry. Her eyes flicked to Hal's crimson and gold, to the lion emblem stitched carefully across his chest. "My lord!" she said, dropping into a swift curtsey. Her hair slipped from behind her ears, only to be returned by the impatient, automatic flick of her fingers.

Hal forced himself not to think about those long pale fingers, not to think about her lustrous hair. He vowed not to realize that her head scarcely came to his chest. She was barely older than a child, looked scarcely old enough to wear the shimmering spidersilk kirtle that glowed in the room as if lit from within. He told himself not to notice the turn of the slender foot that peeked beneath the hem of the girl's sapphire skirt. A sapphire skirt that echoed the color of her eyes . . .

"My lady," he finally remembered to say, and he managed a courtly bow. He was vaguely aware that Farso aped his action, and that Rani and Mair had inclined their heads in gentlewomen's formal curtseys.

"I—we—my lord, we were not aware that you had arrived yet. You should not have been left alone here in the Great Hall. You'll think all Liantines are boors!"

"Hardly, my lady." Hal smiled at her concern. "Kel blessed us as we crossed the ocean. We arrived sooner than we expected."

"King Teheboth—," the girl began.

"I understand—," Hal started at the same time, and they laughed at the confusion.

Hal gestured for the girl to continue, and she swallowed before she said, "King Teheboth is not in the palace. He's ridden in search of the Horned Hind."

"The Horned Hind?"

"Aye. The Spring Hunt is today." At Hal's puzzled glance, she continued. "It's a Liantine custom. On the first day of spring, the king rides forth at dawn, in search of the Horned Hind."

"A *horned* hind? But no female deer bears antlers!"

"No female deer of *our* world." The girl smiled. "The Horned Hind is holy. She is sacred. She holds the world within the basket of her antlers."

"Then it must be unwise to hunt her, lest the world be dropped like an egg."

The girl's laugh was as light as the spidersilk she wore, and Hal found a silly grin spreading across his own lips. She said, "My lord, you jest. King Teheboth slays the Horned Hind on the first hunt of every spring. Her blood restores all Liantine and guarantees the house of Thunderspear will rule another year."

The laughing words shivered through Hal. If the girl had been older, if she had been more schooled in the subtle ways of politics, she might be giving him a warning. She might be telling him that Liantine had ambitions and goals, had intentions to protect its power in all the world. But she was scarcely more than a child. She must be repeating the lessons, religious and civil, that she had heard all her life.

Hal retreated to a safe compliment. "My companions and I were admiring the silk wall hangings."

A flash of emotion darted across the girl's eyes, smoky fire that was smothered in a single breath. "Aye, my lord, they are new. They were only hung a fortnight ago, in honor of my brother's wedding."

Hal heard the slight catch in her voice before the girl said *brother,* and he wondered at the pretty flush that stained her cheeks once again. Her brother's wedding. King Teheboth's fourth son had wed but two weeks before, taking vows with a woman in the mysterious spiderguild. The nuptials had been planned quickly, with little pomp. A fourth son was of no great account in a sprawling royal family. No great account to the royals, that was. But certainly a great coup for a guild. The spiderguild must have tasked its greatest masters with crafting the endless field of silk that draped the room.

Even as Hal recalculated the verdant hangings, the girl's words sank into his skull. King Teheboth's youngest son was this creature's brother. This extraordinary girl must be Berylina—the rabbit-toothed, cross-eyed princess of Liantine.

Hal's ridiculous grin spread as he remembered Duke Puladarati's cool disclaimers that rumors about Berylina had been exaggerated. Exaggerated, indeed. They had been bald-faced lies. "My lady," he began, bowing again.

"I'm sorry, my lord," she said at the same time. "It is not proper for me to stand here speaking to you. With King Teheboth gone to the hunt, you should be received by Lord Shalindor, the king's chamberlain." The beautiful creature glanced across the room, taking in Rani and Mair with her violet eyes, flicking over Farsobalinti. "I'll send a boy to fetch Lord Shalindor."

"The harbormaster has already sent someone, my lady."

"Has he? Very well, then. Lord Shalindor should arrive at any instant. While you wait, allow me to show your maidservants to your quarters, my lord. They can begin to prepare your apartments for your comfort."

Hal's eyes flashed to Rani and Mair, and he caught the indignant words blossoming in Rani's throat. He knew exactly what she would have said if they'd been alone. She must not be discounted as a mere servant, not if she were going to bargain on his behalf. Not if she were to have any credibility negotiating with the Liantines for the Little Army, for Berylina herself.

Hal started to clear his throat, strangely reluctant to make the clarification to the softly smiling princess. Before he could speak, Mair stepped forward. "We're no servants, my lady."

Once again, the dark-haired creature blushed prettily. She looked at Hal in apparent confusion, and his heart went out to her. After all, how was she to know who accompanied him in his travels? How was she to know the positions in the Morenian court? It *was* odd for a king to travel with a merchant and a Touched girl. Heightening the confusion, Mair looked particularly coarse, with her hair still tangled from the sea breeze and her cloak stained with salt water. Rani had at least donned a gown of Morenian crimson, but Mair had taken no steps to disguise her Touched background.

Besides, Berylina was young. She might act composed for a thirteen-year-old girl, but she had scarcely had time to learn the rules for nobility in her father's court, much less for other kingdoms, for distant lands. Better that Hal ease her discomfort gently now. There would be many such lessons in their future, and much might turn on how he guided the princess through this misstep. He made his voice light, and he clarified, "These are my helpmeets, my trusted advisors. Lady Rani. Lady Mair."

"My lady," the princess said seriously, dropping a slow curtsey to Rani, and then her voice caught as she repeated the greeting to Mair. She turned her head fetchingly, as if confused by the titles Hal granted his companions. Hal heard her hesitate and realized that she was embarrassed. He cursed himself silently for letting this first meeting with his prospective bride begin so awkwardly, but he attempted to recover by gesturing to the waiting Farso. "And this is Farsobalinti, my trusted friend and a member of my council."

"My lord," the princess said, and she must have been more at ease, for her smooth curtsey rippled the sapphire silk of her gown, spreading the cloth into a beautiful pool. Farso bowed in a sweeping response.

Hal had to work to push words past the sudden swelling in his throat. "I'm certain that Lady Rani and Lady Mair would be grateful to be shown to their chambers. Kel may have smiled upon us, but our passage was wearing nonetheless. If you could help them to refresh themselves . . ."

What? What had he done wrong now? Rani and Mair were glaring as if he had insulted their parentage. He scarcely had time to wonder before the princess gestured to a curtained doorway across the room. "Of course, my lord. Let me assist the . . . ladies. Lord Shalindor should be here at any moment; I can't think what has detained him."

Hal saw the glare that Rani cast in his direction; she clearly was displeased about being handed off to the princess. But what was Hal to do? It was thoroughly awkward, arriving before they were expected. They would each have to do the best they could. Hal nodded to the women, hoping that his steady gaze would convey his apology at the same time that it issued a command.

As the green silk curtain fell into place behind Rani, Mair, and the extraordinary princess, another was pulled aside, and a tall white-haired man stepped into the room. The man bowed stiffly, sniffing as he touched his nose nearly to his emerald-clad knee. A dragon twined about his chest as if it were frozen in an ecstasy of humility. "My lord. I am Shalindor, King Teheboth's chamberlain. His Majesty was not expecting you until the day after tomorrow, and he regrets that he was not here to greet you. He rides on the Spring Hunt."

"Kel smiled upon us, my lord, and brought us to your hall too soon."

"Not too soon, my lord." Shalindor stretched his thin lips into a rueful smile, as if he regretted contradicting a visitor, a visitor and a nobleman besides. "Not too soon at all. When we made out the flag on your ship, I sent a messenger after King Teheboth. His Majesty should return within the hour."

"That was not necessary!" Hal exclaimed.

"It was no trouble, my lord. Teheboth Thunderspear would certainly have it no other way."

"But the princess said he rode at dawn!"

"The princess?" Shalindor was surprised enough to look Hal directly in the eye. His white eyebrows flew high on his forehead. "You've spoken with Princess Berylina?"

"Aye. She left just as you arrived." Hal recognized surprise in the chamberlain's glance, and he hesitated, wondering if he were getting Berylina in trouble. Perhaps the princess had been forbidden to speak with visitors. Perhaps she was supposed to be taking her lessons—embroidery or lute, or something equally suitable for a young woman of her station.

"The princess?" Shalindor asked, as if in disbelief, but then he seemed to remember himself. "My lady is not usually so forward with . . . strangers," he said at last, shrugging as if he were apologizing.

"She was quite polite," Hal assured the man. "She offered to take my companions to their apartments, so that they could refresh themselves from our journey."

Shalindor seemed to recover, although he still shook his head in surprise. "I trust she'll see to their comfort, then. As I should see to yours." The chamberlain bowed again and gestured toward a door, his bony fingers pointing out a different passage from the one where Berylina had disappeared with Rani and Mair. "My lords?"

Hal nodded congenially and ducked through the doorway with Farsobalinti, following the chamberlain's straight, stiff back.

Farso managed a smile as he adjusted Hal's leather glove. "Are you ready, then, Sire?"

"Farso, this is hardly what I expected to be doing on my first day in Liantine."

Hal looked down at his riding leathers, grateful now that he had followed his former squire's suggestion back in Morenia and had his gear carted across the ocean. Back in Moren, it had seemed ridiculous to pack so much—winter clothes and summer, hunting clothes and ermine-lined capes. All along, Farso had ignored his protests, merely assuring him that one of the marks of kingship was always seeming prepared. Rani had added her agreement—it was important to impress Liantine. If King Teheboth ever suspected the extent of Morenia's need, she reminded him, the princess's dowry would shrink to nothing.

"King Teheboth only intends to honor you, Your Majesty, by including you in this custom."

"I understand that. It's just that it's so early in the year. . . ."

"You won't actually *find* a Horned Hind, Sire." Farso laughed at the ridiculous image. "No females to suffer for today's sport, no fawns to leave orphaned. The king will certainly slay a stag and call it by another name." Farso grinned and mimed a fatal thrust.

"You're looking forward to this, aren't you?"

The young knight shrugged, a smile making his pale eyes sunny. "It's good to ride, Sire. It's good to be out in the fresh air and to feel the horseflesh between your thighs. The hounds baying, the smell of the grass caught underfoot . . . And it's good to eat fresh venison at the end of the day."

Hal knew that most of his nobles felt the same. Nevertheless, his sympathy usually ran with the deer. Not, perhaps, when a joint was roasting over the fire, but during the long chase, with the hounds belling, and dozens of men plotting and planning, holding their iron-tipped spears . . .

Foolishness. If Hal tried to explain his thoughts, Farso would think he was even odder than he was. Hal settled for clapping his hand on his friend's shoulder. "Let us go, then. We wouldn't want to keep our host waiting, not when he's already lost his entire morning, riding back for us."

Nevertheless, the king of all Liantine was pacing impatiently in his cobbled courtyard, attended by a handful of restless nobles. King Teheboth Thunderspear was a man large enough to bear his family name with pride. He stood two handspans taller than Hal, and his chest stretched the green-painted leather that wrapped around it, rolls of fat covering hard muscle. The king's gloves were like sausage casings, barely managing to contain his fingers, and his legs strained at their trews. Teheboth wore his beard in the eastern style, plaited into a long braid down his chin, and the hair atop his head was long and wiry, chestnut shot through with gold and silver.

Hal could not keep from glancing about, from looking for the mammoth horse that could bear Teheboth into the hunt. He was not disappointed—the king of Liantine rode a sturdy battle destrier, a stallion that looked as if it were more fit for weeks of warfare than for a day of hunting.

Beside the battle mount stood a pair of strong riding horses—a roan gelding that tossed its head in the late morning sun and a grey-flecked mare. Hal was enough of a horseman to recognize good beasts when he saw them—these animals would easily rank among the best in all of Morenia.

Hal's admiration was cut short by King Teheboth's exclamation. "My lord! You must excuse our absence when you arrived!" The man's voice was as full as his body, and his greeting echoed off the stone walls of the courtyard. "We are pleased that you will join us! It was fortunate that our riders were able to recall us before we had ridden too far away."

"My lord." Hal smiled, feigning enthusiasm. Hunting was a noble pastime, he reminded himself, and he had spent plenty of long, satisfying afternoons in the Morenian woods—even if he now longed for a hot bath and clean clothes, for a soft pillow and a long rest after the difficult sea crossing. . . .

Longings were not meant for kings.

Before Hal could muster further enthusiasm, he saw Rani and Mair step forward from the shadows of Teheboth's palace. Both women wore riding clothes, and Rani had plaited her long blond hair into a single braid. King Teheboth glanced at the pair, at first dismissing them, but then giving them his full attention as he realized that they were part of Hal's entourage.

"My lady." King Teheboth acknowledged first Rani, then Mair. Hal watched Rani drop a simple curtsey, and Mair mimic the same. The Liantine king scarcely acknowledged the women, saying, "We'll bring back venison for tonight's feast!"

"We look forward to riding with you, my lord." Hal recognized the dangerous sweetness in Rani's tone, and he caught her looking about the courtyard for a mount that she could claim as her own.

"You should stay here, Lady Rani," Hal said. "Help our people settle in after our long journey. We've kept our host long enough, making him ride back to retrieve us. We scarcely have time to find mounts for you, to locate appropriate gear." Hal returned his attention to Teheboth. "The Thousand Gods are smiling upon us, that we were able to reach you before you had ridden too far afield. May Doan look kindly upon our hunt."

Teheboth's bushy eyebrows met in a scowl, and his plaited beard jutted forward in disagreement. "Doan! Your god of the hunt has naught to do with today's ride!" Hal struggled to mask his look of surprise. "You're with the Liantines today, King Halaravilli. We look to the Horned Hind, instead of your clutch of gods."

Hal knew, of course, that the Thousand Gods were little worshiped in Liantine. But he had thought that they still held *some* sway. Before he could find a diplomatic reply, Rani stepped forward, resting a hand on the roan's bridle. She addressed her words to Teheboth, inclining her head gracefully. "Lady Mair and I would ride with you as a token of luck, my lord. While we Morenians have lost the tradition of the Spring Hunt, we can admire a king's quest on behalf of his people. May this be the year that you find the Horned Hind herself, and all the riches at the end of the world."

Of course! Hal remembered now. Along with all that nonsense about the Horned Hind holding the world inside her antlers, there were old stories, ancient legends. The hunter who slew the Horned Hind would find a treasure trove, more wealth than man had ever seen.

"My lady," King Teheboth bowed from his saddle. "You know our customs well."

"Your customs are storied far and wide, my lord. I've seen the Spring Hunt captured in stained glass."

Hal had only a moment to wonder where the window had been located—perhaps in the ruined guildhall or in one of Rani's books. The king of Liantine then said, "We'll return tonight, my lady, with meat for our spring table. In the meantime, I'm sure my people will make you and your companion comfortable."

"My lord—," Rani began again.

Hal interrupted, "Lady Rani, you should not waste more time in the courtyard. I'm sure the princess could use your assistance."

"The *princess*—" Rani bristled, but Teheboth broke in before she could deliver her heated retort.

"My lady, I regret that you cannot join us. The Hind would stand no chance against your determination." There was no room for further argument, and even Rani inclined her head in submission. "Now that we have returned to our courtyard, though, we must drink another stirrup cup, lest the blessed Hind claim we rode without giving fair warning. My daughter toasted us when first we rode, but she is gone about her duties elsewhere in the castle. Will you do us the honor, Lady Rani?"

Teheboth inclined his head toward Rani, who was clearly startled by the request. Hal could see her start to craft some excuse, but he managed to catch her eye, conveying an entire argument in one tight shake of his head. Rani swallowed hard but sank into a reluctant curtsey. "I would be most honored, my lord."

Servants produced wine and a massive gilded cup, and Rani proffered the symbol first to Teheboth. The king, however, waved her over to Hal, indicating that the guest should be honored before the host. Rani rested a hand on Hal's stirrup as she raised the cup into his hands. "I would ride with you, Sire." Her words were scarcely audible.

"We have no choice in this."

"You brought me to bargain for you, and yet you'll make your first bid alone."

"We're in the merchant's house, Rani, living by his rules. What would you have me do?"

"At least hear this. The girl who met us in the Great Hall—"

"Ho there!" Teheboth cried from across the courtyard. "The Horned Hind waits!"

Hal took the golden cup from Rani's fingers, resenting his own flash of gratitude when she relinquished it without further commotion. Of course she had harsh words about Princess Berylina. Of course she was going to make his courtship as difficult as she possibly could. How had he ever expected otherwise?

The wine was sweet on his lips, and he swallowed hard, as if cementing a vow. He could face King Teheboth alone. He could turn the day's ride to his own profit, open the bidding for Berylina and for the return of the Little Army. He did not need Rani by his side constantly.

Hal returned the goblet with tight-lipped silence, and a flash of anger darkened Rani's eyes. Without another word, she turned on her hard leather heel and carried the cup to each of the riders. Farso, and then two of King Teheboth's retainers. She ended with the Liantine king.

Hal watched Rani set a hand on the giant's stirrup, watched words form in her throat. She glanced across at Hal, and he could read her intention as clearly as a story in her precious stained glass. Hal shook his head once more, emphatically, like a stern father. He imagined that he could hear Rani suck in a rebellious breath, but she obeyed. She held up the golden goblet, bowing her head as Teheboth said something that made her flush prettily. The king drank deeply, swallowing once, twice, three times, four, and then he handed the empty goblet back to Rani. She bowed her head and retreated to the shadowed corner of the courtyard, Mair trailing like a ghost.

Hal did not look back as he rode out behind Teheboth Thunderspear.

For nearly an hour, they galloped across the broad Liantine plain, following the course of the Liant River inland. The delta land was rich, and the road was smooth, despite large rocky outcroppings that appeared to either side. Spring had come out in full force across the land, and Hal's eyes feasted on more shades of green than he could count. The horses trod on new-sprung wildflowers, little stars of white and pink. The hunters made good time.

Thinking of Rani's silent submission, Hal avoided the subject uppermost in his mind—Princess Berylina. Even as he cast about for some safe topic, some appropriate opening discussion, the riders slowed their horses, giving the beasts a chance to rest. A groom rode forward, proffering a tooled leather flask to King Teheboth. The Liantine took the container and offered it to Hal. "Brandywine," he said. "It will warm your heart."

Hal took an appreciative swallow, opening his eyes wide at the streak of heat that flowed through his chest. Teheboth acknowledged the compliment with a toothy grin, and then he drank deeply himself, his broad throat convulsing with swallow after swallow. Only after he had passed a hairy hand across his lips did he return the flask to his servant. As the boy dropped back in the ranks, Hal glanced at his face and was surprised to see a livid scar stretched tight across his cheekbone.

An Amanthian. A former soldier in the Little Army, whose birth tattoo had been carved away from his face.

Hal cleared his throat. He'd known that he'd have to address the issue some time, and, frankly, it was the easiest of the topics he'd brought to Liantine. "Are there many of my people serving in your court?"

"Your people?" A quick twitch in Teheboth's cheek showed that he understood the question.

"Amanthians."

Teheboth feigned puzzlement for a moment, and then he pretended to untangle Hal's allusion. "You mean the boy! I'd hardly know he was Amanthian. He seems quite settled into Liantine."

"Nevertheless, the Amanthians are easy enough to find." Hal brushed a hand across his own cheek, indicating a nonexistent scar.

"They serve in Liantine like any of their caste." Teheboth shrugged.

Hal resisted the urge to sigh. He wasn't certain why the Liantine king was pretending to misunderstand, but he knew that it would not be wise to rush matters. Only a fool would directly challenge a king while sitting on that man's own mount, riding in his own hunt, prior to discussing an infinitely more delicate matter of state.

Hal prodded delicately, nodding toward the servant with the flask, who had fallen into a group of grooms. "That boy seems to have learned his way about your court well enough. How long has he been in your service?"

Teheboth laughed, the explosive sound coming from deep in his belly. His braided beard danced as he said, "Do you honestly think I know? Could you tell me when each of *your* servants came to your court? The boy pours wine at my table, my lord. I've never paid him any attention before. And I'm not likely to again, unless it's to punish him roundly for distracting my guest from the hunt. After all, my lord, that *is* why you rode out with us, is it not?"

Hal heard the warning, but he was reluctant to let the matter rest, not now, not knowing how difficult it would be to reopen the discussion if he backed away. "I wonder," he mused, as if the thought had just come to him. "I wonder what caste he was before they carved the tattoo from his face."

"What difference does it make?" Teheboth had turned to stare at Hal.

"Not much at all." Hal rode on for a while, willing to let his words float in the noontime sun. After several peaceful minutes, though, Hal cleared his throat to speak again. "My lord, I'll be honest with you." Teheboth raised one eyebrow and reined his horse in, falling back from the rowdy group of hunters. Hal matched the Liantine's pace until the two men were out of earshot from the others. Hal saw Farso notice, and the former squire started to pull up on his own reins. Hal shook his head, waving one hand in an easy gesture. Farso shrugged and caught up with the Liantine escort.

Hal proffered his open palms as if he bore a gift for Teheboth. "There is no need for us to joust here. You are older and

wiser than I, and you know the sweet waste of honeyed words."
Hal reined his borrowed gelding to a complete stop, swallowing a smile at Teheboth's scarce-masked annoyance. "I must return to my people with news, my lord. I must report to them on
the fate of their Little Army."

"There is no Little Army in Liantine."

"That will not be sufficient. Thousands of children were sent
over here. Thousands of boys and a handful of girls. Their parents still dream of their safe return. What am I to tell my people?"

"Tell your people that their children were sold at market by
their former ruler."

"For what coin?"

Teheboth looked deep in Hal's eyes, and the older man's
hands clenched his reins as if he would wheel his horse about
and ride back toward the Liantine capital. But Teheboth was no
coward. He was not trying to flee Hal's questions. Rather, the
Liantine king was trying to rein in his temper, trying to restrain
a very uncivil rage.

"My lord Halaravilli, I can assure you that this is not a battle you want to fight—not with all the rest that stands between
us." Teheboth lowered his voice; Hal was forced to lean forward to hear him. "The Amanthian bastard, Sin Hazar, sold his
own people. My vassals bought them, clean and clear. The
Horned Hind has no ban against slavery. My guilds, my armies,
my household, we all needed servants, and Sin Hazar offered
us a decent price. I'll tell you this, my lord. No one person
owns a single slave in Liantine. Slaves are owned by groups—
by guilds or societies or by armies. Anything else would be in-
human."

That made no sense at all, Hal wanted to say. Groups were
made of individuals. There was no absolution by saying that a
guild owned a person, that an *army* had made the purchase.
With a clarity that startled him, Hal suddenly saw how he could
turn Teheboth's prickly stubbornness to his own advantage. In
a flash, Hal thought back to lessons he had learned in his nursery, to strategies that he had worked out with his armies of tin
soldiers. The pattern was as clear as the ones that Rani Trader
crafted in glass. Sometimes one needed to lose in order to gain.

Hal lowered his gaze, picking at the fine tooling on his leather saddle. His shoulders sagged, and he looked up through his lashes, as if he were uncertain of his words, of his arguments. "Please, my lord." He let a little of his stress melt into his words. "I ask but one thing. Tell me if there is any chance that I can return Amanthian children to their homes. Tell me if I can bring glad tidings to any Amanthian mother, to any family that aches for its missing sons and daughters."

Teheboth stared at him for a long moment, as if he were measuring out the weight of capitulation. When he spoke, he did not bother to coat his words with regret. "Those children are long gone, my lord. They have spread through Liantine, traveled to the far corners of my realm."

Hal forced himself to meet his rival's gaze, unflinchingly accepting defeat on the issue of the Little Army. "Then you will not help me?"

"I cannot, my lord. It is not in my power to do so. Take heart, though. Some of your people have purchased their freedom through the labor of their hands. Others were granted freedom immediately by kindhearted Liantines. Your *children* have grown, King Halaravilli—some have even fathered their own children, on my Liantine maids. Your Little Army is no more."

There. It was done. Hal had lost this battle. Perhaps in doing so, though, he was in a better position to win the war. He could only hope.

For just an instant, he remembered Rani coming to him in Amanthia, appearing in his camp outside the northern capital. She had been clad in the rags that passed for a uniform in the Little Army, and she was flanked by two brave soldiers, by two boys who had forfeited their innocence for a king's lie.

Rani would not be pleased when she learned that Hal had bartered the Little Army. She would not be pleased to learn that the soldiers were lost, forever beyond recall. But she would be less pleased if Hal lost his other bargaining point, if he had to forfeit Berylina's dowry. Rani was committed to a strong negotiation for the princess; she had pledged as much when she agreed to travel with him.

After all, wasn't that what Rani always tried to teach him? A shrewd merchant must give and take, must recognize the value of yielding on one point, only to snatch up success on the next. That was the lesson that Hal attempted to apply with the Fellowship. He had yielded them some gold—when he could afford the loss—and he hoped for advancement. He could only hope that the strategy would yield success more rapidly here in Liantine.

Besides, Crestman still waited back on Hal's ship. The Amanthian soldier was likely to investigate the Little Army on his own. Who could guess what Crestman might learn, what new facts might change the bargain Hal had just made?

King Teheboth let him sit for a moment, giving him the chance to swallow the acid taste of defeat. Then, before the silence between them could stretch too long, the Liantine lifted one meaty hand to his brow, shielding his eyes from the sun as he scanned the horizon. "We mustn't lose more time, my lord. The winter days haven't grown back to their full summer length yet. You can see the Royal Grove on the horizon there. My master of the hunt is waiting for us, his hounds at the ready. Shall we ride?"

Hal heard the invitation, and he recognized it for what it was—a request to put aside the matter of the Little Army, to declare the dispute completely closed. He nodded grimly. "Aye, my lord. Let us ride."

The sun had barely moved a handspan higher in the sky when they arrived at the Royal Grove. Hal could see that the master of the hunt was busy, attempting to whip in the frantic pack of staghounds. Four boys held leather leashes for the scent hounds, which had already located the trail of deer in the forest. Excitement was palpable in the air.

There was a long moment of disorganization as the Liantine lords sorted themselves out, and King Teheboth held a rapid conference with the master of the hunt. Hal hurriedly met Teheboth's youngest son, Olric, the boy who had wed his spider-guild bride only two weeks before.

Then, the hounds were loosed, and Hal found his gelding eagerly leaping into the Grove. Hal leaned low across the great beast's neck, even though the position made it difficult for him to catch his breath. The horse pounded beneath him, bunching its massive hindquarters to spring over great blocks of stone that were occasionally strewn across the shadowed path. Once, he sat up straighter, eager to help guide the horse over and around stony obstacles, but his cape was grasped by low-hanging branches. Laughing in the forest gloom, Hal abandoned himself to the roan's good sense. He urged the horse forward, yielding to the frenzy of the hunt, to the blood-quest for the Horned Hind.

The hounds' belling echoed in the forest. Occasional shafts of sunlight broke through the canopy of the oak trees, blinding in their brightness. Hal could smell the returning life of spring, the fresh earth churned under hooves, the green crush of first leaves whipped by their passing. Men called to one another, challenges that bounced off the trees with ferocious good cheer.

And then the hounds had found the deer. Their belling changed tone until it was frantic with blood lust. Hal's senses were heightened in the dark wood. He could see the flash of white and brown and black as the dogs leaped through the forest. He could hear the desperate crashes as the prey plummeted through thicker and thicker undergrowth. He could smell the sweat of his horse and of his own body, acrid and strong in the chilled air.

The hunt party plunged through a clearing, and Hal caught his first glimpse of the frantic deer. The Liantines might ride for the Horned Hind, they might dedicate this Spring Hunt to her glory and her power, but the hounds had managed to find a male deer, a virile stag.

The beast was magnificent, his antlers glinting in shafts of the afternoon light that shot through the trees. His powerful haunches gathered as he sprang away from the dogs, and Hal caught his breath as the animal leaped onto a rocky outcropping. The trapped stag turned to face the snarling pack.

The riders quickly drew up, reining their mounts in beside the stony promontory. The dogs were driven into a frenzy by the nearness of their prey, snapping and howling as they tried to leap onto the stony crag. One particularly long-legged beast gained the high ground, but the stag swept toward it, lowering his antlered head and tossing the dog from the rock. The hound yelped loudly as it hit the ground and then lay still—stunned or dead, Hal could not tell.

Other dogs followed suit, maddened now by the proximity of the great beast. One launched itself directly at the stag's throat, and the dog's teeth closed on the russet pelt. The hound lasted for only a moment before the stag struck out with its hooves, slashing at the beast until the dog released its grip and fell, yelping, from the rock.

The smell of deer's blood enraged the pack, and the dogs took grander risks. They leaped from the forest floor onto the escarpment, one, two, three together. The stag lowered his head and tried to sweep the dogs from the rock, but there were too many. Even as the deer's grand antlers connected with a crunching sound, one of the hounds managed to leap behind the stag, to harry the beast's far flank.

And then the hunt was over.

The stag slipped to one knee, permitting two more dogs to leap onto the rock. The dogs' baying chorus crested into one long, sustained note, a note that echoed inside Hal's head, growing and turning and reverberating until his very bones seemed to melt. In a daze, Hal realized that the dogs' cry had been captured in the clarion call of a horn; the master of the hunt was commanding his frenzied hounds to stand down.

King Teheboth strode to the rock, leaping onto its craggy surface with the agility of a much younger man. The king of all Liantine held a long, smooth spear, a weapon tipped with darkest iron.

The stag raised a bleeding foreleg, as if determined to fend off this one last foe. The motion forced the beast to lift its head, to stretch its bleeding, muscled neck into an arch as powerful as the stony crag. Hal thought that he could see the pulse beating beneath the stag's flesh, thought that he could see the noble heart pumping over and over, trying to save the doomed beast.

Teheboth drew back his arm, his own muscles trembling with the force of his grip. Then he thrust forward, piercing the stag's throat, plunging the spear down, down, into the dark meat, into the bloody caverns of the great body.

The canine chorus resumed its frenzied song as the stag's knees buckled and the great beast collapsed onto the stone table. The master of the hunt blew on his horn three more times, and then the boy assistants were in among the dogs, pulling them back, attaching their leashes.

Hal watched as two boys stepped forward, boys with slick scars shining beneath their left eyes. The slaves held iron knives, which they used to salute King Teheboth, and then they set to their labor, plunging iron into deerflesh, cutting, dragging, sawing.

Hal was not certain if the great stag's heart was still beating when one of the boys pried it from the chest, or if the organ only seemed to move with the remnants of life. The servant held up the glistening heart, bringing forth a bellow of approval from the assembled Liantine noblemen. The boy bowed his head and presented the slick, crimson gift to Teheboth.

Teheboth accepted the offering like a victorious conqueror, holding it aloft to another roar of approval. Then the king tossed the heart into the pack of dogs, grinning at the explosion of canine yips and snarls. The lungs followed, and the liver and gut, and the great stag's windpipe last of all.

As the steam still rose from the cooling meat, Teheboth drew his own knife, holding the Zarithian blade high above his head. The king's voice rang out in the forest, bouncing off the trees, off the stone. "Behold, good men of Liantine! Behold the Horned Hind!"

It wasn't a hind, Hal wanted to argue. It wasn't a hind at all. It was a stag, who had fought nobly until the end.

He held his tongue. Hal understood the power of myth. He understood the nature of symbols.

"King Halaravilli!" Teheboth cried. "We thank you for honoring us with your presence at this Spring Hunt. In recognition of your presence, and as a token of the friendship between our houses, I proffer you the Sign of the Hunt."

Hal knew what was expected of him. He strode forward, past the slavering dogs, past the boisterous Liantine nobles. He leaped onto the stony outcropping, using his hands to steady himself for just a moment as his boot slipped in a runnel of blood. He tossed his cloak over his shoulders, baring his gold-shot crimson tunic in the high afternoon sun.

"King Halaravilli," Teheboth proclaimed. "Be welcome in

our court. Speak well of our hospitality, wherever you may ride. Be honored in all of Liantine."

Teheboth raised his Zarithian blade once more, rotating the hilt slightly in his palm. Then, he brought the knife down on the hind's right foreleg, severing the hoof with a single blow. He raised the trophy above his head, eliciting a frenzied clamor from the Liantine men and hounds.

Hal drew himself to his full height as Teheboth came to stand beside him. The burly king looked deep into his eyes, as if he could read all Hal's hopes, all his fears, all his expectations for this journey to Liantine. Teheboth held the severed hoof in his left hand, and he raised his right above Hal's head. "In the name of the Horned Hind, be welcome to Liantine, King Halaravilli."

"In the name of the Horned Hind," Hal murmured, and Teheboth's rough fingers rasped across his brow, painting a holy sign with the stag's blood. Hal shuddered at the touch, silently dedicating the hunt to Doan and all the Thousand Gods.

6

Without thinking, Mareka Octolaris raised her fingers to her glossy black hair, pushing the errant strands behind her ears. She had never imagined how annoying her hair would be, left free from her apprentice braids. It was just as well that she was away from the spiderguild, that she could rapidly make her two braids when she attended her octolaris, here in King Teheboth's palace.

Not that she was allowed to wear the braids now that she had been stripped of her status as an apprentice in the spiderguild.

Not that she was allowed to have the octolaris here in Liantine.

Even now, nearly a month after she had stolen the twenty-four spiders, her heart beat fast at the notion that she had full responsibility for the beasts. No one knew that she had them here—not King Teheboth, not Jerusha, and certainly not the spiderguild itself.

Even as Mareka had stared at the slave girl's body on the day that she was supposed to become a journeyman, she had known that she would be banished from the guildhall. Her mother and father had come to her as soon as they heard about the accident. Her father's hands had still dripped with indigo; her mother's neckpiece was pulled askew. Mareka had pleaded with them, begged them to intervene, to say or do anything to save her from the masters' wrath.

But there was nothing to be done. The masters had listened to the facts, and they passed sentence before the sun had set. The virulent octolaris were to be destroyed, burned upon a pyre of Jerusha and Mareka's own making. The apprentices were to be banished, sent to King Teheboth's capital. They were forbidden to wear apprentice braids, denied the opportunity to don their journeymen armbands. The unspoken condition of their return was financial—they might be reconsidered if they could bring the spiderguild wealth, coins enough to make the masters overlook the shame of an outsider dying from mishandled octolaris, the concrete cost of twenty-four executed spiders.

Jerusha's family succeeded where Mareka's had not. They called upon the masters to finalize a long-pending strategy—marrying a journeyman into the house of Thunderspear. Debts were called in, hasty conferences conducted. A journeyman who had long been groomed to serve as Prince Olric's bride was unceremoniously ousted, and Jerusha granted the status, the title, the responsibility. In the charged financial world of royal marriages, Jerusha's parents let their vast wealth secure a sort of freedom, a type of hope for their shamed daughter.

A mere fortnight ago, Mareka had witnessed the wedding ceremony, standing at Jerusha's side like a loyal sister. All the time, though, she had longed to return to her tiny chamber in King Teheboth's palace. Her fingers had twitched as she imagined plucking markin grubs from her deep, deep basket, digging for them between the layers of yellow riberry leaves. As soon as possible, she had excused herself from the wedding festivities, hurrying off to feed her twenty-four secret spiders from her stash of grubs.

Mareka had not let the vicious octolaris burn. She had been trained since birth to protect spiders, taught that the eight-legged beasts were the Horned Hind's own gift to her guild. She could not burn the virulent octolaris solely because of her mistake. She could not condemn the silk producers because she and Jerusha had fought over a slave girl.

Instead, she had diverted Jerusha's attention, tearfully apologizing over and over for her role in the accident, claiming to accept responsibility, insisting that she—Mareka—feed the offending creatures to the pyre. No master wanted to attend the conflagration; no loyal member of the spiderguild could stand to watch the execution of the creatures in their care. Mareka had stood alone at midnight, poking embers until they turned to ash.

She had harnessed all her creativity, focused all her angry energy, calculating how to get her treasures to Liantine. It had not been easy, but she had managed. She had transported them, hidden in her single travel trunk. She had fed them, collected their abundant silk. She had saved the octolaris, and still Jerusha suspected nothing.

Now, returning from checking on her dangerous secret, Mareka hovered in the shadows of a spidersilk hanging, calculating the best moment to make her appearance at the feast. She had had such fun playing with King Halaravilli ben-Jair that morning. Pitiful, really—he had made the game so easy. Had he not heard about the Liantine princess's rabbit teeth? Did he not know that Berylina's eyes were crossed?

Of course, the king's companions, Rani Trader and Mair, had learned of Mareka's game soon enough. Discovery had been inevitable, with the hallways crawling with servants who knew Mareka's true status, who thought of her as the somewhat inattentive servant of the journeyman Princess Jerusha. Nevertheless, Mareka's game had been worthwhile, if only to watch the blond merchant girl spit her anger as realization dawned. If that one hoped to bargain for success in the Liantine marketplace, she had better learn to marshal her forces with more subtlety.

Mareka reached down to smooth her gown. In honor of the Spring Hunt, she had donned her most delicate spidersilk, the garment she had worn to witness Jerusha's marriage. At first glance, the gown was the white of fresh spring blossoms. As Mareka moved, though, even as she drew breath, the cloth rustled and reflected other shades—glints of cobalt and emerald, ruby and topaz. It was the finest creation her mother and father had ever made, and it comforted her to realize that she walked in the tradition of her guild.

She had further honored that bond by wearing her greatest treasure of all—a rough-cut diamond that her mother had given her the day that she became an apprentice. The clear stone slid on a simple golden chain about Mareka's neck, clasped by eight tiny prongs, eight delicate fingers that twisted like a spider's spinnerets. Looking out at the assembled crowd, Mareka took a deep breath and felt the brilliant gem whisper against her flesh. It was time to join the feast. Time to join the game.

She ducked beneath the spidersilk hanging and stepped into the Great Hall. The room had been transformed since the morning, tables and long benches dragged in. A broad dais had been constructed along the far wall, stretching the length of the room. Even across the hall, Mareka could make out unlit lanterns at the edge of the platform, the mirrors in front of the lamps. The stage was ready for the players, the crown of the evening's entertainment.

In the meantime, the hall was filled with King Teheboth's courtiers. The men still wore their hunting leathers, and many stank of horse. More than one rider had braided beads of antler into his beard—symbol of the Horned Hind that had died that afternoon. Boisterous laughter filled the room, and goblets clanked together as men saluted their king and their goddess. Teheboth Thunderspear had better serve food soon, or some of his lords would be too far gone to sit at table.

The Liantine ladies, of course, were better mannered and far more sober. No proper woman would drink enough to risk public humiliation. Duchesses, countesses, and other noteworthy guests stood against the wall, clustered into small groups to whisper stories in their modulated voices. Mareka saw a number of the women nod in her direction, but none was brave enough to speak to a member of the spiderguild, even an apprentice who had been sent to the Liantine capital in shame. Mareka raised her chin and smiled archly, pushing her hair behind her ears.

So, the men were drinking and the women were gossiping—the Liantine nobility were acting exactly as Mareka expected. They weren't the interesting ones in this room. The interesting ones were the Morenians.

Mareka craned her neck, trying not to be obvious as she sought out the visitors. There, near the dais, was the pale lord who had stood with King Halaravilli. What was his name? Farsobalinti. Baron Farsobalinti.

And apparently the baron had no countess, for the man's hand rested solicitously on the arm of the Touched girl. What

was her tale? From everything Mareka had ever learned about
the odd Morenian castes, the Touched were servants, when they
were permitted to come in contact with nobility at all. What had
the girl—Mair, was that her name?—what had she done to warrant journeying across the ocean? And how had she gained the
attention of a baron?

The easy answer, that the Touched girl was merely a diversion for a traveling man, was belied by Farsobalinti's rapt attention. Clearly, he was trying to deflect some argument;
perhaps Mair was still complaining about being left behind
while the men rode out on the Spring Hunt.

Mareka had heard about the fuss the Morenian women had
made—they had even gone into the courtyard when Teheboth
returned for King Halaravilli. By the Hind's eight horns, didn't
they realize that some things were men's business? Didn't
they realize there were advantages to letting men play their silly
games?

Actually, Mareka suspected that Mair had not made the decision to interfere with the Spring Hunt at all. It seemed more
likely that Rani Trader had led that sortie. Looking across the
Great Hall, Mareka found the blond merchant exactly where
she was expected to be—at Mair's side, looking out unhappily
at the hall. Obviously, Rani Trader was searching for her king.

Well, Mareka was looking for him also. She might as well
stand by the merchant—the Morenian monarch was certain to
find her that way. Pushing back her hair once more, Mareka
glided across the room, skirting a boisterous group of nobles as
she approached her rival.

"My lady," she said, dropping a quick curtsey. She swallowed a smile as Rani Trader registered the diamond that glit-
tered against her flesh.

"Mareka." Rani's tone was cold, and she did not grace the
guildswoman with a title.

Mareka affected a pout. "My lady, I fear you are still disturbed by our misunderstanding."

"Misunderstanding? Nay, there was no misunderstanding,
Lady Mareka." The merchant girl sneered the last two words.
"A misunderstanding implies that one of us stated the truth and
the other misconstrued that truth. This morning, you stated a

falsehood, which was perfectly construed by me. And by my lord, King Halaravilli."

"Is there a problem here?" Mareka was startled by the deep voice, and she raised her eyes to take in the man who stood behind Rani. She had not noticed him across the hall, had not taken in his simple soldier's clothes. He was tall and broad shouldered; he carried himself like a fighting man. The hilt of a curved sword rested easily on his hip, and Mareka was willing to warrant that he had other weapons about him.

She raised her eyes to his face, seeing the steady gaze he held on Rani, his attentive stance as he waited for her reply to his question. Mareka was surprised to see a scar across his cheekbone. A slave, then? An Amanthian bodyguard for King Halaravilli's pet?

"Nay, Crestman." Rani acknowledged the man with greater courtesy than a mere servant would warrant. "Mareka Octolaris and I are only finishing an earlier conversation."

"Mareka Octolaris." The soldier—Crestman—repeated her name as he turned his dark gaze upon her. She was reminded of a stoat's smooth grace. "You are from the spiderguild."

"Aye," she said, and then she had to clear her throat. Why should this hired sword intimidate her? She had served as an apprentice in the spiderguild! She handled poisonous octolaris without a moment's hesitation. "Aye," she said more loudly. "I live in Liantine now, though."

"My people live among yours."

"Your people?"

"The Little Army. The soldiers who were under my command."

The slaves, of course. Unbidden, Mareka pictured Serena's pitiful body; she could hear the child's final, rattling breath. "We have Amanthians among us," she said. Of course she did not say the word *slave* aloud. No proper lady would. Nevertheless, the Amanthian tensed beside her. Mareka watched Rani rest a hand upon his arm, drawing his attention away as surely as Homing distracted a ravenous spider.

Before Mareka could think of something else to say, a voice behind her exclaimed, "Your Majesty!"

Mareka whirled, prepared to offer a curtsey to one of the

Liantine royal princes. Instead, she found herself at arm's length from King Halaravilli. He still wore his crimson-washed riding leathers, following the example set by his Liantine peers. A brown smear across his forehead testified to the success of the hunt. Mareka could make out the ancient emblem of the Horned Hind, rough-drawn on the king's brow. So. King Teheboth had honored this westerner with the spring's first blood. King Halaravilli must be destined for great things in the Liantine court.

"My lord," Mareka said, folding into her deepest curtsey. It took only a small curve of her fingers, a delicate wave of her hand, to direct his attention to the diamond she wore, to the gem that nestled between her breasts.

"My lady," he replied, and fresh blood tinged his cheeks when she caught him staring at the jewel. He reached for her hand, raising her up with a courtly elegance. Mareka let her fingers rest against his palm, trembling slightly. She blinked her blue eyes, and he edged closer, ostensibly shifting to let another man walk behind him. His lips parted as if he were about to speak, but Rani Trader stepped forward, forcing them apart.

"Sire," the merchant girl said to him. "Crestman and I were just speaking with the Lady Mareka."

"Mareka?" The king looked confused. Alas, the game was ending.

"Aye, my liege. May I present to you Lady Mareka Octolaris? She was an apprentice in the spiderguild, before her masters sent her here to court. She serves the guild's journeyman, Princess Jerusha."

So, the little merchant knew something of spiders herself, at least of their venom. Rani Trader could not have made her words more hateful if she had been affianced to the king himself.

King Halaravilli had drawn back his hand from Mareka's palm, and now he looked quite flustered. He shot a worried glance at Crestman, as if he feared the Amanthian's restraint, and then he returned his attention to Mareka. "I'm sorry, my lady. I must have misunderstood." He glanced to Rani Trader and back again. "I thought you were the princess, Berylina. You said that your brother had wed last month, and I—I just assumed . . ."

"As you were meant to do!" Rani Trader spat, in a voice that she must have thought quiet enough not to attract attention.

Mareka lowered her eyes, as if she were ashamed. "I'm sorry, my lord. I was so startled when I saw you! I was expecting the Great Hall to be empty. You must understand—as a mere servant, I am not permitted to cross the Great Hall. If Lord Shalindor learned that I was here earlier . . ." Well, the old man would *want* to punish her, at least that much of her implied tale was true.

The Morenian king's face clouded. "My lady," he said, as if in apology. Mareka forced herself to shrug, pretending to be resigned to an unfair burden. "I am but a guest in King Teheboth's palace, after all. I should not have abused the hospitality of my host by crossing the Great Hall."

"But when you said that Prince Olric is your brother—"

Mareka nearly grimaced. Was the Morenian king usually this slow? "He is, my lord. Now, he is. My guildsister Jerusha married him, a fortnight ago. The husband of my sister is my brother. Is that not the way of things in the west?"

"Well, yes, of course. But . . . your *guild*sister?" This Halaravilli was too much a gentleman to accuse a lady of dissembling, not without more, not without proof. He continued, a bit ruefully: "So now I understand Lord Shalindor's surprise when I told him I had spoken with Princess Berylina. She was nowhere near the Great Hall this morning, was she?"

"She was likely with her nurses, my lord. The king permitted her to offer the stirrup cup when he first left for the Spring Hunt. I understand that the excitement left poor Berylina rather . . . overwrought."

"Overwrought . . . ," King Halaravilli said, clearly disconcerted. Mareka smiled brilliantly. After all, there was more than one way to complete her bid for return to the spiderguild. Jerusha had redeemed herself with the riches of a Liantine prince. How much more rapidly would Mareka rise within the guild if she returned with a bid from a foreign *king*, from the overlord of both Morenia and Amanthia?

Before Mareka could weave a new web from Halaravilli's

dashed expectations, King Teheboth strode up to the knot of westerners. Mareka collapsed into the deep curtsey that her liege lord expected, lowering her head so that her chin touched her chest. Such an obeisance was a small fine to pay if the king permitted her continued access to the visitors. Besides, Mareka knew that her swanlike neck was one of her best features.

"My lord," King Teheboth said, pounding the visiting monarch on his back. "I hope that you will join me for the feast. A place has been prepared at my right hand. They say that the venison is ready to serve, and I would have you savor the first bite of our spring success."

"I would be most honored, my lord," King Halaravilli said easily. His smooth acceptance was marred, though, by the quick look that he cast at his countrymen.

"Lady—er—Mareka, is it?" King Teheboth grunted. "Will you see the king's companions to their places?"

"Certainly, Your Majesty." Mareka inclined her head graciously.

Mareka wasted no time escorting the westerners to the lower tables. There. The Lady Mair would do just fine seated next to King Teheboth's ancient nurse. The old woman was so deaf that she would not hear a word the western girl said, even if the visitor were inclined to protest her treatment. And if Mair had to help the old woman gum her food, well, the Touched girl would just have to manage.

The baron, Farsobalinti, would sit at the end of the bench, then, across from Mareka herself. She would enjoy watching the torchlight flicker on his pale hair. It reminded her of spidersilk.

Rani Trader to her left and Crestman beyond that. It was wise to have a buffer from the Amanthian soldier. There was something wild about his face, something untamed. He was here to cause trouble, more trouble than the normal mating rut in King Teheboth's court, the usual jostling for prestige and position.

Across the room, the high table settled quickly. King Teheboth had indeed saved the place at his right hand for King Halaravilli. Farther down the long table sat Olric, with Jerusha beside her husband, the only woman permitted a place of honor upon the dais. The newlywed princess was radiant, twining her hands about her groom's arm and leaning close to whisper secrets.

Mareka's stomach twitched at Jerusha's display. Undoubtedly, Jerusha hoped to bring home riches—hard gold or the more precious gift of a royal heir—by Midwinter Eve, when all the scattered children of the spiderguild traveled home for the annual Grand Convocation. Jerusha would want to prove that her parents had not spent foolishly when they bought her the title "journeyman."

Well, Mareka was determined that she, too, would be recognized at that gathering. She would stand with her brothers and sisters and offer up the riches that *she* had garnered for her guild. Her stolen octolaris would help with that. Stolen octolaris and contacts with the west. After all, Mareka was only being punished for the death of a slave girl, and a stupid one, at that. No one could be expected to pay forever for such an accident.

Although the nobles settled into their places at the high table, the gilded chair next to King Halaravilli remained empty. The rumors were true, then. Princess Berylina was expected at the feast.

Mareka swallowed a smile. The meal might prove amusing yet, with Berylina present. It was unfortunate that Teheboth's queen had died birthing the princess. By all reports, the queen had been a wise woman, and she might have used some common sense in raising her only daughter. The king, of course, had thrust most of that responsibility on royal nurses, on servants who had long ago grown used to the rough and tumble games of the boys placed in their care. They did not know what to do with a quiet girl, how to nurture a creature who was afraid of her own shadow.

One year in the spiderguild would have brought Berylina into line. She would have learned to fight for what she wanted or perished in the process. But in the royal court, Princess Berylina had been coddled and protected, swaddled like a precious gem. The cruel fate of her ugly teeth and her crossed eyes only made such extravagant care seem more foolish.

Mareka's speculation was cut short by the entrance of the

princess herself. Green and silver spidersilk curtains were
swept away from one of the many side doors. Two nurses entered the Great Hall, sailing forward as if they were sweeping
the room free of marauding pirates. Princess Berylina followed
reluctantly in their wake, clutching the hands of two other attendants.

The child wore a white spidersilk gown, Mareka noted, an
unfortunate echo of her own finery. The princess's garment had
none of the subtlety of Mareka's, though, none of the flashes of
inspired color. It was not cut well for the child's plump body; it
bunched beneath her arms and across her belly. The sophisti-
cated styling might have suited a maiden who had begun to
grow into her woman's form, but for Berylina, the low neckline
seemed a cruel jest. Clearly, the princess was not happy with
the design—she dared to drop the hand of one of her nurses to
tug at the fabric. Repeatedly.

When Berylina realized that all the eyes in the hall were directed at her, she shrank between her attendants. The nurse on
her right leaned forward to whisper encouragement, without
success. The woman on her left tried, as well, bending over the
girl's ear and smiling as she gestured forward. Finally, one of
the advance guards turned about and scowled at the child,
clearly threatening some dread punishment. Berylina's face
wavered as if she were about to burst into tears, but she managed to take a single step. The stern nurse spoke again, and the
girl took another step, then another, and at last she stood before
her father.

All four attendants edged away from their ward, and
Berylina dropped a rigidly formal curtsey. So, Mareka mused.
She had finally mastered that maneuver. But tonight the
princess offered even more surprises. "Sire," she said, locking
her eyes on her father's. It was the first word she had ever proclaimed aloud in a formal court setting.

"My lady Berylina," King Teheboth said, clearly surprised
into a broad smile. "You honor us with your presence." The
compliment was nearly too much for the child; she had not rehearsed a reply. Teheboth salvaged the moment. "I have held a
place for you at my table, next to our most honored guest. Will
you join us, daughter?"

"Aye, Sire." The princess glanced shyly at King Halaravilli, meeting his eyes for an instant before lowering her own. Berylina blushed a crimson as deep as the visiting king's riding leathers, but she stepped up to the dais.

Well. The Horned Hind brought ever-renewed wonders. Mareka listened to the flurry of amazed whispers as her fellow Liantines watched the princess take her seat beside King Halaravilli.

King Teheboth must have feared that his daughter's poise would be short-lived. He raised a commanding hand and caught Lord Shalindor's eye. The skeletal chamberlain inclined his head for one quick moment, and then he pulled back a green-and-silver curtain with a flourish.

Several servants waited in the hallway. The first held an enormous platter decorated with spring flowers. A stag's head was centered in the greenery, its eyes already grown cloudy and grey. The antlers were enormous—Mareka could only guess at the size of the beast that had borne them. Truly, this first kill was a good omen for the coming year. The Horned Hind must intend great things for all of Liantine.

The servants paraded their trophy around the entire hall, accepting salutes from noblemen and squeals from ladies with equal aplomb. Mareka raised her cup as the platter passed, drinking to salute the Horned Hind.

Rani Trader, sitting at Mareka's side, mimicked the gesture. The girl swallowed only once and stared at her cup before setting it back on the table. She must be unused to Liantine drink, to the acidic touch of the greenwine. Well enough. Perhaps she would quaff too much, unaware of the greenwine's alcoholic bite. Perhaps Mareka would learn more about the Morenians, more that would help her ultimate mission.

The servants had clearly been instructed to avoid carrying the stag's head past Princess Berylina. Instead, they circled behind the high table, edging around the most honored nobles until they came to rest at King Teheboth's side. The king raised a heavy goblet in salute to the slain beast, and then he drank deeply. Only when the cup was drained did he climb to his feet.

"My lords! My ladies!" A restless silence fell over the hall. "We have ridden in search of the Horned Hind this first day of spring. Our horses were swift and our dogs were sure—the day was merciful to us. Let us feast on the first fruits of the season and offer up our thanks for another winter survived! To Liantine!"

"To Liantine!" shouted the assembly, and Mareka joined them all by sipping at her greenwine. Rani Trader drank too.

"And we welcome visitors to our court, nobles who have traveled far across the springtime ocean. To King Halaravilli ben-Jair!"

The Liantines had trouble with the visiting monarch's name, and Mareka hid a smile behind her cup as Rani Trader's voice rang a little too clearly in the hall. Another sip of greenwine, and then King Teheboth gestured again to Lord Shalindor. At the chamberlain's command, more servants streamed into the hall, this time carrying platters groaning with venison and new-harvested roots, braces of partridges and loaves of braided bread, all seasoned with expensive eastern spices.

As the food was passed around tables and piled onto trenchers, Mareka continued to concentrate on the high table. King Halaravilli sampled each dish that was placed before him, but he concentrated on addressing Princess Berylina.

He had more grace than Mareka had expected—he managed to look at the princess directly. He avoided staring at her teeth, a rudeness that was known to send the shy child into catatonia. He even avoided the greater danger of speaking to one of her roving eyes or the other—he managed to direct his quiet comments to the middle of her brow. In fact, King Halaravilli actually succeeded in extracting responses from the princess, illustrating the full extent of the Horned Hind's power this spring day.

From across the room, Mareka could not be certain what the child said, but Halaravilli nodded gravely and leaned closer to catch her words. The king raised the flagon of greenwine between them, smiling as he poured more into the princess's goblet.

The meal wore on, and entertainers began to pass among the crowd. Mareka turned away from the jugglers—their work was boring. She had no interest in riddles told by King Teheboth's jester. She could solve most of his tricksy puzzles easily enough, and the more obscure ones were inevitably crude jokes. A madrigal chorus sang sweetly, but their song was poorly chosen, an overly intricate ode to spring that was far better suited to a lady's chamber than to the echoing Great Hall.

At last, the kitchen servants carried in sweetmeats to conclude the meal. In addition to honeyed fruits, there was a monstrous marzipan confection, shaped and tinted to resemble the Morenian lion. King Halaravilli delivered lavish praise for the gilded construction, and then he proffered the tip of the crimson tail to Princess Berylina. The girl was delighted—she even managed a radiant smile before her nerves overcame her and she hid her rabbit teeth behind her palms.

With the marzipan, the players appeared.

The first sign of the troop was a flourish of silk at the Great Hall's double doors. The green and silver hangings were pulled to either side, and the doors flung open. Two stout men carried in iron staffs, the poles wrapped with spidersilk banners. Mareka felt a physical pain in her chest as she saw the pennants—these players were sponsored by her own guild.

Players throughout the land found their sponsors among the guilds and merchant houses, patrons who paid for the troops' passage on the high road, who offered protection and funding. Despite the spiderguild's investment, Mareka had watched the players only a handful of times. As a mere apprentice she had rarely been permitted to observe the players' handiwork when they journeyed to the guildhall.

Now, unfettered by the traditional roles of her guild, Mareka stared in amazement as a giant wrought-iron ball rolled into the room. The structure was easily the height of two men; it barely fit beneath the doorframe. The sphere was a bare framework, bars that had been carefully twisted so that all could see within the core. Segments cut across the interior, presenting everchanging perches and poles.

Two women crouched inside the sphere, clad in the traditional leggings and tight tunics of players. One wore an elaborate headdress, glimmering horns that collected all the light of torches and of candles, snaring the flames and casting them back to the watchers. The other woman was dressed as a hunter, and the tip of her spear was coated in the same reflective gleam.

Mareka's breath caught in her throat as she watched the players' show. The women worked together, rolling the sphere about the floor of the Great Hall. They used their weight to keep the iron ball constantly in motion, moving down the flag-stones, stopping just short of the tables. And all the time that the sphere turned, the women executed a careful dance of death inside its iron bounds.

The hunter stalked the Horned Hind, following her from top to bottom, from side to side. The goddess stretched and folded, tossing her glinting antlers each time that she escaped. The ball rolled and stopped, retreated and advanced, and still the hunter sought her prey. Once, she stabbed with her shining spear. Twice. Three times, four.

The sphere now rested in front of the high table. The Horned Hind and the hunter twisted their bodies, set the metal spinning. For the fifth time, the hunter tried to slay the holy beast. Six times. Seven. The women found themselves directly in front of King Teheboth. The Horned Hind spread within the ball, arms and legs stretched for iron handholds. The hunter paused for perfect timing, then thrust her spear upward, leaning with all of her apparent weight.

The Horned Hind's antlers snagged the iron struts and she died a perfect agony. The sphere stopped dead. The player hunter's arm was frozen, her spear a flawless line.

And then the women moved. They tumbled from their poses and stepped outside their iron cage. They stood before an amazed court, grinning as they brandished their glittering antlers and spears. King Teheboth roared his pleasure as the women bowed like courtiers, and then the players turned about, palming the iron cage to set it rolling. They abandoned the hall as the guests took to their feet, roaring for more.

The spiderguild would be proud.

Mareka sat back on her bench, draining her cup of green-wine, remembering to breathe. Her guild had made the vision possible. Her guild had had the wisdom and foresight to pa-tronize such a brilliant performance.

The players, though, were far from through. While the women had snared the attention of every person in the hall, other members of the troop had quietly set the stage for a more traditional presentation. A jackhand, the all-purpose players' servant, stepped to the front of the dais that ran the length of the Great Hall. With silent efficiency, he lit the row of lanterns at the foot of the platform. The light was immediately captured by the carefully positioned mirrors, throwing the brilliance back toward the stage.

The lanterns called into focus six metal crosiers that were scattered across the dais. The players must have brought them in while everyone was focused on the mimed hunt. Each metal crook was centered in a pool of mirror-light. Each supported a glasswork frame, a stained glass panel that defined a character in the production that was about to begin.

Mareka immediately identified the Prince. Of course, Prince Olric would figure prominently in the players' piece—the recent marriage would be celebrated for months to come. With a fortnight since the nuptials, the players had had ample time to Speak with Olric, to prepare their presentation. As if to draw the crowd's attention, the jackhand tumbled to the intricate glass panel, turning it slightly on its iron hook so that every person present could make out the traditional design of the prince's light-blue cloak, his lead-framed glass sword, the gleaming fillet about his head.

The jackhand stepped back, striking a pose and cocking his head toward the panel. The audience applauded their approval, and the jackhand mimed deafness. The assembled courtiers shouted, then, praising the fine workmanship, and at last the jackhand appeared satisfied. He clapped his hands once, twice, three times, and on the fourth crash, an actor leaped from behind the players' spidersilk curtains. Spinning through a series of fighting forms, the nimble young man came to rest beside the glass panel, frozen into position as he placed his hand on his own sword, raising his chin and gazing nobly at the crowd.

The audience roared, and Prince Olric shouted his approval.

The jackhand then repeated the process, twitching the glass frames into place and summoning the other actors, six in all: the Prince and a Princess, a Cat, a Priest, a Nurse, and the Moon. Mareka had never seen the costume for the Cat before, and she surprised herself by laughing at the player's supple arched back, her twitching black tail.

The jackhand surveyed the tableau he had created, making two small adjustments to the lanterns and their mirrors. Then, with a cheery wave of his hand, he collapsed onto the dais, tucking his chin against his chest and rolling away, head over heels. Before the audience could finish laughing, the Moon began to speak.

"Welcome noble good folk, to our little play. We hope you liked your supper, we hope that you will stay. We've come to tell the story of a noble Prince, who saved a Cat and gained a wife, for happ'ness ever since."

The play was a comedy, then. Mareka far preferred the players' dramas. Comedies quickly became annoying, with their rhymes and their rhythms, their endless, boring patterns. The players found them easier to perform, though. They could quickly Speak to the people who they interpreted; they could craft their stories easily. There was no depth to the comedies.

Dramas, on the other hand . . .

Mareka had Spoken for one drama in her life, the day that she ascended to the eighth level of apprenticeship. To reach the eighth, she had learned how to transfer a brooding female from one box to another. She had sampled octolaris nectar for the first time, using its dilute poison to protect against the bite of any spider she enraged. The nectar had still beat strong in her veins when she met with the players who had been hired to celebrate the apprentices' passage.

She would never forget entering the company's tent, her cheeks glowing from the nectar and her success in handling the octolaris. She had reclined with the players on lush pillows, feeling every fiber of the velvet and spidersilk against her hands, against her bare arms. She remembered watching a perfect golden orb spinning on a chain, a globe that was no larger than the tip of her thumb, spinning, spinning, spinning. A player—a woman scarcely older than a spider journeyman—had told Mareka to count backward, beginning with her age. She had started: sixteen, fifteen, fourteen . . . Then the words were too hard to say, the sounds too difficult to make.

Mareka knew that she *could* open her eyes. She *could* stop the Speaking. . . .

She had not wanted to, though. She had not wanted to resist

telling her story. She answered all the players' questions, told them all her truths. And eight days later, when she watched the play that they performed—a play about her hopes to lead the spiderguild, to bring her guild more honor and pride and wealth than it had ever imagined—Mareka fell into that strange well of peace all over again.

She rediscovered a depth and a calm that she never knew in her daily life, a quiet that told her she did not always need to be thinking; she did not always need to scheme. She did not always need to work to make the spiderguild the strongest, the richest, the most successful guild it could be. She could be quiet. She could be at peace. She could be Mareka.

All of that, from Speaking to the players and watching them tell her story.

Tell her drama, that was. These comedies were a different matter entirely.

Mareka fought to keep from yawning as the players rhymed their way through the tale of how Prince Olric had met Princess Jerusha, when the spiderguild journeyman's pet Cat had escaped into the garden. The players added a few twists of fun— the Nurse protected the chastity of the Princess vigilantly, even as the old woman threw herself against the Priest. The Moon watched over all, making wise and witty comments. In the end, Olric bribed the Moon to duck behind a cloud, and he kissed his sweetheart Princess in the darkness. She agreed to wed him, and the Priest sang out the nuptial rites.

The Moon bowed to the roar of applause. "And so we hope you good folk will find it in your hearts to reward us players richly, paying for our parts."

More applause, more laughter, and all six players scrambled for the coins that were tossed upon the dais. Everyone had enjoyed the silly piece. Some of the nobles were calling out ribald suggestions to the true Prince Olric, giving him ideas of other reasons to bribe the moon. Jerusha blushed prettily, her eyes flashing in triumph as she settled her hand on her husband's arm.

Mareka swallowed a sharp comment, knowing that no one at the table would care that it had been *Mareka's* idea for Jerusha to send her cat out to the king's garden. Mareka had been the one to craft the scheme that had cemented the bond between the spiderguild journeyman and the prince.

Taking a deep breath, Mareka turned to Rani Trader, bracing herself for the inevitable rush of adulation that outsiders showed for the players. She was surprised, to see the merchant girl staring silently at the dais. Rani Trader did not look at Olric or Jerusha; she did not even spare a glance for the players. Instead, the merchant gazed at the glass panels that the jackhand had hung across the stage, eyeing them as if they held all the Horned Hind's secrets.

Mareka watched the merchant as the jackhand lifted down the Moon. The panel slipped a little in the man's hands, but he caught it well before it touched the floor. Rani Trader was half off her bench, though, her hands thrusting forward as if she were a mother protecting a toddling child. The merchant girl scarcely breathed as the jackhand wrapped up the Moon in its spidersilk shroud. Her attention remained gripped by each of the other pieces.

Only when the last of the glass panels had been stowed away did Rani Trader sit back on the bench. She turned to Mareka and breathed, "That was wonderful! Who are these players?"

Mareka sniffed, shrugging to convey the notion that the show had been boring and ordinary. "They're a troop that roams through Liantine. My spiderguild sponsors them." Rani Trader only nodded, drinking in the information like greenwine.

Crestman, though, bristled at the mention of the guild. That action was enough to remind Mareka of the poisoned slave girl, and *that* thought, inevitably, drew Mareka to the virulent octolaris, to the twenty-four hungry spiders that were isolated in her bedchamber, dependent wholly on her to bring them their evening feast of markin grubs.

Mareka rose from the table, a host of lies flooding to her lips. She found that she needed none of them, however. Rani Trader continued to stare at the dais, clutching Crestman's arm and whispering to him of glasswork. The soldier looked uninterested, although he covered the merchant's fingers with his own. Even Mair, the Touched girl, was distracted, leaning toward her pale companion to share some secret.

Mareka was halfway to the doors of the Great Hall when she heard her name called. She turned to find Jerusha, clinging to her husband's arm like a markin grub on an apprentice's finger. Mareka's eyes narrowed to slits, but she forced a veil of courtesy over her words. "Congratulations, sister. The players certainly made a profit on your tale."

Jerusha flashed a chilly smile and said, "The players did, and our guild as well. Our masters will certainly receive great praise for sponsoring such an entertaining troop. Tell me, Mareka. I've brought the house of Liantine to our spiderguild and added to our reputation throughout the land. What plans have you devised for redeeming yourself before our masters?"

Mareka looked down the hall to where King Halaravilli was speaking with Berylina. "I've made my plans, sister," Mareka said to Jerusha. "Just you wait. The spiderguild will profit from me, and I'll join you at the Midwinter Grand Convocation. I'll be a journeyman yet."

7

The sunshine was warm in the viewing stands, and a gentle breeze carried the fragrance of new grass across the Liantine tilting field. On another day, Rani might have been intrigued by the exhibition of horsemen's skill that King Teheboth had arranged as an afternoon diversion. Today, however, she was attempting to conduct a conversation with Hal, under cover of the tourney pageantry.

Rani checked to see that the attention of their host was taken up with preparations for the next round of mock combat before she whispered sharply, "Why did you bother to bring me here if you won't listen to anything I say?"

"Won't listen?" Hal exclaimed, and then he lowered his voice. "Rani, you know I had no choice yesterday. The direct revelation of all the Thousand Gods would not have made Teheboth take you with us on his Spring Hunt. What was I supposed to do, forget the Little Army entirely? Pass up the opportunity to ask about their fate?"

"That is *precisely* what you should have done. You lost everything by moving too soon. You'll have no chance to raise the issue with him again."

Rani was spared Hal's sputtered retort because Teheboth's knights were ready to illustrate their jousting prowess. She forced her attention to the arena, watching as the two riders manipulated their horses to opposite ends of the cleared field. The horsemen had trouble settling their spirited mounts, and the frothy clouds had shifted in the sky by the time they couched their lances.

King Teheboth turned to Princess Berylina, who stood beside him in the viewing stand, and he passed his daughter a length of emerald spidersilk. For a moment, Rani thought that the princess would refuse to accept it, but her father's stern glance proved more fearsome than taking the cloth. Berylina held the gauzy fabric between two fingers, letting it flutter in the breeze. Only when her father nodded did she release the signal.

Both riders leaped forward as the spidersilk left the princess's hand, and Rani's teeth jarred when the knights met in the center of the field. Neither succeeded in unseating the other, although they repeated the process three more times. On the fourth run, Rani was startled by a sharp crack, and she saw one of the knights throw down the splintered remains of his lance. He dismounted with a furious grimace, kneeling before his fellow with ritual, reluctant humility. The winner touched his intact lance to his opponent's breast, only turning to the viewing stand when the other man was pinned by the iron tip.

"Your Majesty," proclaimed the proud knight, bowing toward Teheboth. "Your Highness." He repeated his salute toward Princess Berylina. He inclined his head toward the knot of visiting Morenians but did not address them directly.

Rani joined the viewers in applauding politely. Servants darted onto the playing field, gathering up the shattered bits of lance, and then four attendants began to drag out heavy quintains for another bellicose display. The figures were obviously difficult to set in place—their weighted arms kept whirling about, buffeting the unfortunate servants who were trying to add hoops for tilting riders to capture.

Rani took advantage of the distraction to turn back to Hal. "We have time here in Liantine, my lord. Time for you to gain Teheboth's trust. Yesterday was too soon to drag the Little Army into your discussions."

"Too soon? Have you forgotten that I left a burned and dying city back in Morenia?"

"Do you think I could forget, my lord?" Rani snapped. "Do you truly think that I do not remember Moren?"

She would have been wiser to stay at home. At least in

Moren, she could have guarded against the Fellowship's tricks. She could have watched over Dartulamino's consolidating power as the new Holy Father, measured out the meaning of the church ascending to such heights within the organization. That monitoring might have helped Hal, might have let him calculate an appropriate time to formally announce his own ambitions to the secret group.

By staying in Moren, she might have served her king without the pain that pounded in her chest, without the frustration.

When Hal did not reply, Rani forced her voice to a level tone, prying her attention from the future. Back to Liantine. Back to Moren. "Every day that we are gone, Your Majesty, I think about firelung. I think about starving children. I think about shipments of lumber arriving in Moren, and how we are to pay the waiting tradesmen. Why else do you think that I accompanied you across that Kel-cursed ocean?"

Before Hal could reply, King Teheboth called out, "Ho there! What secrets are you Morenians sharing? Are you placing wagers on my knightly contestants?"

Hal looked up guiltily. "Wagers? Nay, my lord."

With unsuspecting irony, Teheboth said, "That leaves your purse full, then. Full and ready to place a bet with me."

"You have an unfair advantage, my lord." Hal had recovered enough to lighten his tone. "You know your men. You know their skills."

"Come judge them for yourself, then. Each man will take one pass through the course, and then we'll lay our bets. Come! Stand beside my Berylina, that you might judge who is the best."

Hal stretched a smile over his teeth and edged past Rani. She resisted the urge to tangle her fingers in his cloak, to grip his arm and pull him close. She wanted to whisper a warning, to remind him that everything he said, everything he did was under scrutiny. He might think of the Little Army as a separate matter from Berylina, a separate matter from that spiderguild wench who had eyed him all too closely during last night's feast. But they all were interwoven. They all were part of the tangled, twisting pattern that was Liantine.

She restrained herself. She said nothing and stepped aside

so that Hal could watch the course unhindered. She crossed to Crestman. The Amanthian glanced at her quizzically, as if he wanted to know the words she had exchanged with their king. His expectation annoyed her, but she held her tongue even when she felt him shift beside her. She was painfully aware of the sidelong glances that he stole, the way he moved his arm to feel her by his side. She focused on the knights below.

The riders on the field seemed well matched. One rode a spirited little mare, and he used her speed to dart beneath the figures, managing to capture six of the seven quintain rings. The other rider favored a far heavier horse, a battle steed that pounded powerfully around the course. That man also caught six rings, but he wrestled with his mount to make tight turns.

Hal watched seriously, fingering the gold-fringed pouch at his waist. When the exhibition was completed and servants darted out to restore the targets' rings, Teheboth said, "Well? What say you, my lord? What will you wager on a triple run?"

Rani suspected that Hal should place his money on the heavier horse. The little mare had completed the course once, but there was no knowing if she would have the energy for another three passes. Nevertheless, Rani's heart instinctively went out to the rider of the smaller beast.

Crestman scarcely breathed his own reply. "The battle mount." Rani turned to question him, but the soldier's face remained impassive; he might never have spoken.

Hal found a different solution. He bowed to Berylina and said, "My lady? What say you?"

All eyes locked on the princess, who was clearly astonished to find herself the center of such attention. Her crossed eyes darted up to Hal's face and then away, casting unevenly across the playing field. She licked her chapped lips, calling unfortunate attention to the protruding tips of her white teeth. When no one else spoke, she managed to whisper, "My lord?"

"Come now." Hal's voice was as soft and intimate as if they stood alone; Rani could scarce make out his cajoling words. "Your father has permitted me a single demonstration, but I must be protective of my coin. I'd rather have the knowledge of an expert in this court. Who shall I support, my lady? Who will win the triple round?"

Berylina stared out at the riders, her chin quivering. Hal edged closer, taking her plump hand between his own. "Come, my lady. Help a visitor to your father's court. Tell me how to play my wager. I trust you. I trust your knowledge."

Berylina stared down at her trapped hand as if it belonged to another child. She swallowed hard, and then she raised her eyes to Hal's face. She stared at him intensely as she said, "The one that is blessed by Par, my lord."

Hal's smile was quizzical. "By Par?" he asked. Berylina nodded, unable to summon further words. "By the god of the sun?"

"Aye, my lord."

Those last three words proved too great a strain, and Berylina tugged her hand away from Hal, using it to hide her face. Hal appeared not to notice as he turned to King Teheboth. "Very well, then. My lady has spoken. I'll place my wager on the blond man."

The little mare.

"On Charion," Teheboth bellowed. "And will you hold our wagers, daughter?"

Rani thought that the princess would faint away from the attention. Nevertheless, she managed to find the strength to collect a gold coin from her father. When Hal offered his own stake, he took care to place the coin squarely in her palm, folding her fingers around it. "I hope the Thousand Gods have not misled us, my lady," he said with a solemn nod. Berylina blushed the color of Hal's crimson tunic, but she did not pull her hand away.

Rani swallowed hard and turned her attention to the tilting field. Of course Hal needed to court the princess. He needed to please her. He needed to do all in his power to pry her from her shell of shyness. Of course, of course, of course.

Crestman shifted beside her, and Rani scarcely managed to keep from snapping at him. The figures on the field were oddly blurred. The spring breeze was stiffer than Rani had suspected—it must have whipped dirt from the arena into the corners of her eyes. She stealthily swept a hand across them, rubbing them dry. She dared not look, though, to see if Crestman saw her motion.

Whether Berylina had some special knowledge or Hal was lucky, Charion won the competition. The knight manipulated his little mare with daring, snatching twenty of the rings and ducking beneath the last quintain's heavy bag. The other rider managed only eighteen rings and was nearly tossed from his mount by the hearty buffet of a misstruck figure.

Crestman snorted, muttering beneath his breath that the heavier horseman could have won, if he'd sat his horse with greater skill. Hal whooped in pleasure at his victory, his eyes shining with bright fire. Teheboth's automatic scowl turned to a calculating grin as he watched his daughter hand over both coins to the Morenian king. "Well done, my lord," Teheboth said.

"Only through the grace of your daughter," Hal replied courteously.

"Only through the grace of Par," Berylina insisted, with enough force that both men looked at her in surprise.

Rani did not have a chance to talk to Hal again until the end of the riding displays, when the party climbed down from the viewing stand and began a leisurely walk back to the palace. The nobles were expected to refresh themselves in their chambers for the afternoon. Another feast and dancing would be held that night—the players would perform again. Rani looked forward to seeing the glass screens, to studying the fine workmanship.

In the meantime, as Berylina was hustled away by her nurses, Rani purposely dropped back. She hoped that she would have a few moments to conclude her conversation with Hal, and she gestured for Crestman to go on ahead. She was relieved when the Amanthian complied; however, she saw him glance over his shoulder as Hal fell into step at her side.

"Sire," she began as soon as she was certain they would not be overheard. "You know I do not argue with you to be difficult." She swallowed hard. "I know that I have no great grace, and I have no special learning. I try your patience more often than not. But you *must* let me help you when I can. I should have been the one to treat with King Teheboth about the Little Army."

Hal stopped walking and gazed at her steadily. "Do you truly think that he would speak with you? We are not in Morenia here. Teheboth Thunderspear has little need for women's words."

"He will listen when Liantine can benefit. He'd be a fool to overlook advantage solely because he does not care for the messenger."

"Whatever else he might be, Teheboth is no fool. Still, he will not speak with you. You may offer bargains through me, I will say your words, but he must not think you make decisions for me."

"I do not decide what you will do! I offer guidance. I offer counsel."

"He will not make such fine distinctions if you are the one who speaks."

"That is not fair, my lord! If Farsobalinti devised my strategies, you would keep him by your side. You would let him speak his mind before Teheboth, and you would honor him for doing so!"

"The world is rarely fair," Hal said. As Rani started to protest again, he raised a commanding hand. "Besides, Rani, are you prepared to bargain for Berylina?"

Rani's heart twisted in her chest. "Are you certain she is strong enough to meet your needs?"

"She is the only daughter of the house of Thunderspear."

"She is afraid of her own shadow!"

"She was brave enough to speak with me, last night and today. She was certain enough just now to win a gold sovereign from her own father." Rani heard Hal's calm logic, his growing certainty. "Rani, I remember how it felt to sit in a hall, surrounded by people who called me an idiot and thought to deprive me of power."

"My lord, you are no longer the boy who retreated into rhymes to survive!"

"No, Rani. Now I am the king."

"And you need a queen to stand beside you, a queen who

can guide Morenia back from these dark days. Is Berylina the one? Do you truly think that she can do all that you require?"

"Who else would you suggest?"

She could not answer that. She closed her eyes and clenched her hands into fists.

She had not asked for the fire, for the firelung; she had not asked for any of this responsibility. She tried to convince herself that she wanted only to stay in Moren, only to read her books, to work toward being a journeyman. What did Davin's book say? She should learn to pour glass, to cut glass, to set glass. She should lead apprentices and obey masters. She should contribute one quarter of all her worldly goods to her guild.

That was all. She was a guildsman, a simple guildsman.

"Wait, my lord," she said. "Do not make your decision yet. Do not go to Teheboth and ask for Berylina's hand."

"I'll wait for now," Hal said. "I'll wait because I need your plan. I need your strategy to get the princess, along with a dowry large enough to save Morenia."

And then he walked away. He turned his back on her, and he walked across the emerald field, striding fast past Crestman to catch up with Teheboth, with Berylina. Rani started to follow, started to call him back, but she realized she had nothing left to say, no arguments left to make.

A gentle breeze whispered across the grass, and she felt a gossamer touch against her ankles. She looked down and saw the scarf that Berylina had let fall, the spidersilk that had set the men to jousting.

Before she could reach for it, Crestman came up beside her. He scooped up the fragile cloth with a smooth gesture, crumpling it in one tanned hand. "There were Amanthians on that field."

"What?"

"The boys who set the quintains. They were from the Little Army."

She said nothing.

"They did not even look my way. They went about their business like any servant in any noble's household."

Rani did not reply.

"It's like they do not know us, like they have no memory of when they lived in Amanthia."

"Perhaps they don't," Rani said at last. "Perhaps their world has changed, and this is all they know. They were children, after all. They were children when the world they knew was lost." Crestman looked at her strangely, and neither spoke again as they returned to King Teheboth's palace.

"What, exactly, did you think was going to happen here in Liantine?"

Rani huddled by the window, wishing that she could ignore Mair's pointed question. She ran her fingers over the wooden windowsill. The guest apartments that she shared with her friend were bare and cold, even though the palace servants insisted they were the finest in Teheboth's home. The walls were covered with fine paneling, the servants noted often, not the spidersilk trappings found in older rooms.

Now, Rani scarcely cared if she were sleeping in a military tent. She wanted to be gone. She wanted to be back in Moren. She forced herself to answer Mair. "I don't know. I thought that I would speak for Hal. That King Teheboth would listen to me."

"What possibly made you think *that*?"

"Hal asked me to accompany him!"

"He asked you to advise him. He asked you to think of strategies, like a general."

"This isn't a battlefield, Mair."

"What is it, then, Rai? What else would you call it?" Rani did not answer; she had no reply. "You know how this will end, Rai. Let's finish now. Bargain for your king. Tell him the best strategy for negotiating his dowry."

"He has not made his decision yet. He is not certain that he'll ask for Berylina."

"What else can he do? He's waiting for you. He wants you to tell him that he may."

"I do not give the king of all Morenia permission to do anything."

"Precisely," Mair said. "And until you do, he'll wait."

"That's not what I meant, Mair!"

"Perhaps it's the truth, though."

"That's absurd." Rani glared at her friend.

"So you have tried to tell yourself since our boat landed on the Liantine shore. I don't know why we made this journey if you will not follow through." Mair strode away from the window. "Well, I won't sit here any longer."

"Where are you going?"

"Today is market day. I'm going to learn what Liantines use for firelung."

"You don't even know that a single Liantine has ever *suffered* from firelung!"

"I won't find out sitting here."

Rani listened to Mair collect her cloak; she heard a handful of coins clink together. Once, the Touched girl started to speak, but she stopped herself, sighing explosively instead. Mair's footsteps stomped across the floor, echoing off the inlaid wooden panels. The metal latch lifted free of the door, and the leather hinges creaked. Mair paused one last time, and then she stepped smartly over the threshold, grabbing the outside latch with a vicious grunt.

"Wait!" Rani called, just before the door slammed closed. "I'll come with you."

"Of course you will." Mair waited while Rani collected her belongings.

The market square was bustling, and Rani realized how long it had been since she had walked through a thriving trade fair. Even before the fire in Moren, the marketplace had been slow for the winter. Farmers had offered few vegetables, and trade goods were scarce as transport was delayed by snow and other harsh weather.

The Liantine fair, though, was a bustling hive of activity. Children called to one another, and mothers summoned reluctant youths to help carry purchases. Men haggled over tinware and knives and leather belts.

Rani saw one stand that sold nothing but bronze amulets, star-shaped medallions with an image of the Horned Hind soldered to the center. Another table held carved wooden bowls, marked with prices higher than any Morenian merchant would be able to command. There were other wooden pieces—platters and candlesticks, spoons and decorative combs. Many bore the image of the Horned Hind, inlaid or burned into the surface. The merchant boasted that his wares were the latest fashion, the newest treasures, but even so, they were more expensive than Rani or Mair could understand.

"Look," Mair exclaimed once. "Over by the owlboy."

Rani followed her companion's pointing finger, and both girls crossed to study the extensive display of herbs. Some were meant for kitchen work, but others were set aside for healing, for curing, for easing the ill. Mair began to question the handsome young vendor, and Rani's attention wandered.

Both she and Mair had recognized the owlboy, known him for an Amanthian child-scholar, even though his tattoo had been carved away from his face. There were former Little Army children scattered throughout the marketplace, some selling wares, others buying. Some were dressed in rags and had a haunted look of hunger, but most were well clothed, cheerful, talking to companions or studiously searching out bargains.

Mair flourished a large bouquet of dried herbs, laughing when Rani sneezed. "The man says these will help. He says they'll ease the bone-ache and help folks cough the soot from their lungs."

"And if it works? How will you find more?"

"He says it's called lamb's breath. It's common to the east of here. We can find a source in Moren or buy up his stock here."

Rani sniffed at the herbs again, committing the pungent scent to memory. She caught Mair's eye as she straightened. "We both knew that was an owlboy."

"Aye."

"How? He only wears a scar."

"We spent enough time with the Amanthians to know. We learned their castes by living with them, seeing how they carry themselves, how they look." Mair shrugged. "You know that I'm Touched, even when I speak like a noble in the king's own court."

"*Anyone* would know you're Touched, Mair." Rani laughed.

"Ho, there, my lady! Such mirth on market day!" Rani jumped at the loud greeting, whirling about to find the source of the shout. She was startled by the man who stood before her, shocked by his red and black particolored leggings, by his shimmering white spidersilk tunic. "Greetings!" he cried. "Salutations from the Spiderguild Players."

"The Spiderguild Players?" Rani repeated, confused.

"Aye, my lady." The man bowed, sweeping an imaginary hat into the air with a dramatic flourish. "The spiderguild sponsors us. We take their money and turn it into tales!" The man placed his invisible hat on his head, settling its imaginary weight with a wiggle of his wrist. He straightened with an infectious grin.

Something about the precise motion of his hands made Rani recognize him. "You're the jackhand!" she exclaimed. "From last night!"

"Pollino, my lady. At your service. And have you come to the market to Speak with us?"

"Speak with you?" Rani had no intention of speaking with the players; she had not even known that they would be in the marketplace.

"*Speak,* my lady," Pollino said expansively. "King Teheboth has granted us leave to Speak with whoever comes our way, for one entire day and night. We'll leave at dawn tomorrow, packing away our new stories with our spidersilk and glass."

"New stories?" Rani felt like a foolish child, like she could only repeat words given to her. She glanced at Mair to see if the Touched girl understood any more than she. Mair, though, was making her way toward another herbalist.

Pollino cocked his head to one side, as if he were studying her for a portrait. "You've never seen players before, have you?"

"Not players like your company. In my land, in Morenia, there are bards who sing, and pageant men who tell the stories of the Thousand Gods. We don't have companies like yours, though." She licked her lips and ventured one more sentence. "Our players don't have glass."

Pollino darted a glance at her, and she was certain that he saw the yearning on her face. He smiled easily, though, and said, "Your bards, your pageant men, do they Speak to their watchers?"

"Speak?" Once again, she heard his odd emphasis on the word. "I don't know what you mean."

"We Spiderguild Players borrow our stories from those who watch our tales. We invite the watchers to our tents. We charge them a small coin, and then we ask them questions. We learn their stories, and then we give the tales back to others. A watcher's story might last through the ages, if it is clever enough. If it is daring. If it is true. The asking and the telling, that's Speaking."

Rani shook her head uncertainly. "The players in my land do not Speak, then. Your practice seems unfair. You take your watchers' story, and yet you make them pay."

"We take, that is true—coins and tales. But we give, as well. No watcher leaves unhappy, and many come to us again, Speaking as often as we let them." Pollino edged closer, all mirth draining from his face. "And you, my lady? Would you like to Speak with the Spiderguild Players?"

She was about to refuse, about to rejoin Mair and finish prowling the marketplace for treasures. But if she agreed to Speak, Pollino would take her to the players' tents. Their glass would be there. She could see the panels, study the finest glass she had seen since her guild was destroyed. "I—" Her voice broke, and she swallowed hard. "What does it cost?"

Pollino smiled his contagious grin. "A sovereign, my lady. A single sovereign to Speak to the players."

Rani's fingers fell automatically to the pouch at her waist. One gold coin. Just like the coin that Hal had wagered the day before. Just like the coin that he had folded into Berylina's palm.

As a merchant, she knew that she should bargain down the price. She'd be a fool to accept a first bid, to buy without debate. But the wares included *glass,* access to the players' precious panels.

"Done."

Pollino nodded solemnly, as if he heard all the words she did not say, as if he recognized the gravity of the bargain they had struck. "This way, then, my lady."

"A moment, please." Rani looked about for Mair. When she

saw her friend perusing wooden charms, she called out that she was going with the players. Mair shrugged and indicated she could not hear over the noise of the crowd. Rani called a second time and a third, and then she waved Mair back to the market, exasperated.

After all, how long could this Speaking take? How long were the players likely to let Rani peruse their panels?

Rani followed the jackhand through the crowded market, winding her way to the very edge of the square. The players' tents were assembled in a shaded corner, like a small village, brightly colored against the grey of cobblestones. A spidersilk banner flew from the tallest post, snapping smartly in the wind. It was blazoned with a twisting spider, the eight legs picked out in careful black on white.

As Rani approached the tents, she saw players' children chasing each other in an elaborate game. Closer to the largest tent, two grown men held wooden swords, walking around in measured circles. They approached each other and then fell back, joining together and coming apart over and over again. Obviously, they were practicing a fight for some tale.

A girl nearly Rani's age sat on a bench outside the largest tent, biting her lip as she pulled a needle through black spidersilk. It was the Cat's costume, Rani realized. The tail must have come loose.

Pollino nodded to the seamstress as he approached the tent. "Flarissa is inside?"

"Aye." The girl looked up, and a brown-rayed sun was etched across her cheek. Another Amanthian. Another member of the Little Army, peacefully at work in Liantine. Not noticing Rani's stare, the girl nodded at Pollino.

"Is she Speaking with anyone?"

"Nay."

Pollino did not seem disturbed by the girl's short answers. Instead, he grinned to Rani and gestured toward the entrance of the tent. She started to duck through the doorway, but the jackhand gripped her arm. "You pay before you Speak."

Again, Rani knew that she should protest. She knew that she should bargain—pay half first, the rest after. After she had seen this Flarissa.

She reached into her purse and extracted a gleaming sovereign.

Pollino took the coin from her palm, exaggerating the motion by plucking the metal with his forefinger and his thumb. He held it up to the sunlight as if he were checking for shaved edges, but he was clearly pleased with whatever he saw. In a movement too fast for Rani's eyes to follow, he snapped the coin into his own palm, hiding it behind his nimble fingers. "My lady," he said, bowing and pulling open the entrance to the tent.

Rani caught her breath and ducked inside.

Pollino dropped the silk behind her, plunging her into darkness. Rani blinked, and she could see that a little light penetrated the heavy walls. A small brazier burned in the center of the floor, sending up curls of smoke that smelled of pine trees and forest rain. Great bolsters were scattered about, gleaming with the richness of their spidersilk coverings. The spiderguild's patronage served these players well. That, and collecting coins from naive Morenians who agreed to Speak.

Rani blinked again, and she could make out even more in the interior gloom. Trunks were stacked against the far wall, their brass fittings glinting in the gloom. They were of a size to hold the glasswork panels. Glass, wrapped in softest spidersilk, in deepest, darkest velvet . . .

"Be welcome, Speaker."

Rani started at the voice, and she took a step back, clutching at the curtain that Pollino had closed behind her. When she squinted, she could make out the form of a woman on the far side of the brazier, a woman who was turning to face Rani. She was lifting folds of dark blue fabric from her shimmering hair, from hair that was as light as Rani's own. As the woman pulled back her hood, she leaned over the brazier and picked up a fragrant length of incense. The end of the pine-scented stick glowed red as she moved it toward a fat beeswax candle that sat beside the brazier.

The wick took several heartbeats to catch, but when it did, it flared high. Rani could see that the woman was older than she seemed at first, old enough to be Rani's own mother. She had not been in the play the night before. "Please, Speaker," the woman said. "Enter and be at peace."

Rani took a single step forward. At last, she found her voice. "My lady—"

The woman laughed softly. "No lady am I. I am called Flarissa. Be welcome in my tent. Come Speak with me."

"Please, Dame Flarissa. I did not come to Speak."

"No?" A flicker of concern passed across the woman's brow, only to be replaced by a gentle smile. "Why did you come to us, then?"

"I want to see the glass!"

"Glass?"

"I want to see the panels!" Now that Rani was close to the hanging screens, she could scarcely breathe, for all her remembered awe from the night before. Fascination washed over her again, the flush of desire that she had felt when Pollino first hung the Prince on the dais. "Your jackhand put them on the iron stands, before you began your play. Please! I was a glasswright, I was an apprentice learning how to work glass. I was learning how to pour it, how to cut it. I was learning how to set pieces. I was . . . learning."

Rani's words suddenly sounded awkward, frantic and desperate. She wanted this Flarissa to understand. She wanted the woman to know why the panels were so important, why Rani needed to study them. She wanted the player to recognize that Rani was worthy, that she was deserving.

Flarissa nodded. "Come Speak with me, then. Tell me why you stopped learning."

"Please, my lady." Rani surprised herself to find tears in her eyes. "Please let me see the glass!"

"All in good time. Speak first. Then I'll show you the glass. I promise."

Rani was past bargaining. Flarissa had promised. That had to be enough.

Rani crossed to the brazier and stood in front of the player woman.

"Have you ever Spoken before?" Flarissa's voice was calm, soothing.

"No."

"Very well, then. Sit. Make yourself comfortable." Rani forced herself to follow the instructions. Her fingers clenched into fists as she glanced at the trunks across the tent, but she forced her attention back to the brazier. Back to the pine-scented smoke. Back to the ample spidersilk bolsters. Back to Flarissa. "Very good," the woman said, and there was an easy grace behind her words. "Why don't we start with your telling me your name."

Rani stared as if she had been struck dumb. What name was she to give this golden-haired woman? Rani Trader, her birth name? Ranita Glasswright, the name that she had vowed she would not take until her guild was restored? Vows were important, vows were honorable. Nevertheless, she was so close to the glass, so close to what she wanted, what she needed. . . . "Ranita," she whispered.

"Fine, Ranita. Will you join me in a glass of greenwine?"

Rani nodded, eager for something to swallow, something cool, something to ease the pounding of her heart. She had not spoken her guildname for so long. . . .

She took the earthenware goblet that Flarissa offered, raising it with both hands. The glazed edge of the cup was cool against her lips, mercifully, blessedly cool. She drank deeply.

"Good, Ranita. Very well. Let me explain Speaking to you." Flarissa leaned forward and filled the goblet once again. "I am going to ask you to look at something, to look at a trinket. You will concentrate on the bauble. You will watch it closely. While you watch, I will talk to you. I will ask you some questions about the most important day of your life. Those are always the questions we ask first-time Speakers. You need not answer my questions if you choose not to. If you decide that you are through Speaking, all you need to do is open your eyes. If you decide to answer all of my questions, then I will tell you when to open your eyes. Do you think that you can do that?"

Rani's fingers closed around the goblet. She could taste the sharp greenwine at the back of her throat, calming, soothing. She wanted to drink more. Instead, she nodded.

Flarissa smiled. "Very good, Ranita. Have another drink while I get the trinket we will use."

Rani obeyed silently, watching as Flarissa rose from the bolsters. The woman crossed to a basket that was nestled near the trunks, and she rummaged in the container for a long time. She pulled out a strand of pearls and shook her head, dug deeper and considered a single ruby earring. She discarded a golden sphere, a drop the size of Rani's thumb, and then she nodded sharply, closing her hand around something that fit readily into her palm. Rani drank again, running her tongue over lips that were suddenly dry and chapped.

"Fine, Ranita." Flarissa came back to the brazier, taking the time to settle herself amid the bolsters. "Are you comfortable? Would you like to recline? No? Very well, then." Flarissa brought her right hand in front of her, leaving it folded around the hidden object. "Remember, Ranita. You are safe here. You can stop answering my questions whenever you choose. Are you ready?"

"Yes?" Rani could not keep her answer from sounding like a question.

Flarissa nodded and opened her hand. There, in the center of her palm, was a piece of cobalt glass. It was as smooth as a sea-washed pebble, unblemished as a polished stone, perfect as the petal of an anemone. Flarissa turned her palm a little, and the glass winked, capturing the light of the beeswax candle and glowing as if it were illuminated from within.

"There, Ranita. Look at the glass. Look at its color. Look at its purity. Look inside the glass, Ranita. Look inside the glass and imagine it being poured. Imagine the Zarithian apprentice measuring out sand, measuring out color. See the apprentice stirring, stirring, stirring. See the apprentice pouring the glass, pouring the glass onto a stone table. The glass pours evenly, it pours smoothly. The apprentice counts as she pours. Count with her, Ranita. Count with the apprentice."

Rani had read in her books about the fashioning of glass. She could see a girl's hands, measuring out sand. She could see the golden fire kissing the crucible. She could see the grains of color, the precious cobalt tinting the glass. She could see the smooth stone waiting to receive its molten burden. She could see the apprentice, see the glass, hear the girl's voice as she measured out the perfect pour. "One," Rani breathed.

"That's right," Flarissa agreed. "Slowly now. Pour the glass slowly. If you'd like, you may close your eyes." Rani did. "As you pour, breathe in. Breathe out."

"Two."

"Yes," Flarissa said. "Breathe in. Breathe out."

"Three."

"Yes. You may only think the next number. You may say it to yourself, silently."

Rani knew she could say *four*. She knew that she could continue pouring the brilliant cobalt glass. But there was no need to speak, no need to move, no need to stir from the depths of her vision.

Flarissa waited for a long moment, for long enough that the cobalt glass began to set on the pouring stone, began to harden. Rani watched, perfectly content. She was aware that Flarissa was leaning forward, was taking the earthenware goblet from her hands, removing the greenwine. "May we Speak now, Ranita?"

"Yes," Rani whispered.

"I want you to think back, Ranita. Think back to the most important day of your life. To the most important thing that you have ever done. Picture yourself on that day. Picture what you were wearing. Picture where you were standing. Can you see yourself?"

"Yes."

"When you are ready, Ranita, tell me where you are."

The words were hard to say, hard to drag past the soft blanket of relaxation. "I'm in the cathedral."

"Which cathedral?"

"The house of the Thousand Gods. In Moren."

"How old are you?"

"Thirteen."

"What are you wearing?"

Ranita saw her apprentice uniform, her short black cloak, her leggings and tunic. She had worn that costume with pride; she had taken such pleasure in the gold-chased glasswright emblem on her sleeve. Tears pricked behind her eyes, and a sob caught in her throat. Flarissa said calmly, "This happened long ago, Ranita. You need not fear your story. We are only Speaking. Picture the glass pouring. Picture the smooth blue flow. There, Ranita . . . There you are. . . ." Ranita felt the sorrow loosen in her chest. Flarisa crooned, "Now Speak to me. What are you wearing?"

"My guild uniform. I am an apprentice."

"Very good, Ranita. Now, when you are ready, tell me what is happening."

"There is glass."

"Yes?"

"There is glass. Blue glass. And sunlight. Sunlight through the glass." Ranita trailed off, losing herself in her memory of that day, so long ago. She had sneaked into the cathedral, where she had no right to be. She was observing the Presentation of Prince Tuvashanoran, the man's entrance into the church as the Defender of the Faith. She had seen an archer's bow against the glass. . . .

"Speak to me, Ranita. Tell me your story."

"I look through the glass. I see a bow. An archer's bow."

Now, with her eyes closed, sitting beside a brazier in a player's tent in Liantine, Ranita could see every detail of the Morenian cathedral. She remembered the Presentation ceremony as if she were living it again. She told Flarissa how she had cried out, how she had tried to save Prince Tuvashanoran. She told how the prince had stood, how he had grabbed his ceremonial sword from the altar. He had whirled around; he had tried to find the danger. An arrow flew through the cathedral, and it came to rest, quivering and deadly, in his eye.

And all the time Ranita spoke, her voice stayed calm and steady. She could see the story in front of her, see it as clearly as if it were a glass window. She told Flarissa how the King's Men had blamed her, how they had destroyed the glasswrights' guild. She told how she had vowed that she would rebuild the guild one day.

And when she was through, she sat beside the beeswax candle, eyes closed, breath slow, holding on to the memory of her promise.

"Thank you, Ranita." Flarissa's voice was gentle, soothing, smooth as greenwine. "Thank you for Speaking to me."

Ranita heard the words from a distance. She could not feel her fingers, could not feel her toes. She was far away from her body, far away from her mind and her memories and all the problems that spun her through her days.

Flarissa's voice resonated as she said, "Breathe deep, Ranita. Feel the air flow through your lungs, feel it move through your body. Breathe out now. Let your worries flow away. Good, Ranita. Very good. Now, breathe in again. . . ."

Ranita's body tingled, humming with the strength that she breathed in. Exhaling redoubled that power, soothed her, healed her, made her whole.

Flarissa continued speaking. "Remember this power, Ranita. Remember the power of Speaking. Think of it as glass that you can pour within yourself, glass that grows deeper and smoother with every breath. You can return to this power. You can return by yourself, without me. Whenever you need strength and power and peace, you can return here. That is the power of Speaking. Do you understand?"

"Yes."

"Then remember, Ranita. Remember all the questions I have asked, and all the answers you have Spoken. And remember the feelings that you have now, the comfort and security of this place, remember them and feel them when we are through Speaking. Feel them for the rest of today and tomorrow and all the days to come. Very good, Ranita. When you are ready, I want you to count with me, from ten to one. I want you to leave the glass and come back to my tent and my brazier and Liantine. Will you do that, Ranita?"

She did not want to. She wanted to stay with the glass forever. She wanted to stay away from action and responsibility.

But Flarissa said that she could come back to the glass whenever she wished, that she could remember the way that she felt now. Flarissa said that she had the power.

"Ten," Flarissa said. Rani fought the pull.

"Nine," Flarissa said. "Eight."

The numbers thrummed inside Ranita's skull, tugging her, drawing her. "Seven. Six."

"Five," Ranita whispered. "Four." Her voice grew stronger,

matching Flarissa's. "Three." She spoke normally. "Two." She took a deep breath. "One!"

Her eyes flew open.

She still sat in the tent. The pine sticks still curled their smoky incense into the air. The creamy white candle still sat beside the brazier, a little more wax melted around its wick. Rani forced herself to look at Flarissa. "You made me go back to the cathedral."

"You chose to go back there. You chose to Speak that story."

"I was afraid. I did not want to remember Tuvashanoran dying, ever again."

"You were very brave." Flarissa smiled, closing her hands over the cobalt pebble and hiding it away inside her skirts. "How do you feel, Ranita?"

Rani paused to think before she answered the question. Her anger with Hal was gone. Her hopelessness, the feeling that she was trapped—all gone. She felt as if she had run through the streets of Moren, run through every passage of the Merchants' Quarter of her childhood. She felt as if she had combined a perfect glassmaking technique with the powerful patterns that she had created and studied as a merchant child. A smile eased onto her lips. "Wonderful!" she breathed.

Flarissa nodded and climbed to her feet. Rani followed suit, but she was surprised to find the tent pitching wildly around her. "Easy," said Flarissa. "Breathe deeply. Take a moment to find yourself."

Rani clutched the woman's hand for balance. Only when the floor stopped tilting did she dare to look into the player's eyes. "Please, Flarissa. Will you answer a question?"

" 'f course."

Rani struggled, suddenly embarrassed. "I—" She lowered her eyes. "Was—" She could not bring herself to say the words—they were too personal, too secret.

"What, Ranita?"

"Was my story useful?" Rani blurted. "Will the players tell my tale?"

Flarissa did not smile, but she answered immediately. "Aye. The players will tell your story. We'll study it, and then we'll play it well, Ranita Glasswright."

Rani's pride melted across her chest. "Will you show me the glass, then? Will you show me the players' panels?"

"Aye, Ranita Glasswright." Flarissa leaned down to pick up the beeswax candle. Rani followed her to the trunks, trying to remember to breathe, trying to plumb the deep power of the cobalt glass, trying to hold on to the endless peace of Speaking.

8

Hal stood in his Liantine apartments, looking out the window of his receiving room. He tried not to curse the rain that had been falling steadily since dawn. Of course the downpour was necessary for crops. Of course rain was to be expected in spring. Nevertheless, he regretted that he could not walk out of doors. Berylina had agreed to meet with him before noon, and he had hoped to take her outside the palace. He had thought they might return to the jousting field; the site of their little wagering victory might place the princess more at ease around him.

There was, however, nothing to be done for it. Bern, the god of rain, would act as he thought best. So Father Siritalanu had reminded him when they had prayed that morning. Hal had tried to accept the priest's remonstration with good grace.

He sighed now and turned back from the window. "I'm sorry, Farso." He smiled at his friend. "I know you'd rather be anywhere but trapped in here with me."

"Not anywhere, Sire," the nobleman said easily. "My lady Mair returns to the marketplace today, and I'm grateful for the excuse not to look at trade goods in the rain."

"Why would she go out in this downpour?"

"She claims she's found a cure for firelung—some weed they raise far east of here. She's negotiating for bales of it to be delivered. Between the rain and her harsh tongue when she's driving a bargain, I'm more than pleased to stay with you."

"Does she have Rani with her?" Hal realized that he had

asked too quickly when Farso shot him an inquiring glance. "It's just that if Mair's bargaining . . ."

Hal still regretted walking away from Rani at the jousting competition. He knew that she'd been about to say something, about to answer his question about a more suitable match than Berylina. He could certainly imagine what proposals she might make—he'd rehearsed his own responses often enough. Nevertheless, the facts did not change. He was a king. He needed a queen. An heir. He needed five hundred gold bars to begin repaying the church, by no later than midsummer.

For the thousandth time, his thoughts tumbled to the Fellowship. Would Moren have been so needy if Hal had not siphoned off some of his gold to the cabal? Would the kingdom fare better if Hal had not been bidding for secret power? There was nothing to be done for it, though. Hal could not take back the gold that he had given Glair.

Farso shrugged as if he were casting off Hal's own doubts. "I don't believe that Rani will stand with Mair for these negotiations."

"Why not?"

"Sire, you have not heard?"

"Heard what?"

"Rani is spending all her time among the players. She is studying their glasswork, the panels that they use for their productions."

Rani and her glass. Well, that was just as well. Something good should come of this journey. Rani should return to Moren with something she desired.

Before Hal could respond to Farso's announcement, the door to his apartments swung open. Calaratino, the boy who was serving as his page on this expedition, stepped inside. The child's face glowed with excitement, and he thrust out his chest like a bantam rooster.

"Your Majesty! Princess Berylina requests admission to your presence!"

Hal swallowed a sigh. "Thank you, Calo. Please show Her Highness in."

Hal pasted a smile on his face as he looked expectantly toward the door. A pair of nurses entered first, tucking their carefully coiffed heads low enough to show him respect, but not so low that they could not keep an eye on the doorway, on their charge.

Berylina entered like a suspicious cat. She held her head at an awkward angle, half-turned away from the people in the room. She placed each foot cautiously, as if she expected the wooden floors to melt away beneath her slippers. She edged forward, one step, two steps, three, four, and Hal felt his welcoming smile age upon his lips. He abandoned the pretense of joy at seeing the girl and settled instead for a falsely hearty greeting, "Your Highness! You look well today!"

His words confused the poor girl. She started to drop into a curtsey, clearly recalling whatever careful instructions her nurses had provided. She saw Hal's extended hand, though, and hesitated, obviously uncertain about whether she should enter farther into the room. Aching at her indecision, Hal moved forward another few steps. "Please, Your Highness, be at ease. Bid your lady nurses to make themselves comfortable."

Berylina looked about, as if startled to find her nurses so close at hand. She waved her hands at them, like a child shooing flies from honeyed bread, but she seemed apprehensive when they crossed the room, moving to stand in a shadowy, paneled corner. The princess turned back to Hal, as if she expected praise for her action.

He smiled weakly. At least there were only two nurses today, not the four that Berylina might have required. Was that a positive sign? Was that a mark of progress?

"My lady, you remember Baron Farsobalinti? My honored friend?"

The princess cocked her head at Farso, catching him with one of her eyes. She nodded silently, looking as if she would flee the chamber if the tall, pale man took one step in her direction. Hal's concern began to turn to irritation.

One of the nurses cleared her throat, obviously prompting her charge. Berylina remained stubbornly silent, though, clutching the rough-spun linen of her gown with her pudgy fingers. The nurse stepped forward from her shadowed niche. When the princess still failed to act, the woman finally said, "We hope that we have not disturbed you, Your Majesty."

She used the voice of barely restrained exasperation that mothers employ with small children, when they are forced to prompt and prod, teaching by example.

Hal was struck yet again by how young Berylina seemed. At thirteen years of age, she should have learned to speak to nobility, to answer basic questions put to her. Even if the act of speaking caused her embarrassment, she should have been required to do it, required to master it. She was a princess, after all. She did not have the luxury of indulging her fears.

Well, if she were a princess, Hal was a king, and he was well trained in making the best of a bad situation. This current disaster was no different from a dozen other crises he had resolved since taking his throne. He might as well respond to the nurse's question as if it had come from Berylina. He could pretend that the nurse was merely acting as a translator. This entire conversation could be conducted like trade discussions with ambassadors from the distant east, with men who spoke only in harsh words and guttural exclamations that Hal could not have reproduced for all the gold in the world.

He forced himself to smile directly at Berylina. In the few days that he had passed in Liantine, he had become accustomed to the princess's cast vision; it now seemed normal to address her with a slight lack of focus in his own gaze, with an open, easy glance that spared her from turning to one side. It could not be easy for her, viewing the world from two eyes that refused to act in concert.

"Nay, Your Highness. Your visit could never be a disturbance. I was looking out upon the courtyard just before you came. A messenger rode up from your father's docks. He could scarcely be more wet if he had dived from his ship and swum to land."

A ghost of a smile flirted around Berylina's lips, tugging past her teeth. Wonderful, Hal thought. He could almost glean a smile from a child. He must have said something properly, though, for Berylina managed to step forward until she was looking out the window. A gust of wind rattled the lead frame, and the girl crossed her arms over her chest, pulling the heavy linen closer. Hal stepped forward solicitously and said, "Are you chilled, Your Highness? Let me close the shutters."

He started to reach past the princess to pull the insulating wood panels into place, and his palm inadvertently brushed across her arm. Berylina leaped back as if he had burned her, a complicated mixture of shame and urgency flaring in her face. Hal hissed and pulled back, as if he had done something wrong. One of the nurses gasped, "I'm sorry, Your Majesty!"

"There's no need to apologize." Hal recovered quickly, managing to keep his smile on his lips. He spared only a glance for the woman who had spoken, and he could not bring himself to look upon the trembling princess. How could anyone live, so afraid of the surrounding world?

He pulled the shutter closed and latched it carefully. The last thing he wanted now was to have the wooden panel fly open from a gust of wind. *That* would spook Berylina enough that he would never see her again. She'd be like a high-strung new horse, slipping free of a bridle and disappearing over the horizon.

Like a horse . . . Hal toyed with the notion. The princess behaved precisely like a terrified animal. He needed to keep her calm; he needed to keep her from noticing any noose of ownership that he might slip around her neck. He thought of the first scared filly he had ever trained to harness, years ago, outside his father's stables. Turning from the shuttered window, he decided to try a new approach.

"I've always liked rainy days, myself. Farsobalinti can tell you, when I was a boy, I would sit in my nursery and play with my tin soldiers for all the long wet days of spring. Even when my brothers and sisters pestered our nurses to let us play outside, even when they begged to run up and down the palace hallways." Hal cast a quick look at Farso, who nodded as if he recalled Hal's own awkward wordlessness. Berylina seemed to realize that Hal meant her no harm, and her breathing slowed to normal.

Taking the princess's reaction as a good sign, Hal kept up his babbling. "I would sit on a stone bench in a deep window, much like this one. My nurse would bring me warm milk and fresh-baked bread, and crisp autumn apples if we had any. I could spend hours reading books on the history of Morenia, on all the battles fought by my father, and his father, and his father before him. I would study maps and plot those battles, and while away entire days with reading. Reading and writing and drawing."

"I draw."

Hal tried hard to mask his surprise, his relief that the princess had finally said something—anything. He dared not ask her a direct question. Instead, he shrugged and looked down at his hands with a self-deprecating grin. "I drew, but nothing I would show to anyone. I could sketch a map or two, and I could scribble out a coat of arms. But I never was much good at drawing figures."

"I draw figures."

"That takes skill! You must have had good teachers. I never found anyone with the patience to teach me how to draw figures."

"My drawings are in the solar."

"The solar must be cold today." Hal paused, curious to see if she would fill the gap in conversation. Berylina stared at her hands, wringing her fingers as if she could not think of a suitable reply to his statement. Fighting not to sigh, Hal continued. "Spring weather is so unreliable. All this rain would be snow, if it were only a little colder. In Morenia, we get a great deal of snow in winter, and some in spring."

"The solar is very bright when it snows, but it's too late in the year for that now."

Hal fought to hide his surprise—that was the longest speech that Berylina had shared with him. "Alas," he said, trying not to speak too quickly. "The solar is not likely to be bright today. The rain clouds are thick. No, this is a day for torches in the hallways and candles on our writing desks." Still no response. "I think that Bern must be good friends with Tren."

"The god of candles has no friends."

"Why certainly he must! Candles light our way in the dark! They are signs of good cheer. Certainly the god of candles must be the embodiment of that very good cheer. He must be one of the most popular gods!"

"He gives out all his glad tidings in his candles. He has none left for himself."

Hal was stunned. Two consecutive sentences, two complete

thoughts, two statements directly contradicting what Hal himself had said, and the princess was not blushing at all. Clearly, she felt strongly about candles. Or gods. "I'd never heard that about Tren."

Berylina took a deep breath and braved Hal's direct gaze. "I've drawn Tren. Would you like to see him?"

Hal sensed how much the question cost her, how much she longed to flee from him, to run to her nurses and hide her face in their skirts. He saw that she cast a glance toward Farso, that she took in the nobleman's attentive presence as if it physically pained her. Still, she included both of them in her invitation, waving one hand slightly in front of her. Hal made his voice grave, and he bowed a little as he said, "Yes, Your Highness. We would like that very much. *I* would like that."

Berylina turned away without saying anything else, walking determinedly to the door of the chamber. Hal caught an expression of surprise on the face of the younger nurse, the woman who had spoken for the princess when they first entered the room, but the servant quickly masked her emotion. She fell into place behind her mistress, waving the other nurse forward.

They made a strange procession in the hallway. Berylina led the way, her pudgy hands clenched into determined fists at her sides. Both nurses followed behind, wearing the drab black dresses that were expected of their station. The older one turned to look at Hal several times, as if he were a beast harrying them along their way. Farso trailed all of them, a silent honor guard, a chaperon. Hal suspected that the tall nobleman hung back so that he would not be tempted to laugh aloud, so that he would not mock outright his hapless king.

Why should this be so difficult? Hal was not afraid of women! He certainly had no trouble talking to Rani—even fighting with her. There were other women, as well—Mair, and his four sisters, and any number of ladies who were married to his lords. He'd had nurses as a child, and none had left him tongue-tied. None had left him wondering if he held his arms correctly, if he stepped quickly enough, but not too fast.

Of course, none of those women was likely to be his bride.

And none was so afraid of him that her breath sounded like sobs as she led him through the palace hallways.

The solar was reached by a well-sculpted stone stair, a graceful curve that arched to the highest point in the castle's north tower. Berylina paused at the door to the chamber, bowing her head. Her short fingers hovered over the latch like fluttering sparrows, and Hal could almost hear her thoughts, hear her questioning why she had brought a stranger—a man, a suitor!—to her refuge.

She waited for so long that the silence grew awkward, even more uncomfortable than all the other silences she had spawned. Hal waited for one of the nurses to urge her forward, to push the door open, but apparently the women dared not be so aggressive.

Hal glanced at Farso for guidance, but the knight only shrugged. When Hal could no longer bear the tension, he said, "Perhaps, my lady, you can show us the solar another day. It's probably just as well that my companion and I return below. A cup of mulled wine would do all of us well, chase away the chill."

"No."

Berylina could not say more than the one syllable, but she made her fingers close on the iron latch, and she pushed the door open with the grim determination of a prisoner marching toward the headsman's block.

Hal followed her into the solar.

At first glance, the room seemed empty. Great panes of glass were set into three walls, including the one that looked out on the storm-tossed sea. Rain sleeked down the windows, the rivulets making it difficult to decipher clear forms in the city below.

As his eyes grew accustomed to the dim light, Hal could make out dark wooden chairs that hulked against the solid wall, grim with carvings that tangled about their clawed legs. A low table crouched in the center of the room, like a beast skulking before its master. A shuttered lantern was centered on the table, its wrought iron seeming to send out the bitter chill that permeated the room.

One of the nurses shook her head as she stepped over the threshold, muttering something about the wayward whims of children. She eased past her charge and bustled over to the lantern. When she leaned down to tend to the wick, she shielded her work with her black-clad body, but light soon blazed up in the solar, sending shadows scurrying for the corners. The nurse lit a pair of tapers that stood at either end of the table, encouraging further life to enter the room.

Hal could see now that the solar had not been deserted. In fact, there were many signs of the pleasure taken in the room. Lap rugs were draped over two low chairs, and a small book lay open on the floor. A quick glance showed the volume to be an illustrated Book of the Gods, with brilliant blue- and red-illuminated pages devoted to the lives of the Thousand. An ivory comb rested on the low table near the lantern, and Hal could glimpse a single mouse-brown hair trapped between its teeth.

His attention was drawn to an easel that stood by the far windows, as if an artist had looked out over the distant ocean while she worked. Heavy parchment was attached to the board, held in place with a clever arrangement of brass pins. The stand's sturdy tray held sticks of charcoal and white clay crayons and one long piece of reddish chalk.

The parchment presented the detailed outline of a figure, firm lines emerging from the beige background. Hal could see a man's gnarled arms, muscles twisted with some extreme effort. Reins were twined between his fingers, and Hal could just make out a waterspout hitched to the leather, the swirling storm visibly pulling at the restraints. The man's face was contorted with the effort to harness the storm. His cheeks were hollow above a ragged beard that was braided in the Liantine fashion, entwined with shells and bits of flotsam. The man's shoulders were draped with seaweed, and his hair was fashioned from fantastic blocks of coral.

"Kel," Hal said.

"Yes," Berylina said, and she flushed. This time, however, the color in her cheeks was not the burn of shame. It was the powerful shade of pride. She was pleased that Hal had recognized her handiwork.

"You've drawn him well."

"He's not finished." Berylina crossed to the easel and picked up one of the charcoal crayons. The tool seemed to grant her the power of speech. "I started him on the day that you arrived.

You said that Kel had been kind to you, driving your ship across the ocean. I prayed to him in the evening, and he sent me this vision."

"You prayed—" He heard the confidence in her tone, and he registered the strangeness that a child would speak of visions from a god in such an offhand manner. "I understood that your people do not place much faith in the Thousand Gods."

Berylina flushed, but she raised her chin defiantly. Hal tried to ignore the jutting of her rabbitty teeth. "Some of my people know your gods. My nurse, she first taught me of the Thousand Gods."

"Your nurse?"

"Aye." Berylina waved toward the oldest of her attendants. "Her people come from Amanthia." From Amanthia. Like the enslaved Little Army. The nurse was too old to be one of Sin Hazar's soldiers, though. Her family must have come before the Amanthian king began his desperate policy.

But the Little Army soldiers who had entered Liantine in the past several years—they had brought with them their Thousand Gods. Perhaps the slaves were the reason for Teheboth's vehemence in hunting the Horned Hind. Perhaps the Amanthians' faith was sharpening worship in Liantine, turning folks back to their old ways, their dark ways, the mysterious ways of the woodland goddess. . . .

Princess Berylina was holding to her attendant's example: "My nurse taught me. She knows the truth."

"The truth!" Hal started to ask Berylina how she could defy her father, but he bit off his words when he feared they might sound like an accusation. He tried to sound casual when he asked, "May I see the other drawings you have made?"

The princess darted a quick glance at him, as if she feared he mocked her. Hal held his face carefully blank, keeping his expression polite but offering no further pressure. The danger seemed to pass, and Berylina turned to a table in the far corner of the solar.

"Here, my lord. Here are my other drawings."

Hal moved forward, past the two silent nurses, away from Farso. The first drawing was Yen, the god of music. He had a tambour in one hand, and pipes leaned against his feet. His mouth was open in a round *O,* as if he were singing aloud, and his hair flowed around his head in rhythmic curls.

The next parchment showed Glat, the god of snow, with a mantle of fresh flakes across his ancient spidery shoulders. The old man's head was nearly bare, with just a rim of wispy hair at the back of his skull, a circle that might only have been a dusting of snow.

There was Ile, the moon god, and Par, the god of the sun. There were the gods of horses and hawks, and one tiny sketch of the god of cats. Toward the bottom of the pile, there was a drawing of Tren, the god of candles.

As Berylina had said, he was not a happy god. His face was drawn in long lines that spoke of ill temper, of bitterness, as if he had eaten uncooked greens. He extended a candle toward his viewers, apparently luring them forward, drawing them into the sketch. Hal could see what Berylina meant, when she said that the god had no friends. He did his job, he presented his candles, but he had no energy left for good cheer and glad tidings.

The princess's drawings were not perfect. Hal could tell that they were not done by a court painter. In one, an arm was twisted at an unnatural angle; in another, silk robes fell in rigid, impossible folds. Nevertheless, each sprang from the page with an energy and a life all its own, a level of detail that amazed him. It was as if the gods had come to Berylina one by one, journeying to sit beside the princess in her solar, gathering about their attributes so that she could commit them to parchment. Father Siritalanu, with his earnest faith, would be fascinated.

Hal looked up from the drawings and caught Berylina smiling shyly at him. He covered his surprise by saying, "These are very good, you know."

"The gods . . . they come to me. I can see them, and they reach out to hold my hand. They help me draw."

"You must be a very holy person for the gods to speak to you in such a manner."

She shrugged. "They come. I think of them, and I call them by name. Sometimes, I need to pray to get their attention. I've never asked for one to visit me and been refused."

Hal could not keep from probing. "Your father must be very proud of you."

Berylina looked at him oddly. He could not tell if her gaze was skeptical, or if she was merely catching him with one of her skewed eyes. Then she whispered, "My father would have no interest in my drawings."

Hal turned back to the work. He noticed one piece of particularly large parchment turned upside down, peeking out from a pile of completed drawings. "What's this one?"

"Nothing!" Berylina lurched forward and planted her fingers squarely on top of the page.

"Please! Let me see it."

"No, my lord. It was only a drawing that did not work."

"I can't imagine that. All of your drawings work quite well. Better than anything I could ever try."

"Please, my lord!" She was upset enough that she put her hands on his, wrestling with him to take away the parchment. "It was just something I started sketching on the day that you arrived. Before Kel spoke to me. Before I realized that I needed to draw the god of the sea."

"My lady, let me see it!"

His tone was harsher than he intended, and Berylina caught her breath. Her fingers froze into pebbles on the back of the parchment, and then she folded them, one by one, until her hand was a heavy, hopeless fist.

Hal regretted frightening her; he regretted making her cringe from him. Now, though, he had to see what was on the parchment; he had to see the drawing that she would fight to keep from him, when she had shared the others so generously. He moved his hand to cover hers, but she withdrew before he could actually touch her. In fact, she backed away from the table entirely, edging back to hover beside her silent, disapproving nurses. She crossed her arms over her chest, tucking in her hands as if they had become unclean.

Hal took a deep breath and turned over the drawing.

At first, he could not decipher what he saw. An angry hand had slashed red chalk across the parchment, leaving behind rusty streaks that looked like flaking blood. Beneath the red, though, beneath the efforts to deface the work, Hal could make out unsteady charcoal lines.

The ruined drawing had not been made by the same strong hand that had limned the gods. Rather, these marks were tentative, hesitant, barely visible beneath the chalk. Hal turned the parchment a bit to catch the light, and he made out a tangle of hash marks that might have been antlers. He turned the drawing more, and he could see an animal's body, a distorted flank that might belong to a deer.

Recognition dawned. "The Horned Hind."

"Aye, my lord," Berylina whispered, barely audible across the chamber.

"But why did you ruin her?"

For a long moment, he thought that Berylina would not respond, that words would prove too much for her. Her lips trembled, and one tear welled up from her right eye, slipping down her cheek like a silken bead. "I tried, my lord," she gasped at last. "I tried to make her right, but I could not. I could not draw her. I wanted to give her to my father, to make him a gift for the Spring Hunt. The Horned Hind, though, she doesn't speak to me, not like the Thousand Gods. She would not let me draw her."

Hal recovered from the torrent of words, and then he prodded gently, "Would not let you?"

"The Horned Hind grows ever stronger in Liantine, but she has no mercy for one like me."

"Like you?"

Berylina raised her twisted face, made even homelier by the pull of her lips as she tried to restrain her sobs. "The Horned Hind teaches that my eyes mark me, Your Majesty, mark me as one who cannot look on truth. The Horned Hind says that my . . . my teeth are the struggle of good in my body, always fighting to escape. The Horned Hind says that I am evil!"

"You are not evil, my lady!"

"The Horned Hind says I am! My father says I am! He says the Thousand Gods are for slaves and weaklings, and that only the Horned Hind is true!" The girl lunged for the parchment that Hal still held, tugging it away from his unsuspecting grasp and crumpling it into a tortured ball. She clutched the ruined drawing to her belly, stumbling away from the table. One of the nurses folded the sobbing child into her arms, smoothing her hair and crooning helpless words of comfort. The other woman pursed her lips in silent disapproval, glaring at Hal as if he were the source of the princess's distress.

Hal stared in shocked silence, wondering at the agony of a scorned child. Even as his heart went out to Berylina, he plummeted into his own memories, into his own recollections of a father who could not be pleased, a court that believed him an idiot, flawed.

He knew Berylina's anguish. He understood her pain.

Before he could decide what to say, how to act, there was a commotion on the stairs that led to the solar. "Your Majesty!" Hal recognized his page's voice, even as Farsobalinti stepped toward the door to the chamber. When Berylina's sobs grew louder at the newcomer's shout, Hal stepped in front of her, blocking her from Calaratino's sight.

"Your Majesty!" the boy called again.

"King Halaravilli is here, boy," Farso said, reaching out a hand to steady the gasping page. "What message do you bear for him?"

Calaratino staggered forward a step, still gulping for air, and he looked about the solar as if he were in a strange new land. Farso rested a hand on the boy's shoulder, shaking him slightly, as if that would summon a speedier reply.

The page remembered himself enough to sketch a bow toward Hal, and he cast a glance at the sobbing princess. Hal narrowed his eyes, and Farso acted on the implicit order. "Come, Calaratino," the knight said. "What message was so important that you ran to find us here?"

The page extended an oiled tube, with lead caps sealed tight on either end. "A ship just arrived in port, Your Majesty, from Morenia. This missive was entrusted to the captain, with orders that he should deliver it to you directly."

Hal bent closer to study the tube. Beads of water had collected on its side, remnants of the storm that blew against the solar's windows. Hal rubbed his palm over the raindrops, smoothing the oiled surface, and then wiped his moist fingers against his thigh. There was no sign of who had made the urgent dispatch—no seal, no ribbons, no indication whatsoever.

Farso seemed to recognize his uneasiness. "Sire, would you like me to . . . escort the ladies downstairs?"

Hal thought about the panic that such attentions were likely to engender, at least for the poor princess, and he sighed. "No, my lord. We are guests in Princess Berylina's solar. I've intruded enough to bring my business here, no reason to force the ladies to leave."

Nevertheless, the message was urgent; it required his immediate attention. He strode to the rain-slicked windows at the far side of the chamber, snatching one of the lit tapers as he distanced himself from the Liantines. He set the candle on a table and took a deep breath before he opened the tube.

The parchment that slipped into his hand seemed harmless enough. There was a single sheet, curled into a roll that was narrower than his wrist. Again, there were no identifying features, not a wax seal, not a ribbon, not even a distinctive hand. He glanced for a signature, but there was none.

Muttering a prayer to all the Thousand Gods, he unrolled the parchment, turning it toward the taper to make the most of the dim light. He began to read.

"In the name of Jair."

Hal glanced up hurriedly, scanning the oiled tube one last time for any sign of the document's provenance. Nothing. Anonymity cloaked the message, as if it wore a hood, as if it skulked about in the darkest hours of the night.

In the name of Jair. Kingdoms rise and kingdoms fall, all for want of gold. The First Pilgrim offered up his riches, one thousand bars of gold, upon the feast of First God Ait. Jair guides us in all things, blessing body and soul forever. Let all who would be true to their fellow men offer up one thousand bars, gold to serve Jair's cause. The man who strays from the First Pilgrim risks life and limb and peace everlasting but the man who honors Jair finds glory and fame. May Jair protect and keep us, forever and ever.

A cold knife of excitement slid down Hal's spine.

The Fellowship. No one else would call on Jair so explicitly, to the exclusion of all the gods but Ait. No one else would demand one thousand bars of gold—one thousand!—to be true to "fellow" men.

But why? What could the Fellowship intend? Were they raising an army, purchasing Yrathi mercenaries? Were they testing Hal's dedication, ratcheting up their demands because he had produced donations before? Because he had hoped for advancement before? Was this the next test, the next measurement of his devotion, so that he might ascend to a position of authority and leadership in the Fellowship? Why now, when Hal's own treasury was nearly empty?

Hal read the message three times over, hoping that the glimmer of a promise might outweigh the veiled threat. He could not be certain, though. He could not be sure that the letter was anything more than extortion.

He could summon the ship's captain. He could demand to know who had given the man the message, how he had come to bear the scroll. He could rant. He could rave. He could threaten to torture the seaman. But the answer would stay the same. Some Touched child, some merchant brat, some anonymous guildsman or acolyte or noble boy had brought the sealed tube to the dock. The captain had received a bag of gold for his troubles.

Or he had received a new ship, fresh-caulked against the springtime storms.

Or his family had been threatened, his children held hostage against the scroll's safe delivery.

No. That would call attention to deeds better left obscure. Perhaps the captain was a member of the Fellowship himself.

Hal knew his own family history, understood it even better than he did his inclination to court the Fellowship with gold. He knew the legends that surrounded his forefather Jair, the First Pilgrim, the first king of Morenia. Jair was born a Touched child and journeyed through all his kingdom's castes. He discovered the power and the glory of all the Thousand Gods, building the first house in their honor. He took the title, Defender of the Faith, and he offered up a thousand bars of gold to show his dedication to the gods. A thousand bars the first year. Jair prospered as he embraced his faith; his treasury overflowed. And every year, on the feast of First God Ait, Jair had offered up another thousand bars of gold.

A thousand bars . . . That was more than Hal could have spared before the fire. Even for the power that he craved within the Fellowship.

What should he do? He could tell the Fellowship that he would not pay their extortion, could not take the money from needy Moren. After all, the Fellowship had not rewarded him for any of his earlier donations. There was no certainty they would do so now.

But there was a possibility that they might *penalize* him now. The letter contained a threat. The Fellowship might spread rumors of their secret meetings, hints and whispers, enough to rock Hal's sovereignty, if not so much as to expose the actual Fellowship. He would need to explain, then. Justify.

And if the Fellowship spoke, Hal's people would conclude that he was all that they had feared. They would believe that he was weak, that he was manipulated. They would question the secrets he'd told others, the shadows that lurked behind the throne of Morenia. They would wonder if he worked for Liantine, for Brianta, for other lands that hoped to take Morenia for their own.

If Hal wanted to keep his throne, he must pay the Fellowship, regardless of any possible advancement that payment might afford him in the shadowy ranks.

One thousand bars of gold, by the feast of First God Ait. That left him some time—six months. Six months to raise a fortune, when he already owed the church, when he already was committed to paying carpenters and merchants, guildsmen and leeches.

He looked across the room to Berylina, to the disheveled child who was only beginning to recover from her shock at a boisterous page's unexpected entrance. Her eyes were red from crying, and her hair was in disarray. Her rabbit teeth stood out in the dim light, a beacon to her strangeness. Hal looked at her crumpled drawing, the ruined Horned Hind, and he glanced at the stack of parchment, the eerily well-drawn portraits of the gods.

He needed Berylina's dowry. Now. He needed her to stand beside him, to secure his line, to grant him an heir. Only so secured could he imagine taking any stand against the Fellowship. Only so buttressed could he demand the status that he craved within their ranks, the status that would—paradoxically—protect him from scandal. For he *would* advance within the Fellowship. If not this year, then the next, or the year after that. When his own house was in order. When his own line was established. Secure.

He rolled the cryptic parchment tight and shoved it back inside its tube. "My lord Farsobalinti?"

"Yes, Your Majesty?"

"Let us leave these good ladies to their diversions. I am returning to my apartments. Please see that Lady Rani and Lady Mair attend me immediately. If you will excuse me, Princess Berylina."

Another girl might have resented his departure. Another princess might have demanded that he speak with her, that he while away a gloomy afternoon in courtly jest and play. Another bride might have refused to let him leave, to let him meet with ladies of his court.

Berylina, though, looked at him with exhaustion and a hint of relief. "Of course, Your Majesty." She crossed to her easel and picked up her bloodred chalk, beginning to draw before Hal had left the room.

9

Mareka Octolaris leaned her head against the cool window. Rain streaked down the panes, which pulled the heat of her flushed face. She closed her eyes against the silver brightness and reminded herself to take a deep breath, to exhale some of the fire that burned in her blood. The octolaris nectar that she had just consumed was strong, almost too strong.

She had brewed the potion to be more potent than she ever would have dared back at the spiderguild. There, masters would have reminded her that she was only an apprentice, that she did not have the skill to handle the largest doses of dilute octolaris poison. But here, in Liantine, she needed to manipulate the strongest spiders the guild had ever known.

Mareka lifted her head, and the blood in her cheeks flamed hotter. The delicate embroidery of her armband seared into her flesh. She had decided to don the symbol of a spiderguild journeyman, if only in secrecy beneath her formal gown. After all, it had not been *her* fault that she had been kept from her examination. Jerusha had ordered the slave girl to her death. Serena's poisoning was not Mareka's doing.

Trembling in reaction to the infusion in her veins, Mareka crossed to the mantel above her hearth. A pitcher of water—cold, clear water—rested on the wooden shelf. Mareka filled her earthenware goblet carefully, loath to lose even a single drop of the cooling stuff. She swirled the cup, making sure that it incorporated all the pearlescent liquid at the bottom, the remnants of the nectar that she had just consumed. She drank down the water and forbade herself from being distracted by the glinting silver patterns that the nectar tracked around the cup. Twice more she rinsed the goblet, swallowing greedily to quench the thirst that raged at the back of her throat.

There. The power of the nectar radiated from her belly like a spider's web. She set the goblet beside the pitcher, taking care to place it precisely. If she were not cautious, she would move too quickly; she would drag the cup off the mantel and send it crashing onto the floor. She could control the nectar. She could control herself.

After all, she had completed eight years of apprenticeship in the spiderguild.

Once she was a journeyman, Mareka would be trained in all the finer points of octolaris nectar. She would mix the spiders' poison with more and more complex potions, so that she did more than merely immunize herself to the dangerous shimmering venom. Masters in the spiderguild could use nectar to slow their heartbeats, to make their bodies resemble cold and lifeless corpses. They could raise their skin's temperature, so that they could walk through winter nights without a cloak, tread through snowbanks without boots. They could adjust their bodies' cycles, so that they chose when to bear a child, when to bring a pair of squalling twins into the world.

Whatever Mareka did with octolaris nectar here in Liantine was really unimportant, the apprentice assured herself. Certainly no one from the guild would care that she had broken the rules in such a minor way. They would not care that she had mixed the poison, that she had consumed the concoction without supervision. And even if they were concerned, they would forget their wrath when Mareka brought them the rich fruit of her labors, the bountiful harvest of silk from her productive, virulent spiders. The guild could always be assuaged with silk.

With the passage of time, the fire began to lessen in Mareka's veins. When she opened her eyes, the world was still lit with a brilliant silver light; it still shimmered with painful beauty and power. Nevertheless, she could bear to look about her; she could manage to study the rain that streaked outside her window. Silver rain. Glinting rain. Brilliant rain.

She took a few steps toward the door to her chamber, and she almost cried out at the touch of her spidersilk gown across her skin. She could feel each individual fiber of the fabric, each separate strand that had been harvested from a spider's living body. She could sense every pore of her own flesh, every fine hair of the down on her arms. Gasping at the distraction, she stepped into the middle of the room.

She stretched one arm above her head, catching her lower lip between her teeth as her motion pulled her gown tighter across her chest. Lowering her arm slowly was a painful ecstasy. She spread her fingers across the fabric that draped over her thigh, and she cried out at the glinting sensations that fired across her flesh—her fingers, her legs, into the pit of her belly.

Spiders, she reminded herself at last. Octolaris. That was why she had consumed the nectar. That was why she had brewed the potion. She needed to tend to her spiders.

The octolaris were in the corner of the room farthest from the windows. All octolaris were uncertain in drafts, but Mareka's special breed were particularly sensitive. They huddled beneath the stony shelters inside their hastily improvised quarter-cages, all the more pitiful because of these octolaris' giant size.

Still, they had survived their journey. They had not perished on the masters' pyre.

Mareka did everything a guildsman would do back at the spiderguild enclave. She sang the spiders' soothing hymn. She Homed them and gave them markin grubs. She watched their egg sacs, desperate for the approaching day when the spiderlings would hatch. She was afraid of that day, uncertain how she would capture the young, how she would keep them safe and fed. But she would manage. She would do whatever she must to keep the strong octolaris strain alive. At least confining them in her cold, dark chamber reduced their need for food.

For the first time since she had settled her brood in Liantine, it was necessary to move one of the spiders. To Mareka's surprise and shame, one of the brooding females had died. Perhaps it had not received enough markin meat. Perhaps it had become too chilled in the darkened room. Perhaps it had fallen prey to one of the nameless diseases that the guild guarded against in its herds. Whatever the cause, Mareka had discovered the beast's curled body that morning.

She had wept, furious with herself for failing her charge.

When she lifted the corpse from the cage, she was surprised to feel how light it had already become. She had shuddered as she consigned the body to the fire that burned in her grate.

And now, she needed to transfer the dead spider's egg sac to an octolaris that could care for it. This was a difficult operation. Some spiders gorged on their sisters' eggs. Others refused to tend new sacs, refused to rotate the precious bags, to patch them when their silk became torn. Still other octolaris abandoned their own unhatched young, favoring a new sac at the cost of the old.

Mareka could not know how her spiders would react, but she could not let the hundreds of bound hatchlings die without trying to save them. She needed to introduce the orphaned egg sac into a living spider's box. And to do that, she needed to handle a living spider. Thus, she had consumed the octolaris nectar, consumed the strongest tincture that she dared.

It was time.

One, bind your sleeves, gathering up the extra silk that might frighten the spiders. Mareka caught her tongue between her teeth and pulled her silk gown closer. As she wrapped ribbons around her forearms, closing in her loose garment, nectar-induced tremors skipped across her muscles like sparks that danced from flames.

Two, cover your wrists with spidersilk strips, wrapping the bands to protect against bites from leaping octolaris. It was awkward to set the strips alone, but she managed. She lost her concentration twice, losing her awareness in the drumbeat of her pulse, in the frantic, charging flow of her blood from her chest to her fingertips and back again.

Three, block the direct sunlight, approaching the box without glare and with full view of the spider's every movement. There was no sunlight in the chamber, and the dull rain-fed light from the windows was not enough to distract Mareka, even with her nectar-enhanced vision.

Four, sing the hymn, the soothing song that lulled most octolaris into complacence. The tune vibrated up from Mareka's lungs, thrumming across her throat. It hovered on her lips, more subtle than speech, more exciting than any words. Twice she recited the entire hymn, letting the familiar words carry her deeper into the nectar, into the poison, into the octolaris' secret lives.

Five, bow four times, giving the spider a chance to recognize you. The first time, her spidersilk gown caressed her. The second time, it pressed itself against all her flesh at once, melding with her body. The third time, it jangled across her nectar-sensitive skin, sparking like newborn flames. The fourth time, it released her with a lover's reluctance, leaving her panting and flushed.

Six, rattle the riberry branch, forcing the spider from its rocky cave. Mareka could hear the tip of the branch grate against each individual grain of earth on the floor of the octolaris's cage. The smooth riberry bark slipped beneath her fingers, whispering, summoning, luring the spider forward.

Seven, complete the Homing, weaving your fingers in the complicated pattern that signaled dominance, not prey. Mareka stared down at her palms. The creases in her flesh told stories, whispered tales that tried to carry her away. She waggled her fingers as she'd been taught, sending the wordless signal, conveying the silent story. She was friend, not foe. She was companion, not prey. She was spiderguild.

Eight, for brooding females, consume the nectar. Mareka had taken no chances. She had started with the nectar, in case the virulent octolaris leaped too soon. There were no masters to watch her, no other guildsman to say that she had acted out of order.

One, two, three, four. Five, six, seven, eight.

She was ready to approach the brooding spider.

The egg sac was cool and slightly sticky when she collected it from the abandoned spiderbox. She transferred it gently from palm to palm, momentarily snagged in the octolaris nectar's magic. The sac pulled ever so slightly at her skin, plucking her flesh as if she were a stringed lute.

When she opened the new spiderbox, she took her time, settling the wooden lid on the floorboards with exaggerated care. Even with her heightened vision, even with her silver sight, it took her a moment to find the living spider in the new box. The brooding female was huddled over her own clutch of egg sacs.

Of course the spider was nervous. Of course she knew that

something catastrophic had happened. One of her sisters had burned that morning. The spider tasted death in the very air of the room.

Mareka began the octolaris hymn again, drawing out the notes of soothing comfort. The octolaris would never understand words; she would never understand a specific argument of Mareka's desperate need. The apprentice could gain nothing by telling her living spiders that she mourned the death of one of their number. Indeed, the spiders had no way of understanding the complex emotion of loss, no way of measuring sorrow. Instead, they reacted to *fear*—fear that they would be threatened by the flames that had consumed their sister.

Mareka sang her hymn, focusing on broad thoughts of safety and security, of blessed protection. She poured comfort into the song that thrummed across her throat.

The spider responded to her song. The creature crept from beneath her stone, beneath her anchoring riberry branch. She crawled across the rich earth—earth that Mareka could smell with every fiber of her body, could taste with her lips, her tongue, her entire mouth. The octolaris sat back on four of her legs and cocked her head at a sharp angle.

Mareka took a deep breath, transferring the air in her lungs into the final sustained note of the hymn. The nectar pounded through her body, shattered down her arm. She leaned over the box and placed her hand against the earth. The rich earth . . . The fertile earth . . .

She could feel the individual grains of dirt. She could feel three separate hairs that the spider had shed during its confinement. She could feel the tremor as the octolaris registered her presence, as it measured her threat.

Mareka willed her fingers to stay still, to remain flat, even though energy beat through her veins. The nectar was designed to protect her if she were bitten, but it paradoxically made that bite more likely as it stripped away her ability to control the smallest motions of her own body. She reminded herself to breathe, reminded herself to fuel the final hymn note that resonated through the air above the box. She imagined the power of the nectar flowing from her skin, across the cage, through the air to the octolaris.

And the spider moved. It edged forward, first with one leg, then with a pair. It sidled up to Mareka's palm, and it felt at her fingers with its pedipalps. It waved over her as if she were prey, as if she were an egg sac, as if she were a mate. Mareka felt the air of its passing, felt the pressure of its attention, and she caught her own breath, even though that meant stilling her hymn.

The octolaris jumped onto her palm. All eight feet landed at the same time, smoothly, evenly. Mareka could feel the creature's abdomen, heavy against the lines of her palm. She could feel the animal breathing. She could feel the convulsion of the long, thin heart that stretched across the octolaris's body. She raised the lethal creature and held it before her eyes.

The spider crouched on her hand, scrabbling a bit for an adequate purchase; its body filled her palm. Its legs were drawn up beneath it, powerful, ready to spring. Eight eyes stared back at Mareka, grouped in three clumps on the top of the head—three, two, and three again. The eyes were like cabochon onyx; they caught the dim light in the room and glinted it back in silver streaks.

Mareka raised her other hand, the hand that held the egg sac, moving it so that the eight stone eyes could see the thing she held. She kept her fingers flat and smooth, stilling the slightest wriggle that might mimic a markin grub. Slowly, slowly—more slowly than she thought she could do with nectar pounding through her—she brought her hands together.

The octolaris rippled. Its movement started at its pedipalps and rolled back over its body, flipping through the fine black hairs that covered its back. Mareka flinched at the first motion but then regained control. This close, with her silver sight enhanced by the nectar, she could see the spider's jaws. She could see the mouthpieces that glinted with venom. She could see the poison that might be balanced by the strong, strong nectar she had brewed—might, or might not.

The spider reached a leg across the crease between Mareka's palms. One leg, and then another, sampling, testing, edging forward. Mareka felt the swollen abdomen move, felt the spider shift toward the alien egg sac. She concentrated on exuding the scent of the octolaris nectar, sending the power of that infusion through her skin, toward the spider. The octolaris must be comforted, must be made to feel secure. She must feel safe.

There was a long time when Mareka thought that she would fail. The spider hovered, suspended across both of the apprentice's hands. Mareka could feel the octolaris's heartbeat, could read her indecision as if it were a visible organ. And then, when Mareka had almost given up hope, the spider moved. It pulled itself forward until it could lift the egg sac in its front legs. It turned the silken gift over and around, raising the sac to its mouthpieces as if it could smell its dead, departed sister. And then, it passed the egg sac under its body, past its two pairs of middle legs, to the very last pair.

Tears welled up in Mareka's eyes as the spider began to extrude silk from her spinnerets. The wondrous thread emerged from the spider's body as a clear liquid, and then it was snagged on tiny claws, immediately spun and hardened into thick, hard strands. The spider turned the egg sac rapidly, covering the entire container with her own silk. The octolaris had adopted the eggs as her own.

Mareka reveled in the touch of the spider against her hands. She grew warm at the whisper of the turning egg sac, felt weak at the stickiness of the fresh silk. Tears blinded her as the octolaris lifted the new-folded sac in her own legs, as she crouched to protect her treasure. Mareka could scarcely bear to move, to bring her hands back to the earth in the bottom of the spiderbox. She moaned as the spider leaped from her palms, as it crawled past its riberry branch and under its stone. Mareka sighed as the spider added the new egg sac to her old horde.

Mareka replaced the cover on the spiderbox.

She could control the octolaris. She could breed a new line of spiders, new producers of silk. She could make them profitable, make the guild—and herself—rich. Richer even than Jerusha promised, with her last-born prince and her stubborn, Hind-bound house of Thunderspear.

Jerusha. That scheming witch was probably lazing about the royal apartments even now, doing her best to lure her princeling to bed. Jerusha had better find herself with child by the Midwinter Convocation. A prince's heir would be that wretch's only way of proving her continued value to the guild.

Not that Mareka could not do the same, get herself with child.

In fact, Mareka could do better. If she'd been given half a chance with the Liantine dolt, she'd have won Olric over *and* commanded a bride-price paid over to the guild. Well, Olric was lost, but there were other options. Mareka could look higher than a mere prince. She could catch a king inside her web. There were stories of the power of octolaris nectar, rumors of the poison's strength, even among strangers to the spiderguild. . . .

With a quick glance to make sure that all her octolaris were secure, Mareka grabbed a shawl and darted out the door. The octolaris nectar still pounded through her, but its call had softened. Now, its power whispered like well-worked muscles after a footrace, like the clear light after a summer rainstorm. Her armbands still bled heat through her body, and she still continued to count her pulse beneath the protective strips wrapped around her wrists. Now, though, she was certain that the touch of electric spidersilk was pleasure and not pain. She imagined a man's lips, a *king's* lips, roaming across the tight-wrapped strips. She could feel the tremble-touch of Halaravilli's tongue as he drank from her bound flesh.

By the time Mareka had glided through the hallways, she had summoned up more images of King Halaravilli. Certainly, the king appeared meek, with his well-spoken words and his rigid courtesy. She thought of what she could teach him, though, of the lessons that she had already learned from the insistent teacher of her octolaris nectar. She could instruct him in the proper use of his long fingers, for example, in—

She pulled herself to a stop in the doorway of the visiting king's apartments. The door was pushed almost to, as if someone had intended to close it. The wood had warped slightly with the recent rainfall, and it had not caught completely. Mareka glided up to the threshold and caught her breath, the better to hear the discussion within the chamber.

Two voices. One was Halaravilli's. The tone sent a shiver down her spine, and a trace of heat spun out from the web inside her. Oh, what riches she could bring back to her guild!

The other voice belonged to the merchant wench, to Rani

Trader. Both the king and his subject were angry; their voices were raised. The nectar still sharpened Mareka's hearing; she could make out clear words where others might have gathered only the tone of an argument.

"I won't hear of it," Halaravilli said.

"You have nothing to *say* about it! Don't you understand? I can learn from them. I can gain the knowledge I need to rebuild the glasswrights' guild. I can rise to journeyman! That's more important now, my lord. More important, if you are to find a fortune for the Fellowship."

Fellowship? Mareka did not know what Rani Trader meant.

"Rani, I *need* you here. You can't go riding off with a troop of itinerant actors, like a drunken pilgrim on holiday!"

The girl's voice dropped when she replied. Mareka stepped closer, but even then the words were almost too obscure for the nectar to capture. "My lord, when you asked me to come to Liantine, I pledged my help to you. I pledged that I would find a strategy to argue for your bride if you deemed Berylina the woman you would marry. But you yourself have said that King Teheboth will not meet with me. You need my skill, but not my presence."

"So you would leave me here, alone?"

"You're not alone, Sire! You have Lord Farsobalinti; you've got Mair."

"If you go, you're taking Mair." The king's words were so quick that they fell over the merchant's.

When Rani Trader spoke again, there was the faintest smile behind her words. "My lord? You've thought about this, then?"

There was only the faintest uplift to her question, only the shadow of inquiry, and Mareka did not need her octolaris-enhanced senses to tell her that Rani Trader had won. The merchant girl would travel with the players.

"I've thought enough to know that I won't have you wandering alone, across all Liantine."

"Mair would be a welcome companion, Sire."

"A welcome companion." Halaravilli snorted, and Mareka imagined the look of exasperation that framed his words. "She would find more trouble for you than you could find on your own."

"Aye," the merchant girl agreed. "She *will*, my lord."

"And take Crestman, too. He'll keep you safe."

"If he wishes to journey with us, he may. He might learn more of the Little Army, away from Liantine."

"You'll write to me, Rani. Every day. I must know that no harm has come to you. And if I need you . . ."

"If you summon me, I'll return, on the fastest horse that I can find." She paused, then said, "This is best, my lord. What else am I to do here? You have gained the princess's trust; you said yourself that she shared her secret drawings."

"But how am I to make my bid?"

"Directly. With pride and honor. To her father, alone, so that no man may shame him into protecting his fortune."

"He does not consider Berylina a fortune."

"Then use that, my lord. Act as if *you* do not care. Act as if you are ready to return overseas, to journey back to Morenia."

"And if I act too well? If he tells me to be gone?"

"He won't do that. Teheboth wishes to see the princess out of Liantine. Make him pay the price."

"I will not treat her as damaged goods."

"Nay, my lord. She is not damaged. She is not. You are not. None of us is."

There was a pause, a long painful pause, and Mareka wondered what the two were doing, where they were looking, what silent things they said to one another. Then the merchant spoke again, her voice so soft that Mareka pressed her ear against the door. "You must stand firm as you bargain. Make Teheboth Thunderspear pay. Make him raise the dowry so that he can be rid of the goods he does not value."

The king swallowed audibly. "Rani, you know I need the gold. I have no choice—"

"And neither do I, my lord." A brief pause. "Neither do I."

Mareka could not decipher the rustling she heard. Certainly there was silk moving, as if an arm were raised. But whether Rani Trader touched her king, or the king touched his vassal, Mareka could not have said. Rather, she caught a half-swallowed sob, and then footsteps swept across the floor. Mareka scarcely had time to spring back before Rani Trader flung open the door.

"Oh!" the woman cried as she stepped awkwardly to one side. With Mareka's silver nectar-sight, she glimpsed tears welling up in the merchant's eyes, saw the tight lines that were etched beside her mouth as she struggled to hold back surprised words.

"My lady." Mareka dropped a quick curtsey as the other woman fled down the hall, not bothering to look behind her.

Mareka rose up to her full height, taking care to frame herself in the doorway. She pushed her hair behind her ears, preternaturally aware of the motion. She saw confusion flit across Halaravilli's face, measured the time it took for him to recognize her. "My lord," she said, curtseying again.

"My lady," he replied automatically. It took him longer, though, to remember his manners. "I'm sorry. Will you enter? I—I wasn't expecting you."

"Of course you weren't, my lord," Mareka said, gliding over the threshold. She felt the aura of octolaris nectar follow her into the room, spreading like a cloud of incense. The king stared past her, and she could read his transparent desire to follow after the merchant.

Mareka turned back to the door, taking the time to close it carefully. It took an effort to push the oak entirely square within its frame, but she was able to lower the iron latch without making the maneuver seem forced. "My lord!" she exclaimed, turning back to the king. "You look pale! May I pour you a glass of wine?"

"Nay, my lady, don't trouble yourself." He refused to meet her eyes, did not see her smile as she crossed the room. She twitched her skirts as she moved, feeling the nectar against her flesh, sensing it spread.

"It's no trouble, my lord. Certainly no trouble at all." She crossed to the low table smoothly, relishing the nectar-thrum as her gown slid across her thighs. She could smell the greenwine in its pitcher before she poured it into a waiting golden goblet. Some splashed onto her hand and, with her back turned toward Halaravilli, she raised the pale drop to her lips. Its complicated sharpness swept across her tongue, and she caught her breath. When she could speak, she turned and proffered him the cup. "Please, my lord."

She made him walk to her. She made him step away from the place where he had argued with his merchant girl. She raised the cup between them and managed a smile, even as his fingers brushed across her own. She imagined the nectar as a clinging pollen, drifting from her hands to his.

"Thank you, my lady," he said, and his swallows were audible in the room, would have been loud even without her sharpened hearing. When he had drained half the goblet, he dared to meet her eyes. "So, my lady. It seems that you are not the princess I thought you were when first we met."

"Nay, my lord." She started to laugh, but decided only to smile instead. "Not a princess at all."

"You deliberately misled me."

"At first, I did not realize you were confused, and then I was afraid that you would be embarrassed. I did not want your arrival in Liantine to be hard. I tried to explain things to your . . . companions, as soon as I was able." A flicker of emotion pulled across his face as she alluded to Rani Trader. Whatever the bond that stretched between the king and the merchant, it was tight. Painful. "I hope that you can forgive me, my lord."

He sighed. "I had been told what to expect in the princess. I merely—" He shook his head. "I merely wanted her to be otherwise. It's no secret, Lady Mareka. I am a king, and my destiny is to wed to better my crown. My obligation is to serve all of Morenia, and Princess Berylina is the best way I can do that."

"Is she?" Mareka felt the nectar-thrill as Halaravilli's eyes shot to her own. Words thrummed up from her belly, promises to draw the king closer. "There are greater riches in the world than a Liantine princess can bring."

She sifted her fingers through her hair, breathing out slowly. Unbidden, she thought of the octolaris males, drawn to their females when the spiders were ready to lay their eggs. She remembered starlit nights when females wove their mating webs, spinning their sturdiest silk to support themselves and their lovers and their precious globes of eggs. Mareka had watched the spiders; she knew their ways, even though she had never known a man herself. She whispered, "You think you must have Berylina if you will save your kingdom?"

"I must have gold," he breathed, and she felt his words like the touch of his palms.

"Then why waste your time with a princess, my lord? If you want gold, why not trade with the spiderguild? We have gold, my lord. We have all you need."

He did touch her, then. He reached out a hand that trembled, a hand that was rough with urgency. He pulled her closer to him, curving his fingers behind her neck, turning her face to his. She felt the whisper of his breath, and she heard a cry grow and die in the back of his throat. His lips crushed hers, and she drank the greenwine from his mouth, tasted the sweet desperation of a man who needed to save his kingdom, needed to save himself. Her embroidered armbands blazed hot as she closed her eyes and fed King Halaravilli's passion.

10

Rani watched as Mair tugged at the tunic she had borrowed from one of the young players, an itinerant entertainer who had arrived only that morning for the Spring Meet. The Touched girl looked as if she were back in the Moren of her youth, leading her troop of ragged children, exploiting the riches of a city that knew boundless wealth. Rani swallowed a bitter taste as she realized once again that the familiar Moren was lost forever.

Mair, however, was not dwelling on fire or disease or the dangerous plight of Touched children. Instead, she was boasting to the players. "I can easily handle three—it's all in the timing of your entrance."

To prove her point, she backed away, taking five grand steps. "Now. Start turning the ropes. Slowly."

Two of the players held a rope between them, a measure of worsted spidersilk as thick as Rani's thumb. They began to turn the length, and the rope slapped the ground rhythmically, setting up a beat as steady as a drum. Mair nodded and pointed to two more players. "Now, you join them. Stand beside them. Turn now. *Now.*"

As Rani watched, a second length of spidersilk joined the first, also spinning, also striking the ground. There seemed to be more than two ropes at play, more interference in the clear morning air.

"There you go," Mair called. "One more now. Stand next to the others. Start after the next turn, *now.*" Three silken ropes, all turning evenly. Mair watched them, bobbing her head slightly as she traced their arcs. "Keep them steady, now. Keep them turning at the same speed. Don't slow down when you see me move—I'll adjust for the ropes. On three, then. One. Two. Three."

The Touched girl ran between the spidersilk, timing her entrance perfectly. She paused as one rope slapped the ground, then leaped just high enough to let it clear beneath her feet. Again, again, and the players kept twirling. When Mair had bobbed up a dozen times, she skipped free of the ropes, emerging on the near side while the steady rhythm continued.

"Don't stop," she called. "You can run clear through them, too. Tumble between them." To illustrate her point, she paused to count the rhythm, nodding her head once again. "There. On three. One. Two. Three."

Mair sprang at the ropes as if they did not exist, tucking her head and rolling forward, only to land—miraculously—upon both feet. The players let out a shout of collective surprise, and Mair took a mock bow. "All it takes is timing." She grinned, moving to take the end of one of the ropes so that a player could try her tricks.

"Timing and a foolish faith in others," Crestman growled, and Rani jumped, for she had not heard the Amanthian approach.

"Not so foolish," she said, recovering quickly. "If it works, she looks as nimble as a cat. If it fails, she gets slapped by a rope."

"Or falls on her backside. Hard." Crestman winced as a player tumbled down. The young man picked himself up immediately, calling for his companions to give him one more try.

"No great harm done," Rani said.

Crestman scowled. "No great good, either. These players waste their time with children's games."

"Do you honestly believe that? You're not paying attention, then. The players work harder than many other folk I've seen." She read the skepticism in his eyes. "They do! The spiderguild is no easy master. These players pay for their patronage—they deliver stories to the guild, stories of the world and all its workings. The players know more about the world around them than any single merchant, any single guild."

"And I'm certain they have shared this great wisdom with you."

"Some of it, they have." Rani doused her hot retort with the recollection of Speaking. She felt the smooth flow of blue glass like a physical thing; it seemed that she could reach for it just beneath the surface of her thoughts. "Some. And they've promised more—knowledge about their glasswork."

"Then will they answer my questions? Will they share stories of the Little Army?"

Rani shrugged. "You can't know until you ask them. Go ahead. There's nothing to be afraid of."

"I'm not afraid."

"Then come. Let us find Flarissa."

Rani led Crestman through the players' camp. It had taken her scarcely a day to learn her way about the hamlet, around the core of wooden buildings that formed the center of the itinerant players' village. The buildings were simple and sturdy, designed so that they could withstand neglect for the times that the players traveled across Liantine. Flarissa lived in one of the few central buildings, well inside the ever-changing boundaries of tents and wagons. She was regarded as a great leader among the players; she had gathered more stories, Spoken with more visitors than had any other member of the troop. She was honored by a hut built with wooden walls, a thatched roof, and one clear glass window.

Flarissa's hut backed onto the storehouse. Rani had not been permitted inside that structure yet. Flarissa said that it contained great bolts of spidersilk, cloth to be sewn into tents and bolsters and clothing and costumes. It held other tools of the actors' craft—face paints and wigs, and a woodshop for crafting tools for the plays, such as the Old Man's walking stick, the Young Girl's mirror.

And the storehouse contained glass. Rani had heard the players talk about the panels casually, speculate about the screens that defined each play. She understood that the storehouse concealed whitewashed tables for laying out new designs, and lead stripping and glass to create the works. There would be solder, too, to repair broken screens, and silver stain, and paint. . . .

Rani's palms itched as she rounded the corner of the storehouse. A heavy iron lock hung from the oak door, mute testimony to the treasures inside. So far, Rani had needed to content herself with studying the kiln outside the storehouse, looking at the clever brick construction that let air circulate to cool the glass after firing.

Flarissa had promised that the players' glasswright would return that day. He had been on the road, negotiating with the spiderguild, delivering the players' latest news of the kingdom, and bargaining for silk. Any moment, now, he was expected to return for the Spring Meet.

Rani thrust down a flutter of expectation as she knocked on Flarissa's door.

"Come!" the woman called immediately.

Rani glanced at Crestman and was surprised by the hard line of his jaw. He rested a hand upon his curved Amanthian sword before he ducked inside the building, looking as if he intended to storm the place rather than ask assistance. Rani followed, trying to set aside her misgivings about introducing the soldier to the player.

She blinked in the cool richness of Flarissa's hut. She'd visited every day since arriving in the players' camp, and still she was captivated by the accumulation of wealth. A giant curtained bed filled half the room, swathed from floor to ceiling with hangings of the finest spidersilk. The hearth was set with painted tiles, careful designs that captured firelight and reflected it back. Mementos of travels were scattered about—a silver-chased goblet that clearly came from Zarithia, a child's doll that looked to be of Briantan design.

Most striking, however, the floor was covered with fine spidersilk weavings, lush carpets that incorporated a web design. Rays spun out from the center of the room, inviting visitors to step in, to be welcome, to settle into the player's home.

"Ranita!" Flarissa's greeting was light, joyous. She set aside a leather strap that she was mending in the light from the window, a sandal for a player's costume. "I hoped that you would visit me today."

Rani basked in the warmth of the player's greeting. Flarissa reminded her of the feel of a featherbed—soft and warm and

THE GLASSWRIGHTS' JOURNEYMAN

comfortable. For just an instant, Rani thought of her mother, Deela, leaning over Rani's pallet in the long-gone Trader home, crooning her to sleep with a lullaby and a smile.

"Good morning, Flarissa," she said, swallowing the memory like a physical thing.

"You've brought your friend, at last."

"Aye," Rani said, perhaps a little too eager. "Flarissa, this is Crestman. He is a great soldier from Amanthia."

Crestman scowled as he bowed before the player, stiff and uncomfortable. "Amanthia has no great soldiers any longer. We have offered up our arms to Morenia."

Flarissa looked directly at the youth, and she might have been quoting some play when she said, "A soldier's loyalties are never simple."

"I'm loyal to King Halaravilli!"

"I'm certain that you are. That does not mean your path has been easy. Your choices were not lightly made."

Flarissa's words defused some of Crestman's tension, and Rani stepped forward, eager to do more. "I've told Crestman of my Speaking, about how you players gather stories. He is searching for information about the Little Army."

"The Amanthian children." Flarissa's words were not a question; they were quietly resigned. She cast a glance at Crestman. "What were you before your country's war? A lionboy?"

"I was a captain in Sin Hazar's army."

Rani waited for Crestman to explain more about how he came to serve, but Flarissa did not seem surprised by his recalcitrance. Instead, she nodded and said, "We players trade for stories. People pay us, then they Speak."

"What sort of coin?"

"A single sovereign, typically. For you, though, we could work a different exchange."

"What?" Crestman's wariness was like a wild animal's, poised on the edge of a ravine. He was equally ready to scramble down or retreat.

"Show our players how you wield your curved Amanthian sword. Teach them to use the weapon so they may work it into plays."

"And for that?"

"I'll Speak with you. I'll gather up your story."

"You get my labor and my tale."

"And you get the peace of the telling."

Rani hovered, waiting. Suddenly, it was tremendously important to her that Crestman agree. Rani could not explain why. She could not find words, any more than she could describe the cobalt lake that spread beneath her own thoughts. Crestman needed to agree to Flarissa's terms. He needed to reach out to the player, to her bargain, to the healing she could offer.

"Very well, then," Crestman said at last. "I'll teach your players." Rani exhaled her relief. "However—," he continued before Flarissa could reply, "you must give me something else, as well. You must tell me what you know about the Little Army, about my soldiers who are scattered throughout Liantine."

"Crestman," Rani said, "you can't bargain."

"He can," Flarissa contradicted. "*You* bargained to see the glass." Rani flushed as Flarissa turned back to Crestman. "Very well, then. Speak, and I'll tell you what I know about the Little Army. Ranita, if you will leave us now—"

"She can stay," Crestman interrupted.

Flarissa looked at him for a long moment. "You will be safe here. There will be no danger."

"I'm not afraid of your Speaking. But Rani may stay and listen."

At first, Rani thought that Flarissa would protest, would make her leave the hut. The player looked at Crestman's face, studied the hand that still curved around the hilt of his sword. She started to speak, stopped, and then started once again. "Very well, then. She may stay." Flarissa nodded to a low chair that crouched beside the window. "Sit, Ranita. Make yourself comfortable so that you do not interrupt the Speaking."

Rani complied, crossing the room and settling quickly. She tried to seem invisible, tried to mask her breathing, tried even to keep her eyes from flicking back and forth, from Crestman to Flarissa. She listened as the player explained the art of Speaking, outlined what she would ask and how she would guide the conversation. Rani watched as Flarissa collected a single pearl earring, stringing the bauble upon a chain of gold.

She told Crestman to settle on a great bolster beside the hearth, and she waited for him to make himself comfortable.

"Very good, Crestman," Flarissa said. "Remember, you need not tell me anything you wish to keep secret. If you wish to stop at any time, you can open your eyes and walk away. Do you understand?"

"Yes."

"Very well. Look upon the pearl and think back to the most important day of your life. Think. Decide. Choose the story you will tell." Flarissa waited several heartbeats. "Do you see it? Do you see the tale that you will Speak?"

"Yes." Crestman's voice was loud enough that Rani started. He darted his eyes from the pearl to her face. The motion made the white scar upon his cheek leap out.

"Look upon the pearl, Crestman," Flarissa said. "Look upon the pearl and remember your story. Remember the day. How old were you that day?"

"Fifteen." The single word was rough, raw against Flarissa's honeyed tone. He cleared his throat and said again, "Fifteen."

"Very good, Crestman. Relax. Breathe in. Breathe out. Look into the pearl. Think back to the day. You can see it reflected in the pearl. Breathe in. Breathe out. If you wish to close your eyes, you may."

Crestman kept his eyes open, staring at the pearl with unblinking intensity.

"Relax, Crestman. Focus. Take yourself to your story. Breathe in. Breathe out."

"I am breathing!"

"Calm yourself. Focus. Think of this as a training exercise, a chance to build your skills."

"I can't do this!"

"You can, Crestman, if you let yourself. Allow yourself to travel in your thoughts. Look at the pearl. See yourself when you were fifteen. See what you were wearing. Remember how you felt."

"This will never work!" Crestman sprang to his feet, forcing the player woman to sit back abruptly. "I won't be witched by your crooning and your pearls!"

"Crestman!" Rani exclaimed, jumping to her feet.

"No! I will not Speak! I'll learn about the Little Army some other way!"

Before Rani could say anything, before she could beg him to come back and try again, he turned on his heel. His boots clattered on the wooden floor, even through the spidersilk covering, and he yanked the door open. For just a minute, he hovered on the threshold, and then he pulled the door behind him, slamming it with a resounding thud.

"I'm sorry," Rani began. "Flarissa, I never thought that he—"

Before she could complete her apology, the door opened again. Rani whirled about, expecting to see Crestman, but she was shocked into silence by the sight of a grinning stranger.

"Another satisfied customer leaves the player's hearth?" The man crossed the room with familiar ease.

"Do not mock me, Tovin." Flarissa's voice carried a hint of warning, but her flash of annoyance was quickly damped. She turned to Rani. "Some people are not able to Speak with us. Some cannot find their pathways back inside their tales. You can tell your friend that I am willing to try another time. Perhaps when he has come to trust us more."

The man—Tovin—grinned and said, "Or maybe you should have another player try. Some are better at extracting stories than others."

"My lady Flarissa was brilliant at getting me to Speak," Rani answered hotly, stung to defend the player woman. She was surprised to hear Flarissa laugh.

"Ranita! Thank you for your praises. But you need not defend me to this impudent whelp. Ranita, this is Tovin. My son."

Son. Now that Rani looked, she could see the strong line of the man's jaw, the exotic angle of his cheekbones, and she could recognize traces of Flarissa's nose and mouth. Where the player woman was soft, a calm and loving mother, the man was hard. Rani recognized the look immediately. Tovin was a trader. He might live in players' clothing, but he was a merchant man at heart.

"Ranita," Tovin said, pinning her with copper eyes that mirrored his mother's gaze. "You're not from Liantine, are you?"

"I'm from Morenia, sir," Rani said. She tried to keep her voice courteous.

"A westerner, hmm?" He ran his eyes down her body, as if he were appraising horseflesh. She sensed him counting out her name, measuring up her caste. "What guild do you hail from, then?"

"The glasswrights, sir."

"Then you're an outlaw among your people?"

"The glasswrights are no longer outlaw," Rani said stiffly. "We have been recognized by King Halaravilli. We are rebuilding."

"Rebuilding." Tovin rolled the word around on his tongue, and Rani could picture him upon the players' stage. He might take the part of a lord, a noble, a person accustomed to command.

Flarissa interrupted before Rani could elaborate on her hopes for the glasswrights' guild. "Tovin, she's a guest among us players. Don't tease the girl."

Tovin snorted and crossed to the mantel, pouring himself a cup of wine. He was tall, Rani noted, taller than Hal, and he was broad through his shoulders. "Forgive me, Ranita." He offered up the apology without any hint of regret. "My mother thinks that I've been rude."

"You have been," Flarissa remonstrated, but she smiled as she chided. "Don't think that you can ride into camp on the very day of the Spring Meet, come into my cottage, drink my greenwine, and insult my guests."

Tovin laughed and saluted his mother with his goblet before he turned toward Rani. "I trust you will forgive me, Ranita Glasswright? Pardon me before my mother, or I'll never hear the end of her complaints."

Rani tried to remember how she would respond to a merchant boy who teased her, but she was oddly at a loss before Tovin's glinting grin. "There's nothing to forgive," she managed, although she did not reach the light tone that she'd hoped for.

Flarissa nodded indulgently, as if she were pleased to see peace between her squabbling children. "How was your journey, Tovin?"

He shrugged and drained his cup. "Not good. They're driving a hard bargain this time. They claim that they can no longer afford to support a troop of players. The sale of spider-silk is off. The priests are calling for the faithful to give up spidersilk hangings in favor of wood panels, reminders of the Horned Hind."

"When will you go back, then?"

"I'll stay here for the Spring Meet and a bit more. Perhaps a week, all told. Then, I'll conclude our deal." He set his cup upon the mantel. "I've plenty of business to complete, before I return to the road. I just wanted you to know that I am home."

Flarissa glowed with pride. "I'm pleased to see you well."

He bobbed a quick bow and headed for the door, but then turned back to Rani. "Ranita Glasswright. A pleasure to make your acquaintance."

"A pleasure, sir." Rani kept her words short, for she was not at all certain that Flarissa's son pleased her. Not at all sure that it was a pleasure to meet those probing copper eyes. Tovin bowed again and left.

Rani waited for Flarissa's proud smile to fade, and then she asked, "He's been with the spiderguild, then?"

"Aye. He negotiates for us. He buys our silk and settles on our patronage each year."

"The guild must be very strong."

"Strong as spidersilk." Flarissa shook her head. "They don't seem so powerful, if you merely take a glance. Their guildhall is on the high plains, three day's ride from Liantine, two from here. But they spin their webs and measure out their power. Spiders, silk, and poison. The Horned Hind may encroach upon their power, but they are far from beaten yet."

Rani shivered, thinking of the venomous creatures that spawned such wealth. "But enough about the spiderguild!" Flarissa cried. "You must think of all the questions you would ask Tovin."

"Ask him?"

"Of course! Tovin is our glasswright. Did I forget to say that?"

Rani's dismay bubbled up inside her. That man? That unsettling, arrogant . . .

Flarissa smiled. "I'll make sure that he speaks with you tonight. Now sit beside me and keep me company while I finish mending these sandals." Rani settled down beside the player woman and let herself be drawn into conversation, even as she thought about the lessons she might learn from Tovin.

Rani watched Mair rub at her wrist. "You're not a Touched child anymore."

"I didn't fall because I'm old, Rai. I fell because they didn't turn the ropes evenly."

"You're lucky you didn't break that arm again. It's been weak ever since Amanthia."

Mair did not answer, only looked out at the stream. Both girls had been banished from the players' camp, told to stay away for the afternoon and early evening. The players were conducting the most secret part of their Spring Meet, plotting their business deals for the coming year, deciding where they would travel and what they would play. Flarissa had promised to send someone along as soon as the Meet was concluded. Rani and Mair were expected to join in the evening feast.

Rani wondered where Crestman had gone. She had been unable to find him when she and Mair departed for the stream. He was likely spying on the players, counting out the Little Army members they had scattered through their midst. She hoped that he would not offend their hosts.

"So," Rani said to fill the silence. "We were so astonished when Hal received the Fellowship's demand that we scarcely spoke about the reasoning behind it. What do you think that they intend to do with a thousand bars of gold?"

"Break the crown."

"Surely they mean more than that? They must intend to use the gold for something."

Mair pursed her lips. "We already know that they can hire Yrathi mercenaries and turn those soldiers to their will. If they have a treasury so deep, why would they bother collecting a thousand bars of gold from King Halaravilli?"

"It would prove his loyalty. Not a bad plan, that—they test him *and* they get a lot of wealth. Perhaps they intend to do something in Morenia. Something specific to the fire and our rebuilding."

"Aye."

"Or maybe they want to seek out all the Little Army, settle the matter once and for all."

"Aye."

"Or maybe they are going to honor Hal's marriage, to send some gift welcoming his bride."

"Rai, you're making these things up! You have no way of guessing what the Fellowship will do."

"Doesn't it bother you? Not knowing?"

Mair shrugged. "I've never known anything about the Fellowship. From the day I joined them, they kept their secrets. I know they gather power. I know they work in every land. Aside from that, they've kept me ignorant, and I can't lose sleep waiting to learn their next move. I'll protect myself the best I can, use them when I might, and go about living my life."

Rani let Mair's words flow down the stream, disappearing into the deepening twilight. She wished that she could be so dismissive, wished that she could care so little for what the Fellowship planned. "It's not that simple, Mair. Even if they intend to throw the gold into a well, they're affecting things by asking for it. They'll come close to breaking Morenia, just to get their thousand bars."

"He'll pay them from the princess's dowry."

"He won't. He won't be able to bargain for that much. He already owes the church five hundred bars by Midsummer Day—which is fast approaching—and five thousand after that. The most he'll get for Berylina is a thousand."

"You're such an expert in royal trade?"

"I've studied the market." Rani tried to wash the bitterness from her tone. There were many books that she had studied when she was supposed to be focusing on her glasswright skills. She had read the histories of Morenia—and Amanthia, too. She understood the limits on a bride-price. Especially when the groom was desperate.

"He'll find another method, then. He'll raise money some other way."

"Nothing pays that well, Mair."

"Of course things do. Mining gold itself. Slaves. The spider-silk monopoly."

Mining gold—as if Morenia would be lucky enough to find

such deposits in its soil. Slaves—even if Hal *had* been inclined to ransom off his loyal folk, he had seen enough evil in Amanthia to kill the thought. The spidersilk, though . . .

Rani sat up straight. "Spidersilk . . . ," she repeated.

Mair eyed her in the soft darkness. "Don't even think about it. You'd need spiders, Rai. Riberries. Markin grubs."

"How many, though? We could do this, Mair!"

"You're a better merchant than that, Rai. Don't you think others have tried?" Mair shook her head. "They'll protect those spiders, protect the trees—their very lives depend on it. Besides, even if you managed to steal them, how would you build a market overnight? You'd have to find skilled spinners, weavers, dyers. You'd have to send merchants to trade fairs, cart your goods all over Morenia. Amanthia, too."

"I *am* a better merchant, Mair. I'm good enough to see that we'd never succeed if we try to keep the silk trade all to ourselves, the way the guild does now."

"What else would you do?"

Rani saw the plan unfold before her, as if she had turned a page in a book. "We could disperse the silk monopoly among Hal's nobles. We could look at the taxing rolls. Between Morenia and Amanthia, there surely are a hundred landed nobles. Each man could be required to purchase a riberry tree, markin grubs, a handful of spiders. Each man could pay to the crown . . . ten gold bars for the privilege. Ten bars to start, and ten bars every year thereafter, like payments on land, or a marketplace stall—a license. There's Hal's thousand bars for the Fellowship—more, if he obtains more trees."

"License! Why not tax them directly?"

"They will not pay more taxes. They've been assessed heavily—three years ago, for the campaign in Amanthia, two months ago for the first of the fire costs. You know the border lords are restless; they'll rebel at the first hint that they are being squeezed any tighter. But if they *receive* something for their payment, if they become masters of the precious octolaris . . ."

"This is all a fireside tale, Rai. You'll never get the spiders. Never get the trees."

"But if I *could,* Mair. Just imagine, if I could!"

●

"How many Morenian nobles will be able to keep a riberry tree growing? They're tricky, from all we've heard. And the spiders are poisonous."

"What does it matter? They'll pay to try. We'll help them as best we can. If they fail, or if they fear the octolaris, that will be their problem. Ten gold bars is not an unreasonable wager for future riches. Not if a man can become a knight of the Order of the Octolaris!"

"The *what*?"

"Hal can announce a new knightly order. He can order Davin to design a sash or a pendant, something. The nobles are going to *want* to join him in this endeavor!"

Mair shifted her gaze back to the stream, letting the silent night carry away Rani's enthusiasm. "There's only one problem, Rai."

"What?"

"How are you going to get the spiders? How are you going to get the trees?"

"I'll work on that. I'm a trader. I'll figure out how to get the goods."

"All this, just to meet Glair's demands?" Mair's skepticism was clear, even though her face was lost in the darkness.

"What choice do we have? Hal is determined to make his bid within the Fellowship, and they've handed him the perfect opportunity. Maybe Glair does not want Dartulamino to succeed her after all."

"Rai, you have no idea what Glair wants! Maybe Glair and Dartulamino, together, want to ruin the king with this latest request."

"They've miscalculated, then." Rani's voice was firm, loyal.

Mair waited a long time before she asked, "Do you think they have a presence here, Rai? The Fellowship, in Liantine?"

"They must. They have their fingers in every kingdom. I could ask Flarissa."

"You can't!" Mair exclaimed. "You can't tell her about the Fellowship!"

"I won't *tell* her," Rani said. "I'll ask. I'll just see what Flarissa knows."

"What Flarissa knows about what?" The voice was loud in

the darkness, loud and masculine and wholly unexpected. Rani scrambled to her feet and whirled to face the intruder. Tovin was frowning at the girls as he threw wide the shutter on the lantern that he carried.

"Tovin!" Rani exclaimed. How much had the player overheard?

"What did you want to ask my mother about?"

"Glass," Rani extemporized. "I want to know where you get the glass for your panels. I want to know who you trade with."

Tovin looked at her steadily, his copper eyes reflecting the warm lantern light. A small smile curved the edges of his lips, and he raised his eyebrows, as if in disbelief. "Flarissa isn't the person you should speak to, then. I make the glass screens."

"Then I suppose I'd like to speak with you," she extemporized. "I'd like to see the work you do."

"Aye," he nodded. "But wouldn't you rather eat first? The Meet is finally finished for today. Flarissa sent me to bring you back for supper."

The three of them walked back to the main camp. Rani could see that even more tents were being pitched at the edges of the settlement by the last of the players, the ones who had arrived too late to settle in before the serious business began. Carts now ringed the entire camp, and people called out to one another, greeting old friends with jokes and good cheer. The air was charged with excitement as children tumbled between the tents.

Cooking fires sent forth mouthwatering aromas, and many players already huddled over bowls of stew and hunks of fresh-baked bread. Greenwine flowed freely; numerous barrels had been breached. Tovin lost no time finding leather cups for the girls, and Rani realized for the first time that she liked the bite of the drink at the back of her throat. It smelled sharp and clean, and she drank deeply. She collected a bowl of stew, as well, and wandered toward a makeshift stage.

A team of players was practicing Mair's rope tricks, adding to the challenge by holding streamers, by throwing their bodies into impossible poses as they leaped clear of the spidersilk lengths. They called on Mair to join them, and she declined at first, but managed to be cajoled back into the fray, even though she favored her sore wrist.

"Your friend should take care of her arm."

"Tovin!"

"Aye," he said, grinning wolfishly.

"You should not sneak up on people!"

He looked around the open square, at the clusters of people laughing and drinking, sharing snippets of stories and song. "Sneak?"

"You surprised Mair and me by the stream tonight, and I was not expecting you now!"

"I apologize, Ranita." The glint in his eyes gave the lie to his courteous words. "Were you serious tonight, when you said you wanted to learn about our glasswork?"

"I'm a glasswright," she answered immediately. "I hope to be a journeyman by summer's end."

"So my mother said. She told me that I am to show you the storeroom."

"Now?" Rani looked around at the players.

"Aye, if you'd like. The feasting will go on till dawn. You've never been to a players' celebration—we'll be telling tales all night." Rani started to call out to Mair, to say where she was going. The Touched girl was in the middle of the turning ropes, though, engaged in some new trick. "Of course," Tovin said, "if you'd rather wait . . ."

"No!" Rani protested. "I want to learn."

Tovin led her through the crowd easily. When they arrived at the storeroom, he dug into a pouch at his waist, taking only a moment to extract an iron key. He opened the door with a flourish, and Rani inclined her head at his mockingly gallant gesture. Stepping over the threshold, she felt as if she were a lady in one of the players' tales.

The hut was filled with shadows. The far wall was covered with masks—great, ornate faces that leered and frowned and smiled and gaped at the couple who stood before them. Trunks were open along the sides of the room, spilling forth tangles of costumes and finery. Rani huddled near the doorway as Tovin strode forward. With his back to her, he worked some magic with a lantern on the large table that filled the center of the hut, and a warm, yellow glow spread out across the room.

"Come in," he said, and she stepped forward gingerly, catching her breath against the excitement of being in the presence of the glasswork, the masterpieces she had seen on stage in Liantine. "Close the door behind you."

Rani obeyed mechanically, hearing the latch snick closed as she tugged the oak. The lantern light seemed to swell higher then, picking out more details from the costumes, from the gleaming eyes of masks. The room shrank around her, growing close with its secrets, and Rani was reminded of other dark rooms she had been in, of the hidden passages inside Moren's city walls. There were mysteries here among the players, mysteries that she must pay to understand. The hair rose on the back of her neck.

"Over here," Tovin said, gesturing toward the table.

Shivering, Rani reminded herself that this man was Flarissa's son. Flarissa had been kind to her. Flarissa had watched out for her. Flarissa had Spoken with her. Drawing on the peace of that Speaking, on the quiet strength that welled up from the cobalt pool within her mind, Rani found the courage to cross the room.

Glasswork was laid out on the table. Rani could make out the edges of a design sketched on the whitewashed table in dark charcoal. She could see a tangle of flames, narrow pieces of glass, impossibly long, impossibly fragile.

"You'll never cut those," she breathed, her fingers hovering over the colored tongues.

"Of course I will. How else could we play the story of the firebird?" Tovin was not boasting; he merely stated the truth that he understood.

"How?"

"I don't use grozing irons. I use a diamond knife."

"A diamond knife?" Rani had never heard of such a tool.

"We trade for them. They come from kingdoms far to the south of here." Tovin picked up an instrument, an iron haft with a glinting crystal set in the tip. He offered it to Rani, who stepped closer to look at the curious tool. She turned it about in the lantern light, seeing the impossible thinness of the blade, the sharp edge as fine as a hair. She balanced the knife in her left hand and started to test it with her right index finger. "Careful!" Tovin exclaimed.

"I *was* careful!"

"Not careful enough. It's sharper than any blade you've used before. Here." He reached across the table and selected a piece of clear glass. "Cut this."

Rani glanced down at his hands, holding the glass steady. Now, this close to him, she could see the network of scars that traced across his fingers. It had been years since she had seen hands like that, hands marked by a lifetime of cutting glass and being cut by it. She swallowed hard, surprised by the memories that swept over her, the prideful recollections of her too-few days in the guild that she had loved. She pushed down the ache that welled up in her chest.

Switching the knife to her right hand, she set the point against the clear glass. She started to bear down, with all the force that she would apply to a grozing iron. "No," Tovin said, shaking his head impatiently. "Lighter. The blade is not metal. It's not going to force the glass apart. It's going to *cut* it." Rani relaxed her wrist a little, but still he shook his head. "Lighter still. It's like a pen on parchment. Think of it as drawing a design."

Rani was doubtful that she'd be able to cut the line she wanted, but she eased up on the pressure until it seemed that the knife barely skimmed the surface of the glass. Tovin nodded, and she pulled the diamond blade toward her. The thinnest of lines melted onto the clear glass.

Tovin leaned forward and set two fingers on the pieces, pulling them apart easily. Rani gasped in astonishment—it was impossible that he had separated the pane with so little effort. "See?" he asked. "I can make long pieces, because I don't need as much pressure to break them." She nodded slowly, imagining the complicated designs she could craft with Tovin's knife. She clutched the tool with fingers suddenly stiff with longing. The player noticed, nodding as he said, "You've much to learn, Ranita Glasswright, and I can teach you. For a price."

Rani froze for just a moment, and then she set the diamond knife on the table. Suddenly, she was aware of the cut of her

gown, the flow of linen that smoothed across her thighs. She
felt her hair against her neck, curling in the lantern light. She
was standing too close to Tovin, close enough that she felt the
heat of his body. She took a step away and crossed her arms
over her chest. She forced herself to say, "Of course. There's always a price."

For just an instant, Tovin stared at her with his copper eyes,
penetrating and shrewd. Then, he smiled, and he shook his
head. He, too, took a step away from the whitewashed table,
and he held his hands before him, shrugging. The lantern
caught the pathway of glass scars, highlighting the white lines.
"Not what you are thinking, Ranita. We players do not collect
our tolls in flesh."

Rani flushed, but she pulled her arms closer about her.
"What, then?"

"Speak with me. Now."

Rani immediately thought of the pool of cobalt glass that
Flarissa had shown her, of the soothing, powerful path that she
had found. She remembered the peace and the power, the
strength of the Speaking, and a shiver trembled from her neck
to her spine to her limbs.

"I've done that already," she whispered. "I Spoke with
Flarissa."

"Aye, that was one bargain, to see our panels. This is another. To learn how I make them. To learn a journeyman's
skills."

Rani looked at Tovin's hands. She imagined cobalt glass
nudging the white scars. She thought of the glasswright secrets
that he could teach her, lessons beyond diamond knives. When
she raised her gaze to his eyes, she found him staring hard at
her. His breath was even, but she sensed his excitement. His
voice was calm, though, as he said, "You do not need to do this.
No one can force another to Speak."

"I'll do it."

"This is your own choice, Ranita."

"I'll do it," she repeated.

Still he eyed her, nodding slowly. "Very well, then." Tovin
gestured toward a pallet that lay at the far end of the storehouse.
When she hesitated, he said, "I will not touch you, Ranita

Glasswright. You've felt the power of Speech before. You know that I cannot make you do what you do not want to do."

Rani knew that. She knew that he could not force her to tell stories against her will. She remembered the power of Speaking with Flarissa like a physical thing. She longed for it the way a drunkard longed for ale, the way a bride longed for her groom. That ache was what frightened Rani—not Tovin, not the man.

Swallowing her fear, her desire, she crossed to the pallet. When she settled on the edge, her spine was as rigid as wood. She watched as Tovin turned back to the whitewashed table. He moved his hands among the tools there, and he palmed something before he crossed to her. She raised her chin as he approached, brave, defiant.

He laughed. "Relax, Ranita Glasswright. I cannot take anything that you don't offer freely. Take a deep breath." He settled beside her, leaning back on one elbow. His weight forced her to shift on the pallet, and she rested her hands on either side of her body.

"Relax," he repeated. She forced herself to take a deep breath and exhale slowly, unclenching her fists. "That's right," he said. "Breathe in. Breathe out." A child shrieked outside, squealing with laughter, and Rani flinched. "Ignore the noises," Tovin said. "Listen to my voice. You can hear the players, you know that they are there, but they will not bother you. They will not distract you. That's right, Ranita. Breathe in. Breathe out."

She felt herself absorb the rhythm of his words, felt her body sag as she filled her lungs and emptied them. Tovin nodded slowly, and then he moved one closed fist between them. "Here, Ranita. Here's the glass you carved upon the table." He opened his fingers slowly, revealing the curve-edged piece of clear glass. Slowly, cautiously, he tilted it toward her. "Think of cutting the glass, Ranita. Think of the power in your wrist as you hold the diamond knife. Power that flows from your shoulder, down your arm, to your hand, to your fingers. To the knife."

She watched the ripple of light on the cut glass surface, remembered the control and grace that she had possessed while using the diamond blade. Tovin tilted the glass a little farther, and it collected all the lamplight in the room. "That's right, Ranita. Do you see the light? Do you see the glass?"

"Yes."

"Very good, Ranita. Look inside the glass. Look inside it as if it were a mirror. You can see yourself in the glass. Do you see yourself, Ranita?"

"Yes." Rani saw herself sitting on the edge of the pallet, saw Tovin sprawled beside her.

"Very good, Ranita. I'm going to count to ten now, and with every number, you will move further into the mirror. Reach deep into yourself. Deep into the peace. Deep into the Speaking. One. Two. Three."

Rani heard Tovin begin the numbers. She heard each one form on his lips; she absorbed each one with a breath. She pulled herself further into the white light, deeper into the pool of calm awareness that she had crafted with the diamond blade. "Nine," she heard him say. "Ten."

She was aware that her head had drooped, that her chin was resting against the lacy edge of her bodice. She felt the incredible burden of her arms, so heavy that her hands were numb; her fingers were lost. She felt the pallet beneath her, but it seemed a lifetime away.

"Can you hear me, Ranita?" Tovin's voice was clear, sharp, as distinct as an edge of glass. She heard him, and she held on to his presence, even as she moved further away from her self.

"Yes," she tried to say, but she realized that she had only opened her mouth, had only shaped the word.

"Very good, Ranita. You are very good at Speaking. You have power. I knew that you had power when I heard you talk to Mair tonight."

Rani pictured herself beside the stream, pictured the night gathering close about her. She and Mair had been talking about the Fellowship, about her octolaris plan. Secrets. Her breath caught in her throat, and she felt her brow wrinkle into a frown.

"No, Ranita Glasswright. Stay inside the Speaking. Stay inside the mirror. You're safe here. You don't have to tell me anything that you don't want to tell."

Rani let herself be stilled by his words. She let herself slip back into the white comfort, into the weightless, hazy realm in-

side the diamond-cut mirror. Tovin said, "You sat beside the
stream. You spoke with Mair, and you let the water carry away
your words. You let the water wash away, flow away, ease
away. You were worried while you spoke with Mair. You were
afraid. But the stream carried all your burdens. Do you remember the stream, Ranita? Do you remember the water?"

"Yes."

"The water will keep you safe, Ranita Glasswright. It will
keep your secrets. Think of the water, Ranita. Think of it holding you. Covering you. Protecting you."

She felt the water, felt it flowing over her. She felt the cool
stream wash over her toes, her ankles, her legs. She leaned back
into the blood-warm flow, leaned back until her hair streamed
down the riverbed, until she was floating, weightless and cradled in the ever-changing, ever-perfect stream.

"You can speak now, Ranita Glasswright. You can tell the
water your secrets. You can speak them and be safe. Tell the
stream about the Fellowship."

Rani knew she must be cautious. She must not tell Tovin all
that she knew about the Fellowship, all she knew about the cell
led by Glair. Nevertheless, the player had clearly heard something that evening. How could it hurt for her to say a little now?

"We're sisters," she said, and her words swirled into the
flow of the stream.

"Who?"

"Mair and me. We're sisters in the Fellowship."

"Who else is in the Fellowship?"

What had she said beside the stream? What did Tovin already know? "Glair."

"And who else?"

Who else had she named? Had she spoken of Hal? Had she
called him by name? She could not be certain, and she did not
want to tell Tovin more than he already knew. "Others," she
said at last. "Many others."

The stream continued to flow, warm and swift, carrying her
along in a flood of white, white light. She felt a surge of peace
rise within her as she realized that she *was* in control. She *could*
decide not to Speak, not to share Hal's name.

If Tovin worried that she had not answered completely, he gave no sign. "And what does the Fellowship do?"

Do? The question was so large. It stretched across the streambed, filling all the space from one bank to the other. Do? Rani could not begin to form an answer.

Tovin waited, and then he said patiently, "Does the Fellowship gather regularly?"

That, at least, was simple. "No."

"Does the Fellowship ever gather?"

"Yes."

"Tell me of the last time the Fellowship gathered, Rani. Tell me what happened."

Rani paused in the middle of the stream, thinking of the trip that she and Mair had made through the ruined streets of Moren. She could Speak of the Fellowship's meeting. She could share it with Tovin. He already knew that Glair was a member. So long as she kept Hal's name a secret, she could Speak. "It was after the fire. After the fire that ruined Moren."

She heard her voice from a distance, as if the flow of water filled her ears. As she spoke, the words were carried away, washed downstream, moved beyond any place where they could harm her, could harm Hal, could harm Morenia. With every question that Tovin asked, Rani found her burden lightened. The relief of Speaking about the Fellowship nearly made her weep.

She had not realized how difficult it was to keep the shadowy brotherhood secret. Every answer carried her deeper into the safety, deeper into the peace, deeper into the security of the Speaking. She told of the Fellowship's hidden meetings and the black masks that members wore. She told of their shadowy plans for conquering kingdoms, the dreams that the Fellowship harbored. She told of power, raw power, kept chained in secret channels that coursed beneath Morenian politics.

The Speaking protected the telling, protected Rani. It released her from the terrible weight of living her double life. Nothing bad could happen while she was Speaking. The Fellowship could not control her, would not threaten her. It could not make demands of her, as it had of Hal.

She was *right* to Speak. She gained power by Speaking. And

still, she could control her words, she could preserve her secrets. She did not tell Tovin that the king of all Morenia and Amanthia belonged to the Fellowship.

At last, Tovin ran out of questions. Rani floated in the pure, pure stream, and she heard him breathing, heard him swallow. She heard the revelry outside the cottage, but she only waited for Tovin to speak. "Very well, Ranita Glasswright," he said at last. "If you agree, we might Speak of these things again, another day. Is that all right?"

She thought of descending to this calm, quiet place, to the freedom of their honest exchange. "Yes."

"Good. Thank you, Ranita." She felt him shift on the pallet, and she realized that he had moved closer to her as he asked her questions. Still, he had not touched her. He had promised that he would not, and he had held true to that promise.

"It is time for you to leave the stream now. Time to come back to the players' camp. I'm going to count from ten to one, and you'll move with me, back to the camp, back to the storeroom. You'll remember everything we've spoken about, but you will not be afraid. You'll feel rested and awake. Ten. Nine. Eight," he counted slowly. The stream moved more sluggishly. Rani felt herself pulled, dripping and renewed, from the water. "Seven, six, five." She was back in the white light, back in the gleaming mirror. "Four. Three." She could feel her body, feel her fingers, feel her toes. "Two. One."

Her eyes flew open. She was lying on the pallet, her hair spread out behind her. She could not remember reclining on the fragrant mattress; she could not remember slumping so that her legs were sprawled like a child's.

Tovin leaned beside her, his weight still resting on one elbow, his free hand cradling the clear glass. He smiled as she blinked, and he helped her to sit up. "How do you feel?" he asked.

She took a deep breath, and a smile spread across her lips. She felt as if she'd slept for days. She felt as if she'd been breathing the warm aroma of fresh-baked bread for a lifetime. She felt as if she'd been singing for hours. She felt alive and weightless, unburdened. "Free," she said. Tovin helped her to her feet. "And hungry."

"Speaking will do that." He laughed and crossed to the whitewashed table, setting the clear glass beside its companion. "We players can solve that problem, easily enough." Rani was barely aware of his glass-scarred palm at the small of her back as he escorted her from the hut.

11

Hal looked up from the letter he was reading, seeking out Farsobalinti's eyes. "She suggests that we call it the Order of the Octolaris."

"Order of the Octolaris." Farso shook his head, reaching for the parchment and reading the words for himself.

Hal grimaced. Certainly, the idea was creative. Certainly, it would accomplish his most secret goal—gathering together the funds he needed to pay the Fellowship. But it involved octolaris.

Even thinking the word called to mind Mareka. The spiderguild apprentice had left his room a fortnight before, but since that day, she had never been far from his thoughts. Even now, imagining how he might negotiate for spiders, for riberry trees, his pulse quickened. There was something about the woman, some power she held over him. . . .

This was different from the bond he felt with Rani. This had nothing to do with honor and respect and desire to see the woman succeed. With the spiderguild apprentice, he was drawn to remember every touch. He was compelled to relive the sound of her voice, the fragrance of her hair, the silver light that had seemed to jump from her fingertips to his flesh. . . .

"Sire." Hal pulled himself back from his memories, hoping that Farso would keep his eyes upon the letter for a moment longer, until the flush could fade from Hal's shamed cheeks. As if the knight could read his thoughts, Farso stood up to pace, tapping Rani's letter against his palm. "It's easy enough for Rani Trader to say that she'll get you spiders. How does she intend to do that, though? Surely the Liantines have tried before—the spiderguild exists within their very borders!"

"If anyone can do it, Rani can." Hal was resolute. "After all, she unveiled the Brotherhood of Justice after they killed my brother. She faced down King Sin Hazar and liberated the Little Army."

"But poisonous spiders worth a king's ransom?"

"She would not have written if she did not have some plan."

Farso shrugged, accepting his liege lord's quiet conviction. Still, he probed. "I can see your nobles embracing a new-created order. There's been little enough to celebrate of late. I can see them trying to build their own silk trade, trying to get the trees to grow, the spiders to breed. How will you convince them, though, to pay for the privilege? Ten bars of gold, my lord? That is a great deal, on top of all the other taxes they have paid since you took your throne."

"Ten bars is nothing!" Hal protested. How often had he paid ten bars to the Fellowship, after all?

Farso's blue eyes were troubled. "May I speak honestly, my lord?"

"As if you have not before?" Hal waved a hand. "Of course, Farso. You may always speak honestly to me."

Farso sighed. "You say that ten bars are nothing, and in the face of your expenses, you are right. Five hundred you must pay over to the church by Midsummer Day, and five thousand after that. Still, to most of your nobles, my lord, to many of the men who serve you best, ten bars of gold is a massive stake. For many, it will be all that they have saved throughout the years."

"It is a bid for future wealth. Spidersilk will amply repay every man who joins us."

"It will, ultimately. But spidersilk will take great effort. It will take skill, and it will endanger lives. Remember Crestman, and his tale of the child from the Little Army. Octolaris kill. At least some do. I am not saying that your lords will refuse, but this would all be easier if you could explain why such a sacrifice is necessary. The Order of the Octolaris must do more than satisfy a—" He waved his hand in frustration, clearly searching for a word. "—a whim."

Hal stared at Farso. Of course. Hal and Rani, and Mair,

too—they all knew why the Order was necessary, why Hal must find a thousand bars of gold. To Farso, however, to all the rest of Hal's retainers . . . The request must sound greedy. It must sound short-sighted and mean-spirited. He swallowed hard and said, "Is it not enough that I ask it, when I have asked nothing similar in all my time as king?"

"You have, though, Sire." Farso sighed. "Your plans for the order are similar to raising funds for Amanthia. They resemble rebuilding Moren. Why now? What cause do you have to require payment now?"

It would be so easy to tell him. So easy to admit the Fellowship's existence, to admit his desire to lead the shadowy body. The words would take away responsibility, remove the need for skulking and hiding.

And yet Hal could not divulge the secret. There were other lives at stake, anonymous members of the Fellowship who might suffer if they were unveiled. Besides, the Fellowship did have a plan, a grand scheme—one that had largely been hidden from him so far, but one that he firmly believed existed. One that he intended to direct, intended to shape and guide to completion.

He tried a lie. "I need the money because the costs of rebuilding Moren are even more than we predicted. The engineers have said that we must raze even some sections of the city that we thought were secure. While we continue our fight to recover from the fire, disease still spreads. The weed that Mair discovered—the one she hopes will treat firelung—is more costly than any tincture a Morenian leech has ever brewed. Yet, if I announce all this, if I tell my people, I fear that they will lose all heart, and our recovery will be doomed."

Mair's weeds. The lamb's tongue had arrived in Liantine two days before. The farmer who sold it had been overjoyed at disposing of all his crop, and he had crowed over a scant handful of coins. He had even helped to stow the dried bales beneath the deck of Hal's own ship.

Well, Mair was a member of the Fellowship, every bit as much as Hal was. She would have to help him now. She would have to foment one more lie, if Farso ever asked.

Now, Farso stared at Hal, his face even more pale than

usual. When he replied, his words were strangled. "I did not know, my lord. I thought that we had measured all those costs, that the loan you negotiated from the church was enough. I did not realize the burden that you still bear, the fears that must be preying on you, even here in Liantine." He shook his head. "Forgive me, Sire. Of course you know what is best for Morenia. If you say we need the Order of the Octolaris, then you may be certain I agree."

Hal felt like a liar, a cheater, a snake. Nevertheless, he clarified: "Ten gold bars, then, from every landed noble."

Farso nodded and dropped to his knees at Hal's feet. "It will be done, Sire. I ask only that you honor me as the first member of the Order of the Octolaris."

Hal's throat tightened. "Aye, my lord. You will be the first to stand by my side." He raised Farso to his feet, thinking, *assuming I get the riberries.* Assuming I get the spiders. Assuming I can keep myself from Mareka Octolaris and the disaster that will happen if our liaison is ever known, if Teheboth ever finds that I insulted his hospitality and his daughter by bedding a commoner beneath his roof. "The very first. And may I ask another thing of you, an easy thing compared to that?"

"Of course, Sire."

"Please send a letter to Rani Trader. Tell her first that I say, 'It will be so.' She will know you write of spiders. And tell her that I go to speak with Berylina today. I'll ask Teheboth for the princess's hand in marriage before the sun sets."

"I will, Sire." Farso knew enough of Rani that he did not pretend those tidings would be glad.

"Also, write to Davin, back in Moren. Command him to design a pendant for the Order and have it cast one hundred times."

"It will be done, Sire." Farso turned toward the door, confidence quickening his step. Only as he passed over the threshold did Hal call out, "Oh, and Farso? One thing more. Could you send in Father Siritalanu?"

"Again?" the knight asked, clearly speaking before he could stop himself.

"Aye."

Hal had called for the priest often in the past two weeks. In the aftermath of his . . . encounter with Mareka, he had sought the comfort of the church that he had known since childhood. He longed for the reassurance of all the Thousand Gods, even though he was too ashamed to admit to the young religious precisely how he had yielded to temptation, how he had endangered his embassy.

"Sire, if you'd rather that *I* stay . . ."

"I'd rather that you help me where you can do the most good, Farso. Don't look so worried. I'm a bridegroom, or at least I plan to be. It is only natural that I seek the guidance of the Thousand Gods before I go to Princess Berylina."

Farso clearly disagreed with Hal's assessment, but years of serving his lord won out against further protest. "Aye, Sire." Farso bowed again and left the chamber.

Grateful for the man's devotion, Hal crossed his apartment to the small prie-dieu that huddled in the corner. He lowered himself to the wooden kneeler and touched his head to the carved oak upright, calling upon First Pilgrim Jair for guidance. He had spoken to his forefather often in the past fortnight, addressing him as a familiar.

"Jair, you founded my house, and you carved out a line of kings. What temptations did you face? What tests did you fail?"

Hal's prayers were silent, repeating the questions he had asked himself for two full weeks. Even as he settled down to wordless contemplation of his sins, he was interrupted by memories—by the flash of Mareka's eyes in the grey light of his chamber, by the gleam of her supple arm as it whispered from beneath her spidersilk gown. Hal forced himself deeper into his prayers, but he could not forget the heat of his fever, the strange, heady passion that had overtaken him so inexplicably. He lost himself in the recollection of Mareka's kiss, of the heat that had burned from her body into his.

"You called for me, Sire?"

Hal jerked away from his reverie. Father Siritalanu hovered just inside the door, his hands hanging heavy inside their emerald sleeves. The priest was young, as young as Hal—that was one reason that Hal had accepted the cleric into his entourage. Like all the noble priestly caste, Siritalanu was a distant cousin, kin so vague that Hal would need a herald to be certain of the ties that bound them.

"Aye, Father. Thank you for coming," Hal said. "I wanted you to guide me in my prayers."

"Certainly, Sire." The priest closed the door behind him with precision. With the same precision Mareka had used when she had locked out the outside world . . . Hal sucked in his breath, as if he had burned himself on his memories. He would *not* conflate the priest's actions with those of the spiderguild apprentice; he would not sin that gravely.

Siritalanu came to stand beside the prie-dieu, running his hand over the top of the prayer bench. "It is good that you call me when you wish to pray, Your Majesty. It is good to reach out to the Thousand Gods at this changing time in your life. The gods watch over all their children with pride, but they are particularly pleased when we turn to them at times of celebration."

"I am far from home, Father, and I feel the need for comfort."

"Let us pray, then." Hal bowed his head before the young priest. "Let us pray in the name of Fen, the god of mercy."

Hal clenched his hands on the back of the prie-dieu, trying to collect his thoughts. He tried to remember that he was the Defender of the Faith, invested with that office at the same time that he was crowned king of all Morenia. The Thousand Gods should look upon him with favor. With forgiveness.

The priest whispered, "Hail Fen, god of mercy. Forgive us our transgressions, Fen, and find a path for us back to the ways of righteousness."

Hal forced himself to repeat the words, trying to anchor himself upon their familiarity. He let Siritalanu move him from Fen, to Kom, the god of courage, to Lum, the god of love, and—finally—Rit, the god of marriages.

The priest was right, of course. Why not enlist Rit's help before Hal spoke with Berylina? Why not embrace the power of every one of the Thousand Gods? Hal forced himself to relax in Siritalanu's prayerful words. He let himself be lulled by the priest, by the familiar petitions that washed over him, that flowed from his mouth. There was comfort in the prayers, comfort in kneeling humbly, comfort in the familiar silence of the Thousand Gods.

When Hal had completed his appeal to Rit, he left his head bowed for several long minutes. Siritalanu remained kneeling beside him; his presence barely measured by his breathing. Silence enfolded the two men, bonding, comforting, protecting.

But Hal knew that he could not stay at the prie-dieu forever. He could not stay in the paneled apartments that had been assigned to him by King Teheboth, in the chamber where Rani had left him, where Mareka had come to him. The warm coverlet of comfort woven by the prayers began to fray, and Hal forced himself to breathe deeply, as if he were a soldier settling into his gear and heading off to battle.

It was time. Time to go to Berylina.

He stood shakily and leaned against the back of the prie-dieu. The priest clambered to his feet as well, reaching out a hand to steady him. "Are you all right, Your Majesty? You look pale."

"I am fine, Father." Father. The priest was a boy; what could he know of Hal's trepidation? He was no one's *father*. The word shivered through Hal's guilty memories as he remembered Mareka's touch, as he remembered her flesh melting into his. No! Hal was not a father, either. Hal could not be a father. Not yet. Not until he had taken a proper bride. The gods could not be so cruel.

"Your Majesty!" Siritalanu gasped as Hal's knees began to buckle.

"I am fine," Hal repeated, gasping sharply and forcing his head to clear, forcing the dizziness to abate. In the distance, a bell began to toll, and he swallowed hard. "I am expected in Princess Berylina's solar, Father."

"Perhaps you would like me to send her a message, Your Majesty. I can tell the princess that you are not well enough to join her."

"No, Father. That is not possible."

"I'll come with you, then."

Hal started to dismiss the earnest young man. After all, what more could the priest do for him? What more could he do, with

his round eyes and his smooth cheeks, his boyish good nature?
Siritalanu could never understand all the issues at hand.

What could it hurt, though? A priest was proper. A priest belonged on the fringes of a courtship—more than a merchant
did, more than an apprentice. A religious presence would
be . . . appropriate.

Hal raised a hand to the circlet on his brow, as if checking to
make sure that the weight was centered. His head ached, but
that might be from the weight of the fillet, or from his sleeplessness, or from his hunger. . . .

"Come, then, Father," he said grimly. "We mustn't keep the
princess waiting."

"Aye, Your Majesty." The priest made a small bow and followed him out of the chamber.

They passed others in the hallways, Liantines intent on their
daily work about the castle. Hal nodded when he should, looking left and right like the king he was. No one stopped to stare
at him. No one stopped to ogle. His blemished conscience was
not apparent on his face, not marked on his fine robes. For all
these Liantines knew, Hal was the same man he'd always been,
the same moral suitor king.

Even Berylina's nurses were unaware of how he had
changed in the past two weeks.

"My lord!" the youngest said as soon as he stepped into the
solar. Both attendants dropped into pretty curtseys.

"My lady," Hal replied courteously, waving both women to
rise. "Please! Do not stand on ceremony for me!" He forced a
smile across his lips. "Father Siritalanu and I thought that we
would come and partake of the warm spring sunshine here in
the solar." He turned to Berylina and braced himself. "Good
morning, my lady."

"Good morning, my lord," Berylina replied without prompting—a fine sign. She licked her lips nervously, though, drawing unfortunate attention to the rabbit teeth that got in the way
of her tongue.

Hal crossed to the windows, looking down at the Liantine
harbor. He wanted to be on his own ship. He wanted to carry
Mair's firelung weed back to Morenia, to supervise the difficult
labor of tearing down the old city, building up the new. But he

could not leave yet. He must finish his mission here. He forced himself to concentrate, to turn back to the child he was courting. "Have you been drawing today, my lady?"

Berylina flushed shyly, ducking her head to study her hands. Nevertheless, she darted a glance toward her easel, and Hal crossed to study the work in progress.

She had begun the drawing with black charcoal, outlining the figure with determined, heavy lines. The man's cloak fell in neat folds. His legs were sketched with skill, making it appear that he strode off the parchment. A fillet circled his brow, capturing a glint of light, and a heavy chain was strung around his neck. Hal stepped closer to study that chain, and he saw that it was fashioned of interlocking *J*s. *J* for Jair. *J* for the Defender of the Faith. He immediately looked at the figure's face, his stomach tightening as he expected to see his own features reproduced. But Berylina had not yet finished her work. The drawing's visage remained blank.

Hal swallowed hard and darted a glance toward Siritalanu before choosing the safest conclusion. "It's Jair, then."

"Aye," the princess confirmed, apparently grateful that he had been able to identify the portrait. "The First Pilgrim." Hal thought that the girl would not manage any further words, but then she closed her poor, crossed eyes and said, "I thought to draw him as a gift for you. I thought to give him to you when you return to Morenia. When will you be leaving, my lord?"

Hal was touched by her earnest tone, by her naive hope. She must sense that time was disappearing, that Hal's mission was coming to a head. Now, he must speak honestly. He must destroy the princess's fragile hopes and make her recognize her future. He knew now that he would wed her; there had never been any real doubt.

He made his voice as gentle as he could. "Soon, my lady. Soon, we both will leave. I intend to bring you to my home, as my bride."

There was a rustle among Berylina's nurses. Certainly *they* could not be surprised by Hal's announcement. Speculation had been running high throughout all Liantine, from the moment his boat had docked in the harbor. Nevertheless, this was the first time that he had dared to speak of his plans directly to the princess. She blushed furiously and looked away, twisting her hands in her skirts.

Hal felt an answering heat rise in his own cheeks. He should have planned this conversation more completely. He should have figured out precisely what he would say, not left an awkward silence where the princess must respond. Foolishly, he had confessed his intentions on the spur of the moment, inspired by Berylina's drawing and her pathetic question, but now that he had begun, he was bound to continue. He sank to one knee in front of her, capturing one pudgy hand in his. "That is, my lady, if you will have me. If you will allow the crown of Morenia to settle on your brow."

Poor Berylina's fingers were slick between his own, and she looked as if she would dearly love to flee somewhere, anywhere. She glanced at the easel, at the stack of parchment beside the stand, at her expectant nurses. Her throat worked, but she seemed unable to make any sound emerge.

Hal waited patiently, looking up at his intended. The longer he paused, though, the more flustered the princess became. She closed her eyes, and her breath came fast, so fast that he began to fear that she would faint. Her lips trembled, as if she were about to weep. "My lady!" Hal exclaimed, transferring some of his own nervousness to his exclamation.

The cry proved too much for the princess; she pulled her hand from his and whirled away. Before Hal could rise up, Berylina had fled to the far corner of her solar, flinging herself onto her knees. She bent her head and made a holy sign across her chest. Her lips moved in frantic, desperate prayer.

Astonished, Hal clambered to his feet, but he restrained himself from crossing to the distressed child. Father Siritalanu refused to meet his eyes; the priest studied the drawing of Jair as if it held the secrets of all the Thousand Gods. Both nurses looked at their charge with pity, and then the older once said, "I'm sorry, my lord. Her Highness is not well today. She was up quite early, making her drawings, and she must be overtired."

Hal heard the attempt to spare his royal sensitivities, the bid to treat Berylina's actions as normal. He wanted to protest that he had meant her no harm. He had intended to *honor* her with his request. He had thought it would be easier for the child to hear him ask for her hand directly. It wasn't as if she had a say in what would actually happen, after all. It wasn't as if she would be permitted by Teheboth to decide whom she would wed.

"I understand, my lady," Hal forced himself to say graciously to the nurse. He straightened his tunic and looked across at the princess, whose shoulders were now shaking— with either tears or frantic gasps, Hal could not be sure. "I would not disturb Her Highness any more than I already have."

He bowed stiffly and started to turn back to the door, but Berylina cried out. "Your Majesty!" she sobbed, but she would not turn to face him. "I am sorry, my lord!"

Hal's heart twisted inside his chest as he thought what the words must cost her. "No, Your Highness. The sorrow is mine. I did not intend to distress you. By all the Thousand Gods, my lady, that was never my intent."

"B—By all the Thousand Gods," Berylina whispered, her words scarcely audible across the room.

At her faint speech, Father Siritalanu stepped forward, as if he had only just come to life in the solar's bright sunshine. "The Thousand Gods look upon all their children with grace, my lady." The priest's voice was young and earnest, loud in the glass-walled room.

"Yes, Father," Berylina responded, swiveling her splintered gaze to look at the green-clad man.

"The Thousand Gods favor the brave, my lady," Siritalanu continued, stepping out of Hal's shadow.

"Yes, Father," Berylina repeated, and her voice was stronger.

"Will you pray with me, lady? Will you raise your voice to First Pilgrim Jair and all the Thousand Gods?"

"Yes, Father," Berylina said one more time, and then she added, "please."

Siritalanu glanced at Hal, as if asking permission, and the king waved his priest across the room. Anything, he wanted to say. Anything to keep the princess from sobbing, from crying so desperately to be spared the terrible fate of wedding him.

Father Siritalanu nodded as if he were accepting a military

commission, and then he strode across the solar. He knelt beside the princess and took her hands between his own, and if he noticed that they were slick with perspiration, he did not show that knowledge on his smooth, unlined face. Instead, he nodded once, and he pitched his voice so low that Hal could scarcely hear him.

"Have you prayed to Nome before, my lady? Have you prayed to the god of children?"

"Aye," Berylina said. "But not for many weeks."

"Let us speak with him, then. Let us speak to Nome, and then to some of his brethren. In the name of Nome, let us pray." Siritalanu bowed his head then, and the motion brought him even closer to the princess. She followed suit, her unruly hair bobbing as she began to whisper formulaic words with the priest.

Hal watched for a moment. He was grateful to Siritalanu, grateful that the priest would take the initiative to calm the princess. He waited until he heard Siritalanu say, "Let us also pray to Fen. Let us pray to the god of mercy." The priest had mercy on his mind today. Well, Fen had been good enough for Hal to address, so why not send the princess's prayers in that direction, as well?

Hal padded softly to the door. The nurses watched him move as if they were afraid of what he might do, but Berylina seemed entirely unaware of his passage.

Siritalanu knew, though. The priest looked up as Hal reached the doorway, his eyes solemn as they met Hal's across the room. The religious rested a hand on Berylina's wiry hair, spreading his fingers wide, as if he were gathering some precious essence from those unruly strands. His lips curved into a calm smile, a peaceful smile, a smile that Hal could imagine a mother sharing in a private moment with a child. Siritalanu inclined his head slightly, and Hal nodded his gratitude before he left the solar.

Only when he stood outside the room, on the dim landing at the top of the stairs, did he begin to shudder in revulsion. What sort of monster was he? What sort of man so terrified his prospective bride that she ran from him, fled sobbing into a corner, into the arms of a priest? And what horror would Berylina suffer if she knew the full extent of Hal's sin, if she knew the things that he had done with Mareka Octolaris?

If Hal were a true man, he would stride back into the solar and speak to Berylina. He would release her from his schemes, from all his machinations. He would tell her that he never meant to frighten her, that he never intended to force her to be his bride.

And yet, Hal did not have that luxury. He was a warrior-king, fighting to save Morenia, fighting to control the Fellowship, no matter the cost. If one child, one endowered princess, could save his kingdom, what choice did Hal have?

And perhaps Berylina would come to love him. Stranger things had happened. And if she could not love, then perhaps she could come to trust him. And even if she was never able to trust him, perhaps she would one day not be afraid. At least that, by all the Thousand Gods. Let Berylina no longer be afraid.

Hal wound down the twisting stairs. The true business of this transaction was not to be done with the princess. It was time to confront Teheboth Thunderspear.

Hal walked toward the Great Hall, where he knew Teheboth was holding court. The Liantine king had predicted that his cases would occupy him until midday, but he had pledged to spend the afternoon touring the wharf with Hal, showing him the recently completed system the Liantines had installed for docking new and larger trading boats. A system of beams and hoists with iron grappling hooks enabled stevedores to empty a fully laden ship in two days, less than half the time the same ship would take in Moren.

Hal strode into the Great Hall with pretended confidence. As expected, Teheboth was seated on his throne, centered before the glistening green-and-silver spidersilk hangings that had been Jerusha Octolaris's bride-gift. The Liantine monarch looked every inch a ruler, surrounded by nobles and retainers, by attentive lords and scribbling scribes.

For just an instant, Hal regretted that he had not waited, that he had not assembled an entourage to impress Teheboth. Surely Hal should have someone at his side at this auspicious moment—Farso, at the very least.

That was ridiculous, Hal chided himself. He was only seeking a reason to delay. He was only trying to put off the inevitable bargaining. He did not need Farso. He did not need anyone. He was a man in his own right. A noble. A king.

Teheboth flicked a glance toward Hal, but he did not spare his royal visitor a word. Instead, he turned his full attention back to the nobleman kneeling before him.

"Very well, then, Hestaron. You clearly cut down trees that did not belong to you, and the lumber is already lost at sea, lost in the ship that sank. You cannot make remunerations directly for your wrong. You leave me with no choice but to order a restoration of coin."

Hestaron bowed his head, and Hal could read jagged tension across the man's shoulders. His rote response sounded heavy, dull, as he said, "That would be a mercy, Your Majesty."

"You shall pay to your neighbor three times the value of the trees that you cut—three times the value, in gold coin, by no later than the first day of winter."

Hestaron's head shot up, and a look of incredulity crossed his face. "Your Majesty, I cannot make such payment! I lost my goods at sea! In the name of all the Thousand Gods, have mercy!"

"Silence!" Teheboth cut off the man's protest. "The slavish Thousand Gods conduct no business here! For that sacrilegious outburst, you will make an offering to the Horned Hind. You will pay to her priests the value, once again, of all the trees that you cut down."

"Mercy, Your Majesty, I beg of you! Where am I to find such funds? You said, yourself, my ship sank in the first spring storm."

"Aye, Hestaron. Your ship sank. The Hind seeks vengeance in mysterious ways. You will find the funds, or borrow them, or raise them from your vassals, whatever you must do. If not, you will be sold to any honest bidder, and your debts will be paid from your slave-price."

"By all—," Hestaron began again, but then he smothered his words. "Aye, Your Majesty," he managed, barely able to choke out the rest of the expected reply. "Your Majesty is merciful and just."

Teheboth's eyes glinted as he acknowledged the formula, and he waved his nobleman to his feet. "Be gone, then. We'll expect you at our first winter court, with records showing you have paid in full."

Hestaron muttered as he strode past Hal, clenching his hands into fists. The braid of his beard trembled as his lips worked, and Hal quailed before the man's fury. What land was this, where slavery was a threat hanging over vassals' heads? Where calling on the Thousand Gods cost men honest gold? And how had Berylina clung to her faith in a household where the Horned Hind was so firmly entrenched?

"Morenia!" Teheboth shouted from his throne, cutting short Hal's speculation. "Are you ready to break bread with us, then?"

"Aye, my lord," Hal answered, striding down the aisle to meet Teheboth.

The Liantine king gestured expansively to the courtiers assembled in the hall, to the frantic scribes and heralds. "It has been a long morning, with everyone eager to finalize business before the cycle of summer fairs begins. Let us leave this room, so that the clerks can finish their work."

Hal nodded in agreement, following Teheboth to a smaller chamber, a windowed room stripped bare of clinging spidersilk. Wooden panels gleamed in the light, smooth reminders of Teheboth's woodland goddess. A table had already been laid with a fresh-baked loaf of bread, a round of creamy cheese, and a flagon of ale. The king of Liantine poured two cups and proffered one to his guest, all the time discussing the matters that he had heard that morning, the difficult decisions he had made for the good of all his people.

Hal listened to the stories and offered polite agreement when required. Even as Teheboth boasted, Hal tried to calculate a way to broach his own difficult case. Before he could pull the talk around to Berylina, Teheboth set his goblet firmly on the table. His braided beard jutted forward as he said, "So. You want my daughter, and you want me to pay to be rid of her."

Hal was startled by the king's directness. For just an instant, he wished that he had Rani by his side, even if Teheboth would have disregarded her woman's words. "I would have our houses joined in friendship, my lord."

"And that means Berylina, does it not? Unless you're planning on whelping a daughter on some other dam and teaming her with one of my boys."

Hal cleared his throat. "I ask for Berylina's hand in marriage."

"I haven't much to offer in the way of a dowry. Not with four boys to maintain, and the cost of Olric's marriage still smarting."

Hal despised himself for the greedy protest that rose to his lips, but he said dispassionately, "What can you do, then? What gifts does Princess Berylina bring?"

"Two hundred bars of gold." Teheboth set the figure on the table between them, as if he were reciting the cost of bread and cheese. "Along with the usual trappings and finery of a girl of her station, of course."

Two hundred bars. Not even half of what Hal needed, of what he must pay the church on Midsummer Day. Hal forced himself to swallow some ale. "I think that you do not recognize the true value of your only daughter, my lord."

"I value her," Teheboth said. "I value her, but I am realistic. If I offered more for her dowry, my own kingdom would crumple under the pressure. My lords would rise against me if I drained Liantine's treasury, even for our beloved princess."

"Your beloved princess . . ." Hal knew that a shrewd bargainer would mention Berylina's deficits—her straying eye, her rabbit teeth. Rani would certainly do as much if she were here. He could not bring himself to criticize those immutable elements, though, and so he said, "Your beloved princess appears too shy to lead folk here in Liantine. If I may say so, Berylina is a delicate creature, my lord. She must be protected from strain and stress. She should not be burdened with the knowledge that her father counts her value at only two hundred bars of gold."

"Ah," Teheboth sighed. "Perhaps you are correct. But maybe my daughter's shyness would be entirely cured if she learned how much her suitor truly values her. I'd gladly entertain a bid for a bride-price, my lord. Especially because you will take my only daughter so far away."

Teheboth's paternal piety sparked Hal's temper. He was not about to purchase Berylina, to spend his own precious gold on the princess! Morenia was not some outlying swamp, after all. It was a strong kingdom, an old kingdom. The House of Jair had sat its throne for generations, far longer than a Liantine up-start—

Hal forced himself to smother all his angry thoughts. He must remain calm. He must not let himself be provoked. "Surely a princess so beloved would warrant a *greater* price paid by her father. Say, one thousand bars of gold."

Hal wanted to ask for more. He wanted to declare that he would not take Berylina for a sovereign less than two thousand bars. Two thousand bars would let him pay the first installment to both the church and the Fellowship, avoid Rani's still-nascent octolaris plan.

But two thousand bars would never change hands. Teheboth had his own battles to fight in Liantine—honoring the Horned Hind left little room for play. If Hal demanded two thousand bars, he risked being dismissed outright. So he repeated, "One thousand bars."

Teheboth choked on his wine, spluttering, "One thousand! You think me a richer man than even I hope to be!"

"I know you are a rich man," Hal countered, "and a loving father." He put his goblet on the low table, and he snared the gaze of the Liantine king. He kept his voice steady, hoping to convey beyond any doubt that he was through with bargaining. He was through debating. He would have his thousand bars or Berylina would stay in her father's court, perhaps forever. Hal said, "I see the richness of your palace, Teheboth. I drink your fine wine, and I eat your food. I see the new-built palace chambers, with all your fine-carved wooden panels replacing dusty spidersilk. I know what you can pay, when you care to do so. Do not undervalue your daughter. Do not sell her so cheaply that you embarrass her, and yourself, as well."

Teheboth's face flushed crimson, and Hal wondered if he would have dared to be so blunt before Moren's fire, before his kingdom was threatened with ultimate collapse. "Mind your tongue, my lord," Teheboth managed to say.

"Mind your daughter! Mind that you honor her as the only girl your lady ever birthed. Mind that you honor her as the only sister among her brothers, as the bridge that can join our kingdoms forever."

"Five hundred bars," Teheboth countered.

"Eight hundred."

"Done. But the wedding must be held on Midsummer Eve."

"Why Midsummer?" Hal asked in surprise.

"It is a day most blessed by the Horned Hind. Berylina is a potent symbol for my people, my lord. As you have argued so shrewdly, she *is* my only daughter. There are rumors about in Liantine that she holds to the old faith, to the ways of your Thousand Gods. If she weds on Midsummer Eve, my people will be assured of her true beliefs. They will know the holiness of all the house of Thunderspear, and I will not be bothered by fools like that Hestaron you saw this afternoon."

If only Teheboth could know the depths of Berylina's faith. . . . If only the king could see that his daughter spoke with the gods themselves, drew their likenesses as if they were her living, breathing friends. . . . No midsummer ceremony would burn that devotion from the princess. But that was hardly Hal's concern, not when he intended to take his bride to Moren, to a land that understood the Thousand Gods.

Four weeks until the wedding.

"Of course," Teheboth said, as if he could read Hal's thoughts, "you could wait a year. You could celebrate your marriage next summer. And receive the dowry then."

Impossible. The church would not wait a year.

Eight hundred bars of gold, and the wedding in one month.

It was not the arrangement he had hoped for when he arrived in Liantine. Not when he spoke with Teheboth during the Spring Hunt. Not when he forfeited his right to ask about the Little Army, to bid for the return of Amanthian children. He had thought that sacrifice would serve him better here.

Nevertheless, eight hundred bars of gold would let him pay his immediate debts.

And four weeks left him time. Time to recall Rani from the

players' camp. Time to send for Puladarati and the rest of his court. And for four weeks, he should be able to avoid Mareka Octolaris.

Hal extended his hand to his new ally, to the father of the woman he would marry. "Done."

12

Rani nodded as Flarissa gestured to the tight joins in the glass frame. The player's voice was calm and patient as she explained, "You must clean the corners carefully. Too much of the abrasive, and you'll wear away the solder. Too little, though, and the frame won't reflect light properly."

"I understand," Rani said. She picked up her spidersilk rag, running its tight-woven smoothness between her fingers. The players had piles of the spent fabric, ragged from long wear, torn beyond repair. They used clean lengths to wrap their glass for transport.

Rani had spent the better part of the morning studying the fine work. Flarissa had let her review all the glass she wanted, dragging wooden storage bins out of the locked storeroom. Rani had agreed to clean each piece in exchange for the opportunity to learn.

"Aye," Flarissa said now. "You seem to understand a great deal. You've had good teachers in the past."

"Not enough of them. I've learned most of what I know from books."

"But that will change, as you bring your guild back to power." The player's voice was filled with compassion, vivid from the story Rani had Spoken when they first met. "You *will* rebuild it, Ranita," Flarissa said softly. "Have faith."

Rani swallowed hard, and when she spoke, she marveled that her voice was steady. Perhaps even steady enough that Flarissa would not realize that she was changing the topic of conversation. "How many glass panels do the players have, all told?"

"There is one for every character in our plays. I've never thought to count them—ten score perhaps?"

"Ten—" Rani's voice caught at the wonder of it all.

"Aye," Flarissa nodded. "And most of them grimy from our travels."

"I'll clean them," Rani vowed. "I'll clean them all."

Flarissa handed over the tin of scrubbing compound. "Start with the ones that are here. I'll be in my cottage, Ranita. Come and find me if you have any questions." Before the player walked off, she brushed her warm fingers across Rani's cheek, a fond farewell, more personal than any words she might have uttered.

Rani felt the older woman's touch spread through her body like the peace of Speaking. She gathered up her spidersilk rag and began to work the cleaning compound into the joint of the first panel.

She lost track of time as she worked. Her hair kept falling into her eyes as she scrubbed, and she finally sighed with exasperation, wasting precious moments wiping her fingers clean on a fresh cloth before she twisted the blond strands into a braid. Her fingers began to ache from clutching the rag, and the edges of the glass panels cut into the top of her legs. Once, a midge flew into her eyes, and she rubbed away the offending insect without thinking, only to be rewarded by the violent sting of the cleaning compound.

Nevertheless, she marveled at the work that had been entrusted to her care.

Every panel illustrated techniques that Rani had read about but never seen in practice. There, three pieces of glass were held in an intricate framework so that light could play through their layered depths, creating deep, dark shadows of color. And there, long, thin pieces were worked into a figure's hair— pieces so finely cut they must have been created by a master with a diamond knife. And there, wires had been incorporated into the very armature of a stallion so that part of the glass swung free, creating the illusion of a horse's jaunty gait.

This last creation captured Rani's attention most completely.

She had already learned a great deal about designing single planes of glass, about structuring windows. She knew how to sketch a drawing on a piece of parchment and how to scale up that drawing on a whitewashed table. But this craft was different from anything she had tried, anything she had imagined. Like the players' troops themselves, the horse panel needed to be mobile. Rani leaned close over the metalwork, studying how the craftsman had joined the links together, how he had secured the chain to the top of the glass panel.

She could see *what* had been done, but she could not calculate how it had been accomplished. She could imagine creating a design, creating separate sections that worked together to form a complete panel. But even if she had the skill to pour the glass and to cut it, she could not set it properly. She did not know how to make a chain that was smaller than her fingers, certainly not a chain of lead. Lead would twist, crimp, and pull. Some unknown tools must have been used, some unknown skills harnessed to make the stallion's links.

Rani raised both sections of the panel above her face, letting the lead dangle in the sunlight. She could make out the grooves of tiny instruments, of careful workmanship. The implements, though, must be finer than anything she had seen before, than anything she had ever used to pull and temper lead stripping. . . .

"Breathe, girl!"

Rani was so startled that she nearly dropped the horse panel. "Tovin!" she said as Flarissa's son glided to her side.

"So, Mother has set you to work, has she?"

"I volunteered!" Rani rose to the player woman's defense. "I wanted to study the glasswork. We bargained for it when I first Spoke with her."

"There's no better way to study than to touch the pieces."

"Aye," Rani agreed, uncertain whether Tovin was criticizing her. "I was looking at the chains, there. I don't know how you made those."

"Tools, Ranita Glasswright. Surely you know that a workman is only as good as his tools."

She made a face at the trite expression. "But which ones? I've never seen glasswrights' tools to work so fine a chain."

"I could show you, Ranita, but you would need to pay for the knowledge."

Rani shot a glance at the man's smooth face, at his calm features. She was suddenly aware of the glass panel pressing against her thighs, of the heated sunlight splashing across her chest. She felt color rise in her cheeks, and she fumbled for an answer. "What coin, then?"

"The same as before," Tovin said easily. "Speak with me. Tell me more about your homeland."

About her homeland. About the Fellowship, more likely. That was Tovin's interest before. Nevertheless, Rani heard the demand like a thirsty woman listening to a fountain. She longed for Speaking, for the depthless calm of that altered state. And if she should also learn about working the glass, about crafting the magnificent panels . . . She could hear Tovin's dispassionate Speaking voice even now, leading her beside the stream of her memory, further and further into the knowledge that she alone possessed.

She was afraid, though, afraid of that longing, frightened by the strength of the desire that thrummed through her belly. "I've already Spoken with you. I've answered all your questions."

"I've thought of more things I'd like to know." Tovin eyed her steadily.

"I—," Rani began, and then she had to clear her throat. "The Fellowship is secret. No one is supposed to know."

"Aye," Tovin agreed. "The Fellowship is secret. Just as my craft is secret. Just as any guild's workmanship is secret. Your masters would have taught you secrets, if any lived in Morenia still."

Was he agreeing with her or disagreeing? Was he saying that he would avoid the Fellowship and respect her obligations? Rani's hands trembled as she leaned forward to catch his soft words, and the horse panel leaped into motion, its legs mimicking the swinging motion of a true beast. The impossibly tiny chains caught the sunlight, glinting like the light streaks in Tovin's hair.

"The choice is mine," Rani said, but she made the statement a question.

"Aye. You know by now that you control the Speaking."

"And if I don't tell you enough?"

Tovin snared her eyes with his own. "We're both traders, Rani. We know how to measure value. If you fail to deliver true value through the Speaking, then you'll owe some other payment. Cleaning panels, or stitching costumes for the troop."

She raised her chin and tensed her arms, setting the horse's legs swinging once again. "Very well, then." She smothered the panel's motion by snugging it against her body, and then she reached out a hand. "I'll trade with you."

The tradition was an old one, well settled in the marketplace. Tovin hesitated for a moment, and then he clasped her arm at the elbow. She jerked back in surprise, startled to find him using an older symbol than the one that she had offered. Tovin used the soldier's clasp, showing that he had no steel concealed up his sleeves, checking to confirm that she was similarly unarmed. His fingers burned against the meat of her arm and then skimmed past her elbow to her wrist. "Well played, Ranita."

She swallowed hard, wondering if he had lied to her before. Would he truly settle for her cleaning glass frames, in payment for the Speaking? She could not doubt the invitation in his touch; she could not fail to understand the silent offer that his fingers made.

She did not want that, she told herself firmly. She had kissed Crestman, long ago in Amanthia, and the heat that had burned between them still warped their conversations. She had felt Hal's lips upon her hand, a pledge of a future life that tangled her hopes and dreams beyond her comprehension. As little more than a child, she had longed for a soldier man, but he had died with her knife twisted in the small of his back.

She did not want to desire Tovin. He was acting as her guildmaster; he was providing her with glasswrights' lore. Anything else would be confusing, would be frightening, would be wrong.

Tovin must have read her indecision, for he took a step away. "I need to consult with the players, learn what else they intend for me to purchase at the spiderguild. Come find me when you are finished, and we'll complete our work together."

She mumbled some appropriate reply and bent quickly over the glass before her, determined not to watch him walk away. But her intense concentration was broken by someone blocking her light. She looked up to see Crestman looming over her.

"Mair says you're going to bargain for spiders."

"Aye." She recognized the determination in his set jaw, remembered the driven power she had first seen as he commanded his platoon of boys in Amanthia. "We spoke about it while the players had their Meet. We wondered where you'd gone to."

"I was speaking with my soldiers."

"Your soldiers?"

"The slaves within the players' camp."

Rani glanced about her. On the far side of the compound, a dozen players gathered around a low stage, laughing as a juggler attempted to toss five silk-wrapped balls at once. The performer dared to spin about, completing his turn and keeping all the balls in full rotation. He clapped once, twice, three times, all the while juggling well. But when he tried to jump down from the stage, he lost his concentration and bright silk spheres went flying.

A child whooped with laughter and collected three of the balls, jumping onto the platform to try his own hand at the game. Across the courtyard, Rani could just make out a scar glinting on the boy's cheek. She looked back at Crestman. "I'd hardly call them slaves here."

"They seem to be accepted. I've spoken with all of them now—nearly three dozen men, all told. Each once fought for Sin Hazar, and each was sold on reaching Liantine. They've found their way here from other masters. The players are given slaves sometimes in payment for their presentations."

"And? Do your men want to rise up against the troop?"

Crestman shook his head, and she wondered what the admission must cost him. "They do not want to leave the players. They do not want to overturn their lives."

Rani reached out, setting her hand upon his rock-hard arm. "You must honor their decision."

He pulled back, as if she had cut him. "I know that!" He took a deep breath and lowered his voice. "I know that, Rani. I thought that they would follow me. I thought that all the Little Army longed to be free."

"Three years is a long time, Crestman. Three years at least. Some of them were in the earliest shipments from Amanthia—they've been here even longer. They were children when they arrived. They have no family, no home back in Amanthia. Let them be."

"I would, Rani. I would sail for Amanthia tomorrow, but there is still one thing that troubles me."

"What?"

"The tale my scout delivered. The story of the spiderguild. The slave that he described was not like the children here. She was frightened. She was used. She died in service, against her will. I must see my soldiers who are held at the spiderguild. Take me with you."

She wanted to deny him. She wanted to say that Tovin would not do it, would not bring Crestman along. After all, she had yet to secure her own passage. But when she looked into his eyes, when she saw the fierce longing written there, she did not have the heart. "Whatever you find, you will not be content."

"What do you mean?"

"If you find the Little Army happy, you will think that you have failed them. You will believe that you should have rescued them before, brought them home before they could settle here in Liantine. And if you find that they are abused by the spiderguild, you will rage against their fate."

"I'll do more than rage," he said.

"No." Rani shook her head. "You cannot do that. We are guests in Liantine, and there are some things you cannot do. We *need* the spiderguild's cooperation, Crestman. We need spiders and riberry trees."

"For what, Rani? What is more important than the lives of innocent enslaved children?"

The lives in all Morenia, she wanted to say. The lives in Amanthia. The lives in every kingdom touched by the Fellowship. Hal must have the spiders; he must have the riberries, for he must buy new power in the Fellowship.

"You must trust me, Crestman."

"I've had three years of trusting you. Three years of working alone in Amanthia, trying to heal a land without children."

"You must not fight the spiderguild. You must not breach the
peace. If you cannot promise me that, I will not ask Tovin to
take you with us."

She saw his indecision. She knew that he wanted to rage
against her; he wanted to force her to understand, make her
agree to liberate the spiderguild slaves, no matter what the con-
sequences. She watched the arguments rise in his throat, shift
into words, and then die on his lips. His fingers twitched on the
hilt of his Amanthian sword until he clenched them into a fist.

"I have to know," he said at last. "I promise you. No vio-
lence at the spiderguild."

"I'll speak to Tovin, then."

She started to reach out to him, started to touch the scar that
shone across his cheek. He flinched away, though, and then he
turned on his heel, striding fast across the players' camp.

Rani shook her head and reached out for her rags, sifting
through the pile of cloth to find the cleanest one. She dipped a
corner of the fraying silk into her cleaning compound and
turned her attention back to the panels. How ironic that she was
working on the Boy. The glass figure was the consummate
male child, holding a toy horse in one hand and a miniature
bow in another. Rani rubbed accumulated dust from the child's
face and felt her heart falter as she imagined real flesh beneath
her fingers, a real cheek scarred from service in the Little
Army.

She finished that one and turned to the Rosebush, a panel
from an ancient fable about a bloodred vine that grew upon the
graves of tragically denied lovers. Rani knew the story; she had
heard her own mother sing it, years ago in the Traders' shop.
The rosebush grew from the pierced hearts of the maid and her
swain, once they were separated by their families' hatred. The
pungent fumes of the cleaning compound raised tears in Rani's
eyes, and she rubbed her palms across her cheeks in annoyance.

The petals of the roses were a study in flashed glass, she
forced herself to realize. They were doubled over in careful
layers, soldered into shape so that the deepest, darkest colors
held all the mystery of heart blood. Rani never would have

thought to layer the glass petals that way. She never would have thought to link the leading in just that fashion. A master had crafted that panel. Tovin.

As Rani reached for the next panel, the Stargazer, she let her thoughts linger on the master craftsman. How would he respond to her request? Would he take them to the spiderguild—Rani, Mair, and Crestman?

He must. She would do whatever was necessary to convince him.

She scrubbed the Stargazer panel clean, taking special care over the intricate painting that set off the tools in his lead-lined hands. Rani had never been a great draftsman; she found it difficult to paint on glass and create recognizable designs. She could learn, though. With a master to instruct her, a master who was not poisoned by her history with her guild, by the glasswrights' destruction because of Rani's childhood mistakes. . . .

She folded the Stargazer into his spidersilk wrappings and wiped the excess cleaning compound from her hands. Her fingers smarted from the stuff, and she knew that they would be rough in the morning. Small price to pay, of course. Small price for a lifetime lesson. She smoothed her skirts and went in search of Tovin.

She did not have far to wander. Several players were gathered around the stage in the center of the main square. A canopy had been stretched above the planks that formed the platform, shielding the actors from the bright afternoon sun. Iron posts were planted in the stage, indicating where panels would hang, but the players did not bother with the delicate glasswork for their rehearsals. Instead, they relied on all of their acting skills to bring out the nature of the characters they portrayed. Tovin was sprawled on a bench, watching his mother emote from the stage.

"A girl's the thing you likely need, a girl to do the job," Flarissa proclaimed. The watching players laughed as she lifted one arch eyebrow and waggled her hand suggestively. Rani had not seen the play before; she did not know the story, but it was apparent that Flarissa was trying to convince a nervous young man to approach a maid.

"A girl, you say!" the youthful actor cried, making his voice crack comically. "You speak in jest! I daren't attract a mob!"

"Attract a mob? How can that be? Who cares about this feat?"

"This feat is not just any hunt, not any hunt at all. This feat is trav'ling after gold, through to Bramble Hall."

Flarissa's surprise was exaggerated. "The Bramble Hall? Now there's a catch! You'll need to strip to pass those thorns, bare flesh they will not scratch."

"Aye, good dame, you've heard the tales. The Bramble Hall will skin a man, unless he dares its grasp, with naked flesh and naked hands, his, er, covers all unhasped."

The naive young man gestured before him, pointing to the "covers" of his trews and his comically burgeoning "hasp." All the players laughed. The young man tried to keep his expression earnest, even as his hands moved at his waist, mimicking substantial endowment. Flarissa quirked one eyebrow, comically abandoning the play's planned lines. She appraised the boy as if she were suddenly, insatiably curious, and he improvised, responding to her attention with a mocking leer, throwing his arms wide in pretended lechery. Flarissa tried to look shocked and desiring all at once, but she succeeded only in making the troop call out jeers and suggestions.

"Aye, dame, check out the boy's covers," one man called.

"Who cares about his covers?" a woman cried. "I'd check what's underneath the sheets."

"No doubt what's there," a second man jeered, as the boy actor strutted before his companions.

"Not much," a pretty girl called, looking up from a costume she was stitching. "Not much my husband has." She held up a length of limp braid that was shorter than her thumb. Her ribaldry was belied by the swelling of her belly beneath her full skirts.

The company collapsed in good-natured laughter as the actor spluttered a rejoinder. When his protests were ignored, he leaped down from the stage and gathered up the pretty seamstress, bending her back in a swooping kiss, even as he spread a protective hand across their unborn child. The girl feigned indifference to her lover's attentions until he swirled an imaginary cape about them and bent to nibble down her neck, to the ruffle of lace that lined the top of her chemise.

"I give!" the girl squealed. "I give!"

"Aye," growled the actor. "That you have! And will again!" The girl's mock shrieks turned to laughter as the boy tossed away her stitchery.

Flarissa laughed and crossed to Rani and Tovin. "Well, there'll be no bringing him back to his lines for a bit. Not with a wife to distract him from poor Dame Love. And how have you fared this morning, Ranita? Have you made progress on the panels?"

"Aye," Rani said distractedly, staring as the boy threw his arm around his lady's shoulders and coaxed her away from the stage. The company hooted after the couple as they ducked into one of the tents on the edge of the common ground. A clutch of children started to follow the lovers into their retreat, but they were called back by their mothers.

Flarissa pinned Rani with suddenly sharp eyes. "Aye? Then you're finished?"

"Not exactly, lady."

Flarissa started to frown, but the crease in her brow was eased as Tovin said, "I interrupted Rani Trader's work, Mother. We spoke of glasswork and construction, and I kept her from her task."

The player woman tried to direct her dissatisfaction toward her son, but she only succeeded in a self-mocking scowl. "You can help her, then, Tovin. Help her finish the cleaning before you leave for the spiderguild. We'll need those panels for Princess Berylina's nuptials. Midsummer Eve is little more than three weeks away."

"Aye, Mother," Tovin said obediently, and Rani would have marveled at his contrition if she were not stunned by Flarissa's words.

"Princess Berylina's nuptials?" Rani repeated.

"Aye. A messenger rode in this morning from the capital. The princess and your king will wed on Midsummer Eve, and we have been invited to perform at the feast."

"So soon!" Rani said, afraid to trust herself to more.

"Aye. King Teheboth wanted to honor the Horned Hind, and

midsummer is the most auspicious time for that. Oh! I am for-
getting. The messenger carried this for you."

Flarissa handed over a folded letter, and Rani recognized
Farsobalinti's hand, sprawling her name across the parchment.
She took the missive numbly, sliding her finger under the wax
to break the seal. She glanced at the words, scarcely needing to
read them, now that Flarissa had told her the important news
from the capital.

It was done, then. Hal had made his bargain. He was
pledged to Berylina.

"We players have a great deal of work to do between now
and midsummer," Flarissa said. "Reputations can rise or fall for
generations depending on how we play one royal marriage. Of
course, we would stand a better chance to impress if we had
other opportunities to practice wedding plays." The player
woman glanced pointedly at her son; then she said, "Don't dis-
appoint me, Ranita. We'll need all the panels sparkling."
Flarissa bustled off to another knot of players.

Tovin grimaced when Rani turned her attention back to him.
"Don't listen to her scolding. She is only grumpy because she
thinks I should have a wife by now. She wants to hold a grand-
child. Soon enough, she'll be inviting you to sit beside her
hearth, calling you 'daughter.' "

"I can't imagine that!" Rani gasped and stepped away.

"Aye," Tovin continued. "My bride will be her daughter, and
none too soon. She mentions her lack often enough."

"I—," Rani protested. "Why, I never intended . . . I never
thought to . . . I'm not even from Liantine!"

"And I'm not asking to wed you," Tovin said simply, and he
grinned at her discomfort. "Besides, your homeland would
hardly matter to my mother. We're players. We don't count
homes as other people do."

"I—" Rani stumbled for a reply.

"Don't worry, Ranita Glasswright." He shrugged as if he
meant to put her at her ease. "There are too many wenches on
the traveling road to settle down with one. My mother has lived
with disappointment lo these many years, and a few more will
do her no great harm."

How dare he imply that she was not good enough to be a

player's wife! Not good enough, even, to choose over some dalliance on the high road! Especially when she had felt the unspoken offer in his fingertips that very morning, heard his silent bid.

That was ridiculous. Rani had no desire to wed Tovin. She only wanted to learn about glasswork. And to save Moren. She wanted to find Hal the thousand gold bars he needed to answer the Fellowship.

Aloud, she said, "Mothers learn to live with disappointment."

"When did you learn that line?"

"Line?"

"It's from one of the tragedies—Plesandra says it as she watches her son choose the life of a warrior over staying home to farm."

"I haven't seen that play. I haven't seen any of your tragedies."

"They're a grim lot." Tovin shrugged. "The horse panel you were working on this morning is from *Plesandra's Lament*. The stallion's return is the only way the mother learns that her son has died."

Rani shivered, thinking of the story she had held within her hands. "You were going to teach me how to make the chains."

Tovin eyed her steadily. "You were going to Speak with me again. About the Fellowship."

"Aye."

"Come along, then. If you're not afraid, that is." He grinned like a wolf and gestured toward the stage. "If you don't mind building up my mother's hopes."

Rani followed Tovin's pointing fingers, only to find Flarissa staring across the platform at them. The player woman's face was impassive; her arms hung straight at her side. She nodded once as her copper gaze darted from Tovin and then to Rani, and back again. Rani swallowed hard and said, "I am not afraid."

She let him lead her into the storeroom. His hands were steady as he produced the iron key, and he hummed tunelessly as he locked the door behind them. He kindled a lamp with easy grace and led her toward a table in the corner. All the time, Rani was aware of the low bed at the far side of the tent, of the bolsters she had leaned against when she had Spoken with him before.

Tovin, though, seemed to have forgotten that Speaking was part of their bargain. Instead, he took great care in showing her the tools he used to make the fine lead chain. He displayed his adapted goldsmith's equipment, pointed out how he merged the jeweler's delicate art with the brutal skill of a blacksmith. Rani ran her fingers along the handle of improbably curved tongs, and Tovin nodded as she lifted the instrument. His hands cupped hers as he showed her how to manipulate heated lead, how she could use a leather-wrapped hammer to pound the hot links.

The ultimate secret, he explained, was in cooling the chain. He added a powder to the water bath, a powder that came from Zarithia, home of the finest steel blades. He could not tell her what was in the substance, but it cost more than its weight in gold. It set the lead firmly, hardening the tiny links so that they could bear the glass without twisting under the weight.

Rani nodded as she learned. She memorized the heft of the tools, felt how each settled in her palm. She let Tovin adjust her grip on the hammer, shifted her feet for better balance, felt how the power of her muscles rose up through her legs, across her chest, down her arms. She closed her eyes and imagined the panels that she could make—decorative works that turned to capture the sunlight and the breeze.

She imagined the panel that would prove her mastery of the new technique—an emblem for the Order of the Octolaris. She could picture a rounded body crafted from stippled glass, brown glass that had been colored with air-dried silver stain. The head would be attached with lead, the standard soldering that she had mastered long ago. She would make lead chains to attach the legs—long legs, thin legs, legs that she would cut with a diamond knife. Sixteen lead chains. Two for each leg of her octolaris.

When she opened her eyes, Tovin was watching her with an easy grin. "A glasswright's vision, I presume. What did you see?"

"The piece that will test my skill. The piece that would cement my status as a journeyman."

"And that was?"

"A spider."

He did not laugh. He did not tell her that she was a fanciful child, and he did not protest that she had never made a single lead chain, much less sixteen. Instead, he said, "You could do that."

"I've never seen them, though. I mean, the octolaris."

"None have. None outside the spiderguild."

"Take me with you."

"What?" Now he did sound surprised.

"Take me with you when you leave tomorrow. I know you go to complete your bid for patronage. Let me come with you—to see the spiders." And let me make my own bargain, Rani thought. Let me negotiate for Moren, for octolaris and riberry trees worth a thousand bars of gold.

She might have spoken those last thoughts aloud, for the shrewd gaze he leveled on her. "They won't sell their spiders, you know."

"So I've heard."

"Their power is in their monopoly. If any of their breeding stock gets away, they'll lose the value of the entire silk market."

"I understand."

"And yet you want to go."

"Aye. But not alone. Mair would come with me. And Crestman."

She saw the indecision in his face, his uncertainty as he measured out the value of what she asked. He could not afford to alienate the spiderguild, to anger his patrons.

She reached out a hand, settling her fingers against his wrist, as he had touched her that very morning, when they sealed their bargain. His pulse was steady and strong, and its beat gave her the courage to say. "Go ahead, Tovin Player. Let us Speak. Ask me about the Fellowship, and I'll tell you all I know." She swallowed hard. "Everything."

"Every last thing."

"Aye." She wondered at that, even as she agreed. She would

give him Hal's name. Hal's and Mair's and all her other allies. Nothing of value was ever gained without risk. "Everything," she repeated. "If you'll take us to the spiderguild."

"Very well, then," Tovin said at last. "Come Speak with me, Ranita Glasswright."

She let herself be led to the pallet, and she forced her breath to slow as Tovin bade her to look into a pane of crimson glass, a pool of color as deep as blood, as deep as the tone of Hal's own livery. She exhaled and drew herself back to the stream where Tovin first had led her. She imagined herself beside the swift flowing water that carried away all duty and responsibility and fear and respect.

And when Tovin asked her questions, she answered, naming names and sharing secrets and buying her passage to the spiderguild.

She would trade everything for the octolaris and the trees, for a thousand bars of gold. She would trade to pay the Fellowship their ransom. She would answer all Tovin's questions, in hopes of saving Hal and all Morenia.

13

Mareka glanced at the door of her small chamber, wishing again that it had a lock. She had draped her gowns over the spiderboxes, hiding the occupants from anyone who happened to enter. There was no way, though, to hide the huge basket that she had wrestled from beneath her bed, no way to disguise the yellow riberry leaves that were crumbling to dust or the desiccated grubs that she was plucking away from the healthy ones. She needed to determine how many grubs remained, how much longer she could sustain her octolaris horde.

She crossed to the door and placed her ear against its oaken planks, determining that she could hear no one on the other side. This wing of the palace was usually deserted during the day, but she could not be too cautious.

Mareka wondered what she had been thinking when she spirited the virulent octolaris away from the guildhall. They were growing more difficult to handle as hatching time approached. The brooding females repeatedly wrapped their egg sacs in fresh silk, depositing new layers for the hungry new-hatched spiderlings to eat.

At least the impending hatching had reduced the females' appetite. Otherwise, Mareka's stash of grubs would have been long depleted.

Amazingly, even with their reduced diet and their care for the egg sacs, the octolaris continued to spin sheets of lustrous silk, twice as much as normal spiders produced. Even that bounty was becoming a liability. Mareka had never planned on hoarding huge quantities. She could not bring herself to burn the spiders' work, to destroy the product of their hard labor, even though that would have been safer. She had filled her trunk with the stuff, stacked it beneath her bed. She was running out of room.

"There we go," she muttered under her breath, reaching out two strong fingers to pluck sightless grubs from their large container. "Let's see how many of you live."

She shook the creatures into an iron vessel, a pot that she had scrounged from the kitchens when the cook was preoccupied. It would not do to let the grubs escape, to let them writhe blindly through King Teheboth's palace. As she transferred them, she kept a silent tally. One, two, three, four. Five, six, seven, eight. Eight grubs.

The creatures had survived surprisingly well. Nevertheless, they would not spin cocoons in the basket; no markin moths would mature to breed. What would Mareka do when this stash was depleted? The spiderlings would have hatched by then.

Sixteen grubs.

The brooding females were already rotating their egg sacs several times a day, a sure sign that the young would come soon. The hardworking mothers were growing moody from their exertion, though. Mareka had considered dosing herself with nectar just to feed them.

Twenty-four.

What would she do when the spiderlings hatched? How would she contain them without the guild's spiderboxes? How would she keep them from escaping into Liantine?

Thirty-two, she made herself count. Thirty-two grubs.

She had been raised in the spiderguild; she knew that the power of her people was directly dependent on their silk monopoly. If anyone else obtained octolaris, harvested their own spidersilk, they could set their prices at any level, undercutting the guild. They could topple the guild's supremacy, which had been centuries in the making.

Forty.

Even more troubling was the chance that her spiderlings would threaten innocent people with their venom. Outside of the guild, no one was trained to handle the delicate creatures.

No one knew the hymn, no one knew the Homing. No one had nectar to provide protection.

Forty-eight.

By the Hind's eight horns, she never should have taken the octolaris. She never should have brought them outside the enclave. Having realized her mistake, she should have returned to the guild. She could have brought the spiders home, handed them over to the masters. She would be punished for her disobedience, of course, but she would have one thing in her favor—sheet after sheet of perfect spidersilk.

Fifty-six.

It was all King Halaravilli's fault. She was loath to return until she was certain that she could buy her way to journeyman. Certainty, though, would only come with money, with power, with prestige. She could not return until she *knew* that she had the backing of a king. And she was not yet certain that Halaravilli was hers.

Sixty-four.

She had tried to see him. She had lain in wait outside his apartments. She had tracked him through the gardens. She had even taken to attending Father Siritalanu's daily services in celebration of the Thousand Gods. But each time that she approached the king, he was surrounded by his colleagues—the priest, Farsobalinti, even the captain of his ship.

Seventy-two.

He was avoiding her. He was afraid of her. He was afraid of how he had responded to the nectar, of the things that he had said and done. He thought that he had acted like a madman, never dreaming that she had planned it all, that she had come to him, all knowing. Darting her tongue over her lips, Mareka shifted a large cluster of leaves, digging out another clutch of grubs.

Eighty.

If she needed to, she was certain that she could seduce him once again.

Eighty-eight.

If she needed to. She was already three weeks past her time. Her body felt no different, but her mother had always boasted that *she* had caught on her first try. One nectar-spiked encounter for her mother and father to bring Mareka Octolaris into being. By the Hind, she came from strong guild stock.

Ninety-six grubs.

Without warning, the door to the room slammed back on its hinges. "Mareka!" called Jerusha, stepping in as if she belonged there, as if she had the right to walk into the chamber.

"Jerusha!" Reflexively, Mareka stepped in front of the large basket, pushed her iron bowl beneath the bed. "What are you doing here?"

"Prince Olric has asked me—" The princess cut off her own imperious words. "What do you have inside it?"

"Nothing!" Mareka could not keep herself from answering too quickly.

"You have Cook's pot! I heard her screaming at the scullery maid this morning, accusing her of misplacing it. What have you got in there?"

"Nothing!" Mareka repeated, but Jerusha had already stepped closer, was already shoving past Mareka to reach beneath the bed.

The princess froze when she saw the contents. "Grubs! Where are the spiders?"

Mareka set her jaw. "You know that spiders are not allowed outside the spiderguild enclave."

Jerusha's hand flashed before Mareka could measure the danger, and the slap reported in the small room like a clap of thunder. "Don't play games with me!" Mareka shook her head, dazed, raising a palm to her burning cheekbone. "How many spiders did you steal?"

"I am not a thief!" Mareka forced her body between Jerusha and the grubs. "The guild had no interest in those octolaris! They intended to kill them!"

"Intended—" Jerusha started to repeat, and then she seemed to understand the full import of the words. "You took my spiders!"

"They weren't yours!"

"They were the ones I was supposed to care for, the ones I was supposed to feed."

"And a fine job you did of that." Mareka tried not to see the convulsing slave girl, but she could not forget Serena's swollen lips, her broken back.

Jerusha ignored the taunt. "But why would you bring them *here*? To Liantine?"

"Once I saved them from the pyre, how could I leave them back at the guild? They eat more than normal spiders. They eat more so they produce more. Surely you haven't forgotten already?"

"I've forgotten nothing! Let me see them!"

Mareka improvised. "It would be too dangerous. The females cannot be handled without a full dose of nectar. The spiderlings are close to hatching."

"Hatching! You have to get them home!"

"I have one more piece of business first."

"Business? In Liantine?"

Mareka was not about to tell Jerusha about her body's secret. The news was still too precious to her, too important to share with a rival, even as a boast. Instead, she opted to attack. "Who are you to tell me to bring these home? You're jealous, aren't you? You don't want me raised to Journeyman at the Convocation." Anger flashed in Jerusha's eyes, and Mareka rushed in to exploit the raw place. "Have you even explained that to the prince? Have you told him that you'll have to travel from court, return to the guild enclave for midwinter?" No. And from Jerusha's flush of rage, she was afraid to do so. "Perhaps you cannot tell him. Perhaps you realize that he'll set you aside, decide that you aren't worth the trouble of juggling royal obligations with common guildhall needs."

Jerusha's cry was pure fury—Mareka had not realized just how much her gibe would sting. She scarcely had a moment to brace herself, and then Jerusha lunged toward her, reaching out with rigid fingers to scratch her eyes, to claw her face. Mareka sidestepped the first attack, but Jerusha turned back and toppled her with a heavy blow to her chest.

Jerusha straddled her rival, beating at Mareka's face with closed fists. She swung hard, and it took all Mareka's strength to roll onto one side, to set Jerusha off balance. Mareka curled into a ball, fighting to protect her womb.

A quick glance showed Jerusha's face twisted by fury. The

journeyman's nose ran as she sobbed, tears mixing with slime and sweat. Her mouth was curved into a painful grin, and all the time she keened like a desperate animal.

Mareka could not keep fighting. She could not lay upon the wooden floor, waiting for Jerusha to strike a single, perfect blow, waiting for the princess to harm the child that Mareka thought was safe within her.

She waited until Jerusha had leaned back, until she was gasping to fill her lungs. Then, when all was unbalanced, when Jerusha was unprepared with hands and feet and teeth, Mareka sprang up from the floor. She snatched the iron pot from beneath the bed and raced out the door. Jerusha took only a moment to recover, and then she, too, was running through the hallways, screaming taunts and curses. Mareka ducked into the visitors' wing of the palace with the princess close behind, and she was forced to abandon any thought of preserving her privacy, preserving her dignity, preserving the lives of all her octolaris.

Hal grimaced and poured a goblet of greenwine, offering it to Father Siritalanu with a nod. "Drink, man."

"Sire, I do not think that I could swallow his wine."

"If by *his* you mean Teheboth Thunderspear, I must remind you that the man is our host for as long as we stay in Liantine. He is the father of the woman I will marry and a legitimate king set upon his throne by all the Thousand Gods."

"That is the problem, Your Majesty!" And Siritalanu was pacing again. The priest had been crossing back and forth since he had arrived in Hal's chamber, since he had exploded into the room with scarcely a knock to ask permission. "King Teheboth was set upon his throne by all the Thousand Gods, but now he refuses to acknowledge them. He acts as if they have no power over his life!"

"You exaggerate, Father." Hal pressed the cup into the passing priest's hand and watched, pointedly, until the religious swallowed. After one sip, though, Siritalanu returned the goblet to the mantel.

"Exaggerate? You've heard this constant talk about the Horned Hind!"

"She is tradition here, nothing more."

"How can you say that, Your Majesty?" The young priest was shaking with vehemence, anger and shock firming up his words. "You told me yourself that he punished one of his lords for professing belief in the Thousand Gods. He threatened the man with slavery!"

"Hestaron was sentenced because he cut his neighbor's trees."

"And that sentence was increased when he invoked the gods!"

"Hestaron is not our concern, Siritalanu. I will not endanger my wedding to the princess because of some minor court proceeding."

"You have an obligation, Your Majesty! You are the Defender of the Faith."

"What would you have me do, Father? Should I declare holy war against the man who is destined to become my father, because I disapprove of how he handled one case brought before him? Or perhaps you would have me refuse to wed the princess altogether?"

Siritalanu wrung his hands. "At least agree to move your wedding day. It is not seemly for the Defender of the Faith to be joined with his bride on a day sacred to the Horned Hind."

"Her father will not permit the ceremony on any other day." Hal sighed. "You are a man of the cloister, Father Siritalanu. Things may appear simpler to you than they are in fact."

"How complex can they be? A faithful man is penalized for calling on the Thousand Gods! A child is terrorized, told that she is evil because she hears true gods and not the tricksy voice of a false goddess. Is that complicated, Your Majesty?"

Hal made every effort not to take offense at the young priest's exercised tone. He purposely pitched his voice low, hoping to connect with Siritalanu's innate reason. "More so than you imagine. In brokering this marriage, I did not have the luxury of considering some minor Liantine thief. I did not have the luxury of measuring a child's hurt feelings—even the child who will be my bride. I have a kingdom to protect, Father. I have a city to rebuild. I have thousands upon thousands of my own people, looking to me to redeem them."

"But at what cost, Your Majesty? You will ruin yourself, body and soul, if you take to your marriage bed in the name of the Horned Hind."

"Father, the ceremony you loathe is only a symbol, one that will be revisited well before I see any true marriage bed. I hardly need remind you that Berylina is only thirteen years old."

"But you will go to her eventually! You will get your heir on her after having begun your life together beneath the Horned Hind. What hope can you have for a child conceived in an unholy bed? The Thousand Gods will frown upon him!"

"You overstep your bounds, Siritalanu!" Hal's voice shook with anger. "I have let you speak your mind, but you must not forget that I am still your king! Princess Berylina will be my queen. You will not curse my heir."

"My words may anger you, Your Majesty, but the danger is real. Think, Sire! This is the Horned Hind—a spirit tied to blood. She is slain and born anew each year; she takes her power from her *horns*. That is unnatural, Your Majesty. That is perverse! Would you turn your back on all the Thousand Gods and embrace such filth?"

"Father, it is not necessary to choose one faith or the other! Your house already has room for a thousand gods. Surely there is space for one more!" Before the priest could argue back, Hal went on. "Berylina's people expect her to be wed before their goddess. Anything less would nullify the contract of our marriage—Midsummer Eve was a critical condition for Teheboth to agree at all. Certainly the princess understands."

"Perhaps more than you do!"

"Father?" Hal chose to ignore the blatant disrespect, opting to discover Siritalanu's meaning.

The young priest raised his palms to his face, rubbing at his eyes as if he were emerging from deepest sleep. "Sire, your bride sees the Thousand Gods more clearly than anyone I have ever known. They speak to her the way they spoke to your forefathers of old. They visit her, both in her dreams and while she wakes. Princess Berylina understands their words, and she recognizes their power."

"Then she will do whatever is necessary to get to Morenia,

where she may study more of them. *Whatever* is necessary, Sir-italanu. Even naming an extraneous goddess in her wedding vows, if her father so requires."

Father Siritalanu stared at him, his dark eyes sober, like a spaniel's. "You will do nothing, then, Your Majesty?"

"I will do everything, Father. As soon as I am able. As soon as I am on my own soil, with my bride safely at my side and my own men at my back. As soon as Berylina's dowry has gone to repay your church, so that poor Moren might rise up from her ashes. Then, I will denounce the Horned Hind. But not before. Not when I stand to lose everything."

For an instant, the priest seemed to collapse upon himself. Then, he knelt before his king, inclining his head in abject surrender. "Thank you, Sire. I should not have wasted your time."

"It was not a waste at all, Father," Hal said, after only a moment's hesitation. He mistrusted the man's capitulation. "Our discussion has been . . . illuminating."

The priest rose to his feet. "By your leave," he said tonelessly. Hal waved him toward the door.

Siritalanu had scarcely passed over the threshold when there was a flurry of activity in the hallway. Hal looked up in exasperation, certain that this latest disturbance could only add to the ache that had begun to pound behind his eyes.

His belly twisted as he recognized one of the voices. Mareka Octolaris.

He thought that he would stay inside his apartments. He would cross to the window and look out at the harbor in the rain. He would kneel at his prie-dieu and concentrate on prayers to Siritalanu's Thousand Gods. He would reread the latest letter from Rani, her announcement that she planned to travel to the spiderguild, to begin bidding for his Order of the Octolaris. Instead, he reached for the full goblet of greenwine that the priest had left upon the mantel, draining it in one swallow.

The voices were louder now: two women, screaming curses. They sounded like fishwives, screeching, swearing. Hal gritted his teeth together and stormed across the room, throwing open the door and filling his lungs to shout down the chaos.

Before he could speak, before he could do more than pick

out his terrified page huddling at the doorpost, he was pushed aside by a flurry of spidersilk, forced back into the room. The door slammed, the latch clicked, the heavy oak bar locked into place.

Mareka Octolaris leaned against the door, panting as if she had run through all the palace.

Her gown was crumpled, and one sleeve had been shredded. He could glimpse her arm, bruised and bleeding through the silk remains. Her hair was tangled and matted, and she cradled an iron pot against her hip. Her fingers clutched the metal as if it held the secrets of all the Thousand Gods.

"My lady," Hal managed, glancing at the door behind her. Jerusha's voice came shrill through the wood, angry as a wasp. Her fists pummeled the oak, and the princess screeched speculations about Mareka's parents and his own. For just an instant, he worried for the safety of his page, but then the princess swore a terrible oath and stormed away.

"My lord," Mareka said, and she staggered forward, collapsing into a shuddering curtsey.

"Please, my lady!" he protested, raising her up. A bruise was spreading across her cheek, and he could see the clear imprint of someone's hand upon her flesh. Her nose was bleeding, and she had bitten through her lower lip.

Could this be the woman he had been avoiding for a month? Could this be the temptress who had stolen into his dreams, sabotaged his prayers? "What happened, Mareka?"

"It—it is nothing, my lord." Her voice was hoarse and raw, broken.

"Nothing!"

"It is a matter of the spiderguild, between Jerusha and myself."

"You've made it more than that by coming here."

"I did not choose to come this way! She chased me down this hallway! She chased me like a madwoman!"

"Why did she do that?"

Mareka looked down at the pot that she cradled, but she refused to answer.

He sighed and turned to the low table that sat beside his hearth, to a washbasin and pitcher of water. Farso had left them after helping Hal with his morning ablutions, and Teheboth's servants had not yet taken them away. Silently, Hal gathered up a scrap of linen, dipping it in the clean water and offering it to the spiderguild apprentice.

She gazed at him without comprehension until he gestured toward her face. She took the cloth then, touching it to her lip. She gasped at the pain and pulled her hand away, almost dropping her pot.

He reached forward to help by taking the container. "No!" she cried.

"I'm sorry." He did not know what to do, where to look, where to place his hands.

She dabbed at her face again and grimaced when the cloth came away stained with crimson. He saw her steel herself, watched her set her shoulders and her jaw, and then she returned the linen for further ministrations, persevering until the bleeding stopped. Rather than hand him the soiled cloth, she passed in front of him, crossing to the table.

Hal inhaled as she passed, breathing in a storm of memories. He recalled the heat of her body in his arms, the smooth strength of her fingers wrapping about his flesh. He remembered the scent of her hair, the cloud of power that seemed to enfold her. He remembered the hunger that had blossomed from her lips, a hunger that had threatened to consume her, consume him. . . .

But all of it was memory. The heady, mindless desire was gone. She was no longer a temptress, a vixen, the secret love he longed for in the night. She was an ordinary woman. A bruised and breathless, frightened, shaking, ordinary woman.

"I have done something very wrong, my lord." At last. Words. "I have stolen from my people, from my guild."

"Stolen?" He kept the one word neutral. Of course apprentices stole. They took tools, supplies. They wrangled extra garments from the quartermaster, extra food from the larder.

"It's the spiders."

"Aye." He waited for her to explain what she had taken.

"The octolaris."

"Aye."

She glared at him, her eyes sparking like lightning beneath

the storm cloud of her hair. "I stole spiders from the guildhall! I took the octolaris, and I have them here in Liantine!"

Her words hit him like a wave. Octolaris. The base of the spiderguild's monopoly. Here. In Liantine.

"That's impossible."

"It's perfectly possible," she snapped. "I brought them with me when I came to witness Jerusha's marriage."

"But how? Why? Your guild will destroy you if they find out what you have!"

"Precisely," she said, letting the one word speak more than the bruise purpling her cheek, more than the thread of blood that had begun to trickle from her nose once again.

Hal fought against unworthy thoughts. There were octolaris here, in Teheboth's court. *He could take those beasts.* He could spirit them to Moren and sell them to his lords. He could stock the Order of the Octolaris, fully fund his payment to the Fellowship.

He forced himself to speak, to acknowledge Mareka's confession. "And now Jerusha knows," he said. "And she'll inform the spiderguild as soon as she is able."

"Aye," she whispered. "She must be sending a message even now. She'll use the king's own riders, cajole them from her husband. And then she'll dose herself. Take nectar and remove my spiders."

Nectar? What was she babbling about? "So what do you intend to do, then? Ransom the beasts back to the guild?"

"No!" The strength of her protest seemed to hurt her, the one word scraped across a throat already screamed raw. She lowered her voice to almost a whisper and repeated, "No. I cannot return them to the guild. They would be destroyed immediately."

"The spiderguild makes its profit on the sale of silk. Why would it destroy its assets?"

"These . . . assets . . . are too dangerous for the guild. My octolaris' poison is much stronger than that of the average spider."

"They're too dangerous for the guild, and yet you have tended them here? In secret? Alone?"

"We have our ways, my lord. The spiderguild brews a potion

to keep from the spiders' own poison, to keep the octolaris in check. Nectar, we call it. Octolaris nectar." Her face flushed, and her fingers curled about her belly, as if she were hiding something shameful. "It is made from octolaris poison, but it is diluted. It calls to the spiders, soothes them. When we have drunk it, they can sense it on our hands, on our clothes."

Something about her tone made him understand. "You drank the nectar that day. When you came to me before."

Her fingers twined before her, weaving, weaving. She did not meet his eyes. "Yes."

His body seized as he remembered his mystifying passion, the all-consuming heat that had blazed across his flesh. He had not been able to pull his eyes from her, had not been able to step away. Every breath had brought him closer to her, filled his mouth with the scent of her, the taste. . . . "You drugged me."

"Yes."

"But why? What could you hope to gain? I'm hardly a venomous spider that had to be subdued."

She swallowed hard and started to speak, but stopped before she could voice a single, husky word. She closed her eyes, filled her lungs, and then she exhaled slowly. Carefully, bravely, she caught his gaze, looking into his eyes as if there were nothing more important in all the world. She said, "There was no reason, lord. I drank the nectar so that I could tend my spiders. It was a strong brew, stronger than I ever tried as an apprentice at the spiderguild. I finished with the octolaris, but the nectar still burned hot within my veins. I left my chamber and walked through all the hallways, waiting for the drink to exhaust itself. It was only happenstance that I was here when Rani Trader left your rooms. It was only coincidence that brought me to your chamber."

He stared at her, remembering his conversation with Rani, remembering his desolation when the merchant girl announced that she was leaving. He had wanted to reach out for her, to forbid her to leave Liantine. And yet, he had known that she was right. He had known that she must go.

And then Mareka had appeared. Without a plan. Without a mission. By the pure happenstance of all the Thousand Gods.

Warm and willing with the bewitching aura of her octolaris nectar.

He shook his head and forced away the memories. "So, you brought the spiders to Liantine."

"Yes, my lord. And they have thrived! The brooding females have tended to their egg sacs, and the spiderlings are set to hatch."

Brooding females. Spiderlings. The Order of the Octolaris hovered even closer.

"But then?" he prompted. "Jerusha?"

"Jerusha found me in my chamber. I was counting out my markin grubs, seeing how many remain to feed the spiders." Mareka gestured toward the pot. "She found me. She learned about the spiders. And now she'll tell the spiderguild, and they will order all the octolaris destroyed. I won't be able to save them this time. None of them. The brooding females, the egg sacs. All those spiderlings, dead. Because I let Jerusha find me."

"Unless . . ." Hal trailed off, hoping that Mareka would complete his thought.

"Unless what? The guild will never let them live. Not when it condemned them once before."

"Unless the guild cannot reach them."

"They'll get them soon enough. Jerusha is a princess now, in the house of Thunderspear. King Teheboth can enter my chamber at any time. The guild will send a master, and the king will give him access to my spiderboxes."

"Teheboth Thunderspear cannot enter every chamber in this house."

"Are you mad? He's the king!"

"He's the king of Liantine. But I am the king of Morenia, and Amanthia, too. I can claim the right of embassy, and no one from the house of Thunderspear can set foot inside these chambers."

The right of embassy was longstanding, honored for generations. Hal had been assigned these apartments by the king of Liantine when he journeyed east of his own free will. Now, the space within these walls functioned as an outpost of Morenia. Whatever transpired here was separate, apart from Liantine.

Hal waited for Mareka to trace through his plan. She could bring the spiders at once, before Jerusha thought to post a guard outside Mareka's chamber. Save them from certain destruction.

And, Hal told himself, once he had physical possession of the octolaris, he could take them for himself. It would not be theft, he quickly thought. It would be salvation. The guild did not want them; it wanted to destroy them. He could save the spiders. He could spirit them away to Morenia. He could sell them to his nobles, found the Order of the Octolaris. He would have his gold.

The first octolaris outside the spiderguild enclave in generations, and they would be his in a matter of minutes. . . .

"That is impossible, my lord."

"What?" He was astonished.

Her face was lined with pain, but she made her voice firm. "I cannot breach the spiderguild's monopoly. I must obey them." Her voice quivered. "I am their apprentice."

"How long will you keep that rank, once they learn that you have stolen octolaris?"

"If I return the spiders. If I keep the guild's monopoly safe." She spoke the words like a prayer, like a child's chant against ghosts. He realized that she did not fully believe what she said. She was not certain that her guild would keep her. She was afraid. "Even if I let you have the spiders, they would starve. My grubs won't last forever."

"I'll get them food."

"Impossible. You need to feed them markin grubs. From riberry trees. Those only grow at the enclave."

The enclave. Hal's heart beat faster. Rani was heading to the enclave even now. She was mounting her attack, plotting for him, working for his nascent Order. "I will get you riberry trees."

Her laugh was bitter. Hopeless. "Never. I must return the spiders, my lord. I must humble myself before my guildmasters and hope that they show mercy."

Her resignation infuriated him. She was going to throw away his kingdom's hopes for her baseless dreams. "How will you kill the spiders, Mareka Octolaris? How will you execute them, back at your guild?" She flinched, and he stepped closer.

"Will you poison them, give them a dose of their own venom? No? By fire, then."

"By fire," she whispered.

"Are you prepared to do that? Are you prepared to stand by the flames and offer up each spider?"

"I'll do what must be done." Her voice shook.

"You will take them, one by one. You'll have to dose yourself with nectar, no? Your flesh will burn with theirs. Your eyes will see with theirs as you bring them closer, closer—"

"I have no choice!"

"You do!" He caught her arm, gripped her hard, even though he knew the pain that it surely caused her. He must have the octolaris. He could not let them slip away, not now. Not when they were so close. "Don't fool yourself, Mareka. The guild will use you until you bring them back their spiders, and then they'll cast you out forever."

"They won't! They are my people!"

"You have no people. Not any longer. You betrayed your guild." He shook her arm, looming over her and letting his desperate need scorch his words. "You will be alone. You will have no home. You will have no name. All you will possess is a memory, a thought of how you killed the spiders. How you followed their commands and burned your octolaris."

Her eyes brimmed with tears, the first that he had ever seen from her. He tightened his grasp upon her arm.

"They can live, Mareka. Give them to me."

Tears glistened down her cheeks, silent, silver.

Slowly, she nodded her head.

"Say it." Her lips trembled, and he shook her, as if she were a wayward child. "Say that you will give me the octolaris."

"I will, my lord." She caught a sob at the back of her throat. "I will give you all my octolaris. To save them. To keep them from the fire."

He sighed and let her go. Was he a madman? Was he a brutal, raving fiend?

No. He was a king who fought to save his kingdom. A man who fought for power in the Fellowship, for leadership in that strong, secret cabal. He was a man who had just broken the strongest monopoly his world had ever seen. "We have no time to waste. We must get them from your chambers before Jerusha thinks to lock us out."

He was not completely heartless. He took his time collecting his cloak. He gave Mareka a chance to wipe her tears away, to draw herself up, to find her buried pride. He did not stare as she crossed his chamber, as she unlatched the door.

But when she stood on the threshold, framed within the doorway, he looked at her, and he remembered how she had first come to him. He remembered the power of the octolaris nectar, the stunning yearning it had raised within him.

He shoved aside those thoughts. There was no time for foolishness. He hurried through the hallways, eager to bring his octolaris home.

14

"Halt! Speak your name!"

Rani jerked awake, gasping for breath even as she scrambled to her feet. In her first dream-crossed moment of awareness, she glanced at the high walls of the spiderguild enclave, at the ominous gate that was closed until dawn. The guild was not attacking, though. The guild had taken no formal notice of the group that waited for admittance.

Instead, Crestman stood before her, his back lit by the low-burning campfire. He faced the darkness of the high plains with his Amanthian blade drawn, and he called again, "Speak your name! Identify yourself!"

Rani snagged the long knife that she had set beside her saddle just before she fell asleep. She hefted the weapon and tossed her hair from her gaze. Mair materialized before her, swearing fluently and fingering her own blade. Tovin swept up from the darkness, as well, his short sword glittering in the embers' light.

"Rani! Rani Trader!"

Before she could recognize the voice that called her name, Mair tensed beside her. "Farso!" called the Touched girl, and she rushed past Crestman, ignoring his curved and deadly blade.

Baron Farsobalinti stepped into the firelight. He held his hands clear at his side, conspicuously avoiding the hilt of his own sheathed sword, not even moving to embrace Mair. "Well met, Crestman. King Halaravilli would be pleased."

"Who is this?" Tovin asked as Rani sheathed her knife.

"Baron Farsobalinti. King Halaravilli's closest friend." She stepped forward. "What is it, my lord? Has our king fallen ill?"

Farso reached a fleeting hand toward Mair's face, but he answered Rani immediately. "Nay, King Halaravilli is well enough. He sent me with a message, though."

Crestman slapped his sword back into his sheath. He gestured toward their fire and said, "Come then, hand it over."

Farso shook his head. "It is not written. My lord did not want to risk it falling into the hands of his enemies."

"Then speak, man! We are all listening."

Again, Farso shook his head, looking past Crestman. "I must speak with Rani. The king's words are for her alone."

Rani's heart squeezed tight in her chest, and she barely managed to pull in a breath. What had happened in Liantine? Why had Hal sent Farso? Feeling as if another person moved her limbs, she made her way to the tall, pale lord. "Aye, my lord. Let us step aside."

She noticed Mair's look of consternation, the protest that bubbled up to the Touched girl's lips. She heard Crestman mutter something, and she sensed Tovin on the edge of their group, separate, confused. Farso wasted no time; he pulled her into the darkness.

"What, my lord? What news could be so urgent?"

"He told me I must reach you before you enter the spiderguild enclave. I rode out nine horses."

"Tell me, then. What message do you bring from the king?"

The nobleman glanced at the towering wall behind her, and he lowered his voice so that he scarcely breathed his words. "His Majesty has acquired spiders, my lady. Octolaris for your plan."

"What?" Her yelp was loud enough that Crestman took a step closer. She forced herself to whisper to Farso, "How? How did he get them?"

"The spiderguild apprentice in Liantine, Mareka. She stole them from her masters."

For just an instant, Rani pictured the woman's face, her high cheekbones, her calculating eyes. Mareka Octolaris had broken her guild's monopoly, then, smuggled out the spiders. Even now, Rani could remember the manipulative flash of the apprentice's eyes. "And riberry trees? Did she manage those, as well?"

Farso shook his head. "No. There are grubs enough for another month, but after that the spiders will starve. His Majesty commands you to negotiate with the spiderguild for the trees. He thought your mission might be easier if you need not argue for the octolaris, as well."

"Aye," she breathed. Easier. But still not easy. "You did well to ride so fast. This news will make a difference." She shook her head, still wondering how she would negotiate, how she might manipulate the spiderguild. What could she say to them? What bargain could she offer that would convince them to part with the trees? Could she trick them into giving up the riberries, if they did not know Morenia had the spiders? And when would the guild learn that news?

"When did this happen, my lord?"

"Late in the afternoon, the day before yesterday." Rani stared at the nobleman, her surprise transparent. He had not exaggerated about the nine horses—even so, he had ridden faster than she would have thought possible.

"Then the guild cannot know yet."

"Not yet, but they will soon. Princess Jerusha will send them notice, and she will have royal riders at her disposal. They should be here no more than an hour after dawn."

"And that will be an hour too late."

"My lady?"

Rani realized that she had been speaking more to herself than to Farso. "Tovin Player has explained to us. The spiderguild opens its gate but once a day, to protect itself against marauders. Anyone who would enter or leave must stand before the gate at the moment the sun crests the horizon. After that, the gates are closed and all must wait until the next dawn."

"Surely they will open for a rider from the king!"

"Tovin says they will yield to no one, for any amount of money, for any threat. The practice has kept them safe here on the plains for generations."

Farso glanced over his shoulder, at the sky beyond the glowing firelight. "We haven't very long, then."

"No. Not long at all." What could she bargain? What could

she bid? She shook her head. "Thank you for your message, my lord, and for delivering it in time. I fear, though, if I do not release you to speak to Mair, she'll gut us both, and we will have no further spiderguild concerns."

The nobleman smiled and sketched a hasty bow; then he hurried off to the Touched girl. Rani crossed her arms and looked up at the guild's walls. Soon. Soon she would be inside. Soon she would begin negotiating the bargain of her lifetime.

"What news did Farsobalinti have?"

She looked up to see Crestman beside her. "Nothing," she said. At Crestman's skeptical snort, she added, "Nothing that affects your mission here."

"I should know for myself."

"You won't. His Majesty's words were for me alone."

Crestman started to protest, obviously believing that he had the right to stake a claim. Before he could speak, Tovin approached.

"Our plan remains the same, then? You will enter the spiderguild at dawn?"

"Oh, yes. Nothing has changed," Rani said, despite the fact that it had. Everything had changed.

"Very well. We'd best be moving," Tovin said, and his teeth shone out against his lips in the greying darkness. For just an instant, Rani thought of the hours she had spent with the player in the dark storeroom, the hours spent learning glasswrights' secrets, Speaking. Tovin nodded toward the wall. "We must be at the gate when the sun clears the horizon."

Rani turned back to the dying fire and started to gather up her belongings, but Tovin said, "Leave everything. The spiderguild will dispatch a groom to tend our horses while we are inside. Also, leave behind your weapons."

"Weapons?" Rani might never have heard the word before.

"Any knife. Any blade. It will not pass the spiderguild gate."

Rani's hand went to her waist, to the silver-chased dagger that she carried. "I can't go in unarmed."

Tovin's face remained placid. "They'll check. If they find steel, they'll turn you away, before you've had a chance to say one word to plead your cause."

"And if they find me *unarmed*? What danger will I be in then?"

"Rani, these are guildsmen, not soldiers. Why would they attack you, a messenger from another guild? They want to spin their webs, sell their silk. They won't gain power by dragging unsuspecting visitors off to their dungeons."

Rani shrugged and patted her horse's neck, using the motion to gain some time. She knew that Crestman would challenge the edict to go weaponless. Mair, as well, and Farso. Nevertheless, Tovin's claims seemed truthful. He *had* come before the spiderguild many times in the past.

Rani breathed a prayer to Clain, the glasswrights' god, as she slipped her knife into her saddlebag. Let him watch over her—she was only making herself vulnerable for his glory, after all. For his glory and for Hal's.

Tovin nodded and then repeated his warning to Mair and the two western men. As Rani had expected, all three protested. "Do it," Rani said before Tovin could explain once again. "If you are going to accompany me, do what Tovin says."

Mair grimaced, but she slipped her dagger into her own saddlebag. Her dagger, and a small bodkin that she held in a sheath against her wrist. Tovin pinned the Touched girl with hard eyes, a stare that she braved for a long, starlit minute before she sighed and reached beneath the ivory comb that held her hair off her face. Rani was surprised to see the steel picks that she withdrew—surprised because she had not known Mair to take such precautions.

Farso swore softly under his breath, shaking his head as he discarded his own weaponry. Crestman looked as if he would rebel outright, but Rani's imploring glance finally made him comply. He left behind a veritable armory—his Amanthian sword, two short daggers, a long iron spike that had nestled down his boot, and an iron bracelet that opened to reveal two wicked teeth.

Tovin said nothing; he only led the way up to the heavy iron gate that barred entrance to the spiderguild. When all five of them stood before the guild's enclosure, the player glanced over his shoulder, as if he were measuring the time until sunrise. He seemed pleased with what he found—the sky was flushing white behind them. Tovin nodded, and then he stepped forward, taking care to stand in the precise center of a great black flagstone that yawned before the gate. "Come along," he said. "They won't open up if we aren't all standing here."

Crestman started to mutter, but Rani silenced him with a glance. With Tovin standing in the middle of the darkened stone, Rani stepped to his right side, and she waved Mair and Farso over to his left. The Touched girl's eyes sparked, as if she did not care for the command, but she obeyed, pulling Farso with her. Crestman took up his position at Rani's other side, standing close enough that she could feel him breathing, could feel the angry tension that twitched through his flesh, his arms, his very body.

Rani glanced at Tovin for reassurance, but the player said nothing. She thought that she detected a smile on his lips, the faintest of grins, as he turned his eyes forward, staring at the center of the massive ironclad gate.

Rani caught her breath, and she could make out sounds behind the wall. There was the creak of iron, and a rolling, rocking sound, as if a metal rack were jolting along cobbled streets. The noises were vaguely familiar, rising out of Rani's past— the sounds of the Merchants' Quarter swinging into action on a busy morning.

The sun finally moved above the horizon, washing the walls of the spiderguild enclosure with rosy light. Tovin tensed beside her, and Rani heard a muffled order behind the gate. She braced herself, turning to face the entrance. Then, before she could whisper any of the questions that boiled up in her mind, before she could wonder what she was getting herself into, the door in the center of the gate flew open.

Light.

Dazzling, blinding light.

Rani's eyes squinted closed against the brilliance, cloaking her vision in bloodred color. She stumbled, trying to brave the light, trying to make herself look inside the gate, inside the spiderguild's enclosure.

Instead, rough hands seized her. She recognized a soldier's touch, impersonally gripping her shoulders, coursing down her torso, clutching around her legs as he checked for weapons.

Mair swore aloud, and Crestman bellowed, so Rani knew that
her companions must be similarly treated. She was grateful that
she had followed Tovin's advice, that she had left her knife in
her worn leather saddlebags, for it surely would have been discovered.

From the shouted oaths, Rani learned that Mair had not been
so circumspect. "That's *my* knife, you bastard!" the Touched
girl cried.

"Silence!" barked someone, and Rani felt the searching
hands on her own body grow more brutal. She heard Crestman
swear a terrible oath, and then she realized that Mair was being
wrestled to the ground. Farso called out a challenge, and the
spiderguild guards responded with sharp words of their own.

Rani tossed her head, trying to discern what was happening.
By opening her light-blinded eyes to the barest of slits and
twisting away from her captors, she could just see Mair's form,
spread-eagled on the black stone, a spiderguild guard settling
his boot across her neck. Farso was on his knees beside her, his
lashed hands pulled high behind him, involuntarily tightening a
noose that looped around his throat. The nobleman was frozen,
for any gesture that he made would tighten the rope, would cut
off his breath even further.

"Mair!" Rani shouted, but then she caught her breath—she
recognized the prick of a blade against her own throat. The
steel point nestled in the hollow above her breastbone. When
she swallowed, she felt it rise and fall, and she knew that the
sharp tip had nicked her flesh.

As Rani watched through slitted eyes, the spiderguild guards
wrestled Mair to her feet, lashing her hands behind her back
with spidersilk cords. Mair spluttered at the rough treatment,
her Touched tongue filling the air with a complete discourse on
the guards' parentage, on their mothers' unnaturally close alliance with beasts. Farso glared but did not speak a word as one
of the soldiers barked another order. Mair's mouth was suddenly filled with a wad of spidersilk, the gag lashed tight about
her head. The girl continued to thrash, almost breaking free
from her captors, but then the leader hollered, "Hold!"

The bellow echoed off the walls above them, so loud that it
shocked Mair into stillness. The captain took advantage of the

momentary calm to say to the burliest of his men, "I want your knife beside her jugular. Kill her if she swallows."

Crestman caught his breath beside Rani, as if his restraint might provide safety for Mair. Rani's heart pounded, and her pulse raged in the sting at the base of her own throat. The struggle had moved her off the black flagstone, and now she could see inside the city gates. She could make out a complicated system of polished mirrors, dozens of reflective glass plates hanging on rolling iron frameworks. Even as she struggled to make sense of the spiderguild's rough greeting, even as she fought for an escape, she marveled at their cleverness.

The spiderguild opened its gates only at dawn. At dawn, when the sun rose above the horizon . . . The sun, magnified a hundredfold by the carefully positioned mirrors . . . The spiderguild let itself be vulnerable only when it had the power to blind any potential attacker.

And Tovin had known. He had stepped onto the black flagstone, onto the focus of the mirrors' blinding light, with all the confidence of a child settling on his mother's hearth.

Mair's eyes were wild above her gag as she glared a complicated message to Rani. Farso stared up from his own bonds, furiously silent. Before Rani could step forward, before she could try to restore some order to the situation, Tovin spoke. "Well met, spiderguild." The player's voice was wry. He raised his hands slowly, smoothly. Rani knew that he bore no weapon, but his motion was clearly calculated to remind his captors of his helplessness. "We beg leave to meet with the guildmaster."

"Tovin Player, is it?" The guard eyed the tall man suspiciously. "We expected your return, but no one said you'd bring these others."

"I had no time to let you know," Tovin said easily. "They come on their own mission, not on mine."

"Then you do not vouch for them before the guildmaster?"

Tovin's eyes narrowed for a moment. "I'll speak for Ranita Glasswright, for this woman here. The others I'll not condemn, but I do not know their ways, and I do not know their reasons for coming to the spiderguild." He nodded toward Mair. "That one was told not to approach the gate with steel."

"She's with me!" Rani exclaimed, managing not to wince as

her guard tightened his grip on her arms. The pricked spot on her throat pulsed hot. "Tovin says that I am safe, and I say that Mair is!"

"No one has spoken to you, glasswright." The captain did not spare her a glance. He even managed to ignore Crestman at her side, despite the Amanthian's growl. Instead, he pinned all his attention on Tovin. "This is irregular, player."

"Aye," Tovin agreed. "Ranita Glasswright asked me to conduct her here. She has business with your guildmaster."

"What sort of business?"

"Guild business. Beyond the ken of a common player." Tovin shrugged as the soldier glared at him suspiciously. "You'll have to ask the lady for more. I have only guided her here. I do not know the bargain that she hopes to strike."

Rani understood this much about negotiating: she would gain nothing by telling this soldier of her plans. "My words are for your guildmaster alone. I'll do my business with him."

"You will, will you?" the captain growled. "You come to our gates with hidden knives, and you expect to be conducted to Master Anigo?"

Curse Mair for her suspicious mind! Curse her for believing that she was always, unmitigatedly right! Rani forced an even tone into her retort. "My companion feared that we might not be well received here at the spiderguild. She feared that our welcome might be rough, and she vowed to protect herself—and me—from harm."

If the captain appreciated the irony in Rani's statement, he gave no sign. Rather, he glared at her for a long moment, his gaze as hot as the reflecting mirrors' light had been. He stared pointedly at Rani's throat, and she wondered if her blood had begun to trickle down her front, if it had reached the top of her collar. She straightened her shoulders and met the soldier's eyes.

The captain nodded at last. "Very well. Tovin Player, your word will serve for this one, and for the silent solider." He nodded toward Crestman. "The three of you may go before the guildmaster. We'll keep this pair, though, until your business is complete."

Mair squealed through her gag, twisting wildly in her

guards' hands, and Farso lunged forward, gasping as the rope cut across his windpipe. "Please!" Rani exclaimed before the guards could act upon their leader's earlier order to kill Mair. "We cannot leave them here! They're my friends! They thought to protect me!"

"They will not have the chance."

Rani knew enough about the placid simplicity of soldiers to realize that she would not sway this man. Mair had violated the spiderguild's absolute rule. She had approached with steel.

Rani said, "If either of them suffers so much as a bruise at your hands, you'll have the king of all Morenia to answer to. They are dear to King Halaravilli."

The soldier shrugged. "They will be unharmed unless they act rashly, more so than they have already done."

There was nothing else that Rani could do. Surely Mair and Farso would understand. Rani would be foolish to leave the spiderguild with Moren's business undone, now that she was so close. *Now that Hal had the spiders.* She drew herself up, summoning all the regal bearing she had learned in the Morenian palace. "Take care that they are not."

Rani did not look back as she entered the spiderguild's walled compound. She could not measure the betrayal that she was certain to find in Mair's eyes, the impotent rage in Farsobalinti's. Instead, she wiped away the trickle of blood from her throat and followed Tovin into the heart of the spiderguild. Crestman fell in beside her.

She told herself to remember the paths that they trod, so that she could retrace her way to the gate. The task was not easy. The streets met at odd angles, spinning Rani about, upsetting her sense of direction. The guards made abrupt turns—first right, then left, then left and right again.

The spiderguild's stronghold was at the highest point inside the enclosure, and every street was steeper than the one before. As she climbed, Rani could distinguish the ring of turreted walls that surrounded the guild, the ominous stone towers that loomed a mere forty paces apart. Guards stood at attention in each tower, and other soldiers passed on the thick ramparts above the grassy plain.

Before Rani realized how far she had climbed, the group

emerged into a vast central courtyard. Despite her best intentions, despite her vow to remain aloof and unimpressed, Rani could not help but gasp in surprise at the building that occupied the center of the spiderguild's maze.

The courtyard was paved with glittering stone—pure white marble pieced together in a vast, unbuckled expanse. The marble was overlaid by an intricate web of darkest black, stone fitted so closely that it looked as if it had grown there organically. The black pathways spun across the courtyard, completely irregular but perfectly balanced. Gazing across the expanse, Rani recognized the pattern of a spiderweb. Seeing the design, she suddenly understood the twists and turns she had taken to arrive in the courtyard. The streets, too, were patterned after a spiderweb. The guild embraced its treasured octolaris in the very core of its construction.

Tovin smiled at Rani, like a parent who finds his toddler enjoying some bauble. She drew herself up straight. She was not going to gawk like a provincial fool. After all, she was on an embassy from the king of all Morenia. She arrived as the representative of the glasswrights' guild. She would not be dumbfounded by the workings of a clutch of weavers. Mere weavers, that's all the spiderguild contained. Farmers. Harvesters. Spinners. Nothing worth fearing.

So Rani tried to convince herself as she crossed the spider courtyard, with Crestman silent beside her. If only Mair were with her! Mair would not be swayed by the courtyard's stunning appearance. She would make some wry statement, some offhand challenge. She would not be cowed. It took all Rani's will to walk normally, to stride forward without adjusting her gait to tread only on the black stones, or only on the white.

In the center of the courtyard, nestled like a spider in the middle of a web, sat the most curious building Rani had ever seen. It was large—as large as the house of the Thousand Gods back in Moren. A hulking tower rose at each corner, and Rani could decipher the shadowy shapes of bells inside the campaniles. The building's facade formed a massive rectangle, a sheet of marble that towered above the webbed plaza. In the center was a vast window, a field of stained glass that immediately drew Rani's attention. She could make out intricate lead-work, see an expert's hand in the design, although she could not translate the image from the outside, without the brilliance of sunlight streaming through.

The entire facade was a masterpiece of architectural misdirection. Eight ranks of pillars cut across the rectangular stone face. Like everything else under the spiderguild's control, however, the columns reflected the pattern of the city, of the plaza, of the octolaris themselves. The pillars tumbled across the facade as if they radiated from the central stained-glass window. The web spread out in chaotic precision, balanced, harmonious, and not at all predictable. The entire illusion was assisted by intricate stone carving, by sprawling capitals that added to the impression that the building spun out from its center.

Rani swiped once more at the nick on her throat as the guards marched the outlanders across the courtyard and up the steps. Her fingers stung the wound, but they came away dry.

She glanced at Crestman and saw that he, too, was intimidated by the guildhall. His face had paled, and his scar stood out like a dead patch. She caught the rapid flicker of his eyes about the courtyard, and she understood that he was looking for members of his Little Army. Even in the heart of the enemy camp, he was searching for his men.

Summoning all her courage, Rani stepped proudly over the threshold, entering the spiderguild hall as if she were a regal ambassador rather than a mere glasswrights' apprentice.

A large room stretched behind the facade, four bare white walls and a high ceiling. Acting as if the guards did not monitor her every step, Rani moved across the chamber, and then she turned around to face the entrance.

The stained glass window was a masterpiece. She could see evidence of Tovin's glass tools, of diamond knives that had let a master craftsman create long slivers of glass no wider than her thumb. The window depicted the feeding of spiders, a guildsman surrounded by four pairs of eight-legged beasts, each as big as his chest. Riberry trees wove about the edges of the round window, leaning in to offer clusters of yellow leaves, and minute markin grubs were sprinkled across the glasswork like the tiniest flaws in glass.

Rani swallowed hard. The spiderguild had a building finer

than anything Hal could offer. They had glass treasures more delicate than any that she could fashion. She glared defiantly. She *would* bargain with the guild. She *would* obtain the riberry trees. Her king depended on her. All of Morenia relied on her.

By now, the tangle of intricate hallways was familiar. As the guards marched her toward the heart of the guildhall, Rani gave up the dream of tracing her path, of deciphering the twists and turns. She knew now that she was walking a web, that she was edging closer and closer to a core, to a single room that would stand at the heart of all the great guild's power.

And she was not disappointed.

The guards arrived before a pair of doors, rich intarsia fashioned of many colors of wood. Rani was hardly surprised by the story depicted in the intricate inlay: massive octolaris sprawled across the doors, their bodies as long as her forearm, their bent legs nearly the length of Rani's body. Swirling around the spiders in careful detail were scores of riberry trees, their branches picked out in silver grey, each individual leaf set in smooth-polished wood. Focusing on the masterwork, Rani could discern wooden markin grubs in the clusters of yellow at the end of every riberry branch.

Without warning, the doors swung inward. Rani retained just enough sense of drama that she paused on the threshold, resisting her guards' pressure to move forward. She looked about, taking in the room at the core of the guildhall, the man at the center of the room.

There were no windows along the walls—the chamber was too deep in the building for that. There were, however, artful screens set along the edges of the hall, with massive torches burning behind them. Mirrors were placed around the torches, collecting the flickering light and casting it back into the chamber. Rani did not waste time studying the intricate construction of those mirrored lanterns; she knew that they would be related to the instruments that had nearly blinded her at the gate, to the lamps employed by Tovin's players.

Instead, she noticed the slaves who tended the torches. The high-burning lamps made the room close and stuffy; the air was heavy. In an attempt to counter the stillness, slaves were positioned between the torches, slaves who waved heavy fans of silken streamers. Rani felt Crestman stiffen beside her as she took in the scene, and she realized that a dozen soldiers from the Little Army stood near.

The child closest to her was a slight boy; he could not have been more than eight or nine years old when he was shipped to Liantine. The child's scar covered half his cheek, standing out in the flickering torchlight like a patch of diseased flesh. The boy caught his lip with his teeth as he struggled to manipulate his heavy silken fan. He refused to meet her eyes, refused to acknowledge any of the visitors. Instead, he stared ahead as if he were blind, as if he were no longer a child.

Of course, he wasn't. He was a chattel. He was a slave. He belonged to the spiderguild now, as surely as he had belonged to Sin Hazar.

Something about the stalwart child fed the beginning of a plan in Rani's mind. Even as she ran over the possibilities, prodding, testing, she glanced at Crestman, wishing that she could warn him. But there was no way. No way to assure him, to explain her true intention. He would have to have faith. By Cot, the god of soldiers, he would have to believe that she worked in his best interest.

Taking a deep breath, Rani dragged her attention from the child slave and forced herself to meet the guildmaster, the leader of all the spiderguild.

He stood in the center of the room. The man was tall, taller than Tovin, and his head was shaved. Deep wrinkles were carved beside his eyes, the clear effect of years spent on the high windy plains. Although his body was well muscled, there were pockmarks on both his arms, angry scars that spoke of a lifetime tending octolaris.

About his neck, he wore an elaborate weaving, an embroidered, knotted design made entirely of spidersilk. The strange neckpiece cascaded down his bare chest, rising and falling with his deep breath. The guildmaster viewed the newcomers without moving, both fists planted on his hips. The stance made his scarred arms stand out like chiseled stone.

Tovin stepped forward, folding his lanky body into a bow. "My lord Anigo. Many thanks for agreeing to see us on short notice."

"Tovin Player." The spiderguild master's tone was flat, featureless. He shifted his hands, and Rani could see rings on each of his fingers—heavy, golden bands that flashed with inlaid stones. The ostentatious display did not bode well for her plan. She resisted the urge to glance at Crestman.

Tovin straightened and cleared his throat. The sound was a small one, nothing remarkable in another man, but it sent a shiver down Rani's spine. Tovin was nervous. The man who had Spoken with her, the player who was accustomed to standing before endless audiences, *Tovin* was afraid. That realization made Rani more than a little unsure herself, and she scarcely heard the player say, "I beg your indulgence, Lord Anigo, as I present to you two visitors to Liantine. Ranita Glasswright has traveled from distant Morenia to learn about your guild. Crestman is a soldier who accompanies her."

Rani scarcely had time to brace herself before Anigo pinned her with his eyes. She saw the shrewd intelligence behind that gaze, the measured thoughts. She recognized the power immediately—it was the same force that she had seen in her own guildmistress, in Salina, before the guild had been destroyed.

Rani took a single step forward. She had no time to be intimidated, no time to slowly build trust and companionship with the guildmaster. One day. That was all she had. After that, King Teheboth's messenger would arrive, and Anigo would know that Hal had obtained the octolaris. One day for Rani to negotiate for riberry trees. She might as well begin.

"Greetings, Guildmaster." Her voice shook, and she swallowed hard, but she took another step forward, further distancing herself from her companions. Neither Tovin nor Crestman would be pleased with what she was about to say.

"Ranita Glasswright." Anigo nodded as he looked at her, appraising her as if she were horseflesh he debated purchasing. "Your guild was destroyed, though, no? Your guildhall was torn down, and all the glasswrights maimed or killed."

"Those were mistakes, Guildmaster!" The pricked place on Rani's throat smarted as her face flushed with anger. "The glasswrights are rebuilding. We are supported by King Halaravilli!"

Tovin caught his breath at her defiant tone, but she did not spare the player a glance. Out of the corner of her eye, she noted two of the slave boys cringing, drawing back between their torches as if they feared Anigo's physical reprisal. The slaves' reaction made Crestman tense, and Rani knew that she would not have long to work her bargaining. She took another step closer to Anigo.

"King Halaravilli has sent me as his ambassador. He demands that you return the people of his kingdom, the children of the Little Army that you have purchased as slaves."

Anigo threw back his head and laughed, making the elaborate neckpiece sway across his chest. He gestured to the children who lined the room. "And what will your king pay?"

"He'll deliver his payments with soldiers and engines of war, guildmaster." Tovin gasped and grabbed at her arm. She knew the player must be furious; he had not anticipated any such challenge to his patron. She pulled away and said to Anigo, "Even now, my lord, King Halaravilli prepares to wed Princess Berylina. As soon as he has taken his bride, he will send for his soldiers, for his soldiers and Lord Davin."

Anigo's eyes narrowed, and Rani pounced on his recognition. "Aye, my lord. You know Lord Davin's name? He's the man who engineered the undermining of the Swancastle. He's the man who brought down the kingdom of Amanthia, with his devices and his tools. Your guildhall here will provide him with a fine summer diversion."

"Ranita!" warned Tovin, but Rani only stepped closer to the guildmaster.

Anigo glared at her. "You forget yourself, glasswright. My guildhall is a city unto itself. Your king can lay his siege. He can camp out on the plains for months. We have our gardens, and we have the Great Well—we'll outlast any mischief your king might work."

"Will you?" Rani looked about her, as if she were honestly considering the guildmaster's defiance. "Can you wait out a season? Two? Three? What will that do to the market for spidersilk?" Rani pulled her arm free from Tovin's frantic grasp, snarling at the player as he tried to placate her. "I've been in Liantine, my lord! I've seen that your guild is already dying. The Horned Hind holds sway in the capital. King Teheboth has ordered his entire palace reworked in the wood sacred to the Horned Hind, replacing your precious silk. If Halaravilli sets siege to your walls, how long will your guild hold on to its market? How long will the world desire spidersilk when it can live in wool or linen? Not a single shipment out, for all the summer. All the autumn. All the winter. Can you last till spring? Can you last another year?"

Anigo stepped toward her, his scarred forearms quivering with fury. "We paid for our slaves, paid Sin Hazar honorably. You have no right to demand them now."

Rani glanced at Crestman, saw the hope and admiration spread across his face. She wished that she could spare him the course this bargaining was about to take. She wished that she had time to explain. "There is nothing honorable in bargaining for children."

"For soldiers, glasswright."

"For boys. For girls. My king will come to redeem them, with all the might at his command. Unless."

Anigo's eyes were shrewd. "Unless what?"

"Unless you pay him. Pay Morenia for the slaves."

Crestman's cry was strangled, and for the first time since entering the spiderguild enclave she was grateful that the westerners' weapons had been taken from them. Anigo's glance flickered over the captain, and his voice was chilled as he said, "So, your noble king would trade his children for silk?"

"Not silk. For riberry trees."

"What?" Anigo was astonished.

"One score trees for every Amanthian child you keep within the enclave."

"Impossible."

"Twenty trees, or Halaravilli orders his army mobilized. Lord Davin has had three years to devise new engines, three years since Morenia conquered Amanthia."

"Rani, you can't!" Crestman's protest was harsh in the dim room.

"Quiet, Crestman!"

"They are *children*."

"They are soldiers," she snapped at him. "Soldiers sworn to

your king. Your king, who will bring the spiderguild down to its knees. Unless this man pays."

"Ranita," Tovin began, as if he might talk sense into her.

"Silence!" she cried. "I wait to hear from one man in this room. Lord Anigo, what say you? Will you pay in riberry trees? Or will you watch your silk trade die?"

The guildmaster glared at her. His neckpiece rose and fell as his breath came harshly, and beads of perspiration stood out on his shaven head. His eyes were caves, hidden, angry, and she wondered for just a minute how she dared to make this demand, how she dared defy the spiderguild. But then, just as she thought that she would lose, just as she thought that Hal would truly need to summon Davin, Davin and all the army—to rescue her if nothing else—Anigo nodded. Once. A tight inclination of his head, as if his neck were stiff.

"One tree," he said. "One tree for every slave."

"Ten," Rani countered.

Anigo's teeth grated, the scraping clear in the otherwise silent room. Rani caught her breath, frozen, waiting. "Ten."

"No!" Crestman howled, throwing himself toward the guildmaster. A half-dozen soldiers surrounded him, even as Anigo scrambled back four steps. Crestman swore and fought as if his life depended on ripping himself free from the spiderguild guards. He tossed his head like a wild man, struggling to bite his captors, to kick them, to chop at them with his furious fists, but he was subdued quickly by their weapons and superior force.

Rani stared, horrified by what she had provoked. For just an instant, she thought that Crestman might only be playacting, that he actually knew her *true* plan, the one still hidden, but when she saw the vicious hatred flashing from his eyes, she knew that he was lost. "Crestman," she said, her voice barely audible above his harsh panting and the exerted breath of his captors.

"Don't speak to me, traitor!"

She could not respond. She could not tell him her intentions. She could not say that she would bargain for the riberry trees, establish Hal's silk trade, and then return, next year, with gold from the profitable sale of silk, gold that the spiderguild could not resist. She would ransom all the slaves eventually, but for now she could not reveal her plans.

Crestman twisted until he could glare at Anigo. "Take me, then. Make me one of your slaves."

The guildmaster laughed, the grim sound bouncing off the ceiling of the high chamber. "And why would I do that?"

"I can work. I can plow your fields and haul your water. I'll feed your cursed spiders. I'll do whatever you command."

"I could never trust you."

"You'll keep me under guard. You'll keep me without weapons. The other slaves will see me, and they'll know better than to rebel."

Rani wanted to protest. She wanted to tell Crestman that he did not need to do this; he did not need to sell himself for the riberries. He could stand now, walk out of the hall with her, with Tovin. All would be right, within one year.

Anigo nodded slowly, and his blunt fingers stroked his neck-piece. "I won't change my mind. I won't release you when you recognize your foolishness."

"My foolishness was in believing a Morenian would ever hold my own interests at heart. Better that I serve honorably with my soldiers, than that I lap the boots of conquerors."

Anigo stared for a long moment, but then he gestured to his soldiers. "Take him to the slave quarters, then. Issue him a tunic, and send him to the fields, with chains about his ankles. He's on bread and water rations until I say otherwise, and two men will watch over him. Kill him if he takes one false step."

The guards wrestled Crestman to his feet, jostling him with their swords. "Crestman!" Rani cried.

He spat at her.

For just an instant, she was outside of the spiderguild hall, outside of Liantine altogether, and back at the fallen Swan-castle. She stood beside Crestman on the hillside, listening to his tale of bitter disappointment, to the cruelty that had bound him to the Little Army. She remembered the hatred in his eyes, the bitter lust for revenge that had tightened the scar across his cheekbone.

And now, she saw that same raw desire, that same desperate rage. Crestman was lost to her forever.

He turned away without a word, and the guards led him from the hall.

Anigo waited for a long minute, and then he raised a diamond-studded hand. "Done, then. Ten trees for each of my slaves. But not for that one. He was not mine when you drove your bargain."

Rani nodded, sick at heart that anyone—even Anigo—could think that she had meant to profit from Crestman's choice.

Anigo raised a commanding hand, summoning a servant from the shadows. "Very well, then. We will have the papers completed by sunset, and you may sign them then. Ranita Glasswright, you may go about our compound for the daylight hours, but you may not enter any building without a member of the spiderguild."

Rani inclined her head, accepting the restrictions. Before Anigo could leave, Tovin started forward, looking as if he intended to kneel before his lord. "Player," Anigo said. "You, too, are forbidden from entering our buildings."

"My lord, I have negotiations to complete, for the players' cobalt cloth."

"You will not negotiate with us. You chose your side in this charade. The spiderguild has no further interest in the players."

"My lord!"

"Silence!" Anigo's bellow made the floor tremble. "You brought outsiders into our midst. You allowed them to manipulate us. You paved the way for riberry trees to be released into the outside world. The spiderguild will have nothing more to do with you—not with you, and not your troop. You will leave at dawn tomorrow, and you will be denied any further entrance to our enclave."

"My lord, I—"

"One word more, and I will have you taken to the stockade, with the two who broke our laws at the gate."

Tovin's throat worked, and he clearly considered testing the guildmaster's edict. Rani could see that Anigo would not relent, and she reached out one hand to still the player. He shook away her fingers angrily.

"Until sunset, then," Anigo said, inclining his head toward Rani.

The remaining guards led them from the chamber, weapons drawn as they wound through the twisting guildhall corridors. None actually touched Rani with the point or flat of a blade, but they left no question about where she must walk and how quickly. The tangled hallways seemed darker now, gloomier and more twisted.

Rani was relieved at last to find herself in the large reception room, under the glint of colored glass from the octolaris window. Then, she was outside the building altogether, back in the morning sun, looking down on the black-veined marble courtyard. The leader of the guards repeated Anigo's warning to avoid the buildings, and then he led his men away, abandoning Rani and Tovin on the blinding white steps.

Rani waited until the soldiers had left, and her voice trembled as she asked, "Is that all, then? They won't place a guard upon us for the day?"

"What could you do to harm the spiderguild?" Tovin's words were bitter. "All the silk is locked up. The spiders would be death if you handled them. You are locked inside until the gates open at tomorrow's dawn."

Tomorrow's dawn. When the messenger would arrive from King Teheboth.

Rani swallowed hard. "I bargained for Morenia. I got the riberry trees."

"At what cost?" Tovin nearly shouted, his player's voice booming across the courtyard. He clutched at her arm and pulled her close, the force of his fingers strong enough that she knew immediately she would have bruises. "At what cost, Ranita Glasswright? To prove that you could outwit Anigo Octolaris? Without octolaris, your trees are worthless, and for that, you have broken the players!"

"Surely, the players are not broken! Audiences will watch you, even if you play your pieces with ragged curtains."

"This isn't about curtains! Don't you understand? The guild has withdrawn its *support*. We will not be allowed on the Liantine roads without a sponsor. The entire troop will be illegal, banished. Every troop needs a patron, and you have driven ours away!"

Rani had not understood. She had not realized what her bargain cost. Nevertheless, she could not have acted otherwise. She needed the trees. Hal needed them; Morenia did. With the trees, they could rebuild safely, recover from the fire and the illness, escape from under the Fellowship's thumb. . . .

Even if she had needed to bring down the players. Even if she had lost Crestman.

Tovin glared at her. "And you don't even realize, yet, that all your bargaining was for nothing. You'll never keep those trees alive."

"We will. We must."

"Do you know the first thing about riberries, Ranita Glasswright? You should have asked a player. Any one of us could have told you that your plan was foolish. We trade in stories, after all. We trade for knowledge. Our Speaking is not just a way for lonely noble-girls to pass the time."

"I'm a guildsman," she said through set teeth.

"Aye, a guildsman. So what do you know about riberry trees? First, you must protect them from the wind."

"I'll do that. I—I'll design glass screens."

"You must pollinate each tree by hand."

"The children will do that—the Touched and other folk in Moren who were left homeless by the fire."

"You must water each tree twelve times daily, with two full buckets each time."

"We can—" Rani caught herself. "*Twelve* times?"

"Twelve."

"The trees will drown!"

"They are nourished by a moss that grows around their roots."

"We—we can impress people to do that."

"And what will they use for water?"

For the first time since leaving the guildhall, Rani saw that her plan might fail. Her voice shook as she said, "Moren's wells, of course."

"Moren's wells? How deep are they? How much water do they yield, Ranita Glasswright?" She heard her name like a

mocking slur. What could a glasswright hope to know of such
things, of planting and harvesting and husbandry? How could
she be expected to answer?

"How does the spiderguild do it, then?" she spat back in defiance. "We're on a plain here, far from any river." She waved
her hand vaguely to take in the marble courtyard, which had
begun to shimmer in the morning heat.

"The spiderguild has a well. A deeper well than you'll ever
dig in Moren."

"Don't be so sure. When King Halaravilli sets his mind to
something, he can do it." He *can*, Rani told herself. Hal can,
and Davin, and all the people of Moren, who will have no
choice if they wish our land to survive.

For answer, Tovin merely strode away. When Rani hesitated
to follow him, he turned back, his lips twisted into a cruel grin.
"Surely you're not afraid, Ranita Glasswright? Not afraid to
follow me to the truth?"

Rani trotted to catch up to him. She wanted to demand an
answer. She wanted to order him—a player, a man not even
recorded in Morenia's castes—to stop, to listen to her. But
she thought of the power he had held over her, the power of
Speaking, the power of his glasswright skills, and she held
her tongue.

And all the time that she followed him, around the corner of
the guildhall, along the side of the long brick building, through
the ornate, carefully planted gardens, she listened to doubt
grow in her mind. Hal had taken the spiders from Mareka.
Mareka *had* offered the spiders to Hal. What had passed between them? How had their alliance been built? What would
that bond mean to Hal's impending marriage to Berylina?

Tovin brushed past a kitchen garden, pushing through feath-
ery herbs. Beyond the plantings, there was a field of blinding
white stone. The player's boots crunched on the surface, the
sound echoed by Rani's own feet. Tovin headed toward an
unassuming heap of bricks.

A pair of donkeys stood beside the structure, lazily lipping
at grass that struggled in the shadows. The draft beasts trailed
their harnesses, and Rani saw that two massive yokes had been
settled haphazardly against the brick wall. A spider was carved

into each frame, the eight legs creeping across the wood like a cancer.

"What is this?" Rani panted as she caught up with Tovin.

For answer, he pushed open a door, revealing a passage barely wide enough for a laden donkey to pass through. When Rani hesitated to enter, the player crossed his arms over his chest. "Come see what you compete against. Come see how the spiderguild prospers." His words were mocking, condemning, and Rani wanted to explain, wanted to make him understand that she had had no choice but to work for Moren, no choice but to bid for the trees, whatever the cost to the players, to Tovin. To Crestman.

She wanted to explain, and she wanted to turn away, to go back to the front of the guildhall, to the bright morning light. Anything would be better than Tovin's furious superiority. Anything at all.

Swallowing hard, she forced herself to step forward. Over the threshold. Into the darkness.

No. Not darkness. There was no roof overhead. The brick wall was nothing more than a shield to keep the unwary from falling down a steep ramp. Rani looked across the enclosure to a matching hole, another mouthed ramp.

Tovin turned to Rani, half bowing. "My lady," he said with a condescending sneer, and Rani bristled as she began to descend.

The passage was carved from stone, after the first few feet of earth. The ramp curved around a central column of excavated space, the shaft of the well itself. Every ten paces, a window broke through from the enclosed ramp to the shaft.

Taking a deep breath, Rani approached the next gap. When she looked up, she could see two rows of windows above her, cut into the stony column that stretched to the sky. Looking down, she found that windows spiraled beneath her, spinning out like a spiderweb to dot the inside of the stone shaft. She leaned out farther, farther, stretching to see the bottom of the well. "Roan preserve us!" she gasped, calling out to the god of ladders for lack of another protector against the dizzying height. Rani had always liked high places, had always reveled in the power of ladders and scaffolds. But this was nearly too much, even for her. She pulled herself back over the window's stony lip.

Tovin snorted and gestured for her to lead the way down. At the bottom of the well, the walls were damp, traced by rivulets that trickled silently into a vast, spreading pool. Thick wooden planks stretched across the water. Rani wondered how deep it was, but before she could ask, Tovin reached into the leather pouch at his waist. He pulled out a misshapen lump of blood-red glass—a scrap from the players' panels, Rani realized. He held his hand over the water for a moment, and then he released the drop. Rani watched the glass sink through the water, fall into the shadows, disappear into the endless depth of the well. She could not see the bottom; she could not imagine how much water pooled beneath her. The well held more water than many rivers. More water than in all of Moren.

Only when the crimson drop was lost in the shadows at the bottom of the well did Rani dare to speak. "This is what they need, then? The riberry trees?"

"This. Or some other way to get them water."

"Four and twenty buckets a day."

"For each of your trees. For every one that you bought upon a child's back." Tovin's fury had faded to spite. "But you can tell your king that you won your bargain. You won your bargain, and you cut the players off from their sponsor."

"That was not supposed to happen!"

"Of course not." He was mocking her.

"I meant only to help my king."

"Without thought for anyone else. For any*thing* else. You used me, Ranita Glasswright. My players will be lost without a patron—all because you had to prove that you were right. You had to prove that you could best the spiderguild."

"That's not true!" Rani had not bargained for herself at all. She had negotiated on behalf of all of Moren, all the men, women, and children who suffered in the fire's bitter wake. Even now, she could picture the orphans, coughing blood past their sooty lips. She could see the bodies of the dead, stacked like firewood. Like the riberry trees that would also die in Morenia, starved without the water they required. Riberry trees that could only become the faggots to burn the corpses that counted out Rani's failure.

Unless Rani had spoken some version of the truth in Anigo's chamber. If Davin *could* find a way to save Morenia . . . If Davin could construct some massive engine, some pump to convey water to the riberry trees . . .

"That's not true, Tovin," she repeated. Her defiance echoed off the stone shaft, but the player set his fists against his hips and strode over the planks, crossing to the other ramp, to the one that led up from the bottom of the well.

Rani hurried across the pool, refusing to think about how much water was beneath her, how much water she would need for the trees. For Hal's trees. For Hal's spiders. For Mareka's spiders. Once again, she ordered her thoughts away from the manipulative spiderguild apprentice, from the currency she suspected Hal must have paid for the octolaris.

"Tovin!" she cried, and the player was pulled around by the force of the single word. "You must believe that I did not plan to hurt the players! I would not betray you! If you do not believe me, then Speak with me! Let me tell you that way."

"Speak with you." His voice dripped with scorn. "You should know more than that by now, Ranita Glasswright. Anyone can lie while she Speaks. Anyone can tell stories. Speaking does not bind you in any way."

It *had* bound her, though. It had bound her to this tall player, to his satin voice. She needed to know that he did not hate her, that the bond between them was not destroyed. Even here, even now, with Crestman carried away and the Little Army soldiers enslaved above her, Rani could remember the lure of Speaking, the cool blue stream that had called to her, soothed her, drawn her to Tovin. She wanted that water to carry her away, past the spiderguild, past riberry trees and octolaris, past all the bargains that she had made. The bargains that she had made, and Hal as well, in Liantine, with Mareka . . .

"Tovin," she whispered, and the sound curved back along the stone ramp.

He paused by the first window, framed in the diffuse light that glimmered down the well shaft. Rani could see the stiffness in his shoulders, the hard line of his jaw.

She strode up the ramp.

He was taller than she was; she circled half-around so that she did not have to look up at his face. Her fingers on his spidersilk tunic were certain; her palm lay flat against his chest, absorbing the beat of his heart through the fabric.

For just an instant, Rani was catapulted into her past. Years ago, she had stood before a man this way. She had felt her blood stir at his strong, handsome face, her breath come short beneath the power of his gaze. He had given her an almond cake, and she had thought that she might love him. But she had been tricked, driven by forces beyond her control. She had killed that other man.

And Crestman. Crestman who was a slave now, who had forfeited his birthright, and his commission in the Little Army. Crestman who had been the first man to kiss her.

Things were different now. Tovin was no soldier. Rani was not controlled by others. She could make her own choices.

She leaned forward and brushed her lips against the startled player's. He started to draw back, but she closed her hands in his tunic. "You must believe me," she whispered. "I meant you no harm. Not you or the players. Not back there, with Lord Anigo. And not now." His mouth was hot beneath hers, and she felt him respond to the urgency of her words.

"Ranita," he warned, the sound almost lost in the rustle of fabric. He raised a hand to the *V* of flesh at her throat, and she felt a salty sting when he touched the raw nick from the spider-guild guards.

"Hush." She enforced the command by lacing her fingers with his. "I am a guildsman, Tovin Player. I can sponsor your players' troop. I can grant you passage on all the roads."

"Not in Liantine." His voice was husky. "Not here. Ranita, you don't know what you're doing."

"I know." She swallowed hard and met his gaze. "I know precisely what I'm doing. You have taught me, Tovin Player. You taught me how to cut glass, how to set it. I am a glass-wright, and I have the power of all Morenia behind me. I can help your players, if you will let me."

His copper eyes were dark, nearly black in the well's gloom. Still, she understood the questions that he asked her, the answers he demanded. "I will, Tovin Player," she said, and then she pulled their hands between them, drawing him close, close enough that he knew all her promises, all her plans, all her desires that flowed beside the Speaking stream, just beneath the surface of her thoughts.

15

Hal watched Mareka, measuring the concern that etched her face as she glanced about his apartments. "We still have no word from the spiderguild, my lord?"

"This is the first day that my people *could* return. The first day, if they were not detained by your masters."

"Not mine," she said. "Not mine any longer." He noted her tone, both the resignation and the anger. "They ceased to be my masters the day you took their spiders from me."

"I did not take them, lady. You gave them of your own free will. You could have brought them back to your guildhall. You could have turned them over to certain death."

"That is not fair, my lord! Admit that you have used me! You used me for your own gain, after all that passed between us."

Hal flushed, betrayed by a sudden memory of her flesh hot beneath his hands. "You came to *me*, Mareka. You came to me with your cursed octolaris nectar. You may not pass responsibility for that."

She clutched at her skirts, gathering up the spidersilk between her fingers and freeing it to fall in crinkled planes. Her temper sparked in her eyes, and once again Hal saw the woman who had manipulated him in Liantine's Great Hall, the schemer who had led him to believe she was a princess, the woman that he meant to court. Her voice was low when she replied, so low that he had to take a step closer to make out her words. "Is that the way King Teheboth would see things? Is that what the house of Thunderspear will think, if they hear that you took another woman beneath their very roof when you were courting the only daughter of the king?"

"You would not dare, Mareka. You would not dare to tell your tales of lying and seduction."

"Why not, my lord? What have I to lose? Not a crown. Not a dowry."

"A reputation, though. Mareka Octolaris, to all the world outside these doors, you are a brave apprentice who dared to save your spider brood. You acted to protect a precious treasure that your close-eyed guildmasters would have destroyed. You allied yourself with me—with the enemy—because you had been raised to that duty since birth."

"You forget, my lord. I am not bound to you in any formal way. I could save my spiders still, by offering them up to Teheboth."

Hal had not thought of that option. He had believed Mareka to be under his control. Nevertheless, he answered sharply, "And *you* forget, my lady. Teheboth has taken in Jerusha Octolaris as his daughter. He is tied to the spiderguild now. He is their ally. Give him the spiders and they die, as surely as if you returned them directly to the guildhall."

"Are you truly so naive that you cannot imagine King Teheboth breaking with the spiderguild? It's only Jerusha that he's taken in, after all—a girl rebellious enough to ignore her masters and let a slave girl die! What would the house of Thunderspear do to break the monopoly of the spiderguild? To break that power? Imagine the wealth King Teheboth might gain—and the only thing barring him is Jerusha." Mareka settled her hands across her belly, as if she enclosed the swollen promise of a child. "What would Prince Olric need to say, my lord? That Jerusha was barren? That she could bear the prince no heir? He'd be within his rights, then. He could set her aside."

"And what would you do, Mareka? Would you go to Olric to offer up your spiders? Would you dose yourself with octolaris nectar, and take him unawares?"

"I could, my lord. I have the power."

"Then you're nothing but a whore."

He did not see her hand move, did not see the flat of her palm before the slap resounded in the chamber. His cheek stung as if she had branded him, and he caught at her wrist before she could land another blow.

"Let me go!" She twisted loose. "Let me feed my spiders!"

"*My* spiders," he said. "You gave them into my keeping."

Her eyes were hot as she stalked to the cages that lined the walls of his apartments. "Only because I saw no other course, my lord. Only because I saw no other way to protect my charges."

"There is no other way, Mareka. I am the only guarantee those octolaris will live until their eggs hatch. Not Teheboth. Not Olric. Only me."

She turned away, dismissing him with all the arrogance of a princess. He watched her cross to the basket, to the container of markin grubs. She counted out the octolaris' morning meal, transferring her squirming white victims to a silver platter that she kept there for the purpose. It took her only a moment to tie back the sleeves of her gown, to lace up the flowing garment so that the spiders would not be provoked. She bound silk strips about her wrists, providing further protection.

Mareka hummed as she approached the spider cages, filling the room with a song that vibrated across her ribs and up her throat. She paused before the first of the octolaris, and she waved her hands in a pattern that was becoming familiar to Hal, a pattern that he had seen dozens of times since he took possession of her treasures. She had explained to him that she was Homing the spiders, that she was announcing her presence so that they did not mistake her fingers for food.

Then, she did something Hal had never seen her do before— she repeated the pattern a second time, and then a third. She took the time to waggle her fingers through a fourth repetition. She must fear the octolaris. She must worry that her agitation would provoke them. Nevertheless, she reached for the silver tray.

The markin grubs clung to her fingers like burrs. Hal thought of those same fingers slipping down his spine, and a frisson tingled through him, raising the hairs on his arms.

What would he do if she actually did go to Teheboth? What if she told Thunderspear of her tryst with Hal?

Even now, Hal might escape condemnation. After all, he

could argue, men were meant to do their jousting before they settled into married life. He had lain with Mareka before his intentions for the princess were formally announced. He could claim foolishness, fear, nervousness about the change that he faced. His indiscretion would prove embarrassing, but it might not destroy his pending marriage to Berylina. If he painted himself as a fool. As a boy. As a weakling swayed by women.

But if Mareka took the *spiders* to Teheboth, what then? Hal needed the spiders. He needed the income they would generate, the base they would provide for his fledgling Order of the Octolaris. Without the spiders, Hal could not pay the Fellowship. He could never ascend to the leadership of that organization, never work toward the shadowy goals of the Royal Pilgrim.

Watching the spiderguild apprentice sway as she fed her charges, Hal realized that he could set aside Berylina. He could set aside his advisors' plans, thrash their expectations that he marry a noblewoman, a princess. He could offer his hand to Mareka Octolaris. Then, her threats to go to Teheboth would die forever. Then, she would be bound to come to Morenia, to tend her spiders and their young, to guide Hal's new knightly Order.

For just an instant, Hal imagined the outrage of his council lords, their incredulity as he announced his decision. He could see their astonishment, and he imagined the accusations against him. They would say that he had thrown over Berylina, left her behind because of her looks, because of her shyness.

He pictured himself explaining. He pictured himself standing before his council with the octolaris in their boxes, with the riberry trees that Rani was even now negotiating for him.

Rani.

If he set aside Berylina, how could he take a guildswoman for his bride? How could he turn to Mareka, when there were so many better choices?

Besides, if Hal abandoned Berylina, he abandoned her dowry. He lost the immediate payment that he owed to the church; the installment that must be made in one short week, on Midsummer Day. He must have Berylina. There was no way around that.

Berylina and payment to the church. Mareka and payment to the Fellowship.

He could not have both.

Bells began to toll steadily, marking noon. Damnation! He was expected in Berylina's solar. This was the last day that he could visit his bride before the wedding. By Liantine custom, bridge and groom must be estranged for one week before the marriage ceremony. "Mareka," he began.

"Go," she said, without turning away from Homing the second spider. "Go to your princess, my lord."

Hal could hear the smile behind her words, the mockery that straightened her shoulders, that surely quirked her smile. The bells stopped tolling. He was late. "My lady," he said, and he bowed stiffly, even though she never turned around.

He hurried through the Liantine hallways, walking fast enough that his poor page had to trot to keep up. Only on the solar stairs did he take the time to straighten his tunic, to run his palms through his unruly hair. He hovered by the door, angry that he had nearly forgotten his obligation to visit Berylina. He could not afford to make diplomatic mistakes. Not now. Not with so much depending on rules and custom and obligation.

He waved the questioning Caralatino to silence and listened to the sounds coming from inside the aerie room. He could just discern the murmur of voices low in conversation, and then a tentative giggle, like a wild bird chittering on a tree branch. So. Berylina *could* laugh. Maybe not around him—she was still too shy for that—but at least she was capable of mirth.

Hal sighed and stepped into the solar.

Berylina stood at an easel, a charcoal crayon held fast between her fingers and her thumb. She was studying her parchment carefully, her head turned at an appraising angle, a perspective that hid for just a moment the crossed lines of her sight. She even managed to disguise her rabbit teeth, for her lips were pulled back in a wide grin, a smile that matched the trilling laugh that filled the room. "Don't look directly at me!" she said. "Bain would not look directly at a mere mortal."

Bain. The god of flowers.

Hal knew the princess's words were not meant for him, and

he glanced across the room, following Berylina's gaze. He was surprised to see Father Siritalanu sitting on one of the ornately carved chairs that lined the walls of the chamber. The priest had spread his green robes about his feet, and he had permitted Berylina—Berylina or her nurses—to cover the cloth with flowers. Three great lilies cascaded across the front of the fabric, and a waterfall of forget-me-nots tumbled down his front. There were irises and daffodils, and a careful garland of early roses that wound about his shoulders.

At Hal's entrance, the religious started to stand, upsetting the careful display. Berylina, not noticing the intruder, exclaimed, "No! Don't move yet! I haven't finished."

"Forgive me!" Siritalanu exclaimed, and in the quick embarrassment of the moment, Hal was not certain if the priest spoke to him or to the princess.

Trying to make the best of things, Hal waved the priest back to his chair as he crossed to Berylina's handiwork. "What have you created there, my lady?"

It was too late for his jovial question. Berylina's smile had faded, replaced by a rapid twitch that she tried to hide by turning her face toward the window. For a long minute, Hal thought that she would not answer at all, but then she whispered. "Nothing, Your Majesty. Only a drawing."

"Let me see." He tried to sound boisterously happy, like an eager groom courting his bride.

"Please, Your Majesty. It's only a pastime, a trifle—"

Hal brushed away her protests and circled behind the easel. He was surprised enough that he could not keep from exclaiming as he saw what she had drawn.

Siritalanu's face was identifiable in the work. The young priest grinned openly, as if he were a young man caught at horseplay with his peers. His hands were open in his lap, long fingers twining through the flowers. The blooms themselves were perfectly depicted, exactly shaped and shaded, the black lines carefully contrasted with the creamy parchment.

And yet, the drawing was not merely a portrait. Berylina had captured something more, some alien air, some hint of differentness, of—Hal hesitated before admitting the word—holiness. She had taken the physical presence of Father Siritalanu and transformed it into the image of a god.

"This is quite remarkable, my lady!"

She blushed, as red as the roses that glowed against the priest's green robe across the room. "It's nothing, Your Majesty!"

"You've captured the essence of Bain."

"Only because Father Siritalanu helped me," the princess insisted, her shy words gaining strength from her religious fervor. "Only because we prayed before I began my drawing." The mention of prayer seemed to give her even more confidence, and she hastened to add, "Father Siritalanu has been most generous with his time, Your Majesty. I am grateful that you have let him attend to my spiritual preparation for what is to come."

"Well—er—yes." Hal scarcely recognized how many words Berylina had strung together. Rather, he was flummoxed by what he was supposed to say. She used the phrase "what is to come" as if summoned to her execution.

One of Berylina's nurses stepped forward and chided her mistress, "You have not shown King Halaravilli any hospitality, Your Highness. You must offer him a cup of wine."

"Oh!" Berylina started, and she set her charcoal crayon beside the easel. She fumbled as she dropped into a curtsey, and all her new-built eloquence fled as she struggled to get out her words: "Please, Your Majesty, forgive me!"

Hal forced himself to convert his grimace into an honest smile. "No forgiveness is necessary, my lady. And please, do not interrupt your work. When you complete your drawing, we will set it under glass. We will preserve it, and you can keep it in your solar in your new home, in Morenia. You can look upon it to remind you of Bain's hand, guiding you in all your efforts to grow new things."

The princess blushed and averted her eyes, twisting her fingers about each other and smearing charcoal dust across both hands.

What? Hal wanted to exclaim. He only meant new things— like their marriage. Like the bond between their houses. By all the Thousand Gods—she was only a *child*! He could not have meant anything more by his words! Hal cleared his throat and tried to smooth over his suggestion. "We have many lovely gardens in Moren, my lady. You will be pleased to see Bain's handiwork, I think."

After one of the nurses glared and cleared her throat peremptorily, Berylina whispered, "I should like that, Your Majesty." The admission proved too much for her, and she blushed again, gathering up her skirts with her sooty fingers.

"Yes. Well, then." Hal looked at Father Siritalanu, but the religious gave no hint of where he might take the conversation safely. "Well, I should be going, then. I should let you finish your drawing."

Berylina remained silent until the nurse prompted her with an urgent nod. Then the princess said, "Yes, Your Majesty. Thank *you.*"

"No," Hal stumbled. "Thank *you.*"

And he left the solar. Shaking his head, muttering under his breath, cursing his own awkwardness, he closed the oaken door behind him and collapsed against its solid support. He ignored Calaratino's questioning look, ignored the possibility that a nurse, or Siritalanu, or—may First god Ait protect him—the princess herself would choose that moment to leave the solar.

She was only a child, he told himself. Of course she was awkward. Of course she was afraid. He was hardly helping things, stumbling over his own words as if he were no more than a page. All would be better, he promised, after they were wed. Then both of them would know that they were meant to be together, that they would have to work together, for Morenia's sake. Then, they would find ways to speak to each other, to communicate beyond their horrible, uncomfortable blurted words and silences. Their joining before the Thousand Gods would make all right.

But would the Thousand Gods truly bless their union? Would the gods look upon him with favor when he came before them with a clouded heart? For he could not say that he truly wanted to wed Berylina, the girl. He wanted Berylina, the endowered princess. He wanted eight hundred bars of gold.

Then again, what princess *wasn't* desired for her dowry? What king's daughter wasn't meted out as a source of income and stability? And what king had the luxury of wedding for love, for companionship, for happiness?

Before Hal could begin to measure his true response, he heard footsteps on the stairs—fast, eager strides. He forced himself to stand straight, and he threw his shoulders back as if he had just left the solar, ever the enthusiastic bridegroom.

He took only two steps before Baron Farsobalinti burst around the curve of the stairwell. "Sire!"

"Farso! You've returned!"

"Aye, my lord. With Mair and Rani Trader."

"And your mission? You reached them in time?"

"Aye. Before Teheboth's messenger arrived at the spider-guild."

Hal's heart soared. "What happened, then? Did you speak with the guildmaster? Did Rani? Were you successful?"

Farso flushed a curious shade of crimson, and he refused to meet Hal's eyes. "I did not enter the spiderguild enclave, my lord. I was . . . detained at the gate."

"Detained . . . What happened, Farso?" Hal barely managed to lower his voice, remembering that they spoke on a public staircase, in the middle of the Liantine castle. His urgency ripped through his words. "Did you get the trees?"

"Aye, my lord. Rani Trader is seeing to them even now."

Swallowing a wave of relief more powerful than he had ever expected, Hal smothered his other questions. He hurried down the stairs and out to the main courtyard, with Farso and his page straggling behind.

Everything was chaos. Liantine servants bustled around two great carts. Teams of draft horses snorted, shying as people bustled by. Hal heard Mair's Touched growl before he saw her, before he found her snapping at a pair of hapless servants. "Take care wi' them! It's th' yellow leaves we maun keep safe. Dinna jostle th' puir things!"

And Rani's voice rose loud, as well. "Saw those barrels in half, then, and fill them with water. Don't disturb the moss around the base of the trees. Set them in water for now. We'll do better, we'll have to, before they ship to Morenia. Three of them in each barrel. Careful!"

And everywhere, there were riberry trees. Riberry saplings, at least, each as tall as Rani. They were strapped upright on the two carts, lashed together. Filthy silk wrappings wove about their roots, holding in mud at the base of each tree. Twenty, forty . . . Hal approximated his counting. Five hundred trees.

"Water," Rani cried. "Each tree needs water! They've dried out during transport. I don't care if it sucks dry all the wells in Liantine, these trees must get their water now!"

She brushed a wisp of hair back from her face, leaving a streak of mud in its place. Hal took a deep breath and crossed the courtyard. "Well met, Rani Trader."

"Your Majesty," she said, bobbing into a distracted curtsey. "Careful!" she called, looking beyond Hal's shoulder. "Do not knock the earth from the roots!"

He waited until that tree had been settled to Rani's satisfaction. "You were successful, then."

"Aye, Sire."

"And what have I paid for these trees?"

For just a moment a shadow crossed her features. His heart clenched hard in his chest as he dreaded what she would say, as he feared the accounting she would deliver. She swallowed hard, though, and met his eyes. "Nothing for now, my lord."

"Nothing?" His amazement was shrill.

"I threatened the spiderguild with your army, with Davin's war engines. I bartered across the backs of the Little Army."

The Little Army. Hal glanced around the courtyard, suddenly looking for Crestman. He had gone with Rani to the players' camp. Certainly, he must be somewhere amid the trees. Hal glanced around but did not see the dour soldier. He forced himself to ask, "And Crestman?"

Rani's glinting tears might have been brought out by the wind. "He's gone, my lord. He stayed behind at the spiderguild. He stayed with his men."

He heard her sorrow, her disappointment, her fear, but he himself felt a strange shadow of relief. The Amanthian captain had been vehement about freeing the children, about tracking down and releasing the enslaved Little Army. And yet, Hal had not known how to do that, had been told by Teheboth Thunder-spear that such redemption was impossible. Hal had other missions here in Liantine. He could not be the leader to all his people, not every one at once.

Rani swallowed noisily and said, "We'll get them yet, my lord. With the trees and your spiders, we'll have the gold, even after you pay . . . your other debts." To the Fellowship, she did not say aloud. "We'll redeem the spiderguild slaves come next spring."

Hal heard the exhaustion behind her words, heard the shadow of an untold story about crossing the plains with the trees, about bargaining for their possession. Now that he looked for it, he could see the slump of her shoulders, the smudges beneath her eyes, the weariness throughout her body. "Aye, Rani. We'll speak of that later."

"You must send notice to Davin immediately, my lord."

"To Davin?"

"Aye. He must figure out a way to get water for the trees. At the spiderguild, there is a well. . . ." She trailed off, and her fingers strayed toward her throat, toward a new-healed wound and a scab that spoke of danger. She shook her head, though, as if she were thrusting away some private vision. "We must find a way to get the trees the water they need—twenty-four buckets, every day, for every tree."

"Twenty-four . . ."

"Davin can do it. He must."

"I cannot reach him now. Puladarati, Davin, all the council lords—they all have taken ship for the wedding."

"The wedding!" Rani said, as if she had forgotten their initial reason for coming to Liantine.

"Aye. One week."

"Then we'll speak to Davin as soon as he arrives. He can begin his planning here, and send orders home." She nodded, and he could see the way that she adjusted her thoughts, the way that she shifted her plans to keep pace with the facts. Her face was drawn as she asked, "And you, my lord? How go your negotiations with Liantine?"

It's not enough, he wanted to say. I have Berylina's dowry, which will keep the church at bay, but I cannot pay the Fellowship. Or, I have the spiders, which will pacify the Fellowship, but the church's demands will go unmet. Berylina or Mareka. Mareka or Berylina.

He started to explain, but he saw the shadows of fatigue on Rani's face, the tight lines beside her lips as she glanced beyond him at the trees.

"Rest, Rani. Come to me this evening, and I'll tell you of our plans."

She started to protest, but her words were nearly drowned in a yawn that she fought to turn into a cough. "Yes, my lord. I'll see to the trees, then come to you tonight."

Hal paced his chamber, measuring the steps with the impatience of a young child. Fifteen paces to the door. Turn about. Fifteen to the window. Turn about. Door. Window. Door. Window. With every pass, he reminded himself not to look at his wedding raiment, already hanging on a wooden stand. Not to look at the octolaris cages nestled against the walls.

Farso had spent the better part of the afternoon in Hal's chamber, filling in the details of the visit to the spiderguild. Although the noble had never made it past the stockade, he knew how Rani had outsmarted the guildmaster, how she had made her bid for the riberry trees. Farso had listened as Rani told Mair every detail about forcing the spiderguild to collect the trees that very afternoon, about pledging gold for draft horses and drays.

Waiting to leave the spiderguild, Farso himself had seen the carts lined up just inside the enclave's gates. He had watched the mirrored racks drawn into place before dawn; he had listened to the barked commands as King Teheboth's rider was blinded, was searched, was conducted inside the walls.

Teheboth's man had protested his treatment, had argued that he should have been permitted entrance the day before. The rider had been so indignant that he had not paid attention to the two draped carts beyond the mirrored racks. He had not realized that his embassy was lost before it had begun.

All that, Farso told, even as he laid out Hal's wedding finery. Hal insisted that his servants would attend to the crimson-

and-gold cloth, that there were days left before the ceremony, but Farso only shook his head. He had served his lord in Morenia. He would not forfeit that honor in a foreign land.

And so Hal now paced inside his chambers, waiting for Rani. He hoped she would have an answer, some guidance, any instruction as he asked himself—Berylina or Mareka? Liantine or spiderguild? Church or Fellowship?

Who would be appeased?

Could all be pleased? Would all be seized?

He shook his head. It had been years since his mind played its rhyming tricks on him, since the chittering voices had come to whisper their twisted versions of the truth. He would not yield to them now. He had not given in to their seductive whisper in nearly three years, since he had camped on the Amanthian Plain, believing that Rani was dead and buried, left to rot in the cold, northern earth.

As if summoned by his memory, there was a knock at the door, and Hal's page entered. Calaratino bowed deeply and said, "Ranita Glasswright, Your Majesty."

"Send her in, then."

The boy stepped aside, ushering Rani into the chamber. "Thank you," Hal said to the page. "Please see that we are undisturbed."

Hal waited until the door closed before he let himself look at Rani. She had clearly rested since her labors in the courtyard. She wore a simple gown, clean lines of somber grey. As if to compensate for the quiet attire, her hair was plaited in an intricate braid, a style that made her seem older, more worldly.

"The trees are settled, then?"

"Aye, my lord. King Teheboth is already complaining that his wells will run dry with the effort to water all of them."

"Will they?"

"Not for the short time the trees will stay here. We must take fresh water in barrels, though, for the ocean crossing. We'll likely lose some trees, no matter what precautions we take. Tovin says they are very sensitive."

"Tovin?"

Hal was surprised to see Rani blush. "Tovin Player. The man who took us to the spiderguild."

"He's from the players' troop? The one that performed after the Spring Hunt?"

"Aye." The troop that Rani had run after. The people she had left him to join—left him after they had argued. Before Mareka came to his chambers.

Hal cleared his throat. "The players are sponsored by the spiderguild, are they not? Did Tovin bargain for you, then?"

"No!" She answered too quickly, and he wondered at the story she did not tell. She must have realized how harsh her answer sounded, for she swallowed hard and said, "No, my lord. Tovin did not bargain for Morenia. He feared that our request would anger the spiderguild. He was right."

"Then he was put between his patrons and Morenia."

"Aye, my lord. But not for long. Anigo Octolaris decided that Tovin had turned traitor, and the spiderguild withdrew its sponsorship of the guild. Anigo ordered Tovin from the guild-hall."

"Then they are left without a patron?" Hal could not keep concern from his voice. He had seen the players, the sort of awe that they inspired in the Liantine court. If charismatic souls like that were alienated . . . What deviltry could they work throughout the land? What stories could they spread about Morenia?

"Not precisely, Sire." Rani swallowed and licked her lips. "They needed a guild to sponsor them. The glasswrights have undertaken that responsibility."

"What!"

"I have agreed that they may go forward under my guild's name. I have pledged responsibility for their actions on the high roads, and I have agreed to fund their playacting, to the extent that I am able."

"Here? In Liantine?"

Again, she swallowed. She bent her head to study her clasped hands, and the action highlighted the careful braiding in her hair. "No, Sire. The players will follow me. They will come to Morenia, after the wedding."

"And they *agreed* to this?"

"They had no true choice, my lord. In Liantine, no troop may travel without a sponsor. The spiderguild withdrew its support immediately upon the conclusion of our . . . negotiations for the riberry trees."

Hal heard the story she did not tell—how angry Tovin must have been, how cheated he must have felt. Hal reached out and covered Rani's clasped hands with one of his own, and he tried to ignore how she flinched. "Did he hurt you, Rani? Is that why you took on such an obligation?"

"No!" Her head shot up, and she jerked her hands away from his. "No, Sire, it was not like that!"

Not like that. Then precisely how *was* it, Hal found himself wanting to ask. What exactly passed between the two of you? Astonished, he watched a blush steal across Rani's cheeks, and he could not ignore the sudden catch in her voice.

As if in answer to the questions he could not bring himself to ask, one of the octolaris shifted in its cage behind Hal. The spiders moved often as they wrapped and rewrapped their egg sacs. The sound should not have surprised him, but this time it made him start, made him remember his own manipulations, his own actions that had led to the acquisition of the spiders. . . .

Who was he to question Rani? Who was he to question the price of a bargain fairly made?

He stepped back, crossing toward the octolaris cage. He gestured toward the beasts, even as he made sure to keep a careful distance from the venomous spiders. "Very well, then. The players made their choice, and you completed your negotiations. We have the riberry trees, and—for now—we have the spiders."

"For now?"

"Mareka Octolaris informed me this morning that she might take the beasts. She might offer them to Teheboth."

"But he would destroy them! Farso said the spiderguild wants them dead."

"The spiderguild does. But Teheboth might not yield to the desires of the guild. Things are shifting here in Liantine; they've changed even in the months that we have been here." Hal gestured to the cages, struggling to put into words the transitions he had witnessed. "When we arrived, the spiderguild still held some power—they had just wed their journeyman to the king's youngest son. Now, though, the Horned Hind is taking hold, more thoroughly than ever before. I think it has to do—at least in part—with the Little Army, with its faith in the Thousand Gods. Teheboth wants to distance himself from slaves, from everything base, and so he pulls even closer to the Hind, to the Hind and her wooden symbols. As a result, the price of silk is falling, even on a daily basis."

"Aye." Rani nodded, and he could see shrewd calculation behind her eyes. "I've seen the markets, of course. I've seen the stands selling wool and linen."

"There was a time when Teheboth would not have dared to defy the spiderguild. But now? With spiders in his own palace? With riberry trees, as well?"

He watched Rani calculate the threat. "You think he'll take them for his own, then?" she said. "He'll take a stand against the guild, to crush them for his own advance?"

"I cannot say. I believe Teheboth still intends for me to marry Berylina. He wants to get her out of Liantine."

"Then you'll take the princess and her dowry, and we'll sail for Morenia immediately following the wedding."

"Except that Mareka might act then. She might offer Liantine the spiders—" Hal paused to clear his throat. "—out of spite, when Berylina and I are wed."

Out of spite. There. That should serve as his confession. If Rani were half the negotiator she claimed to be, she should understand. She should know the hold Mareka had over him.

He caught his breath to see how long it took for her to process his words, to weigh their true meaning. The turnings of her merchant mind were nearly visible as she glanced from the octolaris cages to Hal, as she flicked her eyes toward his inner apartments. "So," she said at last. "The spiderguild apprentice might act out of spite if you marry Berylina." He could not read Rani's tone, could not find acceptance or rejection, or even resignation in her words. Rather, she was a merchant, counting out her wealth, measuring up her position in the marketplace. "She'll offer up her spiders to Teheboth, and we'll lose our Order of the Octolaris. We can have the princess's dowry—and pay the church immediately—or we can have the spiders and the trees—and pay the Fellowship over time."

Hal's relief was nearly palpable. Of course Rani saw the problem clearly. "Precisely," he said.

Rani glanced at the octolaris cages once again, started to speak, but then she stopped herself. Instead, she took a deep breath and raised a hand to her throat, to the remnant of her small, healing wound. Who had hurt her? How had she received the nick?

Hal resisted the fleeting temptation to follow her hand, to set his own fingers against her injury. Instead, he said, "You see the problem, then. How are we to do both? How are we to satisfy the church and the Fellowship?"

"And keep from earning Liantine's enmity, all at the same time." Rani strode across to the window, looking out over the city. "You must let me think on this, my lord. Let me see what I can devise."

"We haven't much time, Rani."

"Hardly any time at all." Her answer was so soft that he had to strain to hear her words. She gazed into the distance, and her fingers strayed to her throat once again. After a moment, she shook her head, and the motion seemed to set aside her vague and distant mood. "We must prepare for what we can, though. The players will come to you tonight, my lord. They'll speak with you, in preparation for the festivities following your wedding."

"Why do they wish to speak to me?"

"No. *Speaking.*" There was a curious emphasis as she said the word. "They will prepare a play for you, a story to tell in honor of your wedding. After the feast, of course. After the houses of Morenia and Liantine are joined."

"This . . . speaking. Is it difficult?"

She turned and smiled at him—the first untarnished smile she had shown him since her return to Liantine. "Oh, yes, my lord. It is difficult. You will be asked to share your stories, your secrets, your deepest thoughts. It is difficult, my lord, but well worth the labor. Speaking will change your world forever."

Hal heard her words and barely kept himself from muttering a petition to the Thousand Gods. He needed to change his world. He needed to create a way to keep both the church and the Fellowship at bay. And if, along the way, he could experience this . . . speaking, this change that made Rani Trader glow, then he was willing to try. He was a desperate man, and he was willing to try nearly anything. "You'll think on this, Rani? You'll find a way for me to keep both church and Fellowship content?"

"I'll see what I can do, my lord." She nodded and turned back to the window. "I'll see what I can do."

16

"Sire, this is most irregular."

Hal whirled around to face the Holy Father. He had already fought this battle with Dartulamino, already explained why the leader of the Morenian church was expected to watch over a heathen wedding ceremony—to watch over *and* to give his blessing. "Yes, Father, it is." Hal's page jumped at the anger in the king's voice, stumbling as he backed away to the edge of the tent. Hal scarcely spared a glance for the wooden casket that Calaratino held, for the jewels that glinted on their velvet bed.

Hal could hear the crowd outside the pavilion, the rising pitch of excited voices as people gathered on the edge of the woods. The morning fog had burned off, and the sun was hot on the spidersilk tent. Hal knew that the hour must be approaching noon, that it was almost time for his wedding service to begin. He waved at the page. "Go ahead, Calo. Tell them that I'll be ready in a few moments. I wish to pray with the Holy Father."

The boy's eyes were as big as trenchers as he bowed his way out of the pavilion. "Yes, Sire," he said.

"And make sure that we are not interrupted," Hal said as Calaratino reached the door.

"Yes, Sire." The page seemed incapable of any further words. That was just as well. The last thing Hal needed was a child spreading rumors about a squabble that he had overheard, a jagged dispute between the crown and the church. Hal waited until the spidersilk folds of the door had fallen into place, until he had regained as much privacy as was possible amid this farce of a wedding spectacle.

"Father," he said, stepping closer to Dartulamino and lowering his voice. How many times must he explain himself? How many times must he state that he had had no choice regarding the blasphemous rites? "Father," he began, after a deep, steadying breath. "You know the danger that I faced. You know that I had no choice here. I must gain Princess Berylina's hand in marriage. I must have her dowry, if Moren is to be rebuilt."

"Some costs are too great, Sire."

"But not this one!" Hal fought to lower his voice, remembering that anyone could hear through spidersilk. "Not this one, Father. Don't you understand? It is more important than ever for me to wed Princess Berylina. She *believes* in the Thousand Gods. She embraces them with her very soul. She is endangered staying here in Liantine, here in the heart of the territory held sacred to the Horned Hind. If I can help her escape by wedding her here, today, then I am obliged to do so. And if I can get her dowry for Morenia at the same time, so much the better."

"You risk your very soul, Your Majesty. You chance having the Heavenly Gates locked against you forever!"

"Who says that, my lord? Is that the Holy Father speaking? Or is it the Fellowship of Jair?"

The priest gaped, seeming astonished that Hal had dared to name the shadowy cabal aloud. "My lord, if you think for one instant—"

"I think *every* instant. I think that the church would like nothing better than to have the crown forfeit on its obligations. I think that the priests would like me to fail to make my first repayment, fail to render up my first usurious return tomorrow. You would shake your head in sorrow, and you would sigh at the dishonor, but you would gather up my power all the same."

"Sire—"

"But," Hal continued, not permitting Dartulamino to interrupt, "that is nothing compared to how you would gloat if I fail to pay the Fellowship. I still don't understand precisely what test the Fellowship has set me, Father, what they intend to do with the bars of gold I'll pay. I recognize the power of the

Fellowship, though—the power of its promise. The power of its threat. The power of the Royal Pilgrim. I *will* meet the Fellowship's demand, and by giving, grow stronger. You may not want me as a rival, but you will not drive me away, Dartulamino. I know my obligations, and I begin to understand my potential."

"Your *potential* is lost if you give yourself to Liantine, if you sell yourself to the Horned Hind."

"I'm selling no one. I'm fighting to preserve what is mine, in any way that I see fit. And if that fight requires wedding a Liantine princess atop a wooden platform on the edge of a sacred grove, then that is what I will do. If I must kneel before a horned hind, then I will. If I must take my child bride on a bed of holy fir boughs, I will. I will not give up on Morenia, Dartulamino. I will not let you have my kingdom without a fight!"

Before the Holy Father could respond, the tent flap opened, and Teheboth Thunderspear ducked inside. The king of Liantine looked like an invading warrior—he had set aside his resplendent silks for riding leathers painted with the green and silver of his homeland. Teheboth's beard was braided with bits of pierced antler, and his hair was clouted back, held at his neck with a fantastic bronze medallion, shaped like the stylized Horned Hind he had painted on Hal's brow months before. In his hand was a massive spear, an ancient token of his house that glinted with deadly iron at the tip.

"I beg your pardon, my lord," Teheboth said, scarcely sparing a glance for the Holy Father. "I was told that you were praying."

"I was," Hal said, refusing to elaborate. Let the Liantine wonder at the method of prayer for followers of the Thousand Gods.

"I trust you've found the spiritual guidance you require, then," Teheboth said after only a moment's pause. "Our people are waiting to witness the joining of our houses."

Hal nodded and settled his crimson cloak about his shoulders, the resplendent garment glinting even in the dull light that sifted through the tent. He paused for one moment, reaching into the wooden casket that the page had held to withdraw a heavy chain of interlocking *J*s. *J* for Jair. *J* for the Defender of the Faith.

He turned to Dartulamino. "Father? Will you assist me?"

Hal watched the Holy Father weigh his options. The man could take the chain of office. He could settle the golden *J*s around Hal's neck. He could give his blessing to the wedding, to the joining of Morenia and Liantine.

Or he could refuse. Without explaining about the Fellowship, without letting people know his reasons. He could gather up his holy entourage and abandon King Halaravilli.

Dartulamino was no fool. He understood the political world. He sighed and stepped forward, taking up the golden chain. No emotions flicked across his sallow face as he said, "In the name of all the Thousand Gods, Sire." He raised the necklace over Hal's head. "In the name of First Pilgrim Jair."

"In the name of Jair," Hal murmured, accepting the silent challenge. Dartulamino might have yielded as the Holy Father, but there were battles left to fight. The Fellowship remained a tangled skein—a glittering, unknown mystery.

Teheboth shook his head and muttered something under his breath, which might have been a prayer to the Horned Hind. He refused to acknowledge the Holy Father as he turned back to the entrance of the tent. Lifting the flaps of spidersilk with a warrior's disdain, the Liantine gestured Hal to walk before him. Hal scarcely had a chance to see that Dartulamino stalked behind, furious.

Even though Hal knew the assembly that waited for him, he was still surprised. Hundreds of people stood on the edge of the forest, resplendent in their finest clothes. The Morenians wore spidersilk and velvet—all Hal's council lords, and Davin, and various nobles who had managed the journey to Liantine. Hal caught Puladarati's eye as he strode nearer the assembly, and he nodded gravely. The former regent had worked his magic once again, gathering together the finest of Morenian and Amanthian nobility, regardless of the short time for planning, regardless of the straitened times.

There were Liantines, too, dozens of Teheboth's lords. Hal recognized many of them now, after his days in the foreign court. Prince Olric stood with Jerusha at his side, almost lost in the swirl of the royal family. The followers of the Horned Hind were obvious throughout the crowd—each man wore riding leathers, his beard braided with antler and wooden decorations. Even the Liantine ladies sported bronze medallions, the symbol of their faith.

Hal looked across the field to the edge of the forest, to the platform that had been erected beneath the shadow of the trees. A woman stood there, all alone. She was clad in chestnut-colored velvet, a long, straight gown, with sleeves that covered her wrists. Her hair was pulled back into an elaborate head-dress, a carefully woven construction that hinted at antlers, at horns that were captured and lost in the shifting sunlight on the edge of the trees.

So that was the priestess, sacred to the Horned Hind. That was the woman who would watch over Hal's joining with Berylina. She gazed at him across the field, and he measured her cool appraisal. He might not be content with what was to happen. He might have fought battles against his nobles, against his own priests. But the priestess of the Horned Hind must have her own reservations, her own concerns about joining the house of Liantine to a heathen.

Hal knew that Berylina was not yet present. Teheboth had briefed him the day before on Liantine custom, on the traditions that this wedding ceremony would follow. Hal, in turn, had told Puladarati, had ordered all his followers to be prepared for the foreign observances. He could only hope that the Morenians would follow his lead.

The crowd fell silent as Teheboth escorted Hal across the field. Morenians and Liantines alike clustered near, pressing closer to the wooden platform at the edge of the forest. Teheboth acknowledged his people as he moved, nodding here, touching a shoulder there. The procession was nothing like Morenian pomp, nothing like the regal service that would take place if Hal were marrying his bride in the house of the Thousand Gods.

Hal wondered if he was expected to make the same casual recognition of his retainers. He could not, though. They would not know what to make of a royal smile, of a comradely touch as their king moved toward one of the holiest moments of his royal life. Hal contented himself with seeking out the eyes of his favorites among the crowd.

Puladarati first, of course. The other council lords—Count Edpulaminbi, Count Jerumalashi. Davin, scowling, his deep-lined face dark beneath the summer sun. Farso, standing near the front.

And beside Farso was Mair. The Touched girl wore a simple gown, unadorned linen in Farsobalinti's glinting blue. Hal wondered for an instant if there were a message there, if there were other nuptials to be celebrated. Not today, though. No such distraction for today.

Rani stood beside Mair. Hal swallowed hard and met her gaze. They had not spoken since the day that she returned from the spiderguild—both had been swept up in duty and responsibility. Each day, he had hoped to see her, hoped at least for some missive as she outlined a plan to save him, to save Morenia and Amanthia both. He had waited for her to set forth a strategy, to tell him how he might keep both his dowry and his octolaris.

But she had failed him. She had not found a solution. They must act, separately, solving the problems in order. First they would take Berylina's dowry on this Midsummer Eve. Then, they could repay the church. Then they would find a way to meet the Fellowship's demands. With Mareka's spiders if she cooperated. Without, if necessary.

With a curious twist of pride, Hal saw that Rani wore his crimson, her gown brilliant against the gold of her hair. She glanced toward the dais, and then across the field, to the pavilion where Princess Berylina waited. She swallowed hard, and he longed to go to her, to seek her blessing. There was no time, though, no opportunity. Besides, before he could take a step, before he could make the decision to follow Teheboth's casual example, Rani reached for the arm of the man who stood beside her; she leaned close to whisper something to her companion.

Tovin. Tovin Player. Hal had not known the man when Rani returned from the spiderguild, but Hal had asked Farso, and Farso had demanded information from Mair. So, Tovin Player had taught Rani her glasswork. He had guided Rani to the spiderguild. He had accepted her sponsorship for his troop, when the spiderguild denounced the players. Even now, Hal knew the players were gathering their belongings, preparing to take ship for Morenia as soon as the wedding festivities were ended.

After Rani's request, Hal had Spoken with the players—quickly and without much concentration. A woman named Flarissa had come to him, and she had swung a pearl drop before his eyes, calming him and asking him questions. He had answered briefly, recalling the day that he first heard Berylina's name.

Nonsense. There was no power in the Speaking, no force to explain Rani's reverential tones when she discussed the players. The troop played games, dressing in their amusing costumes, standing on their makeshift stage. Entertainment, yes, but a power to change people's lives? Not at all. At least not when the questions he was asked concerned Berylina. If the players had asked him other things, delved into other secrets, closer to his heart . . . Hal set aside the thought.

And, as Hal watched, Tovin Player covered Rani's fingers with his own. The intimacy sent a shudder down Hal's spine, a chill that set his jaw and made him think of angry commands. Before he could even summon up words, Hal's gaze slipped to the edge of the crowd, to a figure clad in white.

Mareka Octolaris. No, no longer *octolaris*. As expected, the spiderguild had denounced its shamed apprentice. It had made formal demand for its spiders, for the twenty-three beasts that even now crowded along the walls of Hal's apartments in the palace. The spiderguild had raged, but Teheboth had stood fast. The right of embassy had held. So far. Perhaps Hal had only imagined the problems Mareka had threatened. Perhaps she had only been playing with him; she had never truly intended to back out of their arrangement and proffer up her spiders to Liantine.

Mareka stared at Hal across the field of grass, and she seemed the very model of decorum. The passion she had shown him, the heat of the octolaris nectar, might all have been a dream. Now, her hair fell demurely down her back, like a girl's. Her brilliant white gown hung straight. She had worn the spidersilk at Hal's first feast in Liantine; the cloth was shot through with delicate glints of color. Mareka's fingers were laced before her, serenely folded, as if she waited patiently for some long-expected announcement.

"My lord Halaravilli ben-Jair!" Teheboth's words boomed across the grassy field, forcing Hal's attention to the foot of the dais. "I bid you welcome in Liantine! Welcome to our court, and to a taste of our hospitality, beneath the sky, beneath the watchful eyes of the Horned Hind."

The Morenians murmured as the priestess stepped forward. The woman did not speak, as a priest of the Thousand Gods would do under such circumstances. Instead, she inclined her head, with all the grace of a deer, of a noble beast caught on the edge of the forest. She raised her hands in a complicated gesture, as if she were summoning some elemental force to look upon the proceedings on the edge of the forest.

Hal crossed to the man who would become his father, and he spoke loudly enough that all could hear him. "My thanks, Teheboth Thunderspear. I am grateful for this opportunity to join you in the summer fields." Hal extended his hand as they had agreed before, clasping Teheboth's forearm in the time-honored show of friendship and faith. Teheboth's eyes glinted above his beard.

"Please, my lord," Teheboth said. "I bid you welcome and pray that you will partake of the hospitality of the house of Thunderspear. I fain would offer up a humble gift in recognition of the honor that you do my house today."

Hal forced an easy smile across his face. He and Teheboth had discussed this presentation. He knew what was to come. Hal let himself be led to a majestic chair that stood just below the raised dais. The chair—a throne, really—was crafted of finest oak, smooth-grained wood that had been carved and polished by an expert craftsman. The arms had been worked to resemble the trunks of mammoth trees, and the back of the chair was a medley of whorls. Branches broke out at the top of the chair, wild and unruly, shadowy limbs that mimicked the horns of a magnificent twenty-pointed stag.

Hal inclined his head to Teheboth and crossed to the chair. The seat was easily broad enough for two grown men. Teheboth had explained that it was called a marriage bench, that it was the first of many symbols of man and woman being joined together beneath the Horned Hind. As the ceremony progressed, Berylina would come to sit beside him, come to join him beneath the horns.

Only when Hal was settled did he realize that his slippered feet rested on spidersilk. The oaken throne had been set atop a woven tapestry, a magnificent length of cloth that was even now being ground into the earth. If the occasion had been less solemn, Hal might have smiled at the outrageous symbolism. Teheboth was determined to make his point, determined to carve the once-powerful spiderguild out of the affairs of his court.

The king of Liantine waited until his guest was settled, standing patiently until Hal felt the wood behind his spine. He knew the image he presented; he knew that the horns would seem to grow from his own crowned head. Defiantly, Hal sought out the Holy Father's gaze on the edge of the crowd, nodding slightly as the sallow priest grimaced and glanced away.

"Halaravilli ben-Jair, you came to us on an auspicious day. You arrived in Liantine on the day of the Spring Hunt, on the day each year when the Horned Hind offers up her life for the betterment of all her most true worshipers. You rode out with my men on that hunt, and you stood beside the Hind as she died her yearly death. The Hind spoke to me as she fell beneath my spear; she told me to mark you as one of hers, to gather you into the house of Thunderspear. And so I made the mark of the Horned Hind upon your brow, and I welcomed you into my court."

Hal's expression did not change, but he could see the consternation among his followers. Puladarati, Dartulamino, all the others—they had not been present for the hunt. They had no idea what bloody symbol Teheboth had made. Ah, well . . . As Hal had said to Father Dartulamino, there would be time enough to make all right with the Thousand Gods. Time enough when he and his bride were on the far side of the ocean.

"And now, Halaravilli ben-Jair, I come to do the Horned Hind's bidding once again. I come to see you joined to the house of Thunderspear—joined in more than word, in more than deed. I come to see you sit before me as my son, as the last of the male children of my house. For you, Halaravilli ben-Jair, will take from me my daughter. You will be joined with Berylina Thunderspear, with the last of my children, with the most delicate of all the gifts in my house. And for this, Halaravilli ben-Jair, I bid you thanks. I bid you thanks, and gratitude, and the long devotion of my land and all my people."

Hal wanted to say something. He wanted to acknowledge the generous words. He felt awkward, sitting upon his throne-like chair, looking up at the man who was bestowing such alleged riches upon him. And yet, he had been told the formula. He had been told to sit, and to wait. To wait for Berylina to come to him.

Teheboth raised one great hand, gesturing toward a pavilion on the far side of the crowd, as distant from the one that Hal had used as was possible in the festival space. "And so, Halaravilli ben-Jair, I call to my daughter, Berylina. I bid her come out from the tent of her father, to come to the side of her husband."

Teheboth paused. There was no motion at the distant pavilion. Even though they were too far away to hear the king's words, a servant should have been appointed to watch for the royal gesture. Hal imagined the chaos inside that tent, the nurses who were even now struggling to collect their charge. He pictured Berylina's unruly hair, her roaming eye, her rabbity teeth chewing away at her lower lip. He regretted the panic that he was certain she felt, but he knew that the time had come. Berylina was to become a queen without delay.

Teheboth raised his voice and continued. "I call to my daughter, Berylina, that she might witness the traditions of our people, the presentation of the gifts to the groom, and the granting of boons." Again, Teheboth paused, but there was still no motion at the distant pavilion.

Disconcerted, Teheboth sought out Lord Shalindor, his chamberlain. The white-haired man hovered at the very edge of the Liantine crowd, looking as if he had smelled some foul odor amid the guests. Shalindor made the slightest of shrugs, and then he waved his hand by his side, gesturing to a velvet-covered wain beside him. Continue, the man seemed to say.

Move on with the ceremony and let Berylina's nurses work their magic.

Teheboth frowned, but he turned to Hal and bowed deeply. "But let me make the first offering, the first gift to the groom. It is only appropriate that this presentation be made without the presence of the bride, for no woman should know the true price her father places upon her."

Teheboth glared at his courtiers, and obedient laughter went up. Teheboth ignored them. "Halaravilli ben-Jair, I present to you the dowry for Princess Berylina. No father has loved his daughter more than I have loved mine. I pray in the name of the Horned Hind that this sorry symbol of my honor and respect for Berylina can see her kept well and sound in Morenia."

Shalindor waited until Teheboth nodded once again, and then the chamberlain issued his own tight flurry of gestured signals. A dozen burly soldiers stepped forward, each attired in the green-painted leathers of the Liantine court. The fighting men set their shoulders to the edge of the wain, and Hal watched the muddy wheels edge forward, gouging the spidersilk covering on the ground. The wagon creaked under its velvet-shrouded burden, coming at last to rest immediately before the throne.

Shalindor stepped up then, moving to the front right corner of the cart. He nodded carefully, as if he were making one last precise measurement, and then he pulled away the velvet with a flourish.

Gold bars glinted beneath the noon sun—hundreds of them, stacked neatly on the platform. Hal wondered at the foolishness of dragging all that wealth out of the palace, of carting it across the field. Foolish, perhaps, but the gold bars were impressive. And, of course, they were safe. They were heavy, and the finest flower of all the Liantine and Morenian military stood ready to protect them.

Hal started to rise from his throne, but one quick glance from Teheboth reminded him of the expected procedure. Instead, he inclined his head graciously and slipped into the royal plural. "We thank you, Teheboth Thunderspear. Brilliant as this gold is beneath the noonday sun, it is but a shadow of the honor and respect we hold for Princess Berylina. She will be welcome in Morenia for as long as we draw breath." Hal paused a moment, hoping that he sounded like an eager groom. Then, he continued, "But as we understand your customs, each person who presents a gift to the groom is entitled to ask for a boon."

Teheboth's eyes glinted. "Aye, Halaravilli ben-Jair."

"Then what would you have of us, Teheboth Thunderspear? What bounty may we grant to you in gratitude for the fine gifts you make to us this day?"

"I ask this, Halaravilli ben-Jair: that you honor my daughter, and you respect her. That you keep her by your side for as long as you both shall live. And when you get children on her body, that you raise those children under the sign of the Horned Hind."

Hal whirled to look at the priestess who stood behind him, but she had made no movement on the dais. She still stood directly behind his throne, clad in brown velvet, caught beneath her horned headdress. Hal turned back to Teheboth slowly. He had not expected this, had not expected to bind his *children* to the Liantine faith.

Dartulamino stepped forward, his face turning scarlet above his smooth, green robes. Other Morenians shifted on the grass, glancing from the silent priestess to their king to the spluttering Holy Father. Hal cast his eyes across to Berylina's pavilion. Illogically, he cursed her delay. It seemed that if she had been present, Teheboth would not have made such a demand, would not have cornered Hal so publicly.

Still, Berylina was thirteen years old. Hal would not be "getting heirs upon her body" for two years at the least. Two years to begin the work, and nearly another one before he would see the product of his efforts. What could change in three years? How many ways could he reshape his promises by then?

Hal met Teheboth's gaze. "Aye, Teheboth Thunderspear. I grant you this boon. All the children I conceive with Princess Berylina shall be raised under the sign of the Horned Hind."

There was an explosion of disbelief among the Morenians, and many nobles cried out to the Thousand Gods. Dartulamino threw back his shoulders, taking a step forward as if he would interrupt the proceedings. Hal glared at Puladarati, who made his own steps, clutching the Holy Father's arm as if he looked to give support, or take it. Dartulamino started to shake off the lion-maned retainer, started to snarl at the former regent, but Puladarati said something too soft for anyone to overhear. The Holy Father spat a reply, but Puladarati shook his head, gripping the priest's arm more tightly. Dartulamino glared up at the dais, nearly spitting at Hal's throne, but the priest allowed himself to be pulled back into the crowd.

Hal swallowed hard and looked back to Teheboth. The Liantine king was nodding slowly. "Very well, Halaravilli ben-Jair. I thank you for your most generous boon. Welcome, son, into the house of Thunderspear."

Farsobalinti was next to approach the marriage bench, for he had spoken with Hal before the ceremony. They had agreed that Farso would be the first of the Morenian nobles, would pave the way for the show of support Hal required. The pale-haired lord knelt upon the spidersilk tapestry, inclining his head until his chin touched his chest. "Rise, Baron Farsobalinti," Hal said. "Stand before me like a brother."

"Like a brother I come to you," Farso said, and a smile flirted about his lips despite the solemnity of the occasion. "I come to you, and I bear you a gift, in recognition of your marriage to Princess Berylina." Farso gestured for two pages to step forward, and they dragged a box between them. "I hardly think my showing worthy, Your Majesty, before the princess's generous dowry, but still I would offer up to you a symbol of my happiness at your good fortune this day." Farso nodded, and the boys opened the box, counted out ten bars of gold. They settled the riches on the corner of Teheboth's wain.

For just an instant, Hal wondered at Farso's resourcefulness. Certainly, they had spoken about Farso making up this offering, but Hal had never imagined that his friend would have the actual gold on hand. He had expected a certificate, a pledge, nothing more. He looked into Farso's eyes, smiling as he saw the pale blue depth of friendship. "We thank you, cherished Farsobalinti. And what boon would you request of the groom?"

"Only this, Your Majesty. That I might be decorated in the Order of the Octolaris by your own hand."

A murmur went up from the assembled guests. What was this new Order of the Octolaris? What well-wrought play was being acted out before them?

Hal inclined his head and rose from the throne, ignoring Teheboth's sudden scowl. Hal had given in to nearly every one of the Liantine's demands about the service. Teheboth could damn well let Hal move from the marriage bench.

Hal looked over to his own retainers and saw that Davin had edged to the front of the crowd. He held a velvet pouch in his age-spotted hands, and he lifted it slightly when he caught Hal's gaze. Hal nodded and waved the old man forward.

Davin did not bother with bowing as he approached his lord. Instead, he inclined his head and muttered under his breath. "One hundred brooches, and no more than a month to make them. No respect for an old man, no respect at all."

Hal merely extended his hand, waiting for the velvet bag. Davin handed it over with a loud sigh, and then he melted back into the crowd. Hal made a show of holding up the velvet reticule, opening its strings slowly. He tipped it over when he knew that he had the attention of all the nobles on the field, Morenian and Liantine alike, and when Davin's handiwork spilled out, he held it up for all to see.

The brooch was fashioned on an iron base, with a clever clasp that promised to stay fastened. As Hal turned the piece about, he saw that Davin had chosen enamelwork to display the pride of the Order—crimson paint upon a golden background. An octolaris was splayed across the brooch, its eight legs curled around an image of the Morenian crown. Hal could not have asked for a finer symbol.

Swallowing hard, Hal turned back to Farso. He fastened the brooch on the other man's cloak, taking care to position it squarely over Farso's heart, and he whispered, "Thank you, brother."

"Sire," was Farso's only reply, and then the nobleman turned about, striding back to the ranks of the Morenians with his badge of honor flashing upon his breast.

As the assembly murmured and jostled for a better view of Davin's handiwork, Hal cast a look at Dartulamino. The Holy Father nodded once, clearly taking the measure of the ten bars of gold. The priest had been close enough to hear Davin's grumbling; he could count the gold that Hal might command from all his nobles, beyond Princess Berylina's dowry. Dartu-lamino's eyes narrowed to slits, but the man stayed silent.

Hal's attention was reclaimed by Teheboth. The man was clearly embarrassed, and he glanced toward his daughter's pavilion with more than a little exasperation.

"If you will excuse me, son." The title was strange in Hal's ears, but he nodded to the Liantine king. "Princess Berylina should witness at least some of the gifts to the groom. With your indulgence, I will send one of my lords to bring her forth."

"Of course, my lord. As you think best."

Teheboth nodded to Shalindor. The chamberlain slipped through the crowd like a stork, looking neither left nor right as people let him pass. All eyes stayed on the white-haired man as he stalked across the field.

"Your Majesty." Hal was surprised by the voice he knew so well, and he turned back to the gift-giving with a start of shame.

"Rani Trader."

"I would offer up a gift, in honor of your wedding."

She was braver than he was. She was looking at him, staring into his face. Her brow was smooth, unconcerned, and she collapsed into a graceful curtsey.

"Please!" he exclaimed, and he reached out hurriedly to raise her up. Her humility was more than he expected, before all the watchful eyes. As his hand closed around hers, he learned that she was not quite so composed as she had seemed. Her fingers trembled like leaves in a breeze.

"Your Majesty," she said, and she swallowed hard. "Sire, I would make you a gift of riberry trees. Five hundred and thirty riberry trees await you in King Teheboth's courtyard."

A rumble rolled through the ranks of the wedding guests. Many of the Liantines had arrived in their king's city only that morning. They had not seen the courtyard, the barrels filled with water, the slaves toting bucket after bucket to the trees. Events had unfolded so rapidly that many people did not know that Rani had negotiated for the spiderguild's treasure.

Five hundred and thirty trees. Fifty-three children, sold into Liantine slavery in the spiderguild alone. Fifty-four, with Crest-man. Out of how many thousand Amanthian children who had been shipped across the sea? How many of his people were lost forever in Liantine?

The riberry trees, however, would buy their freedom eventually, he could hope. The trees would ultimately pay for their passage home.

Hal would take the riberries and Mareka's octolaris, and he would find his place in the Fellowship of Jair. He would build the Order of the Octolaris, and he would come back to redeem whatever children he could. Some—maybe even most—had already been lost forever. But others would survive. They would crave freedom, and he would give it to them. Later. After he had married Berylina and made his peace with Liantine. With the church. With the Fellowship. Then Hal could save whatever children were left. And all because Rani had managed to bargain for the riberry trees.

"Thank you, Rani Trader. Thank you for your gift. And what boon would you ask of me?"

Her throat worked for a moment, and he had a chance to imagine all the things that she might ask, all the demands she might make, all the favors she might beg. He thought of their fights in Morenia, their bitter disagreements, about his crown, about his kingdom, about the Fellowship.

But she smiled a brilliant smile, and he knew that he need not fear any of those things. He need not fear Rani Trader.

"As you know, Your Majesty, my glasswrights' guild was destroyed in the year before you took the throne. All the master glasswrights have left Morenia. I seek to rebuild my guild, and in that pursuit, I have studied the duties of a journeyman. I can pour glass, and I can cut it. I can set it. I can supervise apprentices. I have offered the fourth part of all my earnings to the crown, in the form of the riberry trees that sit in King Teheboth's courtyard even now. I ask that you declare me a journeyman in my guild."

Hal faltered. He did not doubt Rani for a moment. He knew that she would not lie about her standing, would never lie about her glasswork. But who was he to pass judgment? Who was he—a noble—to say that she should be elevated within the structure of a guild?

"Rani," he began. "Ranita Glasswright. I am no master guildsman."

"There is one who would speak for me, a master in his own right. If you would sanction his evaluation, then it might bear weight enough, enough for Morenia, which has no glass-wrights' guild of its own."

"Then let him stand forward." Hal watched as Tovin Player stepped to Rani's side. The man bowed fluidly, gracefully, as if this were a play he had performed numerous times in the past. Hal saw the possessive way the player stood beside Rani, and his own heart beat faster in his chest. He forced himself to say, "Glasswright, do you speak for this one? Do you say that she is qualified as a journeyman?"

"She speaks the truth, Your Majesty." Tovin's honeyed tones flowed over the assembly, easily reaching the wedding guests who stood at the back of the crowd. Even with that volume, even with that force, it did not seem that the player raised his voice. "She has met the duties of a journeyman. Justice requires that she be elevated to that rank."

"Very well, then." Hal forced himself to meet Rani's eyes, to see the excitement glinting there. "Ranita Glasswright, I com-mend thee to thy guild, and I welcome thee to the rank of journey-man. May your guild prosper long in Morenia."

"Thank you, Sire." Her smile was dazzling as she sank into a deep curtsey. This time, Tovin raised her up. The player es-corted her back to the ranks of Morenian nobles.

Hal forced himself to look away from Tovin's protective hand on Rani's arm, from the quiet glance that the two of them shared. Instead, he turned to Teheboth, to the Liantine king's impatient sigh. Teheboth was glaring across the field, as if he would set fire to Berylina's pavilion with the power of his gaze. Shalindor was nowhere in sight.

Even as Hal wondered what course he should pursue, he turned back to find another wedding well-wisher. Mareka Oc-tolaris knelt before him. "My lady," he said and reached out to raise her up.

"Your Majesty," she said. He looked at her more shrewdly. Never before had Mareka acknowledged his sovereignty, not in any of her gamesmanship. She saw that he caught the difference in her wording, and she smiled. "I would offer up a gift, Your Majesty."

"Aye?" He did not waste time with titles, with courtesy. After all, what was he to call the woman now? She was a disgraced apprentice, an outcast from her guild.

"I offer to you spiders, Your Majesty. Twenty-three brooding females. Their eggs will hatch within a week, and all the spiderlings I give to you, as well."

There was a roar through the wedding guests—most of them had not heard the tale of Mareka's banishment from her guild. The Liantines who had been mystified by Rani's presentation exclaimed aloud, and Hal could count the heartbeats until people put the pieces together. Riberry trees. Octolaris.

The spiderguild was broken. The silk monopoly was all but destroyed. Farsobalinti's Order of the Octolaris now made sense. Liantines chattered among themselves, and Morenians cried out questions, desperately seeking information about the gifts and their meaning.

Hal waited for the furor to die down, and then he said to Mareka, "My thanks, lady. Your gift is a generous one, and it will be spoken about in Morenia for generations. And now I ask what boon would you request, in exchange for the offering you have made."

The crowd edged forward, eager to hear Mareka's response. The woman who had broken the spiderguild's hold could demand anything in the world. She could ask for a king's ransom, and it would certainly be hers.

Mareka unlaced her fingers, laid them to rest across her belly. She took a deep breath, as if she gathered strength from the sparkling spidersilk beneath her fingers, and then she raised her eyes to look at him directly. "Your hand in marriage, Sire. I ask that you raise up the mother of your child and set her beside you on your throne. Marry me, Your Majesty, and make the child that I bear—your child—your heir."

Hal's cry of outrage was drowned by Teheboth's. The Holy Father bellowed a question, and even the Horned Hind priestess stepped forward on the dais. The crowd surged closer, those nearest to the platform repeating Mareka's words for those who stood farther away.

Mareka looked at him unwaveringly, her fingers spread protectively, suggestively.

One time, he wanted to cry out. One cursed time!

But he knew Mareka was no fool. He knew that she would not make her claim if she bore no child. She would submit herself to any proof, agree to drink any truthteller's potion.

He would lose Berylina. He would lose the Liantine dowry. He would fail to repay the church. After all his planning, all his manipulations, all his careful, careful calculation, he would forfeit the power of his crown to the Holy Father.

The snare of the octolaris nectar had a longer reach than Hal had ever imagined.

Even as his mind reeled, even as he sought to phrase some answer, some denial, some refusal, he raised his eyes to Berylina's pavilion. How would the princess react? She would be ashamed, of course, and angry. But could she fail to be relieved? Could she fail to be grateful that she was released from her obligations? Even now, the door to Berylina's tent was pulled aside, even now she was emerging—at last—to face the man who she thought was her bridegroom.

But Berylina did not step out of the tent.

Shalindor emerged instead. The chamberlain stumbled out of the pavilion, running back to the wedding guests, to the edge of the forest. He lost one slipper in the grass, and still he lurched ahead, throwing himself through the crowd, up to the dais.

"The princess is gone!" Shalindor cried. "Princess Berylina is gone!"

17

Rani whirled toward the chamberlain, staring at his scarlet face as he fought to the front of the dais. The impeccable retainer's hair stood out from his head in wisps, and his hands shook as he stumbled before his king.

"What are you saying, man?" Teheboth bellowed.

"They're gone!"

"Who? Berylina and who?"

"That western priest. Siritalanu. The nurses have been drugged, and now they are tied up, all four of them, bound and gagged."

Teheboth roared in fury and rounded on Hal. "I don't know what you thought to gain by this, but you will pay!"

Rani could see that Hal was every bit as surprised as Teheboth. The king of all Morenia looked about him as if he had just awakened from a dream. He opened his mouth and closed it again, obviously struggling for appropriate words, for a proper retort. Helplessly, he gestured toward Berylina's tent, and then to Mareka Octolaris, who still stood before him in all the finery of her spiderguild. "My lord," Hal managed at last. "I know nothing of this matter. I am as surprised as you."

Teheboth swore succinctly, the oath of a frustrated, angry man. Before Hal could react, the Liantine king turned on his heel and stormed through the crowd, striding across the field to the princess's tent. Rani turned to Mair.

"What happened?"

"I dinna know, but I can imagine." Mair's Touched patois

coated her voice as she glanced about excitedly. "Th' wee mouse 'ad more t' 'er than we thought!"

"But where would she go?"

"If I 'ad t' guess, I'd say t' th' docks. I'd say tha' she's on a boat right now, 'er 'n' tha' priest. She's sailin' fer Morenia, 'n' prayin' tha' th' Thousand Gods 'll keep 'er safe from 'er da."

"From her *da* and from her intended," Farso said, nodding toward Hal. The king, though, was engaged in a furious whispered confrontation with Mareka Octolaris. His hand had closed on the woman's arm, and he towered over her. Her simple white shift and her straight falling hair made her look more childish than ever before.

Rani knew at once that the spiderguild apprentice's claims must be true; Hal had as much as admitted he had been with the woman. But how had he let himself be trapped in the age-old bonds of fatherhood? Certainly he needed an heir to his throne, but he should have known that a foreign commoner would never meet with his lords' approval. He should have been more careful.

As if to underscore Rani's thoughts, the crowd was murmuring behind her, the chatter of their questions rapidly rising in volume. She heard exclamations of amazement and surprise, of disdain. Puladarati was bellowing for order, already gathering up the core of Morenia's knighthood. Liantine lords had begun to cross the field, stumbling toward the princess's pavilion. Hal needed to follow them, needed to make his own arguments now, before it was too late.

Setting her teeth, Rani stepped forward, placing herself on the edge's of Hal's vision.

"By Nome," Hal was saying to Mareka, swearing by the god of children. "You could have come to me, Mareka!"

"And what would you have done, then? Would you have called off your wedding? Would you have set aside Princess Berylina?"

"I would have considered all my options! I would have measured right and wrong."

"And you would have questioned every man in King Teheboth's court, to find if someone else could be the father. You know the truth already, though. You know I knew no man before you."

Rani watched as Hal spluttered a reply, and she felt color rising in her own cheeks. The argument that she listened to was far too similar to one that she had longed to have with Hal herself, to one that she had imagined often in the long years that she had spent in the Morenian court. Rani clutched at the fabric of her crimson gown, gathering up the spidersilk in tight fists. The feel of the cloth reminded her of the truth, of how so many things had changed.

For just a moment, she glanced at Tovin Player. He was watching her. He was standing in the middle of the chaos, a calm smile painted across his lips, as if—even at that distance—he knew what she thought. He knew her good thoughts and her evil ones, and still he stood there, waiting for her to return. And yet, what did she truly know of him? How could she truly measure his intentions? He had done no ill by her, not yet. No ill at all . . . She flushed and raised her chin, nodding once. A comforting warmth flooded her limbs as Tovin returned the gesture.

Then Rani cleared her throat and stepped between Hal and Mareka. "Sire," she said.

"Not now, Rani."

"Yes, now, my lord. You must go with Teheboth. You must seek out the truth of what happened in Berylina's tent. Do not let him tell the story as he sees fit."

Hal started to snap at her, but Rani saw him catch the words at the back of his throat. He closed his eyes and took a deep breath, holding it for several heartbeats. When he exhaled, long and slow, he threw back his shoulders. His crimson cloak caught the glint of the sunlight, reflecting color onto his pale cheeks. "Yes, Rani. Ranita." But then he looked at Mareka again. "We will finish this talk, my lady."

The spiderguild apprentice collapsed into a curtsey, her only concession to her delicate condition a single hand cupped about her belly. "Of course, Your Majesty."

Hal looked as if he were going to say more, as if he had swallowed some bitter seed that he longed to spit out. Instead, he sought Puladarati in the crowd. "My lord duke!"

"Your Majesty." Puladarati's reply was immediate, grave, flawlessly polite.

"Stay here beside the gold. We must make sure that the excitement does not lead to . . . mistakes in the counting of such gifts."

"Aye, Sire." Puladarati turned to four of his fellow councilmen, appointing them to stand at the corners of the wain. "Go ahead, Your Majesty. We will watch over the field."

Hal strode after Teheboth with all the determination of a general in the midst of battle. Rani took one look at her companions, and then she followed her king. Her friends were close behind.

They had to fight their way into the princess's pavilion, elbowing past the restless crowd. Teheboth was towering over the oldest of Berylina's nurses, bellowing questions at the woman. She knelt upon the floor of the pavilion, looking up at him dazedly. She tossed her head as if she heard a ringing in her ears, and she blinked her eyes with every few words. Teheboth took a step closer. "Speak up, woman! I cannot hear a word you say!"

"I—I am sorry, Your Majesty." The nurse's words were slurred. "I cannot think straight, my head feels like it's floating."

"I'll show you floating!" the Liantine king grumbled, and he reached for the sword hilt at his waist. A ripple went through the crowd, a whispered exclamation, and Hal leaped forward.

"Hold, my lord! Let me try to speak to this good woman."

Teheboth clearly thought to ignore Hal at first, but then he muttered a curse and stepped back. "Do your best, if you can make any sense out of her. She's babbling like a goose."

Hal came to stand before the nurse. For just an instant, he looked at Berylina's other three attendants, but those women remained stretched out on a pallet on the far side of the tent. Only the faintest motion of their chests confirmed that they still lived, that they still drew breath despite their drugged sleep.

Shaking his head, Hal pitched his voice low, soft enough that Rani was forced to catch her own breath to overhear his words. "Come now, dame. What happened here? Where is Princess Berylina?"

The nurse looked about the tent, clearly puzzled by the disarray. Her gaze settled on the brilliant wedding gown that was still laid out across the princess's bed. In keeping with Liantine tradition, the garment was velvet, deep, golden finery that reflected the shadows of sunlight on moving leaves. Branchwork was picked out across the shoulders, delicate embroidery that echoed the marriage bench Hal had sat on.

"We arrived with my lady at dawn this morning," the nurse began, a puzzled tone behind her words. "The princess was frightened, poor dear, and she insisted on setting up her easel."

Rani followed the woman's floating gesture, looked across the tent to the wooden stand. A scrap of parchment was pinned to the surface, and firm charcoal lines stood out, even in the gloom. Rani recognized the outline of a golden cup, the swirl of a cape limned in a thousand colors. First God Ait. The father of all the Thousand Gods.

Hal nodded toward the drawing. "So, you let her draw."

"Aye. It seemed to soothe her, poor thing. She was so frightened. So afraid. But she was more at peace when he arrived."

"Who?" Hal's voice was mild, as if he were merely chatting with the woman. Rani saw Teheboth shift in frustration.

The nurse scowled, and for a moment, she looked as if she would not respond to the westerner questioning her. She continued, at last. "Father Siritalanu, of course. He said he'd come to pray with her, just as they have prayed every day."

"Just—," Hal started to repeat, apparently surprised, but he caught himself. Rani saw the quick glance he cast at Dartulamino; she understood that Hal was wondering if Siritalanu had been put up to this disappearance by the Holy Father, by the church he served. Dartulamino, though, looked just as surprised as Hal. Rani nodded to herself. Whatever had happened here, Dartulamino had not planned it. Neither the church nor the Fellowship had plotted Berylina's escape.

"Aye," the nurse said. "He told her it was a western custom. He said that she would never be acceptable to you if she did not pray to all the Thousand Gods. She was eager to behave, poor thing. She would have done anything the priest asked."

This last admission proved too much for Teheboth, for a man who thought that he had saved his daughter from other ways of worship. "So what did that dog do to her?" the Liantine demanded, shouldering forward.

The nurse dropped her head, nearly prostrating herself in an effort to pacify her king. "I do not know, Your Majesty, I cannot say! Please do not hurt me, I cannot tell you more, I truly cannot!"

Hal eased himself between Teheboth and the nurse. "And why can you not say more?"

"The priest! He—he drugged me! All of us—he gave us nurses a cup of wine. He said that it was necessary, that it was how you westerners . . ." She trailed off, as if she feared to cast aspersions on the man who stood between her and her furious lord, and then she managed to whisper, "how you began your wedding ceremonies. How you honored your gods."

Hal sighed. "And so you drank."

"Yes, my lord."

"And then you fell asleep."

"Yes, my lord."

While the nurse delivered her trembling confession, Rani maneuvered along the edge of the tent, toward the princess's easel. There was something about the edge of the drawing, something about the corner of the artwork. . . .There! Rani reached out and touched the parchment, freeing a note that had been pinned to the easel beneath the drawing. Whoever had left the message did not intend for it to be found immediately.

"Your Majesty," Rani called. She crossed to Hal and handed him the message.

"That is Berylina's hand!" exclaimed the nurse.

Hal unfolded the parchment, tilting it to catch a better stream of light from the doorway. "Father," he began to read. He looked up to Teheboth, raising an eyebrow and half offering the letter. The king of Liantine shook his head once, a grim rejection, and Hal swallowed before he continued to read aloud. "Father, I know you will be displeased when you find this letter. I know that you intended to honor me with marriage to King Halaravilli. I am not meant for marriage to any man, though. I am pledged to all the Thousand Gods. Please do not be angry, Sire. I go with Father Siritalanu, to the birthplace of First Pilgrim Jair. I go to find the voices of the gods who have spoken to me all my life. I go to escape your false goddess of the Horned Hind, to find the true and everlasting secret of the Thousand Gods. Your daughter forever, Berylina Thunderspear."

Teheboth's cry of rage was wordless—raw, elemental fury. Before Rani could read his intention, before she could warn Hal or take any action herself, the Liantine king shifted his grip on his spear. He bellowed as he pulled it back, and then he thrust the iron tip into the hapless nurse's breast. As he drove the weapon home, he howled, "You did this! You and your sisters, determined to protect her from the Horned Hind!"

The motion was so sudden, the blow so direct, that the woman did not have time to cry out. She raised her hands as if she were warding off a blow, and then her fingers scrambled about the shaft of the spear. She opened her lips, and Rani thought her dying words would be a protest, but only a trickle of blood emerged.

Even as the nurse collapsed back to the ground, even as her blood began to pool upon the spidersilk beneath her, Hal leaped forward with a cry of outrage. "That was wrong, my lord!" he exclaimed. "That poor woman was not the cause of this disaster."

"If she had guarded my daughter's virtue as she was charged to do, none of this would have happened!"

"Your daughter's virtue is *yet* unsullied!"

"My daughter has run off with a heathen dog. She's fled to rut with your priest, and if you were any sort of a man, you'd hunt her down and kill her like the strumpet that she is!"

"Hold your tongue, Thunderspear." Hal's voice was pure winter, bitter ice that hissed against Teheboth's rage. "Do not say more that you'll regret."

"My only regret is that I did not see my daughter's failings more clearly before. I knew she told tales of your cursed western gods, but I thought that she would hold true to the ways of her people. I thought that she would yield to the wisdom of the Horned Hind once she had submitted to a man." Teheboth slammed his fist into his gloved palm, letting his rage carry him around the princess's wedding pavilion. He knocked Berylina's easel to the ground, mashing her drawing of First God Ait beneath his boots, and he glared at the still-drugged trio of nurses. "Her eyes marked her from the day that she was born, her eyes, and her jaw, and her cursed, blasted shyness. She killed her dam, and she was marked for evil the instant she drew her first breath."

"She is the flesh of your flesh, Thunderspear."

"She is outcast! She is dead to this house." Teheboth whirled about, tossing his head until his eyes lit upon his chamberlain, Shalindor. "You! See to this mess! Have those women cast in chains, and see that this pavilion is burned to the ground. Then be certain that the dowry gold is returned to my treasury."

The dowry gold. The ingots that stood between Hal and the church. Teheboth could not take back Berylina's bride-price.

"Hold!" Rani cried.

Her voice was high, spinning out across the tent like a tentative web. She cleared her throat, flashing back to the players, to their tricks for making themselves heard in a grand hall. Rani reached inside her memories, gathered together the strength that she had known when she had Spoken with Tovin, with Flarissa. A kingdom depended on the words she uttered next, and she must not risk it by talking too softly, by being too meek.

Teheboth laughed, the bark of a madman. "The *journeyman* speaks?"

"Aye, my lord. I, Ranita Glasswright. The leader of the glasswrights in my land."

"And what would you say that any of us should hear on this dark day?"

Rani looked across at Hal. She saw the tension in his face, his drawn features. She saw the way Mareka Octolaris lurked behind him, a shimmering white shadow. She saw how Hal raised a hand to the chain of office about his neck, to the necklace of interlocking *J*s, how he nodded to her even now.

Hal did not know what she would say. He did not know how she would speak, what she would do. But he placed his faith in her. He placed his kingdom in her hands.

Rani took a step forward, as if she were easing back into the negotiations that she and Hal had begun so long ago, in the king's private apartments in Moren. She remembered how the light had glinted on Hal's chain then, how the candles had shone across the table. She remembered the ancient Holy Father, the spent and broken man.

Rani looked across the tent now, at the new Holy Father. She saw Dartulamino watching her, narrowing his eyes. He was waiting for her; he expected something of her. For just an instant, she wondered at the pattern that the man envisioned, the path he saw before her. Did he see it as a holy man, as a priest of the Thousand Gods? Or did he see it as a Morenian, as a countryman loyal to his king? Or did he see it as a member of the Fellowship, a soldier in the cabal that she continued to question, to challenge?

Whatever drove the man, whatever sparked his attention, Rani knew that she must act. She must step forward now and pour her glass, spread it on the cooling stone before it reached the brittle, breaking stage. She must hold her diamond knife at the ready, cut the new glass with a strong, straight line. She must stand prepared to set the pieces of Morenia, to shape her land.

"Hold, Teheboth Thunderspear. You will not have Shalindor take back the gold."

"My daughter is dead to the world. Your king could not wed her corpse, even if he had not plowed the spiderguild's fields."

"Your daughter may be lost to Liantine, but she is far from dead. She comes to the Thousand Gods as a penitent, as a pilgrim. Even now, she travels to the homeland of holy Jair, where she will don a Thousand-Pointed Star and begin a sacred pilgrimage under the tutelage of Father Siritalanu."

"She will be no bride."

"But she will enter the house of the Thousand Gods." Rani saw the answer spread out before her, flow past her like leaves spun across a swirling stream. "She will enter the house of the Thousand Gods, and she will fall under the protection of the Defender of her Faith. She will be accepted as a pilgrim, accepted as a wise and holy woman, once she has offered up her worldly goods."

Rani remembered her own brief time as a pilgrim, her own humbling before the Holy Father now dead and burned in Morenia. She had had nothing but a doll to offer up, a child's poppet. Berylina had so much more. "The gold will buy Berylina's entrance into the house that has waited for her all her life. Offer up her dowry to Morenia's Defender of the Faith. To Halaravilli ben-Jair."

"Never!" Teheboth bellowed.

"It is already done, my lord." Rani forced her voice into a certain register, into the ringing tones of a merchant who closes a deal. She sounded like a marketplace trickster, sniffing out a certain bargain. She stepped closer to Teheboth, edging between him and Hal. She felt her own king beside her, knew that his breath came fast as he let Rani drive her deal. "*Think,* Teheboth Thunderspear. Would you have it said that you have no control over your very house? That you let your own daughter flee with a man unknown to you? That your Horned Hind failed to discern the resolution of this tale, failed to see how the house of Thunderspear would be betrayed? Would you have your people say that? Would you have that story told?"

Teheboth's throat worked, and his face flushed crimson. He reached for his plaited beard, tugged at the bits of antler worked into the design. He glanced outside the door of the tent, as if he sought wisdom in the forest, from the priestess who had not deigned to step inside.

Rani spoke even more quietly, forcing the man to move closer to her. "Do not answer, King Teheboth, until you have thought through all the points. You have already committed to the dowry. You counted it gone from your treasury. You counted yourself lucky to marry off your daughter. Her broken gaze will never darken your palace again, and her jutting teeth will be gone forever, all reminder of her so-called sin. You thought to buy the friendship of Morenia with your eight hundred bars, and you can have it still. Just leave. Leave the wain and return to your castle. Take your people and fashion whatever stories you care, to forget about today. But leave the gold. Leave the gold behind."

Teheboth's hands twitched, opening and closing as if he longed for his spear. He glared at Rani, and then at Hal. "So, Halaravilli ben-Jair. You let this one speak for you?"

"She speaks the truth," Hal said.

"And you would steal my gold? You? Who lay with a

woman beneath my roof, in the very days that you courted my daughter?"

"Your daughter is dead to you, Teheboth Thunderspear."

Rani thought that Hal might have spoken too glibly, might have pushed the man too far too soon. For just an instant, the Liantine king looked as if he would grasp his spear from the nurse's body, send it back to finish its gory work.

But then Teheboth stopped himself. He looked from Hal to Rani to Mareka, and he muttered a curse beneath his breath. "Very well, Morenia. You win this round. Be gone from Liantine by noon tomorrow. You and your women and your priests—be gone."

Rani heard the words and felt a rush of satisfaction, a tangible breath of relief. Her strategy had worked. She had gained the dowry. The dowry, the spiders, the riberries—Morenia had all.

She looked across the tent to Dartulamino, measured how the Holy Father accepted the news of his defeat. For a moment, anger flashed across his sallow face, sparking in his eyes, settling in the shadows beneath his bony cheeks.

Then he nodded slowly. His anger washed away, and it was replaced by a more subtle look, by a more delicate shading. Rani wondered if Dartulamino thought of the eight hundred bars of gold, the dowry that would release the church's immediate claim against Hal's crown. She wondered if he thought about Farso's ten bars, about the Order of the Octolaris, made real by the spiders and the trees that waited back in Liantine's courtyard.

After all, what did the Fellowship intend to do with its thousand bars of gold? What did it intend to build through its secret tax? How would Hal's payment affect Moren, affect all of Morenia?

Rani could not know. She could not imagine. But looking across the pavilion, she saw the Holy Father's shadowy smile, and then he lifted an imaginary cup. He held his hand as if he toasted her victory across the spidersilk tent. He flourished his wrist for just a moment, and Rani ducked her chin, acknowledging the gesture.

And then, all unaware of the drama that had passed between

Rani and Dartulamino, Teheboth Thunderspear stalked from the tent, calling orders to all his waiting men. He told them that the tent should be struck, that the silk should be burned. He told them that they were never to speak the name of his dead daughter. He told them they were to make an offering to the Horned Hind, a sacrifice of wine and bread, that very afternoon. And he told them to leave the wain behind.

18

The breeze tugged at Rani's hair, and the ship's sails belled out, as if they, too, yearned to return to Morenia. She watched Hal raise a golden cup and swallow fine Liantine wine, and then he held the goblet toward Mareka. After she drank, Holy Father Dartulamino accepted the goblet and raised his hands in blessing. "May the Thousand Gods look over your union, Halaravilli ben-Jair and Mareka Octolaris. May your union be fruitful and prosperous. May you bring glory to First God Ait and all the Thousand Gods. And let us say, Amen."

The assembled witnesses mouthed the word *Amen* and then Dartulamino gathered up the spring-green shawl that had cloaked the shoulders of the bride and groom. Farso stepped forward to congratulate his lord, and he bowed toward his new queen. Mareka blushed prettily at the attention, but then she glanced at the sun, which stood directly overhead.

"I beg your pardon, lords and ladies, Holy Father. The octolaris must be fed. It grows close to their time." She moved toward her cabin, sheltered in the foredeck, but then she looked back to the Morenians. Her smile was shy, like a child's, as she reached a hand toward King Halaravilli. "Please, my lord. Will you assist me with the spiders?"

Hal hesitated for a moment. He looked to Dartulamino, blushing from his throat to the roots of his hair. The Holy Father nodded, however, for he had seen scores of shamefaced bridegrooms. Mareka passed through the doorway to the cabin, already pulling the sleeves of her gown close about her forearms, preparing to tend her brood. Hal turned to follow her.

As he passed by Rani and Tovin, the ship bucked, hitting the trough of a wave and making Hal stumble. The player reached out a quick hand, steadying the king even as Rani caught her breath. Hal paused then and looked at her. He hesitated, but then he said, "Ranita Glasswright."

"My lord."

"I bid you a joyous Midsummer Day."

Her belly flipped at the layers of meaning in his voice, at the greeting, the apology, the slightest hint of challenge. As Rani struggled for words, she felt Tovin step behind her; she felt the heat of his body close to hers. "I feared this day, Sire," she said. "I feared the counting out of debts."

"The Holy Father has received his payment from the funds I have as Defender of the Faith."

Rani nodded, knowing that there were other debts, other countings. The breeze caught her hair, whipping an errant strand across her eyes. Hal reached out to brush it from her face, but then he stopped himself. He stood, frozen, uncertain. Rani wanted to speak to him, wanted to tell him that she understood, that she knew he had choices to make, choices for a kingdom. But the words sat in her belly like stones, and she stayed silent until he turned away, until he crossed the deck and followed Mareka into her spider lair.

Tovin waited until the door was closed. When he spoke, he stood close enough that she could feel his words trembling through her spine. "This one ship bears all of Morenia's salvation."

"Salvation?"

"A good king. Gold for debts. Spiders for the future, and riberry trees. Lamb's breath to treat firelung. A dedicated guildsman who gives what she must so that her kingdom might survive."

"But what if the king chose wrong? What if the gold is not enough and the spiders die, and the riberries shrivel to nothing? What if the lamb's breath does not ease the firelung—if the merchants were wrong in Liantine?"

"Then you'll find other answers, Ranita Glasswright. You'll find other patterns. You'll pour your glass and cut your designs and set your pieces until they work."

She sighed. "I fear I do not have the skill."

"You do. You must."

"And why is that? Why must *I* manage this?"

"Your king depends on you. Your king, and your mysterious Fellowship, and a troop of feisty players who even now take ship for Morenia."

Fellowship. The way Tovin said the word sent shivers down her spine. He knew all that she did of the fellows. She had told him, Spoken with him, never dreaming that she would be bringing him into their midst. What would Tovin do with his knowledge? How would he play out the game?

Rani sighed, unable to predict what the future would bring. "More people. More people who rely on me, who lay claim to me."

"Aye, Ranita Glasswright. But more you can depend on. More you can rely upon to help you."

She shook her head. "I have done so much wrong. The Little Army remains in Liantine. Crestman is lost. The Fellowship . . ."

"The majority of the Little Army is safe and grown. You'll see some with our players, when they arrive in Morenia. You'll redeem the few who are still unwilling slaves come spring. And Crestman . . . He made his choice."

"He did not know."

"He had no faith."

"Faith . . ." Rani breathed the word, thinking about the faith that a princess had, to defy her father, to leave her home, to travel in search of the Thousand Gods. She thought about the faith that she—Rani—had placed in Tovin, in an itinerant player who admitted that he traded tales and information, all to better his people, his players' troop.

Tovin said, "When you first Spoke to Flarissa, you told her the story of the most important day in your life. You went on faith and paid a coin and told your tale. Was that a bargain well made?"

A coin, a single sovereign, for all that had happened in Liantine. The players she had come to sponsor, the riberry trees she had negotiated for, the dowry she had wrested from Teheboth Thunderspear. The man who stood beside her.

"No answer?" he asked as she remained silent beside him. "You think your bargain poor? Perhaps I must sweeten the deal?"

She started to protest, started to explain, but he shook his head with a smile. His long fingers reached out to cup her face, but then he pulled back, feigning startlement. She saw the glint of gold between his fingers, and he displayed a new-minted sovereign, as if he had found it in her hair. Despite herself, she laughed.

She reached out for the coin, but Tovin shook his head. He closed his fingers around the gold piece, and when she tapped his fist, he uncurled his fingers to reveal two coins. Still, he would not let her take them; he folded his hands about the sovereigns and made as if he would drop them into her outstretched palm.

No coins fell from his fist, though.

Instead, he poured a length of lead chain from his hand to hers, careful links as delicate as the ones that he had shown her a lifetime before, in the players' storeroom. She gathered up the chain and held it to the light, and now she could make out the marks of the tools he had used, the goldsmith's pliers and clamps that he had adapted to his needs. Now she understood how the chain was made, and how it had been tempered, how it had been made strong enough to support a complete frame of glass.

With her journeyman's eyes, she knew.

She stretched the chain between her hands and then looped it about his wrist. "Faith, then. Tell me, Tovin Player, what stories do you tell of faith? What stories of the Thousand Gods, and kings and guildsmen and players?"

"I have tales to last for all this journey, Ranita Glasswright. For all this journey and more."

"Then you should start the telling now." She leaned closer, and he settled an arm about her shoulders. She turned her face and rested her cheek against his broad chest, listening carefully lest she lose a single word of his players' knowledge to the wind that bore her home.

ABOUT THE AUTHOR

Mindy L. Klasky lives near Washington, D.C., which has been her home since she took her first professional job, as a trademark and copyright attorney at a major law firm. After six years of working as a litigator, Mindy became a librarian, and now she manages a law library's reference department. In her spare time—when she is not reading or writing—Mindy swims, bakes, and quilts. Her cats, Dante and Christina, make sure that she does not waste too much time sleeping.

Dennis L. McKiernan

HÈL'S CRUCIBLE Duology:

In Dennis L. McKiernan's world of Mithgar, other stories are often spoken of, but none as renowned as the War of the Ban. Here, in one of his finest achievements, he brings that epic to life in all its magic and excitement.

Praise for the HÈL'S CRUCIBLE Duology:

"Provocative...appeals to lovers of classic fantasy—the audience for David Eddings and Terry Brooks."—*Booklist*

"Once McKiernan's got you, he never lets you go."—Jennifer Roberson

"Some of the finest imaginative action...there are no lulls in McKiernan's story."
—*Columbus Dispatch*

Book One of the **Hèl's Crucible Duology**
INTO THE FORGE 0-451-45700-5

Book Two of the **Hèl's Crucible Duology**
INTO THE FIRE 0-451-45732-3

AND DON'T MISS McKiernan's newest epic which takes you back to Mithgar in a time of great peril—as an Elf and an Impossible Child try to save the land from a doom long ago prophesied....

SILVER WOLF, BLACK FALCON 0-451-45803-6

To order call: 1-800-788-6262

Mindy L. Klasky

THE GLASSWRIGHTS' PROGRESS
Living in the palace of Morenia's new king, Rani Trader
struggles to rebuild the banished glasswrighs'
guild while an enemy of the kingdom assembles a
very unusual army
45835-4

THE GLASSWRIGHTS' APPRENTICE
If you want to be safe...mind your caste.

In a kingdom where all is measured by birthright,
moving up in society is almost impossible. Which is why
young Rani Trader's merchant family sacrifices nearly
everything to buy their daughter an apprenticeship in the
Glasswrights' Guild—where honor and glory will be
within her reach.
45789-7

To order call: 1-800-788-6262

Wen Spencer

TAINTED TRAIL
Half-man, half-alien Ukiah Oregon is tracking a missing woman when he discovers he may actually be the long-lost "Magic Boy"—who vanished back in 1933...
45887-7

ALIEN TASTE
by Wen Spencer
Living with wolves as a child gave tracker Ukiah Oregon a heightened sense of smell and taste. Or so he thought—until he crossed paths with a criminal gang known as the Pack. Now, Ukiah is about to discover just how much he has in common with the Pack: a bond of blood, brotherhood...and destiny
45837-0

To order call: 1-800-788-6262